THE HOUSE WITH THE GREEN SHUTTERS

THE HOUSE WITH THE GREEN SHUTTERS

GEORGE DOUGLAS

JAMES THIN
1983

THE MERCAT PRESS,
EDINBURGH

ISBN 0901824 72 0

Printed in Scotland by
John G Eccles Printers Ltd, Inverness

WITHDRAWN

THE HOUSE WITH THE GREEN SHUTTERS.

CHAPTER I.

THE frowsy chambermaid of the " Red Lion " had just finished washing the front door steps. She rose from her stooping posture and, being of slovenly habit, flung the water from her pail straight out, without moving from where she stood. The smooth round arch of the falling water glistened for a moment in mid-air. John Gourlay, standing in front of his new house at the head of the brae, could hear the swash of it when it fell. The morning was of perfect stillness.

The hands of the clock across " the Square " were pointing to the hour of eight. They were yellow in the sun.

Blowsalinda, of the Red Lion, picked up the big bass that usually lay within the porch, and carrying it clumsily against her breast, moved off round the corner of the public-house, her petticoat gaping behind. Halfway she met the hostler, with whom she stopped in amorous dalliance. He said something to her, and she laughed loudly and vacantly. The silly *tee-hee* echoed up the street.

A moment later a cloud of dust drifting round the

corner, and floating white in the still air, showed that she was pounding the bass against the end of the house. All over the little town the women of Barbie were equally busy with their steps and door-mats. There was scarce a man to be seen either in the Square, at the top of which Gourlay stood, or in the long street descending from its near corner. The men were at work ; the children had not yet appeared ; the women were busy with their household cares.

The freshness of the air, the smoke rising thin and far above the red chimneys, the sunshine glistering on the roofs and gables, the rosy clearness of everything beneath the dawn—above all, the quietness and peace —made Barbie, usually so poor to see, a very pleasant place to look down at on a summer morning. At this hour there was an unfamiliar delicacy in the familiar scene, a freshness and purity of aspect—almost an un-earthliness—as though you viewed it through a crystal dream. But it was not the beauty of the hour that kept Gourlay musing at his gate. He was dead to the fairness of the scene, even while the fact of its presence there before him wove most subtly with his mood. He smoked in silent enjoyment because on a morning such as this everything he saw was a delicate flattery to his pride. At the beginning of a new day, to look down on the petty burgh in which he was the greatest man filled all his being with a consciousness of importance. His sense of prosperity was soothing and pervasive ; he felt it all round him like the pleasant air, as real as that and as subtle ; bathing him, caressing. It was the most secret and intimate joy of his life to go out and smoke on summer mornings by his big gate, musing over Barbie ere he possessed it with his merchandise.

He had growled at the quarry carters for being late in setting out this morning (for, like most resolute dullards, he was sternly methodical), but in his heart he was secretly pleased. The needs of his business were so various that his men could rarely start at the same hour and in the same direction. To-day, however, because of the delay, all his carts would go streaming through the town together, and that brave pomp would be a slap in the face to his enemies. "I'll show them," he thought proudly. "Them" was the town-folk, and what he would show them was what a big man he was. For, like most scorners of the world's opinion, Gourlay was its slave, and showed his subjection to the popular estimate by his anxiety to flout it. He was not great enough for the carelessness of perfect scorn.

Through the big green gate behind him came the sound of carts being loaded for the day. A horse, weary of standing idle between the shafts, kicked ceaselessly and steadily against the ground with one impatient hinder foot, clink, clink, clink upon the paved yard. "Easy, damn ye; ye'll smash the bricks!" came a voice. Then there was the smart slap of an open hand on a sleek neck, a quick start, and the rattle of chains as the horse quivered to the blow.

"Run a white tarpaulin across the cheese, Jock, to keep them frae melting in the heat," came another voice. "And canny on the top there wi' thae big feet o' yours; d'ye think a cheese was made for *you* to dance on wi' your mighty brogues?" Then the voice sank to the hoarse, warning whisper of impatience—loudish in anxiety, yet throaty from fear of being heard. "Hurry up, man—hurry up, or he'll be down on us like bleezes for being so late in getting off!"

Gourlay smiled grimly, and a black gleam shot from his eye as he glanced round to the gate and caught the words. His men did not know he could hear them.

The clock across the Square struck the hour, eight soft, slow strokes, that melted away in the beauty of the morning. Five minutes passed. Gourlay turned his head to listen, but no further sound came from the yard. He walked to the green gate, his slippers making no noise.

"Are ye sleeping, my pretty men ? " he said softly. . . . " *Eih ?* "

The " *Eih* " leapt like a sword, with a slicing sharpness in its tone that made it a sinister contrast to the first sweet question to his " pretty men." " *Eih ?* " he said again, and stared with open mouth and fierce, dark eyes.

"Hurry up, Peter," whispered the gaffer, " hurry up, for God sake. He has the black glower in his een."

" Ready, sir ; ready now ! " cried Peter Riney, running out to open the other half of the gate. Peter was a wizened little man, with a sandy fringe of beard beneath his chin, a wart on the end of his long, slanting-out nose, light blue eyes, and bushy eyebrows of a reddish gray. The bearded red brows, close above the pale blueness of his eyes, made them more vivid by contrast ; they were like pools of blue light amid the brownness of his face. Peter always ran about his work with eager alacrity. A simple and willing old man, he affected the quick readiness of youth to atone for his insignificance.

"Hup, horse ; hup then ! " cried courageous Peter, walking backwards with curved body through the gate, and tugging at the reins of a horse the feet of which struck sparks from the paved ground as they stressed painfully on edge to get weigh on the great wagon behind. The cart rolled through, then another, and another, till twelve of them had passed. Gourlay stood aside to watch them. All the horses were brown ; " he makes a point of that," the neighbours would have told you. As each horse passed the gate the driver left its head, and took his place by the wheel, cracking his whip, with many a " Hup, horse ; yean, horse ; woa, lad ; steady ! "

In a dull little country town the passing of a single

cart is an event, and a gig is followed with the eye till it disappears. Anything is welcome that breaks the long monotony of the hours and suggests a topic for the evening's talk. "Any news?" a body will gravely inquire. "Ou ay," another will answer with equal gravity: "I saw Kennedy's gig going past in the forenoon." "Ay, man; where would *he* be off till? He's owre often in his gig, I'm thinking." And then Kennedy and his affairs will last them till bedtime.

Thus the appearance of Gourlay's carts woke Barbie from its morning lethargy. The smith came out in his leather apron, shoving back, as he gazed, the grimy cap from his white-sweating brow; bowed old men stood in front of their doorways, leaning with one hand on short, trembling staffs, while the slaver slid unheeded along the cutties which the left hand held to their tooth-less mouths; white-mutched grannies were keeking past the jambs; an early urchin, standing wide-legged to stare, waved his cap and shouted, "Hooray!"—and all because John Gourlay's carts were setting off upon their morning rounds, a brave procession for a single town! Gourlay, standing great-shouldered in the middle of the road, took in every detail, devoured it grimly as a homage to his pride. "Ha, ha, ye dogs!" said the soul within him. Past the pillar of the Red Lion door he could see a white peep of the landlord's waist-coat—though the rest of the mountainous man was hidden deep within his porch. (On summer mornings the vast totality of the landlord was always inferential to the town from the tiny white peep of him revealed.) Even fat Simpson had waddled to the door to see the carts going past. It was fat Simpson—might the Universe blast his adipose—who had once tried to in-fringe Gourlay's monopoly as the sole carrier in Barbie. There had been a rush to him at first, but Gourlay set his teeth and drove him off the road, carrying stuff for nothing till Simpson had nothing to carry, so that the local wit suggested " a wee parcel in a big cart " as a new sign for his hotel. The twelve browns prancing past would be a pill to Simpson ! There was no smile about Gourlay's mouth—a fiercer glower was the only sign of his pride—but it put a bloom on his morning, he felt, to see the suggestive round of Simpson's waistcoat, down yonder at the porch. Simpson, the swine ! He had made short work o' *him !*

Ere the last of the carts had issued from the yard at the House with the Green Shutters the foremost was already near the Red Lion. Gourlay swore beneath his breath when Miss Toddle—described in the local records as " a spinster of independent means "—came fluttering out with a silly little parcel to accost one of the carriers. Did the auld fool mean to stop Andy Gow about *her* petty affairs, and thus break the line of carts on the only morning they had ever been able to go down the brae together ? But no. Andy tossed her parcel carelessly up among his other packages, and left her bawling instructions from the gutter, with a portentous shaking of her corkscrew curls. Gourlay's men took their cue from their master, and were contemptuous of Barbie, most unchivalrous scorners of its old maids.

Gourlay was pleased with Andy for snubbing Sandy Toddle's sister. When he and Elshie Hogg reached the Cross they would have to break off from the rest to complete their loads ; but they had been down Main Street over night as usual picking up their commissions, and until they reached the Bend o' the Brae it was unlikely that any business should arrest them now. Gourlay hoped that it might be so; and he had his desire, for, with the exception of Miss Toddle, no customer appeared. The teams went slowly down the steep side of the Square in an unbroken line, and slowly down the street leading from its near corner. On the slope the horses were unable to go fast—being forced to stell themselves back against the heavy propulsion of the carts behind; and thus the procession endured for a length of time worthy its surpassing greatness. When it disappeared round the Bend o' the Brae the watching bodies disappeared too; the event of the day had passed, and vacancy resumed her reign. The street and the Square lay empty to the morning sun. Gourlay alone stood idly at his gate, lapped in his own satisfaction.

It had been a big morning, he felt. It was the first time for many a year that all his men, quarrymen and carriers, carters of cheese and carters of grain, had led their teams down the brae together in the full view of his rivals. "I hope they liked it!" he thought, and he nodded several times at the town beneath his feet, with a slow up-and-down motion of the head, like a man nodding grimly to his beaten enemy. It was as if he said, "See what I have done to ye!"

CHAPTER II.

ONLY a man of Gourlay's brute force of character could have kept all the carrying trade of Barbie in his own hands. Even in these days of railways, nearly every parish has a pair of carriers at the least, journeying once or twice a week to the nearest town. In the days when Gourlay was the great man of Barbie, railways were only beginning to thrust themselves among the quiet hills, and the bulk of inland commerce was still being drawn by horses along the country roads. Yet Gourlay was the only carrier in the town. The wonder is diminished when we remember that it had been a decaying burgh for thirty years, and that its trade, at the best of times, was of meagre volume. Even so, it was astonishing that he should be the only carrier. If you asked the natives how he did it, " Ou," they said, " he makes the one hand wash the other, doan't ye know ? "—meaning thereby that he had so many horses travelling on his own business, that he could afford to carry other people's goods at rates that must cripple his rivals.

" But that's very stupid, surely," said a visitor once, who thought of entering into competition. " It's cutting off his nose to spite his face ! Why is he so anxious to be the only carrier in Barbie that he carries stuff for next to noathing the moment another man tries to work the roads ? It's a daft-like thing to do ! "

" To be sure is't, to be sure is't ! Just the stupeedity

o' spite ! Oh, there are times when Gourlay makes little or noathing from the carrying ; but then, ye see, it gies him a fine chance to annoy folk ! If you ask him to bring ye ocht, ' Oh,' he growls, ' I'll see if it suits my own convenience.' And ye have to be content. He has made so much money of late that the pride of him's not to be endured."

It was not the insolence of sudden wealth, however, that made Gourlay haughty to his neighbours ; it was a repressiveness natural to the man and a fierce contempt of their scoffing envy. But it was true that he had made large sums of money during recent years. From his father (who had risen in the world) he inherited a fine trade in cheese ; also the carrying to Skeighan on the one side and Fleckie on the other. When he married Miss Richmond of Tenshillingland, he started as a corn broker with the snug dowry that she brought him. Then, greatly to his own benefit, he succeeded in establishing a valuable connection with Templand-muir.

It was partly by sheer impact of character that Gourlay obtained his ascendency over hearty and careless Templandmuir, and partly by a bluff joviality which he —so little cunning in other things—knew to affect among the petty lairds. The man you saw trying to be jocose with Templandmuir was a very different being from the autocrat who " downed " his fellows in the town. It was all " How are ye the day, Templandmuir ? " and " How d'ye doo-oo, Mr. Gourlay ? " and the immediate production of the big decanter.

More than ten years ago now Templandmuir gave this fine, dour upstanding friend of his a twelve-year tack of the Red Quarry, and that was the making of Gourlay. The quarry yielded the best building stone in a circuit of thirty miles, easy to work and hard against wind and weather. When the main line went north through Skeighan and Poltandie, there was a great deal of building on the far side, and Gourlay simply coined the money. He could not have exhausted the quarry had he tried—he would have had to howk down a hill— but he took thousands of loads from it for the Skeighan folk; and the commission he paid the laird on each was ridiculously small. He built wooden stables out on Templandmuir's estate—the Templar had seven hundred acres of hill land—and it was there the quarry horses generally stood. It was only rarely—once in two years, perhaps—that they came into the House with the Green Shutters. Last Saturday they had brought several loads of stuff for Gourlay's own use, and that is why they were present at the great procession on the Monday following.

It was their feeling that Gourlay's success was out of all proportion to his merits that made other great-men-in-a-small-way so bitter against him. They were an able lot, and scarce one but possessed fifty times his weight of brain. Yet he had the big way of doing, though most of them were well enough to pass. Had they not been aware of his stupidity, they would never have minded his triumphs in the countryside; but they felt it with a sense of personal defeat that he—the donkey, as they thought him—should scoop every chance that was going, and leave them, the long-headed ones, still muddling in their old concerns. They consoled themselves with sneers, he retorted with brutal scorn, and the feud kept increasing between them.

They were standing at the Cross, to enjoy their Saturday at e'en, when Gourlay's " quarriers "—as the quarry horses had been named—came through the town last week-end. There were groups of bodies in the streets, washed from toil to enjoy the quiet air; dandering slowly or gossiping at ease; and they all turned to watch the quarriers stepping bravely up, their heads tossing to the hill. The big-men-in-a-small-way glowered and said nothing.

" I wouldn't mind," said Sandy Toddle at last—" I wouldn't mind if he weren't such a demned ess ! "

" Ess ? " said the Deacon unpleasantly. He puckered his brow and blinked, pretending not to understand.

" Oh, a cuddy, ye know," said Toddle, colouring.

" Gourlay'th stupid enough," lisped the Deacon ; " we all know that. But there'th one thing to be said on hith behalf. He's not such a ' demned ess ' as to try and thpeak fancy English ! "

When the Deacon was not afraid of a man he stabbed him straight ; when he was afraid of him he stabbed him on the sly. He was annoyed by the passing of Gourlay's carts, and he took it out of Sandy Toddle.

" It's extr'ornar ! " blurted the Provost (who was a man of brosy speech, large-mouthed and fat of utterance). " It's extr'ornar. Yass, it's extr'ornar ! I mean the luck of that man—for gumption he has noan, noan whatever ! But if the railway came hereaway I wager Gourlay would go down," he added, less in certainty of knowledge than as prophet of the thing desired. " I wager he'd go down, sirs."

" Likely enough," said Sandy Toddle ; " he wouldn't be quick enough to jump at the new way of doing."

" Moar than that ! " cried the Provost, spite sharpening his insight, " moar than that—he'd be owre dour to abandon the auld way. *I'm* talling ye. He would just be left entirely ! It's only those, like myself, who approach him on the town's affairs that know the full extent of his stupeedity."

" Oh, he's a ' demned ess,' " said the Deacon, rubbing it into Toddle and Gourlay at the same time.

" A-ah, but then, ye see, he has the abeelity that comes from character," said Johnny Coe, who was a sage philosopher. " For there are two kinds of abeelity, don't ye understa-and ? There's a scattered abeelity that's of no use! Auld Randie Donaldson was good at fifty different things, and he died in the poor-house! There's a dour kind of abeelity, though, that has no cleverness, but just gangs tramping on ; and that's——"

"The easiest beaten by a flank attack," said the Deacon, snubbing him.

CHAPTER III.

WITH the sudden start of a man roused from a day-dream Gourlay turned from the green gate and entered the yard. Jock Gilmour, the " orra " man, was washing down the legs of a horse beside the trough. It was Gourlay's own cob, which he used for driving round the countryside. It was a black—Gourlay " made a point " of driving with a black. " The brown for sturdiness, the black for speed," he would say, making a maxim of his whim to give it the sanction of a higher law.

Gilmour was in a wild temper because he had been forced to get up at five o'clock in order to turn several hundred cheeses, to prevent them bulging out of shape owing to the heat, and so becoming cracked and spoiled. He did not raise his head at his master's approach. And his head being bent, the eye was attracted to a patent leather collar which he wore, glazed with black and red stripes. It is a collar much affected by ploughmen, because a dip in the horse-trough once a month suffices for its washing. Between the striped collar and his hair (as he stooped) the sunburnt redness of his neck struck the eye vididly—the cropped fair hairs on it showing whitish on the red skin.

The horse quivered as the cold water swashed about its legs, and turned playfully to bite its groom. Gilmour, still stooping, dug his elbow up beneath its ribs. The animal wheeled in anger, but Gilmour ran to its head with most manful blasphemy, and led it to the stable door. The off hind leg was still unwashed.

" Has the horse but the three legs ? " said Gourlay
suavely.

Gilmour brought the horse back to the trough, mutter-
ing sullenly.

" Were ye saying anything ? " said Gourlay. " *Eih ?* "

Gilmour sulked out and said nothing ; and his master
smiled grimly at the sudden redness that swelled his neck
and ears to the verge of bursting.

A boy, standing in his shirt and trousers at an open
window of the house above, had looked down at the
scene with craning interest—big-eyed. He had been
alive to every turn and phase of it—the horse's quiver
of delight and fear, his skittishness, the groom's ill-
temper, and Gourlay's grinding will. Eh, but his father
was a caution ! How easy he had downed Jock Gilmour ! The boy was afraid of his father himself, but
he liked to see him send other folk to the right about.
For he was John Gourlay, too. Hokey, but his father
could down them !

Mr. Gourlay passed on to the inner yard, which was
close to the scullery door. The paved little court,
within its high wooden walls, was curiously fresh and
clean. A cock-pigeon strutted round, puffing his gleaming breast and *rooketty-cooing* in the sun. Large, clear
drops fell slowly from the spout of a wooden pump, and
splashed upon a flat stone. The place seemed to enfold
the stillness. There was a sense of inclusion and peace.

There is a distinct pleasure to the eye in a quiet brick
court where everything is fresh and prim ; in sunny
weather you can lounge in a room and watch it through
an open door, in a kind of lazy dream. The boy, standing at the window above to let the fresh air blow round
his neck, was alive to that pleasure ; he was intensely
conscious of the pigeon swelling in its bravery, of the
clean yard, the dripping pump, and the great stillness.
His father on the step beneath had a different pleasure
in the sight. The fresh indolence of morning was

round him too, but it was more than that that kept him gazing in idle happiness. He was delighting in the sense of his own property around him, the most substantial pleasure possible to man. His feeling, deep though it was, was quite vague and inarticulate. If you had asked Gourlay what he was thinking of he could not have told you, even if he had been willing to answer you civilly—which is most unlikely. Yet his whole being, physical and mental (physical, indeed, rather than mental), was surcharged with the feeling that the fine buildings around him were his, that he had won them by his own effort, and built them large and significant before the world. He was lapped in the thought of it.

All men are suffused with that quiet pride in looking at the houses and lands which they have won by their endeavours—in looking at the houses more than at the lands, for the house which a man has built seems to express his character and stand for him before the world, as a sign of his success. It is more personal than cold acres, stamped with an individuality. All men know that soothing pride in the contemplation of their own property. But in Gourlay's sense of property there was another element—an element peculiar to itself, which endowed it with its warmest glow. Conscious always that he was at a disadvantage among his cleverer neighbours, who could achieve a civic eminence denied to him, he felt nevertheless that there was one means, a material means, by which he could hold his own and reassert himself—by the bravery of his business, namely, and all the appointments thereof, among which his dwelling was the chief. That was why he had spent so much money on the house. That was why he had such keen delight in surveying it. Every time he looked at the place he had a sense of triumph over what he knew in his bones to be an adverse public opinion. There was anger in his pleasure, and the pleasure that is mixed with anger often gives the keenest thrill. It is the delight of triumph in spite of opposition. Gourlay's house was a material expression of that delight, stood for it in stone and lime.

It was not that he reasoned deliberately when he built the house. But every improvement that he made —and he was always spending money on improvements —had for its secret motive a more or less vague desire to score off his rivals. " *That*'ll be a slap in the face to the Provost ! " he smiled, when he planted his great mound of shrubs. " There's noathing like *that* about the Provost's ! Ha, ha ! "

Encased as he was in his hard and insensitive nature, he was not the man who in new surroundings would be quick to every whisper of opinion. But he had been born and bred in Barbie, and he knew his townsmen— oh yes, he knew them. He knew they laughed because he had no gift of the gab, and could never be Provost, or Bailie, or Elder, or even Chairman of the Gasworks ! Oh, verra well, verra well ; let Connal and Brodie and Allardyce have the talk, and manage the town's affairs (he was damned if they should manage his !)—he, for his part, preferred the substantial reality. He could never aspire to the provostship, but a man with a house like that, he was fain to think, could afford to do without it. Oh yes ; he was of opinion he could do without it ! It had run him short of cash to build the place so big and braw, but, Lord ! it was worth it. There wasn't a man in the town who had such accommodation !

And so, gradually, his dwelling had come to be a passion of Gourlay's life. It was a by-word in the place that if ever his ghost was seen, it would be haunting the House with the Green Shutters. Deacon Allardyce, trying to make a phrase with him, once quoted the saying in his presence. " Likely enough ! " said Gourlay. " It's only reasonable I should prefer my own house to you rabble in the graveyard ! "

Both in appearance and position the house was a worthy counterpart of its owner. It was a substantial two-story dwelling, planted firm and gawcey on a little natural terrace that projected a considerable distance into the Square. At the foot of the steep little bank shelving to the terrace ran a stone wall, of no great height, and the iron railings it uplifted were no higher than the sward within. Thus the whole house was bare to the view from the ground up, nothing in front to screen its admirable qualities. From each corner, behind, flanking walls went out to the right and left, and hid the yard and the granaries. In front of these walls the dwelling seemed to thrust itself out for notice. It took the eye of a stranger the moment he entered the Square. " Whose place is that ? " was his natural question. A house that challenges regard in that way should have a gallant bravery in its look ; if its aspect be mean, its assertive position but directs the eye to its infirmities. There is something pathetic about a tall, cold, barn-like house set high upon a brae ; it cannot hide its naked shame ; it thrusts its ugliness dumbly on your notice, a manifest blotch upon the world, a place for the winds to whistle round. But Gourlay's house was worthy its commanding station. A little dour and blunt in the outlines like Gourlay himself, it drew and satisfied your eye as he did.

And its position, " cockit up there on the brae," made it the theme of constant remark—to men because of the tyrant who owned it, and to women because of the poor woman who mismanaged its affairs. " 'Deed, I don't wonder that gurly Gourlay, as they ca' him, has an ill temper," said the gossips gathered at the pump, with their big, bare arms akimbo ; " whatever led him to marry that dishclout of a woman clean beats *me!* I never could make head nor tail o't ! " As for the men, they twisted every item about Gourlay and his domicile into fresh matter of assailment. " What's the news ? "

asked one, returning from a long absence ; to whom the
smith, after smoking in silence for five minutes, said,
" Gourlay has got new rones ! "   " Ha—ay, man, Gourlay has got new rones ! " buzzed the visitor ; and then
their eyes, diminished in mirth, twinkled at each other
from out their ruddy wrinkles, as if wit had volleyed
between them.   In short, the House with the Green
Shutters was on every tongue—and with a scoff in the
voice, if possible.

CHAPTER IV.

GOURLAY went swiftly to the kitchen from the inner
yard. He had stood so long in silence on the step, and
his coming was so noiseless, that he surprised a long,
thin trollop of a woman, with a long, thin, scraggy neck,
seated by the slatternly table, and busy with a frowsy
paper-covered volume, over which her head was bent
in intent perusal.

"At your novelles?" said he. "Ay, woman; will
it be a good story?"

She rose in a nervous flutter when she saw him; yet
needlessly shrill in her defence, because she was angry
at detection.

"Ah, well!" she cried, in weary petulance, "it's an
unco thing if a body's not to have a moment's rest after
such a morning's darg! I just sat down wi' the book
for a little, till John should come till his breakfast!"

"So?" said Gourlay. "God, ay!" he went on; "you're
making a nice job of *him*. *He'*ll be a credit to the house.
Oh, it's right, no doubt, that *you* should neglect your
work till *he* consents to rise."

"Eh, the puir la-amb," she protested, dwelling on the
vowels in fatuous, maternal love; "the bairn's wearied,
man! He's ainything but strong, and the schooling's
owre sore on him."

"Poor lamb, atweel," said Gourlay. "It was a
muckle sheep that dropped him."

It was Gourlay's pride in his house that made him

harsher to his wife than others, since her sluttishness
was a constant offence to the order in which he loved to
have his dear possessions. He, for his part, liked everything precise. His claw-toed hammer always hung by
the head on a couple of nails close together near the
big clock ; his gun always lay across a pair of wooden
pegs, projecting from the brown rafters, just above the
hearth. His bigotry in trifles expressed his character.
Strong men of a mean understanding often deliberately
assume, and passionately defend, peculiarities of no importance, because they have nothing else to get a repute
for. " No, no," said Gourlay ; " you'll never see a
brown cob in *my* gig—I wouldn't take one in a present ! "
He was full of such fads, and nothing should persuade
him to alter the crotchets, which, for want of something
better, he made the marks of his dour character. He
had worked them up as part of his personality, and his
pride of personality was such that he would never consent to change them. Hence the burly and gurly man
was prim as an old maid with regard to his belongings.
Yet his wife was continually infringing the order on
which he set his heart. If he went forward to the big
clock to look for his hammer, it was sure to be gone—
the two bright nails staring at him vacantly. " Oh," she
would say, in weary complaint, " I just took it to break
a wheen coals ; " and he would find it in the coal-hole,
greasy and grimy finger-marks engrained on the handle
which he loved to keep so smooth and clean. Innumerable her offences of the kind. Independent of these,
the sight of her general ·incompetence filled him with a
seething rage, which found vent not in lengthy tirades
but the smooth venom of his tongue. Let him keep the
outside of the house never so spick and span, inside was
awry with her untidiness. She was unworthy of the
House with the Green Shutters—that was the gist of it.
Every time he set eyes on the poor trollop, the fresh
perception of her incompetence which the sudden sight

of her flashed, as she trailed aimlessly about, seemed to
fatten his rage and give a coarser birr to his tongue.

Mrs. Gourlay had only four people to look after—her
husband, her two children, and Jock Gilmour, the
orra man. And the wife of Drucken Wabster—who
had to go charing because she was the wife of Drucken
Wabster—came in every day, and all day long, to help
her with the work. Yet the house was always in confusion. Mrs. Gourlay had asked for another servant, but
Gourlay would not allow that ; " one's enough," said he,
and what he once laid down he never went back on.
Mrs. Gourlay had to muddle along as best she could,
and having no strength either of mind or body, she let
things drift, and took refuge in reading silly fiction.

As Gourlay shoved his feet into his boots, and stamped
to make them easy, he glowered at the kitchen from
under his heavy brows with a huge disgust. The table
was littered with unwashed dishes, and on the corner
of it next him was a great black sloppy ring, showing
where a wet saucepan had been laid upon the bare board.
The sun streamed through the window in yellow heat
right on to a pat of melting butter. There was a basin
of dirty water beneath the table, with the dishcloth
slopping over on the ground.

" It's a tidy house ! " said he.

" Ach, well," she cried, " you and your kitchen-
range ! It was that that did it ! The masons could
have redd out the fireplace to make room for't in the
afternoon before it comes hame. They could have
done't brawly, but ye wouldna hear o't—oh no ; ye bude
to have the whole place gutted out yestreen. I had
to boil everything on the parlour fire this morning ; no
wonder I'm a little tousy ! "

The old-fashioned kitchen grate had been removed
and the jambs had been widened on each side of the
fireplace ; it yawned empty and cold. A little rubble
of mortar, newly dried, lay about the bottom of the

square recess.   The sight of the crude, unfamiliar scraps
of dropped lime in the gaping place where warmth
should have been, increased the discomfort of the
kitchen.

" Oh, that's it ! " said Gourlay.   " I see ! It was
want of the fireplace that kept ye from washing the
dishes that we used yestreen.   That was terrible !   However, ye'll have plenty of boiling water when I put in
the grand new range for ye ; there winna be its equal
in the parish !   We'll maybe have a clean house
than."

Mrs. Gourlay leaned, with the outspread thumb and
red raw knuckles of her right hand, on the sloppy table,
and gazed away through the back window of the kitchen
in a kind of mournful vacancy.   Always when her first
complaining defence had failed to turn aside her husband's tongue, her mind became a blank beneath his
heavy sarcasms, and sought refuge by drifting far away.
She would fix her eyes on the distance in dreary contemplation, and her mind would follow her eyes in a
vacant and wistful regard.   The preoccupation of her
mournful gaze enabled her to meet her husband's sneers
with a kind of numb, unheeding acquiescence.   She
scarcely heard them.

Her head hung a little to one side as if too heavy
for her wilting neck.   Her hair, of a dry, red brown,
curved low on either side of her brow, in a thick,
untidy mass, to her almost transparent ears.   As she
gazed in weary and dreary absorption her lips had fallen
heavy and relaxed, in unison with her mood ;   and
through her open mouth her breathing was quick, and
short, and noiseless.   She wore no stays, and her slack
cotton blouse showed the flatness of her bosom, and
the faint outlines of her withered and pendulous breasts
hanging low within.

There was something tragic in her pose, as she stood,
sad and abstracted, by the dirty table.   She was scraggy

helplessness, staring in sorrowful vacancy. But Gourlay eyed her with disgust. Why, by Heaven, even now her petticoat was gaping behind, worse than the sloven's at the Red Lion. She was a pr-r-retty wife for John Gourlay! The sight of her feebleness would have roused pity in some : Gourlay it moved to a steady and seething rage. As she stood helpless before him he stung her with crude, brief irony.

Yet he was not wilfully cruel ; only a stupid man with a strong character, in which he took a dogged pride. Stupidity and pride provoked the brute in him. He was so dull—only dull is hardly the word for a man of his smouldering fire—he was so dour of wit that he could never hope to distinguish himself by anything in the shape of cleverness. Yet so resolute a man must make the strong personality of which he was proud tell in some way. How, then, should he assert his superiority and hold his own ? Only by affecting a brutal scorn of everything said and done unless it was said and done by John Gourlay. His lack of understanding made his affectation of contempt the easier. A man can never sneer at a thing which he really understands. Gourlay, understanding nothing, was able to sneer at everything. "Hah ! I don't understand that ; it's damned nonsense ! "—that was his attitude to life. If "that" had been an utterance of Shakespeare or Napoleon it would have made no difference to John Gourlay. It would have been damned nonsense just the same. And he would have told them so, if he had met them.

The man had made dogged scorn a principle of life to maintain himself at the height which his courage warranted. His thickness of wit was never a bar to the success of his irony. For the irony of the ignorant Scot is rarely the outcome of intellectual qualities. It depends on a falsetto voice and the use of a recognized number of catchwords. " Dee-ee-ar me, dee-ee-ar me ; "

" Just so-a, just so-a ; " " Im-phm ! " " D'ye tell me
that ? " " Wonderful, serr, wonderful ; " " Ah, well,
may-ay-be, may-ay-be "—these be words of potent irony
when uttered with a certain birr. Long practice had
made Gourlay an adept in their use. He never spoke to
those he despised or disliked without " the birr." Not
that he was voluble of speech ; he wasn't clever enough
for lengthy abuse. He said little and his voice was low,
but every word from the hard, clean lips was a stab.
And often his silence was more withering than any utterance. It struck life like a black frost.

In those early days, to be sure, Gourlay had less occasion for the use of his crude but potent irony, since the
sense of his material well-being warmed him and made
him less bitter to the world. To the substantial farmers
and petty squires around he was civil, even hearty, in
his manner—unless they offended him. For they belonged to the close corporation of " bien men," and
his familiarity with them was a proof to the world of
his greatness. Others, again, were far too far beneath
him already for him to " down" them. He reserved his
gibes for his immediate foes, the assertive bodies his
rivals in the town—and for his wife, who was a constant
eyesore. As for her, he had baited the poor woman so
long that it had become a habit ; he never spoke to her
without a sneer. " Ay, where have *you* been stravaiging
to ? " he would drawl ; and if she answered meekly, " I
was taking a dander to the linn owre-bye," " The Linn ! "
he would take her up ; " ye had a heap to do to gang
there ; your Bible would fit you better on a bonny
Sabbath afternune ! " Or it might be : " What's that
you're burying your nose in now ? " and if she faltered,
" It's the Bible," " Hi ! " he would laugh, " you're turning godly in your auld age. Weel, I'm no saying but it's
time."

" Where's Janet ? " he demanded, stamping his boots
once more, now he had them laced.

"Eh?" said his wife vaguely, turning her eyes from the window. "Wha-at?"

"Ye're not turning deaf, I hope. I was asking ye where Janet was."

"I sent her down to Scott's for a can o' milk," she answered him wearily.

"No doubt ye had to send *her*," said he. "What ails the lamb that ye couldna send *him*—eh?"

"Oh, she was about when I wanted the milk, and she volunteered to gang. Man, it seems I never do a thing to please ye! What harm will it do her to run for a drop milk?"

"Noan," he said gravely, "noan. And it's right, no doubt, that her brother should still be abed—oh, it's right that he should get the privilege—seeing he's the eldest!"

Mrs. Gourlay was what the Scotch call "browdened * on her boy." In spite of her slack grasp on life—perhaps, because of it—she clung with a tenacious fondness to him. He was all she had, for Janet was a thowless † thing, too like her mother for her mother to like her. And Gourlay had discovered that it was one way of getting at his wife to be hard upon the thing she loved. In his desire to nag and annoy her he adopted a manner of hardness and repression to his son—which became permanent. He was always "down" on John; the more so because Janet was his own favourite—perhaps, again, because her mother seemed to neglect her. Janet was a very unlovely child, with a long, tallowy face and a pimply brow, over which a stiff fringe of whitish hair came down almost to her staring eyes, the eyes themselves being large, pale blue, and saucer-like, with a great margin of unhealthy white. But Gourlay, though he never petted her, had a silent satisfaction in his daughter.

---

* *Browdened.* A Scot devoted to his children is said to be "browdened on his bairns."

† *Thowless*, weak, useless.

He took her about with him in the gig, on Saturday afternoons. when he went to buy cheese and grain at the outlying farms. And he fed her rabbits when she had the fever. It was a curious sight to see the dour, silent man mixing oatmeal and wet tea-leaves in a saucer at the dirty kitchen table, and then marching off to the hutch, with the ridiculous dish in his hand, to feed his daughter's pets.

*   *   *   *   *   *

A sudden yell of pain and alarm rang through the kitchen. It came from the outer yard.

When the boy, peering from the window above, saw his father disappear through the scullery door, he stole out. The coast was clear at last.

He passed through to the outer yard. Jock Gilmour had been dashing water on the paved floor, and was now sweeping it out with a great whalebone besom. The hissing whalebone sent a splatter of dirty drops showering in front of it. John set his bare feet wide (he was only in his shirt and knickers) and eyed the man whom his father had " downed " with a kind of silent swagger. He felt superior. His pose was instinct with the feeling : " *My* father is *your* master, and ye daurna stand up till him." Children of masterful sires often display that attitude towards dependants. The feeling is not the less real for being subconscious.

Jock Gilmour was still seething with a dour anger because Gourlay's quiet will had ground him to the task. When John came out and stood there, he felt tempted to vent on him the spite he felt against his father. The subtle suggestion of criticism and superiority in the boy's pose intensified the wish. Not that Gilmour acted from deliberate malice ; his irritation was instinctive. Our wrath against those whom we fear is generally wreaked upon those whom we don't.

John, with his hands in his pockets, strutted across the yard, still watching Gilmour with that silent, offen-

sive look. He came into the path of the whalebone.
" Get out, you smeowt ! " cried Gilmour, and with a
vicious shove of the brush he sent a shower of dirty
drops spattering about the boy's bare legs.

" Hallo you ! what are ye after ? " bawled the boy.
" Don't you try that on again, I'm telling ye. What are
you, onyway ? Ye're just a servant. Hay-ay-ay, my man,
my faither's the boy for ye. *He* can put ye in your place."

Gilmour made to go at him with the head of the
whalebone besom. John stooped and picked up the
wet lump of cloth with which Gilmour had been washing
down the horse's legs.

" Would ye ? " said Gilmour threateningly.

" Would I no ? " said John, the wet lump poised for
throwing, level with his shoulder.

But he did not throw it for all his defiant air. He
hesitated. He would have liked to slash it into Gilmour's face, but a swift vision of what would happen
if he did withheld his craving arm. His irresolution
was patent in his face ; in his eyes there were both a
threat and a watchful fear. He kept the dirty cloth
poised in mid-air.

" Drap the clout," said Gilmour.

" I'll no," said John.

Gilmour turned sideways and whizzed the head of
the besom round so that its dirty spray rained in the
boy's face and eyes. John let him have the wet lump
slash in his mouth. Gilmour dropped the besom and
hit him a sounding thwack on the ear. John hulla-
balooed. Murther and desperation !

Ere he had gathered breath for a second roar his
mother was present in the yard. She was passionate in
defence of her cub, and rage transformed her. Her
tense frame vibrated in anger ; you would scarce have
recognized the weary trollop of the kitchen.

" What's the matter, Johnny dear ? " she cried, with
a fierce glance at Gilmour.

" Gilmour hut me ! " he bellowed angrily.

" Ye muckle lump ! " she cried shrilly, the two scraggy muscles of her neck standing out long and thin as she screamed ; " ye muckle lump—to strike a defenceless wean !—Dinna greet, my lamb ; I'll no let him meddle ye.—Jock Gilmour, how daur ye lift your finger to a wean of mine ? But I'll learn ye the better o't ! Mr. Gourlay 'll gie *you* the order to travel ere the day's muckle aulder. I'll have no servant about *my* hoose to ill-use *my* bairn."

She stopped, panting angrily for breath, and glared at her darling's enemy.

" *Your* servant ! " cried Gilmour in contempt. " Ye're a nice-looking object to talk about servants." He pointed at her slovenly dress and burst into a blatant laugh : " Huh, huh, huh ! "

Mr. Gourlay had followed more slowly from the kitchen, as befitted a man of his superior character. He heard the row well enough, but considered it beneath him to hasten to a petty squabble.

" What's this ? " he demanded with a widening look. Gilmour scowled at the ground.

" This ! " shrilled Mrs. Gourlay, who had recovered her breath again — " this ! Look at him there, the muckle slabber," and she pointed to Gilmour, who was standing with a red-lowering, downcast face, " look at him ! A man of that size to even himsell to a wean ! "

" He deserved a' he got," said Gilmour sullenly. " His mother spoils him, at ony rate. And I'm damned if the best Gourlay that ever dirtied leather's gaun to trample owre *me*."

Gourlay jumped round with a quick start of the whole body. For a full minute he held Gilmour in the middle of his steady glower.

" Walk," he said, pointing to the gate.

" Oh, I'll walk," bawled Gilmour, screaming now that anger gave him courage. " Gie me time to get *my* kist, and I'll walk mighty quick. And damned glad I'll be to get redd o' you and your hoose. The Hoose wi' the Green Shutters," he laughed, "hi, hi, hi!—the Hoose wi' the Green Shutters!"

Gourlay went slowly up to him, opening his eyes on him black and wide. "You swine!" he said, with quiet vehemence; "for damned little I would kill ye wi' a glower!"

Gilmour shrank from the blaze in his eyes.

"Oh, dinna be fee-ee-ared," said Gourlay quietly, "dinna be fee-ee-ared. I wouldn't dirty my hand on 'ee! But get your bit kist, and I'll see ye off the premises. Suspeecious characters are worth the watching."

"Suspeecious!" stuttered Gilmour, "suspeecious! Wh-wh-whan was I ever suspeecious? I'll have the law of ye for that. I'll make ye answer for your wor-rds."

"Imphm!" said Gourlay. "In the meantime, look slippy wi' that bit box o' yours. I don't like daft folk about *my* hoose."

"There'll be dafter folk as me in your hoose yet," spluttered Gilmour angrily, as he turned away.

He went up to the garret where he slept and brought down his trunk. As he passed through the scullery, bowed beneath the clumsy burden on his left shoulder, John, recovered from his sobbing, mocked at him.

"Hay-ay-ay," he said, in throaty derision, "my faither's the boy for ye. Yon was the way to put ye down!"

CHAPTER V.

In every little Scotch community there is a distinct type known as " the bodie." " What does he do, that man ? " you may ask, and the answer will be, " Really, I could hardly tell ye what he does—he's juist a bodie ! " The " bodie " may be a gentleman of independent means (a hundred a year from the Funds), fussing about in spats and light check breeches ; or he may be a jobbing gardener ; but he is equally a " bodie." The chief occupation of his idle hours (and his hours are chiefly idle) is the discussion of his neighbour's affairs. He is generally an " auld residenter ; " great, therefore, at the redding up of pedigrees. He can tell you exactly, for instance, how it is that young Pin-oe's taking geyly to the dram ; for his grandfather, it seems, was a terrible man for the drink—ou, just terrible. Why, he went to bed with a full jar of whisky once, and when he left it he was dead, and it was empty. So, ye see, that's the reason o't.

The genus " bodie " is divided into two species—the " harmless bodies " and the " nesty bodies." The bodies of Barbie mostly belonged to the second variety. Johnny Coe and Tam Wylie and the baker were decent enough fellows in their way, but the others were the sons of scandal. Gourlay spoke of them as a " wheen damned auld wives." But Gourlay, to be sure, was not an impartial witness.

The Bend o' the Brae was the favourite stance of the bodies : here they forgathered every day to pass judg-

ment on the town's affairs.   And, indeed, the place had
many things to recommend it.   Among the chief it was
within an easy distance of the Red Lion, farther up
the street, to which it was really very convenient to
adjourn nows and nans.   Standing at the Bend o' the
Brae, too, you could look along two roads to the left
and right, or down upon the Cross beneath, and the three
low streets that guttered away from it.   Or you might
turn and look up Main Street, and past the side of the
Square, to the House with the Green Shutters, the
highest in the town.   The Bend o' the Brae, you will
gather, was a fine post for observation.   It had one
drawback, true : if Gourlay turned to the right in his
gig he disappeared in a moment, and you could never
be sure where he was off to.   But even that afforded
matter for pleasing speculation which often lasted half
an hour.

It was about nine o'clock when Gourlay and Gilmour
quarrelled in the yard, and that was the hour when the
bodies forgathered for their morning dram.

" Good-moarning, Mr. Wylie ! " said the Provost.

When the Provost wished you good-morning, with a
heavy civic eye, you felt sure it was going to be good.

" Mornin', Provost, mornin' ! Fine weather for the
fields," said Tam, casting a critical glance at the blue
dome in which a soft, white-bosomed cloud floated high
above the town.   " If this weather hauds, it'll be a
blessing for us poor farming bodies."

Tam was a wealthy old hunks, but it suited his humour
to refer to himself constantly as " a poor farming bodie."
And he dressed in accordance with his humour.   His
clean old crab-apple face was always grinning at you
from over a white-sleeved moleskin waistcoat, as if he
had been no better than a breaker of road-metal.

" Faith ay ! " said the Provost, cunning and quick ;
" fodder should be cheap "—and he shot the covetous
glimmer of a bargain-making eye at Mr. Wylie.

Tam drew himself up. He saw what was coming.

" We're needing some hay for the burgh horse," said the Provost. " Ye'll be willing to sell at fifty shillings the ton, since it's like to be so plentiful."

" Oh," said Tam solemnly, " that's on-possible! Gourlay's seeking the three pound! and where he leads we maun a' gang. Gourlay sets the tune, and Barbie dances till't."

That was quite untrue so far as the speaker was concerned. It took a clever man to make Tam Wylie dance to his piping. But Thomas, the knave, knew that he could always take a rise out the Provost by cracking up the Gourlays, and that to do it now was the best way of fobbing him off about the hay.

" Gourlay! " muttered the Provost, in disgust. And Tam winked at the baker.

" Losh," said Sandy Toddle, " yonder's the Free Kirk minister going past the Cross! Where'll *he* be off till at this hour of the day? He's not often up so soon."

" They say he sits late studying," said Johnny Coe.

" H'mph, studying! " grunted Tam Brodie, a big, heavy, wall-cheeked man, whose little, side-glancing eyes seemed always alert for scandal amid the massive insolence of his smooth face. " I see few signs of studying in *him*. He's noathing but a stink wi' a skin on't."

T. Brodie was a very important man, look you, and wrote " Leather Mercht." above his door, though he cobbled with his own hands. He was a staunch. Conservative, and down on the Dissenters.

" What road'th he taking? " lisped Deacon Allardyce, craning past Brodie's big shoulder to get a look.

" He's stoppit to speak to Widow Wallace. What will he be saying to *her*? "

" She's a greedy bodie that Mrs. Wallace: I wouldna wonder but she's speiring him for bawbees."

" Will he take the Skeighan Road, I wonder? "

" Or the Fechars ? "

" He's a great man for gathering gowans and other
sic trash.   He's maybe for a dander up the burn juist.
They say he's a great botanical man."

" Ay," said Brodie, " paidling in a burn's the ploy
for him.   He's a weanly gowk."

" A-a-ah ! " protested the baker, who was a Burnso-
maniac, " there's waur than a walk by the bank o' a
bonny burn.   Ye ken what Mossgiel said :—

> 'The Muse nae poet ever fand her,
> Till by himsel' he learned to wander,
> Adown some trottin' burn's meander,
>   And no thick lang ;
> Oh sweet to muse and pensive ponder
>   A heartfelt sang.' "

Poetical quotations, however, made the Provost uncomfortable.   " Ay," he said dryly in his throat ; " verra
good, baker, verra good !—Who's yellow doag's that ?
I never saw the beast about the town before ! "

" Nor me either.   It's a perfect stranger ! "

" It's like a herd's doag ! "

" Man, you're right !   That's just what it will be.
The morn's Fleckie lamb fair, and some herd or other'll
be in about the town."

" He'll be drinking in some public-house, I'se warrant, and the doag will have lost him."

" Imph, that'll be the way o't."

" I'm demned if he hasn't taken the Skeighan Road ! "
said Sandy Toddle, who had kept his eye on the minister.   Toddle's accent was a varying quality.   When
he remembered he had been a packman in England it
was exceedingly fine.   But he often forgot.

" The Skeighan Road ! the Skeighan Road !   Who'll
he be going to see in that airt ?   Will it be Templandmuir ? "

" Gosh, it canna be Templandmuir ; he was there
no later than yestreen ! "

" Here's a man coming down the brae ! " announced Johnny Coe, in a solemn voice, as if a man " coming down the brae " was something unusual. In a moment every head was turned to the hill.

" What's yon he's carrying on his shouther ? " pondered Brodie.

" It looks like a boax," said the Provost slowly, bending every effort of eye and mind to discover what it really was. He was giving his profoundest cogitations to the " boax."

" It *is* a boax ! But who is it though ? I canna make him out."

" Dod, I canna tell either ; his head's so bent with his burden ! "

At last the man, laying his " boax " on the ground, stood up to ease his spine, so that his face was visible.

" Losh, it's Jock Gilmour, the orra man at Gourlay's ! What'll *he* be doing out on the street at this hour of the day ? I thocht he was always busy on the premises ! Will Gourlay be sending him off with something to somebody ? But no ; that canna be. He would have sent it with the carts."

" I'll wager ye," cried Johnny Coe quickly, speaking more loudly than usual in the animation of discovery— " I'll wager ye Gourlay has quarrelled him and put him to the door ! "

" Man, you're right ! That'll just be it, that'll just be it ! Ay, ay—faith ay—and yon'll be his kist he's carrying ! Man, you're right, Mr. Coe ; you have just put your finger on't. We'll hear news *this* morning."

They edged forward to the middle of the road, the Provost in front, to meet Gilmour coming down.

" Ye've a heavy burden this morning, John," said the Provost graciously.

" No wonder, sir," said Gilmour, with big-eyed solemnity, and set down the chest ; " it's no wonder, seeing that I'm carrying my a-all."

" Ay, man, John.   How's that na ? "

To be the centre of interest and the object of gracious condescension was balm to the wounded feelings of Gilmour.   Gourlay had lowered him, but this reception restored him to his own good opinion.   He was usually called " Jock " (except by his mother, to whom, of course, he was " oor Johnny "), but the best merchants in the town were addressing him as " John."   It was a great occasion.   Gilmour expanded in gossip beneath its influence benign.

He welcomed, too, this first and fine opportunity of venting his wrath on the Gourlays.

" Oh, I just telled Gourlay what I thocht of him, and took the door ahint me.   I let him have it hot and hardy, I can tell ye.   He'll no forget *me* in a hurry "— Gilmour bawled angrily, and nodded his head significantly, and glared fiercely, to show what good cause he had given Gourlay to remember him—" he'll no forget *me* for a month of Sundays."

" Ay, man, John, what did ye say till him ? "

" Na, man, what did he say to you ? "

" Wath he angry, Dyohn ? "

" How did the thing begin ? "

" Tell us, man, John."

" What was it a-all about, John ? "

" Was Mrs. Gourlay there ? "

Bewildered by this pelt of questions, Gilmour answered the last that hit his ear.   " There, ay ; faith, she was there.   It was her was the cause o't."

" D'ye tell me that, John ?   Man, you surprise me.   I would have thocht the thowless trauchle * hadna the smeddum left to interfere."

" Oh, it was yon boy of hers.   He's aye swaggerin' aboot, interferin' wi' folk at their wark—he follows his faither's example in that, for as the auld cock craws the young ane learns—and his mither's that daft aboot him

* *Trauchle*, a poor trollop who trails about ; *smeddum*, grit.

that ye daurna give a look! He came in my road when
I was sweeping out the close, and some o' the dirty
jaups splashed about his shins. But was I to blame for
that?—ye maun walk wide o' a whalebone besom if ye
dinna want to be splashed. Afore I kenned where I
was, he up wi' a dirty washing-clout and slashed me
in the face wi't! I hit him a thud in the ear—as wha
wadna? Out come his mither like a fury, skirling
about *her* hoose, and *her* servants, and *her* weans. ' Your
servant!' says I—' your servant! You're a nice-looking trollop to talk aboot servants,' says I."

" Did ye really, John? "

" Man, that wath bauld o' ye."

" And what did *she* say? "

" Oh, she just kept skirling! And then, to be sure,
Gourlay must come out and interfere! But I telled
him to his face what I thocht of *him*! ' The best Gourlay that ever dirtied leather,' says I, ' 's no gaun to
make dirt of me,' says I."

" Ay, man, Dyohn! " lisped Deacon Allardyce, with
bright and eagerly inquiring eyes. " And what did he
thay to that na? *That* wath a dig for him! I'the
warrant he wath angry."

" Angry? He foamed at the mouth! But I up and
says to him, ' I have had enough o' you,' says I, ' you
and your Hoose wi' the Green Shutters,' says I. ' You're
no fit to have a decent servant,' says I. ' Pay *me my*
wages, and I'll be redd o' ye,' says I. And wi' that I
flang my kist on my shouther and slapped the gate
ahint me."

" And *did* he pay ye your wages? " Tam Wylie probed
him slyly, with a sideward glimmer in his eye.

" Ah, well, no—not exactly," said Gilmour, drawing
in. " But I'll get them right enough for a' that. He'll
no get the better o' *me*." Having grounded unpleasantly on the question of the wages, he thought it best
to be off ere the bloom was dashed from his importance,

so he shouldered his chest and went. The bodies watched him down the street.

"He's a lying brose, that," said the baker. "We a' ken what Gourlay is. He would have flung Gilmour out by the scruff o' the neck if he had daured to set his tongue against him!"

"Faith, that's so," said Tam Wylie and Johnny Coe together.

But the others were divided between their perception of the fact and their wish to believe that Gourlay had received a thrust or two. At other times they would have been the first to scoff at Gilmour's swagger. Now their animus against Gourlay prompted them to back it up.

"Oh, I'm not so sure of tha-at, baker," cried the Provost, in the false, loud voice of a man defending a position which he knows to be unsound; "I'm no so sure of that at a-all. A-a-ah, mind ye," he drawled persuasively, "he's a hardy fallow, that Gilmour. I've no doubt he gied Gourlay a good dig or two. Let us howp they will do him good."

For many reasons intimate to the Scot's character, envious scandal is rampant in petty towns such as Barbie. To go back to the beginning, the Scot, as pundits will tell you, is an individualist. His religion alone is enough to make him so; for it is a scheme of personal salvation significantly described once by the Reverend Mr. Struthers of Barbie. "At the Day of Judgment, my frehnds," said Mr. Struthers—"at the Day of Judgment every herring must hang by his own tail!" Self-dependence was never more luridly expressed. History, climate, social conditions, and the national beverage have all combined (the pundits go on) to make the Scot an individualist, fighting for his own hand. The better for him if it be so; from that he gets the grit that tells.

From their individualism, however, comes inevitably

a keen spirit of competition (the more so because Scotch
democracy gives fine chances to compete), and from
their keen spirit of competition comes, inevitably again,
an envious belittlement of rivals. If a man's success
offends your individuality, to say everything you can
against him is a recognized weapon of the fight. It
takes him down a bit, and (inversely) elevates his
rival.

It is in a small place like Barbie that such malignity
is most virulent, because in a small place like Barbie
every man knows everything to his neighbour's detri-
ment. He can redd up his rival's pedigree, for example,
and lower his pride (if need be) by detailing the disgraces
of his kin. " I have grand news the day ! " a big-
hearted Scot will exclaim (and when their hearts are big
they are big to hypertrophy)—" I have grand news the
day ! Man, Jock Goudie has won the C.B."—" Jock
Goudie "—an envious bodie will pucker as if he had
never heard the name—" Jock Goudie ? Wha's *he* for a
Goudie ? Oh ay, let me see now   He's a brother o'—eh,
a brother o'—eh " (tit-tit-titting on his brow)—" oh, just
a brother o' Drucken Will Goudie o' Auchterwheeze !
Oo-ooh, I ken *him* fine. His grannie keepit a sweetie-
shop in Strathbungo." There you have the " nesty "
Scotsman.

Even if Gourlay had been a placable and inoffensive
man, then, the malignants of the petty burgh (it was
scarce bigger than a village) would have fastened on his
character simply because he was above them. No man
has a keener eye for behaviour than the Scot (especially when spite wings his intuition), and Gourlay's
thickness of wit and pride of place would in any case
have drawn their sneers. So, too, on lower grounds,
would his wife's sluttishness. But his repressiveness
added a hundredfold to their hate of him. That was
the particular cause which, acting on their general
tendency to belittle a too-successful rival, made their

spite almost monstrous against him. Not a man among
them but had felt the weight of his tongue—for edge
it had none. He walked among them like the dirt below
his feet. There was no give and take in the man ; he
could be verra jocose with the lairds, to be sure, but he
never dropped in to the Red Lion for a crack and a dram
with the town-folk ; he just glowered as if he could
devour them ! And who was he, I should like to know ?
His grandfather had been noathing but a common
carrier !

Hate was the greater on both sides because it was
often impotent. Gourlay frequently suspected offence,
and seethed because he had no idea how to meet it—
except by driving slowly down the brae in his new gig
and never letting on when the Provost called to him.
That was a wipe in the eye for the Provost ! The
" bodies," on their part, could rarely get near enough
Gourlay to pierce his armour ; he kept them off him by
his brutal dourness. For it was not only pride and
arrogance, but a consciousness also that he was no
match for them at their own game, that kept Gourlay
away from their society. They were adepts at the under
stroke, and they would have given him many a dig if
he had only come amongst them. But, oh no, not he ;
he was the big man ; he never gave a body a chance !
Or if you did venture a bit jibe when you met him, he
glowered you off the face of the earth with thae black
een of his. Oh, how they longed to get at him ! It
was not the least of the evils caused by Gourlay's black
pride that it perverted a dozen characters. The " bodies "
of Barbie may have been decent enough men in their
own way, but against him their malevolence was monstrous. It showed itself in an insane desire to seize on
every scrap of gossip they might twist against him.
That was why the Provost lowered municipal dignity to
gossip in the street with a discharged servant. As the
baker said afterwards, it was absurd for a man in his

" poseetion." But it was done with the sole desire of
hearing something that might tell against Gourlay.
Even countesses, we are told, gossip with malicious
maids about other countesses. Spite is a great leveller.

" Shall we adjourn ? " said Brodie, when they had
watched Jock Gilmour out of sight. He pointed across
his shoulder to the Red Lion.

" Better noat just now," said the Provost, nodding
in slow authority—" better noat just now! I'm very
anxious to see Gourlay about yon matter we were speaking of, doan't ye understa-and ? But I'm determined
not to go to his house! On the other hand, if we go
into the Red Lion the now, we may miss him on the
street. We'll noat have loang to wait, though ; he'll be
down the town directly, to look at the horses he has at
the gerse out the Fechars Road. But *I'm* talling ye, I
simply will noat go to his house—to put up with a
wheen damned insults! " he puffed in angry recollection.

" To tell the truth," said Wylie, " I don't like to call
upon Gourlay either. I'm aware of his eyes on my
back when I slink beaten through his gate, and I feel
that my hurdies are wanting in dignity ! "

" Huh ! " spluttered Brodie, " that never affects me.
I come stunting out in a bleeze of wrath and slam the
yett ahint me ! "

" Oh, well," said the Deacon, " that'th one way of
being dignified."

" I'm afraid," said Sandy Toddle, " that he won't be
in a very good key to consider our request this morning,
after his quarrel with Gilmour."

" No," said the Provost ; " he'll be blazing angry !
It's most unfoartunate. But we maun try to get his
consent, be his temper what it will. It's a matter of importance to the town, doan't ye see, and if he refuses
we simply can-noat proceed wi' the improvement."

" It was Gilmour's jibe at the House wi' the Green
Shutters that would anger him the most, for it's the

perfect god of his idolatry. Eh, sirs, he has wasted an awful money upon yon house ! ”

“ Wasted's the word ! ” said Brodie, with a blatant laugh. “ Wasted's the word ! They say he has verra little lying cash ! And I shouldna be surprised at all. For, ye see, Gibson the builder diddled him owre the building o't.”

“ Oh, I'se warrant Cunning Johnny would get the better of an ass like Gourlay. But how in particular, Mr. Brodie ? Have ye heard ainy details ? ”

“ I've been on the track o' the thing for a while back, but it was only yestreen I had the proofs o't. It was Robin Wabster that telled me. He's a jouking bodie, Robin, and he was ahint a dike up the Skeighan Road when Gibson and Gourlay forgathered — they stoppit just forenenst him ! Gourlay began to curse at the size of Gibson's bill, but Cunning Johnny kenned the way to get round him brawly. ‘ Mr. Gourlay,’ says he, ‘ there's not a thing in your house that a man in your poseetion can afford to be without, and ye needn't expect the best house in Barbie for an oald song ! ’ And Gourlay was pacified at once ! It appeared frae their crack, however, that Gibson has diddled him tremendous. ‘ Verra well then,’ Robin heard Gourlay cry, ‘ you must allow me a while ere I pay that ! ’ I wager, for a' sae muckle as he's made of late, that his balance at the bank's a sma' yin.”

“ More thyow than thubstanth,” said the Deacon.

“ Well, I'm sure ! ” said the Provost, “ he needn't have built such a gra-and house to put a slut of a wife like yon in ! ”

“ I was surprised,” said Sandy Toddle, “ to hear about her firing up. I wouldn't have thought she had the spirit, or that Gourlay would have come to her support ! ”

“ Oh,” said the Provost, “ it wasn't her he was thinking of ! It was his own pride, the brute. He leads the woman the life of a doag. I'm surprised that he ever married her ! "

" I ken fine how he married her," said Johnny Coe. " I was acquaint wi' her faither, auld Tenshillingland owre at Fechars—a grand farmer he was, wi' land o' his nain, and a gey pickle bawbees. It was the bawbees, and not the woman, that Gourlay went after ! It was *her* money, as ye ken, that set him on his feet, and made him such a big man. He never cared a preen for *her*, and then when she proved a dirty trollop, he couldna endure her look ! That's what makes him so sore upon her now. And yet I mind her a braw lass, too," said Johnny the sentimentalist, " a braw lass she was," he mused, " wi' fine, brown glossy hair, I mind, and— ochonee ! ochonee !—as daft as a yett in a windy day. She had a cousin, Jenny Wabster, that dwelt in Tenshillingland than, and mony a summer nicht up the Fechars Road, when ye smelled the honeysuckle in the gloaming, I have heard the two o' them tee-heeing owre the lads thegither, skirling in the dark and lauching to themselves. They were of the glaikit kind ye can always hear loang before ye see. Jock Allan (that has done so well in Embro) was a herd at Tenshillingland than, and he likit her, and I think she likit him ; but Gourlay came wi' his gig and whisked her away. She doesna lauch sae muckle now, puir bodie ! But a braw lass she——"

" It's you maun speak to Gourlay, Deacon," said the Provost, brushing aside the reminiscent Coe.

" How can it be that, Provost ? It'th *your* place, surely. You're the head of the town ! "

When Gourlay was to be approached there was always a competition for who should be hindmost.

" Yass, but you know perfectly well, Deacon, that I cannot thole the look of him. I simply cannot thole the look. And he knows it too. The thing'll gang smash at the outset—*I'm* talling ye, now—it'll go smash at the outset if it's left to me. And than, ye see, you have a better way of approaching folk ! "

" Ith that tho ? " said the Deacon dryly. He shot a suspicious glance to see if the Provost was guying him.

" Oh, it must be left to you, Deacon," said the baker and Tam Wylie in a breath.

" Certainly, it maun be left to the Deacon," assented Johnny Coe, when he saw how the others were giving their opinion.

" Tho be it, then," snapped the Deacon.

" Here he comes," said Sandy Toddle.

Gourlay came down the street towards them, his chest big, his thumbs in the armholes of his waistcoat. He had the power of staring steadily at those whom he approached without the slightest sign of recognition or intelligence appearing in his eyes. As he marched down upon the bodies he fixed them with a wide-open glower that was devoid of every expression but courageous steadiness. It gave a kind of fierce vacancy to his look.

The Deacon limped forward on his thin shanks to the middle of the road.

" It'th a fine morning, Mr. Gourlay," he simpered.

" There's noathing wrong with the morning," grunted Gourlay, as if there was something wrong with the Deacon.

" We wath wanting to thee ye on a very important matter, Mithter Gourlay," lisped the Deacon, smiling up at the big man's face, with his head on one side, and rubbing his fingers in front of him. " It'th a matter of the common good, you thee ; and we all agreed that we should speak to *you*, ath the foremost merchant of the town ! "

Allardyce meant his compliment to fetch Gourlay. But Gourlay knew his Allardyce, and was cautious. It was well to be on your guard when the Deacon was complimentary. When his language was most flowery there was sure to be a serpent hidden in it somewhere.

He would lisp out an innocent remark and toddle away, and Gourlay would think nothing of the matter till a week afterwards, perhaps, when something would flash a light; then " Damn him, did he mean ' *that* ' ? " he would seethe, starting back and staring at the " *that* " while his fingers strangled the air in place of the Deacon.

He glowered at the Deacon now till the Deacon blinked.

" You thee, Mr. Gourlay," Allardyce shuffled uneasily, " it'th for your own benefit just ath much ath ourth. We were thinking of you ath well ath of ourthelves ! Oh yeth, oh yeth ! "

" Ay, man ! " said Gourlay, " that was kind of ye ! I'll be the first man in Barbie to get ainy benefit from the fools that mismanage our affairs."

The gravel grated beneath the Provost's foot. The atmosphere was becoming electric, and the Deacon hastened to the point.

" You thee, there'th a fine natural supply of water— a perfect reservore the Provost sayth—on the brae-face just above *your* garden, Mr. Gourlay. Now, it would be easy to lead that water down and alang through all the gardenth on the high side of Main Street—and, 'deed, it might feed a pump at the Cross, too, to supply the lower portionth o' the town. It would really be a grai-ait convenience. Every man on the high side o' Main Street would have a running spout at his own back door ! If your garden didna run tho far back, Mr. Gourlay, and ye hadna tho muckle land about your place " —*that* should fetch him, thought the Deacon — " if it werena for that, Mr. Gourlay, we could easily lead the water round to the other gardenth without interfering with your property. But, ath it ith, we simply cannoat move without ye. The water must come through your garden, if it comes at a-all."

" The most o' you important men live on the high side o' Main Street," birred Gourlay. " Is it the poor folk at the Cross, or your ain bits o' back doors that you're thinking o'?"

"Oh—oh, Mr. Gourlay!" protested Allardyce, head flung back, and palms in air, to keep the thought of self-interest away, "oh—oh, Mr. Gourlay! We're thinking of noathing but the common good, I do assure ye."

"Ay, man! You're dis-in-ter-ested!" said Gourlay, but he stumbled on the big word and spoiled the sneer. That angered him, and, "It's likely," he rapped out, "that I'll allow the land round *my* house to be howked and trenched and made a mudhole of to oblige a wheen things like you!"

"Oh—oh, but think of the convenience to uth—eh—eh—I mean to the common good," said Allardyce.

"I howked wells for myself," snapped Gourlay. "Let others do the like."

"Oh, but we haven't all the enterprithe of you, Mr. Gourlay. You'll surely accommodate the town!"

"I'll see the town damned first," said Gourlay, and passed on his steady way.

CHAPTER VI.

THE bodies watched Gourlay in silence until he was out of earshot. Then, " It's monstrous ! " the Provost broke out in solemn anger ; " I declare it's perfectly monstrous ! But I believe we could get Pow-ers to compel him. Yass ; I believe we could get Pow-ers. I do believe we could get Pow-ers."

The Provost was fond of talking about " Pow-ers," because it implied that he was intimate with the great authorities who might delegate such " Pow-ers " to him. To talk of " Pow-ers," mysteriously, was a tribute to his own importance. He rolled the word on his tongue as if he enjoyed the sound of it.

On the Deacon's cheek bones two red spots flamed, round and big as a Scotch penny. His was the hurt silence of the baffled diplomatist, to whom a defeat means reflections on his own ability.

" Demn him ! " he skirled, following the solid march of his enemy with fiery eyes.

Never before had his deaconship been heard to swear. Tam Wylie laughed at the shrill oath till his eyes were buried in his merry wrinkles, a suppressed snirt, a continuous gurgle in the throat and nose, in beaming survey the while of the withered old creature dancing in his rage. (It was all a good joke to Tam, because, living on the outskirts of the town, he had no spigot of his own to feed.) The Deacon turned the eyes of hate on him. Demn Wylie too—what was he laughing at !

" Oh, I dare thay you could have got round him ! "
he snapped.

" In my opinion, Allardyce," said the baker, " you
mismanaged the whole affair. Yon wasna the way to
approach him ! "

" It'th a pity you didna try your hand, then, I'm
sure ! No doubt a clever man like *you* would have
worked wonderth ! "

So the bodies wrangled among themselves. Somehow or other Gourlay had the knack of setting them by
the ears. It was not till they hit on a common topic
of their spite in railing at him that they became a band
of brothers and a happy few.

" Whisht ! " said Sandy Toddle suddenly ; " here's his
boy ! "

John was coming towards them on his way to school.
The bodies watched him as he passed, with the fixed
look men turn on a boy of whose kinsmen they were
talking even now. They affect a stony and deliberate
regard, partly to include the newcomer in their critical
survey of his family, and partly to banish from their
own eyes any sign that they have just been running
down his people. John, as quick as his mother to feel,
knew in a moment they were watching *him*. He hung his
head sheepishly and blushed, and the moment he was
past he broke into a nervous trot, the bag of books
bumping on his back as he ran.

" He's getting a big boy, that son of Gourlay's," said
the Provost ; " how oald will he be ? "

" He's approaching twelve," said Johnny Coe, who
made a point of being able to supply such news because
it gained him consideration where he was otherwise
unheeded. " He was born the day the brig on the
Fleckie Road gaed down, in the year o' the great flood ;
and since the great flood it's twelve year come Lammas.
Rab Tosh o' Fleckie's wife was heavy-footed at the time,
and Doctor Munn had been a' nicht wi' her, and when

he cam to Barbie Water in the morning it was roaring wide frae bank to brae ; where the brig should have been there was naething but the swashing of the yellow waves. Munn had to drive a' the way round to the Fechars brig, and in parts o' the road the water was so deep that it lapped his horse's bellyband. A' this time Mrs. Gourlay was skirling in her pains and praying to God she micht dee. Gourlay had been a great crony o' Munn's, but he quarrelled him for being late ; he had trysted him, ye see, for the occasion, and he had been twenty times at the yett to look for him. Ye ken how little he would stomach that ; he was ready to brust wi' anger. Munn, mad for the want of sleep and wat to the bane, swiire back at him ; and than Gourlay wadna let him near his wife ! Ye mind what an awful day it was ; the thunder roared as if the heavens were tumbling on the world, and the lichtnin sent the trees daudin on the roads, and folk hid below their beds and prayed—they thocht it was the Judgment ! But Gourlay rammed his black stepper in the shafts, and drave like the devil o' hell to Skeighan Drone, where there was a young doctor. The lad was feared to come, but Gourlay swore by God that he should, and he garred him. In a' the countryside driving like his that day was never kenned or heard tell o' ; they were back within the hour ! I saw them gallop up Main Street ; lichtnin struck the ground before them ; the young doctor covered his face wi' his hands, and the horse nichered wi' fear and tried to wheel, but Gourlay stood up in the gig and lashed him on through the fire. It was thocht for lang that Mrs. Gourlay would die ; and she was never the same woman after. Atweel, ay, sirs, Gourlay has that morning's work to blame for the poor wife he has now. Him and Munn never spoke to each other again, and Munn died within the twelvemonth— he got his death that morning on the Fleckie Road. But, for a' so pack's they had been, Gourlay never looked near him."

Coe had told his story with enjoying gusto, and had told it well—for Johnny, though constantly snubbed by his fellows, was in many ways the ablest of them all. His voice and manner drove it home. They knew, besides, he was telling what himself had seen. For they knew he was lying prostrate with fear in the open smiddy-shed from the time Gourlay went to Skeighan Drone to the time that he came back, and that he had seen him both come and go. They were silent for a while, impressed, in spite of themselves, by the vivid presentment of Gourlay's manhood on the day that had scared them all. The baker felt inclined to cry out on his cruelty for keeping his wife suffering to gratify his wrath ; but the sudden picture of the man's courage changed that feeling to another of admiring awe : a man so defiant of the angry heavens might do anything. And so with the others ; they hated Gourlay, but his bravery was a fact of nature which they could not disregard ; they knew themselves smaller, and said nothing for a while. Tam Brodie, the most brutal among them, was the first to recover. Even he did not try to belittle at once, but he felt the subtle discomfort of the situation, and relieved it by bringing the conversation back to its usual channel.

"That was at the boy's birth, Mr. Coe ? " said he.

" Ou ay, just the laddie. It was a' richt when the lassie came. It was Doctor Dandy brocht *her* hame, for Munn was deid by that time, and Dandy had his place."

" What will Gourlay be going to make of him ? " the Provost asked. " A doctor or a minister or wha-at ? "

" Deil a fear of that," said Brodie ; " he'll take him into the business ! It's a' that he's fit for. He's an infernal dunce, just his father owre again, and the Dominie thrashes him remorseless ! I hear my own weans speaking o't. Ou, it seems he's just a perfect numbskull ! "

" Ye couldn't expect ainything else from a son of Gourlay," said the Provost.

Conversation languished. Some fillip was needed to bring it to an easy flow, and the simultaneous scrape of their feet turning round showed the direction of their thoughts.

" A dram would be very acceptable now," murmured Sandy Toddle, rubbing his chin.

" Ou, we wouldna be the waur o't," said Tam Wylie.

" We would all be the better of a little drope," smirked the Deacon.

And they made for the Red Lion for the matutinal dram.

CHAPTER VII.

JOHN GOURLAY the younger was late for school, in spite of the nervous trot he fell into when he shrank from the bodies' hard stare at him. There was nothing unusual about that; he was late for school every other day. To him it was a howling wilderness where he played a most appropriate *rôle*. If his father was not about he would hang round his mother till the last moment, rather than be off to old " Bleach-the-boys "—as the master had been christened by his scholars. " Mother, I have a pain in *my* heid," he would whimper, and she would condole with him and tell him she would keep him at home with her—were it not for dread of her husband. She was quite sure he was ainything but strong, poor boy, and that the schooling was bad for him; for it was really remarkable how quickly the pain went if he was allowed to stay at home; why, he got better just directly! It was not often she dared to keep him from school, however; and if she did, she had to hide him from his father.

On school mornings the boy shrank from going out with a shrinking that was almost physical. When he stole through the green gate with his bag slithering at his hip (not braced between the shoulders like a birkie scholar's), he used to feel ruefully that he was in for it now—and the Lord alone knew what he would have to put up with ere he came home! And he always had the feeling of a freed slave when he passed the gate on his return, never failing to note with delight the clean smell of the yard after the stuffiness of school, sucking it in through glad nostrils, and thinking to himself, " O crickey, it's fine to be home ! " On Friday nights, in particular, he used to feel so happy that, becoming arrogant, he would try his hand at bullying Jock Gilmour in imitation of his father. John's dislike of school, and fear of its trampling bravoes, attached him peculiarly to the House with the Green Shutters ; there was his doting mother, and she gave him stories to read, and the place was so big that it was easy to avoid his father and have great times with the rabbits and the doos. He was as proud of the sonsy house as Gourlay himself, if for a different reason, and he used to boast of it to his comrades. And he never left it, then or after, without a foreboding.

As he crept along the School Road with a rueful face, he was alone, for Janet, who was cleverer than he, was always earlier at school. The absence of children in the sunny street lent to his depression. He felt forlorn ; if there had been a chattering crowd marching along, he would have been much more at his ease.

Quite recently the school had been fitted up with varnished desks, and John, who inherited his mother's nervous senses with his father's lack of wit, was always intensely alive to the smell of the desks the moment he went in ; and as his heart always sank when he went in, the smell became associated in his mind with that sinking of the heart—to feel it, no matter where, filled him with uneasiness. As he stole past the joiner's on that sunny morning, when wood was resinous and pungent of odour, he was suddenly conscious of a varnishy smell, and felt a misgiving without knowing why. It was years after, in Edinburgh, ere he knew the reason ; he found that he never went past an upholsterer's shop, on a hot day in spring, without being conscious of a vague depression, and feeling like a boy slinking into school.

In spite of his forebodings, nothing more untoward befell him that morning than a cut over the cowering shoulders for being late, as he crept to the bottom of his class. He reached "leave," the ten minutes' run at twelve o'clock, without misadventure. Perhaps it was this unwonted good fortune that made him boastful when he crouched near the pump among his cronies, sitting on his hunkers with his back to the wall. Half a dozen boys were about him, and Swipey Broon was in front, making mud pellets in a trickle from the pump.

He began talking of the new range.

"Yah! Auld Gemmell needn't have let welp at *me* for being late this morning," he spluttered big-eyed, nodding his head in aggrieved and solemn protest. " It wasna *my* faut! We're getting in a grand new range, and the whole of the kitchen fireplace has been gutted out to make room for't ; and my mother couldna get my breakfast in time this morning, because, ye see, she had to boil everything in the parlour—and here, when she gaed ben the house, the parlour fire was out !

"It's to be a splendid range, the new one," he went on, with a conceited jerk of the head. " Peter Riney's bringin'd from Skeighan in the afternune. My father says there winna be its equal in the parish ! "

The faces of the boys lowered uncomfortably. They felt it was a silly thing of Gourlay to blow his own trumpet in this way, but, being boys, they could not prick his conceit with a quick rejoinder. It is only grown-ups who can be ironical ; physical violence is the boy's repartee. It had scarcely gone far enough for that yet, so they lowered in uncomfortable silence.

"We're aye getting new things up at our place," he went on. "I heard my father telling Gibson the builder he must have everything of the best ! Mother says it'll all be mine some day. I'll have the fine times when I leave the schule—and that winna be long now, for I'm clean sick o't ; I'll no bide a day longer than I need !

I'm to go into the business, and then I'll have the times.
I'll dash about the country in a gig wi' two dogs wallop-
ping ahin'. I'll have the great life o't."

" Ph-tt ! " said Swipey Broon, and planted a gob of
mud right in the middle of his brow.

" Hoh ! hoh ! hoh ! " yelled the others. They hailed
Swipey's action with delight because, to their minds, it
exactly met the case. It was the one fit retort to his
bouncing.

Beneath the wet plunk of the mud John started back,
bumping his head against the wall behind him. The
sticky pellet clung to his brow, and he brushed it angrily
aside. The laughter of the others added to his wrath
against Swipey.

" What are you after ? " he bawled. " Don't try
your tricks on me, Swipey Broon. Man, I could kill ye
wi' a glower ! "

In a twinkling Swipey's jacket was off, and he was
dancing in his shirt sleeves, inviting Gourlay to come
on and try't.

" G'way, man," said John, his face as white as the
wall ; " g'way, man ! Don't have *me* getting up to ye,
or I'll knock the fleas out of your duds ! "

Now the father of Swipey—so called because he always
swiped when batting at rounders—the father of Swipey
was the rag and bone merchant of Barbie, and it was
said (with what degree of truth I know not) that his
home was verminous in consequence. John's taunt was
calculated, therefore, to sting him to the quick.

The scion of the Broons, fired for the honour of his
house, drove straight at the mouth of the insulter. But
John jouked to the side, and Swipey skinned his knuckles
on the wall.

For a moment he rocked to and fro, doubled up in
pain, crying " *Ooh !* " with a rueful face, and squeezing
his hand between his thighs to dull its sharper agonies.
Then with redoubled wrath bold Swipey hurled him at

the foe. He grabbed Gourlay's head, and shoving it down between his knees, proceeded to pommel his bent back, while John bellowed angrily (from between Swipey's legs), "Let me up, see!"

Swipey let him up. John came at him with whirling arms, but Swipey jouked and gave him one on the mouth that split his lip. In another moment Gourlay was grovelling on his hands and knees, and triumphant Swipey, astride his back, was bellowing "Hurroo!"— Swipey's father was an Irishman.

"Let him up, Broon!" cried Peter Wylie—"let him up, and meet each other square!"

"Oh, I'll let him up," cried Swipey, and leapt to his feet with magnificent pride. He danced round Gourlay with his fists sawing the air. "I could fight ten of him! —Come on, Gourlay!" he cried, "and I'll poultice the road wi' your brose."

John rose, glaring. But when Swipey rushed he turned and fled. The boys ran into the middle of the street, pointing after the coward and shouting, "Yeh! yeh! yeh!" with the infinite cruel derision of boyhood.

"Yeh! yeh! yeh!" the cries of execration and contempt pursued him as he ran.

*　　　*　　　*　　　*　　　*　　　*

Ere he had gone a hundred yards he heard the shrill whistle with which Mr. Gemmell summoned his scholars from their play.

CHAPTER VIII.

ALL the children had gone into school. The street was lonely in the sudden stillness. The joiner slanted across the road, brushing shavings and sawdust from his white apron. There was no other sign of life in the sunshine. Only from the smiddy, far away, came at times the tink of an anvil.

John crept on up the street, keeping close to the wall. It seemed unnatural being there at that hour; everything had a quiet, unfamiliar look. The white walls of the houses reproached the truant with their silent faces.

A strong smell of wallflowers oozed through the hot air. John thought it a lonely smell, and ran to get away.

" Johnny dear, what's wrong wi' ye ? " cried his mother, when he stole in through the scullery at last. " Are ye ill, dear ? "

" I wanted to come hame," he said. It was no defence ; it was the sad and simple expression of his wish.

" What for, my sweet ? "

" I hate the school," he said bitterly ; " I aye want to be at hame."

His mother saw his cut mouth.

" Johnny," she cried in concern, " what's the matter with your lip, dear ? Has ainybody been meddling ye ? "

" It was Swipey Broon," he said.

" Did ever a body hear ? " she cried. " Things have come to a fine pass when decent weans canna go to the school without a wheen rag-folk yoking on them ! But what can a body ettle ? Scotland's not what it used to be ! It's owrerun wi' the dirty Eerish ! "

In her anger she did not see the sloppy dishclout on the scullery chair, on which she sank exhausted by her rage.

" Oh, but I let him have it," swaggered John. " I threatened to knock the.fleas off him. The other boys were on *his* side, or I would have walloped him."

" Atweel, they would a' be on his side," she cried. " But it's juist envy, Johnny. Never mind, dear ; you'll soon be left the school, and there's not wan of them has the business that you have waiting ready to step intil."

" Mother," he pleaded, " let me bide here for the rest o' the day ! "

" Oh, but your father, Johnny ? If *he* saw ye ! "

" If you gie me some o' your novelles to look at, I'll go up to the garret and hide, and ye can ask Jenny no to tell."

She gave him a hunk of nuncheon and a bundle of her novelettes, and he stole up to an empty garret and squatted on the bare boards. The sun streamed through the skylight window and lay, an oblong patch, in the centre of the floor. John noted the head of a nail that stuck gleaming up. He could hear the pigeons *rooketty-cooing* on the roof, and every now and then a slithering sound, as they lost their footing on the slates and went sliding downward to the rones. But for that, all was still, uncannily still. Once a zinc pail clanked in the yard, and he started with fear, wondering if that was his faither !

If young Gourlay had been the right kind of a boy he would have been in his glory, with books to read and a garret to read them in. For to snuggle close beneath the slates is as dear to the boy as the bard, if somewhat diverse their reasons for seclusion. Your garret is the true kingdom of the poet, neighbouring the stars ; side-windows tether him to earth, but a skylight looks to the heavens. (That is why so many poets live in garrets, no doubt.) But it is the secrecy of a garret for him and his books that a boy loves ; there he is lord of his imagination ; there, when the impertinent world is hidden from his view, he rides with great Turpin at night beneath the glimmer of the moon. What boy of sense would read about Turpin in a mere respectable parlour ? A hay-loft's the thing, where you can hide in a dusty corner, and watch through a chink the baffled minions of Bow Street, and hear Black Bess—good jade !—stamping in her secret stall, and be ready to descend when a friendly hostler cries, " Jericho ! " But if there is no hay-loft at hand a mere garret will do very well. And so John should have been in his glory, as indeed for a while he was. But he showed his difference from the right kind of a boy by becoming lonely. He had inherited from his mother a silly kind of interest in silly books, but to him reading was a painful process, and he could never remember the plot. What he liked best (though he could not have told you about it) was a vivid physical picture. When the puffing steam of Black Bess's nostrils cleared away from the moonlit pool, and the white face of the dead man stared at Turpin through the water, John saw it and shivered, staring big-eyed at the staring horror. He was alive to it all ; he heard the seep of the water through the mare's lips, and its hollow glug as it went down, and the creak of the saddle beneath Turpin's hip ; he saw the smear of sweat roughening the hair on her slanting neck, and the great steaming breath she blew out when she rested from drinking, and then that awful face glaring from the pool.—Perhaps he was not so far from being the right kind of boy, after all, since that was the stuff that *he* liked. He wished he had some Turpin with him now, for his mother's periodicals were all about men with impossibly broad shoulders and impossibly curved waists who asked Angelina if she loved them. Once, it is true, a somewhat too florid sentence touched him on the visual nerve : " Through a chink in the Venetian blind a long pencil of yellow light pierced the beautiful dimness of the room and pointed straight to the dainty bronze slipper peeping from under Angelina's gown ; it became a slipper of vivid gold amid the gloom." John saw that and brightened, but the next moment they began to talk about love and he was at sea immediately. " Dagon them and their love ! " quoth he.

To him, indeed, reading was never more than a means of escape from something else ; he never thought of a book so long as there were things to see. Some things were different from others, it is true. Things of the outer world, where he swaggered among his fellows and was thrashed, or bungled his lessons and was thrashed again, imprinted themselves vividly on his mind, and he hated the impressions. When Swipey Broon was hot the sweat pores always glistened distinctly on the end of his mottled nose—John, as he thought angrily of Swipey this afternoon, saw the glistening sweat pores before him and wanted to bash them. The varnishy smell of the desks, the smell of the wallflowers at Mrs. Manzie's on the way to school, the smell of the school itself—to all these he was morbidly alive, and he loathed them. But he loved the impressions of his home. His mind was full of perceptions of which he was unconscious, till he found one of them recorded in a book, and that was the book for him. The curious physical always drew his mind to hate it or to love. In summer he would crawl into the bottom of an old hedge, among the black mould and the withered sticks, and watch a red-ended beetle creep slowly up a bit of wood till near the top, and fall suddenly down, and creep patiently again—this he would watch with curious interest and remember always. " Johnny," said his mother once, " what do you breenge into the bushes to watch those nasty things for ? "

" They're queer," he said musingly.

Even if he *was* a little dull wi' the book, she was sure he would come to something, for, eh, he was such a noticing boy.

But there was nothing to touch him in " The Wooing of Angeline ; " he was moving in an alien world. It was a complicated plot, and, some of the numbers being lost, he was not sharp enough to catch the idea of the story. He read slowly and without interest. The sounds of the outer world reached him in his loneliness and annoyed him, because, while wondering what they were, he dared not look out to see. He heard the rattle of wheels entering the big yard ; that would be Peter Riney back from Skeighan with the range. Once he heard the birr of his father's voice in the lobby and his mother speaking in shrill protest, and then—oh, horror !—his father came up the stair. Would he come into the garret ? John, lying on his left side, felt his quickened heart thud against the boards, and he could not take his big frighted eyes from the bottom of the door. But the heavy step passed and went into another room. John's open mouth was dry, and his shirt was sticking to his back.

The heavy steps came back to the landing.

" Whaur's *my* gimlet ? " yelled his father down the stair.

" Oh, I lost the corkscrew, and took it to open a bottle," cried his mother wearily. " Here it is, man, in the kitchen drawer."

" *Hah !* " his father barked, and he knew he was infernal angry. If he should come in !

But he went tramping down the stair, and John, after waiting till his pulses were stilled, resumed his reading. He heard the masons in the kitchen, busy with the range, and he would have liked fine to watch them, but he dared not go down till after four. It was lonely up here by himself. A hot wind had sprung up, and it crooned through the keyhole drearily; "*oo-woo-oo,*" it cried, and the sound drenched him in a vague depression. The splotch of yellow light had shifted round to the fireplace; Janet had kindled a fire there last winter, and the ashes had never been removed, and now the light lay, yellow and vivid, on a red clinker of coal and a charred piece of stick. A piece of glossy white paper had been flung in the untidy grate, and in the hollow curve of it a thin silt of black dust had gathered—the light showed it plainly. All these things the boy marked and was subtly aware of their unpleasantness. He was forced to read to escape the sense of them. But it was words, words, words, that he read; the subject mattered not at all. His head leaned heavy on his left hand and his mouth hung open, as his eye travelled dreamily along the lines. He succeeded in hypnotizing his brain at last, by the mere process of staring at the page.

At last he heard Janet in the lobby. That meant that school was over. He crept down the stair.

"*You* were playing the truant," said Janet, and she nodded her head in accusation. "I've a good mind to tell my faither."

"If ye wud——" he said, and shook his fist at her threateningly. She shrank away from him. They went into the kitchen together.

The range had been successfully installed, and Mr. Gourlay was showing it to Grant of Loranogie, the foremost farmer of the shire. Mrs. Gourlay, standing by the kitchen table, viewed her new possession with a faded simper of approval. She was pleased that Mr. Grant should see the grand new thing that they had gotten. She listened to the talk of the men with a faint smile about her weary lips, her eyes upon the sonsy range.

"Dod, it's a handsome piece of furniture," said Loranogie. "How did ye get it brought here, Mr. Gourlay?"

" I went to Glasgow and ordered it special. It came
to Skeighan by the train, and my own beasts brought
it owre. That fender's a feature," he added complacently ; " it's onusual wi' a range."

The massive fender ran from end to end of the fireplace, projecting a little in front ; its rim, a square bar
of heavy steel, with bright, sharp edges.

" And that poker, too ; man, there's a history wi' that.
I made a point of the making o't. He was an ill-bred
little whalp, the bodie in Glasgow. I happened to say
till um I would like a poker-heid just the same size as
the rim of the fender ! ' What d'ye want wi' a heavy-
heided poker ? ' says he ; ' a' ye need's a bit sma' thing
to rype the ribs wi'.' ' Is that so ? ' says I. ' How do
you ken what *I* want ? ' I made short work o' *him !*
The poker-heid's the identical size o' the rim ; I had it
made to fit."

Loranogie thought it a silly thing of Gourlay to concern himself about a poker. But that was just like him,
of course. The moment the body in Glasgow opposed
his whim, Gourlay, he knew, would make a point o't.

The grain merchant took the bar of heavy metal in
his hand. " Dod, it's an awful weapon," he said, meaning to be jocose. " You could murder a man wi't."

" Deed you could," said Loranogie ; " you could kill
him wi' the one lick."

The elders, engaged with more important matters,
paid no attention to the children, who had pushed between them to the front and were looking up at their
faces, as they talked, with curious watching eyes. John,
with his instinct to notice things, took the poker up
when his father laid it down, to see if it was really the
size of the rim. It was too heavy for him to raise by
the handle ; he had to lift it by the middle. Janet was
at his elbow, watching him. " You could kill a man
with that," he told her, importantly, though she had
heard it for herself. Janet stared and shuddered.

Then the boy laid the poker-head along the rim, fitting edge to edge with a nice precision.

"Mother," he cried, turning towards her in his interest, "mother, look here! It's exactly the same size!"

"Put it down, sir," said his father with a grim smile at Loranogie. "You'll be killing folk next."

CHAPTER IX.

" ARE ye packit, Peter ? " said Gourlay.

" Yes, sir," said Peter Riney, running round to the other side of a cart, to fasten a horse's bellyband to the shaft. " Yes, sir, we're a' ready."

" Have the carriers a big load ? "

" Andy has just a wheen parcels, but Elshie's as fu' as he can haud. And there's a gey pickle stuff waiting at the Cross."

The hot wind of yesterday had brought lightning through the night, and this morning there was the gentle drizzle that sometimes follows a heavy thunderstorm. Hints of the farther blue showed themselves in a lofty sky of delicate and drifting gray. The blackbirds and thrushes welcomed the cooler air with a gush of musical piping, as if the liquid tenderness of the morning had actually got into their throats and made them softer.

" You had better snoove away then," said Gourlay. " Donnerton's five mile ayont Fleckie, and by the time you deliver the meal there, and load the ironwork, it'll be late ere you get back. Snoove away, Peter ; snoove away ! "

Peter shuffled uneasily, and his pale blue eyes blinked at Gourlay from beneath their grizzled crow nests of red hair.

" Are we a' to start thegither, sir ? " he hesitated. " D'ye mean—d'ye mean the carriers too ? "

" Atweel, Peter ! " said Gourlay. " What for no ? "

Peter took a great old watch, with a yellow case, from

his fob, and, " It wants a while o' aicht, sir," he volunteered.

" Ay, man, Peter, and what of that ? " said Gourlay.

There was almost a twinkle in his eye. Peter Riney
was the only human being with whom he was ever really
at his ease. It is only when a mind feels secure in itself
that it can laugh unconcernedly at others. Peter was
so simple that in his presence Gourlay felt secure ; and
he used to banter him.

" The folk at the Cross winna expect the carriers till
aicht, sir," said Peter, " and I doubt their stuff won't
be ready."

" Ay, man, Peter," Gourlay joked lazily, as if Peter
was a little boy. " Ay, man, Peter. You think the
folk at the Cross winna be prepared ? "

" No, sir," said Peter, opening his eyes very solemnly,
" they winna be prepared."

" It'll do them good to hurry a little for once," growled
Gourlay, humour yielding to spite at the thought of his
enemies. " It'll do them good to hurry a little for once.
Be off, the lot of ye ! "

After ordering his carriers to start, to back down and
postpone their departure, just to suit the convenience
of his neighbours, would derogate from his own importance. His men might think he was afraid of Barbie.

He strolled out to the big gate and watched his teams
going down the brae.

There were only four carts this morning because the
two that had gone to Fechars yesterday with the cheese
would not be back till the afternoon ; and another had
already turned west to Auchterwheeze, to bring slates
for the flesher's new house. Of the four that went down
the street two were the usual carriers' carts, the other two
were off to Fleckie with meal, and Gourlay had started
them the sooner since they were to bring back the ironwork which Templandmuir needed for his new improvements. Though the Templar had reformed greatly

since he married his birkie wife, he was still far from
having his place in proper order, and he had often to
depend on Gourlay for the carrying of stuff which a
man in his position should have had horses of his own
to bring.

As Gourlay stood at his gate he pondered with heavy
cunning how much he might charge Templandmuir for
bringing the ironwork from Fleckie. He decided to
charge him for the whole day, though half of it would
be spent in taking his own meal to Donnerton. In that
he was carrying out his usual policy—which was to make
each side of his business help the other.

As he stood puzzling his wits over Templandmuir's
account, his lips worked in and out, to assist the slow
process of his brain. His eyes narrowed between peering lids, and their light seemed to turn inward as he
fixed them abstractedly on a stone in the middle of the
road. His head was tilted that he might keep his
eyes upon the stone ; and every now and then, as he
mused, he rubbed his chin slowly between the thumb
and fingers of his left hand. Entirely given up to
the thought of Templandmuir's account, he failed to
see the figure advancing up the street.

At last the scrunch of a boot on the wet road struck
his ear. He turned with his best glower on the man
who was approaching ; more of the " Wha-the-bleezes-
are-you ? " look than ever in his eyes—because he had
been caught unawares.

The stranger wore a light yellow overcoat, and he had
been walking a long time in the rain apparently, for the
shoulders of the coat were quite black with the wet,
these black patches showing in strong contrast with the
dryer, therefore yellower, front of it. Coat and jacket
were both hanging slightly open, and between was seen
the slight bulge of a dirty white waistcoat. The newcomer's trousers were turned high at the bottom, and
the muddy spats he wore looked big and ungainly in

consequence. In this appearance there was an air of dirty and pretentious well-to-do-ness. It was not shabby gentility. It was like the gross attempt at dress of your well-to-do publican who looks down on his soiled white waistcoat with complacent and approving eye.

"It's a fine morning, Mr. Gourlay," simpered the stranger. His air was that of a forward tenant who thinks it a great thing to pass remarks on the weather with his laird.

Gourlay cast a look at the dropping heavens.

"Is that *your* opinion ? " said he. "I fail to see't mysell."

It was not in Gourlay to see the beauty of that gray, wet dawn. A fine morning to him was one that burnt the back of your neck.

The stranger laughed : a little deprecating giggle. "I meant it was fine weather for the fields," he explained. He had meant nothing of the kind, of course ; he had merely been talking at random in his wish to be civil to that important man, John Gourlay.

"Imphm," he pondered, looking round on the weather with a wise air ; "imphm ; it's fine weather for the fields."

"Are *you* a farmer, then ? " Gourlay nipped him, with his eye on the white waistcoat.

"Oh—oh, Mr. Gourlay! A farmer, no. Hi—hi ! I'm not a farmer. I dare say, now, you have no mind of *me ?* "

"No," said Gourlay, regarding him very gravely and steadily with his dark eyes. "I cannot say, sir, that I have the pleasure of remembering *you*."

"Man, I'm a son of auld John Wilson of Brigabee."

"Oh, auld Wilson, the mole-catcher ! " said contemptuous Gourlay. "What's this they christened him now ? 'Toddling Johnnie,' was it noat ? "

Wilson coloured. But he sniggered to gloss over the

awkwardness of the remark. A coward always sniggers when insulted, pretending that the insult is only a joke of his opponent, and therefore to be laughed aside. So he escapes the quarrel which he fears a show of displeasure might provoke.

But though Wilson was not a hardy man, it was not timidity only that caused his tame submission to Gourlay.

He had come back after an absence of fifteen years, with a good deal of money in his pocket, and he had a fond desire that he, the son of the mole-catcher, should get some recognition of his prosperity from the most important man in the locality. If Gourlay had said, with solemn and fat-lipped approval, " Man, I'm glad to see that you have done so well," he would have swelled with gratified pride. For it is often the favourable estimate of their own little village—" What they'll think of me at home "—that matters most to Scotsmen who go out to make their way in the world. No doubt that is why so many of them go home and cut a dash when they have made their fortunes; they want the cronies of their youth to see the big men they have become. Wilson was not exempt from that weakness. As far back as he remembered Gourlay had been the big man of Barbie; as a boy he had viewed him with admiring awe; to be received by him now, as one of the well-to-do, were a sweet recognition of his greatness. It was a fawning desire for that recognition that caused his smirking approach to the grain merchant. So strong was the desire that, though he coloured and felt awkward at the contemptuous reference to his father, he sniggered and went on talking, as if nothing untoward had been said. He was one of the band impossible to snub, not because they are endowed with superior moral courage, but because their easy self-importance is so great that an insult rarely pierces it enough to divert them from their purpose. They walk through life wrapped comfortably round in the wool of their own conceit. Gourlay,

though a dull man—perhaps because he was a dull man
—suspected insult in a moment.　But it rarely entered
Wilson's brain (though he was cleverer than most) that
the world could find anything to scoff at in such a fine
fellow as James Wilson.　A less ironic brute than Gourlay would never have pierced the thickness of his hide.
It was because Gourlay succeeded in piercing it that
morning that Wilson hated him for ever—with a hate
the more bitter because he was rebuffed so seldom.

"Is business brisk?" he asked, irrepressible.

Business!　Heavens, did ye hear him talking?　What
did Toddling Johnny's son know about business?　What
was the world coming to?　To hear him setting up his
face there, and asking the best merchant in the town
whether business was brisk!　It was high time to put
him in his place, the conceited upstart, shoving himself
forward like an equal!

For it was the assumption of equality implied by
Wilson's manner that offended Gourlay—as if mole-
catcher's son and monopolist were discussing, on equal
terms, matters of interest to them both.

"Business!" he said gravely.　"Well, I'm not well
acquainted with your line, but I believe mole traps are
cheap—if ye have any idea of taking up the oald trade."

Wilson's eyes flickered over him, hurt and dubious.
His mouth opened—then shut—then he decided to
speak after all.　"Oh, I was thinking Barbie would be
very quiet," said he, "compared wi' places where they
have the railway.　I was thinking it would need stirring up a bit."

"Oh, ye was thinking that, was ye?" birred Gourlay,
with a stupid man's repetition of his jibe.　"Well, I
believe there's a grand opening in the moleskin line, so
there's a chance for ye.　My quarrymen wear out their
breeks in no time."

Wilson's face, which had swelled with red shame,
went a dead white.　"Good-morning!" he said, and

started rapidly away with a vicious dig of his stick upon the wet road.

" Goo-ood mor-r-ning, serr ! " Gourlay birred after him ; " goo-ood mor-r-ning, serr ! "   He felt he had been bright this morning   He had put the branks on Wilson !

Wilson was as furious at himself as at Gourlay.   Why the devil had he said " Good-morning " ?   It had slipped out of him unawares, and Gourlay had taken it up with an ironic birr that rang in his ears now, poisoning his blood.   He felt equal in fancy to a thousand Gourlays now—so strong was he in wrath against him. He had gone forward to pass pleasant remarks about the weather, and why should he noat ?—he was no disgrace to Barbie, but a credit rather.   It was not every working-man's son that came back with five hundred in the bank.   And here Gourlay had treated him like a doag ! Ah, well, he would maybe be upsides with Gourlay yet, so he might !

CHAPTER X.

" SUCH a rickle of furniture I never saw ! " said the Provost.

" Whose is it ? " said Brodie.

" Oh, have ye noat heard ? " said the Head of the Town with eyebrows in air. " It beloangs to that fellow Wilson, doan't ye know ? He's a son of oald Wilson, the mowdie-man of Brigabee. It seems we're to have him for a neighbour, or all's bye wi't. I declare I doan't know what this world's coming to ! "

" Man, Provost," said Brodie, " d'ye tell me tha-at ? I've been over at Fleckie for the last ten days—my brother Rab's dead and won away, as I dare say you have heard—oh yes, we must all go—so, ye see, I'm scarcely abreast o' the latest intelligence. What's Wilson doing here ? I thought he had been a pawnbroker in Embro."

" Noat he ! It's *whispered* indeed, that he left Brigabee to go and help in a pawmbroker's, but it seems he married an Aberdeen lass and sattled there after a while, the manager of a store, I have been given to understa-and. He has taken oald Rab Jamieson's barn at the bottom of the Cross—for what purpose it beats even me to tell ! And that's his furniture——"

" I declare ! " said the astonished Brodie. " He's a smart-looking boy that. Will that be a son of his ? "

He pointed to a sharp-faced urchin of twelve who was busy carrying chairs round the corner of the barn, to the tiny house where Wilson meant to live. He was a red-haired boy with an upturned nose, dressed in shirt

and knickerbockers only.   The cross of his braces came
comically near his neck—so short was the space of shirt
between the top line of his breeches and his shoulders.
His knickers were open at the knee, and the black stock-
ings below them were wrinkled slackly down his thin
legs, being tied loosely above the calf with dirty white
strips of cloth instead of garters.   He had no cap, and it
was seen that his hair had a " cow-lick " in front ; it
slanted up from his brow, that is, in a sleek kind of
tuft.   There was a violent squint in one of his sharp
gray eyes, so that it seemed to flash at the world across
the bridge of his nose.   He was so eager at his work that
his clumsy-looking boots—they only *looked* clumsy because the legs they were stuck to were so thin—skidded
on the cobbles as he whipped round the barn with a
chair inverted on his poll.   When he came back for
another chair, he sometimes wheepled a tune of his own
making, in shrill, disconnected jerks, and sometimes
wiped his nose on his sleeve.   And the bodies watched
him.

" Faith, he's keen," said the Provost.

" But what on earth has Wilson ta'en auld Jamieson's
house and barn for ?   They have stude empty since I
kenna whan," quoth Alexander Toddle, forgetting his
English in surprise.

" They say he means to start a business !   He's made
some bawbees in Aiberdeen, they're telling me, and he
thinks he'll set Barbie in a lowe wi't."

" Ou, he means to work a perfect revolution," said
Johnny Coe.

" In Barbie ! " cried astounded Toddle.

" In Barbie e'en't," said the Provost.

" It would take a heap to revolutionize *hit*," said the
baker, the ironic man.

" There's a chance in that hoose," Brodie burst out,
ignoring the baker's gibe.   " Dod, there's a chance, sirs.
I wonder it never occurred to me before."

"Are ye thinking ye have missed a gude thing?" grinned the Deacon.

But Brodie's lips were working in the throes of commercial speculation, and he stared, heedless of the jibe. So Johnny Coe took up his sapient parable.

"Atweel," said he, "there's a chance, Mr Brodie. That road round to the back's a handy thing. You could take a horse and cart brawly through an opening like that. And there's a gey bit ground at the back, too, when a body comes to think o't."

"What line's he meaning to purshoo?" queried Brodie, whose mind, quickened by the chance he saw at No. 1 The Cross, was hot on the hunt of its possibilities.

"He's been very close about that," said the Provost. "I asked Johnny Gibson—it was him had the selling o't —but he couldn't give me ainy satisfaction. All he could say was that Wilson had bought it and paid it. 'But, losh,' said I, 'he maun 'a' lat peep what he wanted the place for!' But na; it seems he was owre auld-farrant for the like of that. 'We'll let the folk wonder for a while, Mr. Gibson,' he had said. 'The less we tell them, the keener they'll be to ken; and they'll advertise me for noathing by speiring one another what I'm up till.'"

"Cunning!" said Brodie, breathing the word low in expressive admiration.

"Demned cute!" said Sandy Toddle.

"Very thmart!" said the Deacon.

"But the place has been falling down since ever I have mind o't," said Sandy Toddle. "He's a very clever man if he makes anything out of *that*."

"Well, well," said the Provost, "we'll soon see what he's meaning to be at. Now that his furniture's in, he surely canna keep us in the dark much loanger!"

Their curiosity was soon appeased. Within a week they were privileged to read the notice here appended:—

"Mr. James Wilson begs to announce to the inhabitants of Barbie and surrounding neighbourhood that he has taken these commodious premises, No. 1 The Cross, which he intends to open shortly as a Grocery, Ironmongery, and General Provision Store. J. W. is apprised that such an Emporium has long been a felt want in the locality. To meet this want is J. W.'s intention. He will try to do so, not by making large profits on a small business, but by making small profits on a large business. Indeed, owing to his long acquaintance with the trade, Mr. Wilson will be able to supply all commodities at a very little over cost price. For J. W. will use those improved methods of business which have been confined hitherto to the larger centres of population. At his Emporium you will be able, as the saying goes, to buy everything from a needle to an anchor. Moreover, to meet the convenience of his customers, J. W. will deliver goods at your own doors, distributing them with his own carts either in the town of Barbie or at any convenient distance from the same. Being a native of the district, his business hopes to secure a due share of your esteemed patronage. Thanking you, in anticipation, for the favour of an early visit,
    "Believe me, Ladies and Gentlemen,
            "Yours faithfully,
                "JAMES WILSON."

Such was the poster with which "Barbie and surrounding neighbourhood" were besprinkled within a week of "J. W.'s" appearance on the scene. He was known as "J. W." ever after. To be known by your initials is sometimes a mark of affection, and sometimes a mark of disrespect. It was not a mark of affection in the case of our "J. W." When Donald Scott slapped him on the back and cried, "Hullo, J. W., how are the anchors selling?" Barbie had found a cue which it was not slow to make use of. Wilson even received letters addressed to " J. W., Anchor Merchant, No. 1 The Cross." Ours is a nippy locality.

But Wilson, cosy and cocky in his own good opinion, was impervious to the chilly winds of scorn. His posters, in big blue letters, were on the smiddy door and on the sides of every brig within a circuit of five miles; they were pasted, in smaller letters, red on the gateposts of every farm; and Robin Tam, the bellman, handed them about from door to door. The folk could talk of nothing else.

"Dod!" said the Provost, when he read the bill, "we've a new departure here! This is an unco splutter, as the oald sow said when she tumbled in the gutter."

"Ay," said Sandy Toddle, "a fuff in the pan, I'm thinking. He promises owre muckle to last long! He lauchs owre loud to be merry at the end o't. For the loudest bummler's no the best bee, as my father, honest man, used to tell the minister."

"Ah-ah, I'm no so sure o' that," said Tam Brodie. "I forgathered wi' Wilson on Wednesday last, and I tell ye, sirs, he's worth the watching. They'll need to stand on a baikie that put the branks on him. He has the considering eye in his head—yon lang far-away glimmer at a thing from out the end of the eyebrow. He turned it on mysell twa-three times, the cunning devil, trying to keek into me, to see if he could use me. And look at the chance he has! There's two stores in Barbie, to be sure. But Kinnikum's a dirty beast, and folk have a scunner at his goods; and Catherwood's a drucken swine, and his place but sairly guided. That's a great stroke o' policy, too, promising to deliver folk's goods on their own doorstep to them. There's a whole jing-bang of outlying clachans round Barbie that he'll get the trade of by a dodge like that. The like was never tried hereaway before. I wadna wonder but it works wonders."

It did.

It was partly policy and partly accident that brought Wilson back to Barbie. He had been managing a wealthy old merchant's store for a long time in Aberdeen, and he had been blithely looking forward to the goodwill of it, when jink, at the old man's death, in stepped a nephew, and ousted the poo-oor fellow. He had bawled shrilly, but to no purpose; he had to be travelling. When he rose to greatness in Barbie it was whispered that the nephew discovered he was feathering his own nest, and that this was the reason of his sharp dismissal. But perhaps we should credit that report to Barbie's disposition rather than to Wilson's misdemeanour.

Wilson might have set up for himself in the nippy northern town. But it is an instinct with men who have met with a rebuff in a place to shake its dust from their shoes, and be off to seek their fortunes in the larger world. We take a scunner at the place that has ill-used us. Wilson took a scunner at Aberdeen, and decided to leave it and look around him. Scotland was opening up, and there were bound to be heaps of chances for a man like him! "A man like me," was a frequent phrase of Wilson's retired and solitary speculation. "Ay," he said, emerging from one of his business reveries, "there's bound to be heaps o' chances for a man like me, if I only look about me."

He was "looking about him" in Glasgow when he forgathered with his cousin William — the borer he! After many "How are ye, Jims's" and mutual speirings over a "bit mouthful of yill"—so they phrased it; but that was a meiosis, for they drank five quarts—they fell to a serious discussion of the commercial possibilities of Scotland. The borer was of the opinion that the Braes of Barbie had a future yet, "for a' the gaffer was so keen on keeping his men in the dark about the coal."

Now Wilson knew (as what Scotsman does not?) that in the middle 'fifties coal-boring in Scotland was not the

honourable profession that it now is.   More than once,
speculators procured lying reports that there were no
minerals, and after landowners had been ruined by
their abortive preliminary experiments, stepped in,
bought the land, and boomed it.   In one notorious case
a family, now great in the public eye, bribed a laird's
own borers to conceal the truth, and then buying the
Golconda from its impoverished owner, laid the basis of
a vast fortune.

   " D'ye mean—to tell—*me*, Wellyum Wilson," said
James, giving him his full name in the solemnity of the
moment, " d'ye mean—to tell—*me*, sir "—here he sank
his voice to a whisper—" that there's joukery-pawkery
at work ? "

   " A declare to God A div," said Weelyum, with equal
solemnity, and he nodded with alarmed sapience across
his beer jug.

   " You believe there's plenty of coal up Barbie Valley,
and that they're keeping it dark in the meantime for
some purpose of their own ? "

   " I do," said Weelyum.

   " God ! " said James, gripping the table with both
hands in his excitement—" God, if that's so, what a
chance there's in Barbie !   It has been a dead town for
twenty year, and twenty to the end o't.   A verra little
would buy the hauf o't.   But property 'ull rise in value
like a puddock stool at dark, serr, if the pits come round
it !   It will that.   If I was only sure o' your suspeecion,
Weelyum, I'd invest every bawbee I have in't.   You're
going home the night, are ye not ? "

   " I was just on my road to the station when I met
ye," said Weelyum.

   " Send me a scrape of your pen to-morrow, man, if
what you see on getting back keeps you still in the same
mind o't.   And directly I get your letter I'll run down
and look about me."

   The letter was encouraging, and Wilson went forth

to spy the land and initiate the plan of campaign. It was an important day for him. He entered on his feud with Gourlay, and bought Rab Jamieson's house and barn (with the field behind it) for a trifle. He had five hundred of his own, and he knew where more could be had for the asking.

Rab Jamieson's barn was a curious building to be stranded in the midst of Barbie. In quaint villages and little towns of England you sometimes see a mellow red-tiled barn, with its rich yard, close upon the street; it seems to have been hemmed in by the houses round, while dozing, so that it could not escape with the fields fleeing from the town. There it remains and gives a ripeness to the place, matching fitly with the great horse-chestnut yellowing before the door, and the old inn further down, mantled in its blood-red creepers. But that autumnal warmth and cosiness is rarely seen in the barer streets of the north. How Rab Jamieson's barn came to be stuck in Barbie nobody could tell. It was a gaunt, gray building with never a window, but a bole high in one corner for the sheaves, and a door low in another corner for auld Rab Jamieson. There was no mill inside, and the place had not been used for years. But the roof was good, and the walls stout and thick, and Wilson soon got to work on his new possession. He had seen all that could be made of the place the moment he clapped an eye on it, and he knew that he had found a good thing, even if the pits should never come near Barbie. The bole and door next the street were walled up, and a fine new door opened in the middle, flanked on either side by a great window. The interior was fitted up with a couple of counters and a wooden floor; and above the new wood ceiling there was a long loft for a storeroom, lighted by skylights in the roof. That loft above the rafters, thought the provident Wilson, will come in braw and handy for storing things, so it will. And there, hey presto! the transformation was achieved, and Wilson's Emporium stood before you. It was crammed with merchandise. On the white flapping slant of a couple of awnings, one over each window, you might read in black letters, " JAMES WILSON : EMPORIUM." The letters of " James Wilson " made a triumphal arch, to which " Emporium " was the base. It seemed symbolical.

Now, the shops of Barbie (the drunken man's shop and the dirty man's shop always excepted, of course) had usually been low-browed little places with faded black scrolls above the door, on which you might read in dim gilt letters (or it might be in white)

" LICENS'D TO SELL TEA & TOBACCO."

" Licens'd " was on one corner of the ribboned scroll, " To Sell Tea & " occupied the flowing arch above, with " Tobacco " in the other corner. When you mounted two steps and opened the door, a bell of some kind went " *ping* " in the interior, and an old woman in a mutch, with big specs slipping down her nose, would come up a step from a dim little room behind, and wiping her sunken mouth with her apron—she had just left her tea—would say, " What's your wull the day, sir ? " And if you said your " wull " was tobacco, she would answer, " Ou, sir, I dinna sell ocht now but the tape and sweeties." And then you went away, sadly.

With the exception of the dirty man's shop and the drunken man's shop, that kind of shop was the Barbie kind of shop. But Wilson changed all that. One side of the Emporium was crammed with pots, pans, pails, scythes, gardening implements, and saws, with a big barrel of paraffin partitioned off in a corner. The rafters on that side were bristling and hoary with brushes of all kinds dependent from the roof, so that the minister's wife (who was a six-footer) went off with a brush in her bonnet once. Behind the other counter were canisters in goodly rows, barrels of flour and bags of meal, and great yellow cheeses in the window. The rafters here were heavy with their wealth of hams, brown-skinned flitches of bacon interspersed with the white tight-corded home-cured—"Barbie's Best," as Wilson christened it. All along the back, in glass cases to keep them unsullied, were bales of cloth, layer on layer to the roof. It was a pleasure to go into the place, so big and bien was it, and to smell it on a frosty night set your teeth watering. There was always a big barrel of American apples just inside the door, and their homely fragrance wooed you from afar, the mellow savour cuddling round you half a mile off. Barbie boys had despised the provision trade, heretofore, as a mean and meagre occupation ; but now the imagination of each gallant youth was fired and radiant—he meant to be a grocer.

Mrs. Wilson presided over the Emporium. Wilson had a treasure in his wife. She was Aberdeen born and bred, but her manner was the manner of the South and West. There is a broad difference of character between the peoples of East and West Scotland. The East throws a narrower and a nippier breed. In the West they take Burns for their exemplar, and affect the jovial and robustious—in some cases it is affectation only, and a mighty poor one at that. They claim to be bigger men and bigger fools than the Eastern billies. And the Eastern billies are very willing to yield one half of the contention.

Mrs. Wilson, though Eastie by nature, had the jovial manner that you find in Kyle ; more jovial, indeed, than was common in nippy Barbie, which, in general character, seems to have been transplanted from some sand dune looking out upon the German Ocean. She was big of hip and bosom, with sloe-black hair and eyes, and a ruddy cheek, and when she flung back her head for the laugh her white teeth flashed splendid on the world. That laugh of hers became one of the well-known features of Barbie. "Lo'd-sake!" a startled

visitor would cry, "whatna skirl's tha-at!" "Oh,
dinna be alarmed," a native would comfort him, "it's
only Wilson's wife lauchin at the Cross!"

Her manner had a hearty charm. She had a laugh
and a joke for every customer, quick as a wink with her
answer; her gibe was in you and out again before you
knew you were wounded. Some, it is true, took exception to the loudness of her skirl—the Deacon, for instance, who "gave her a good one" the first time he
went in for snuff. But "Tut!" quoth she; "a mim cat's
never gude at the mice," and she lifted him out by the
scruff of his neck, crying, "Run, mousie, or I'll catch
ye!" On that day her popularity in Barbie was assured
for ever. But she was as keen on the penny as a
penurious weaver, for all her heartiness and laughing
ways. She combined the commercial merits of the East
and West. She could coax you to the buying like a
Cumnock quean, and fleece you in the selling like the
cadgers o' Kincardine. When Wilson was abroad on his
affairs he had no need to be afraid that things were mis-
managing at home. During his first year in Barbie
Mrs. Wilson was his sole helper. She had the brawny
arm of a giantess, and could toss a bag of meal like a
baby; to see her twirl a big ham on the counter was to
see a thing done as it should be. When Drucken Wabster came in and was offensive once, "Poo-oor fellow!"
said she (with a wink to a customer), "I declare he's in
a high fever," and she took him kicking to the pump
and cooled him.

With a mate like that at the helm every sail of Wil
son's craft was trimmed for prosperity. He began to
"look about" him to increase the fleet.

CHAPTER XI.

THAT the Scot is largely endowed with the commercial imagination his foes will be ready to acknowledge. Imagination may consecrate the world to a man, or it may merely be a visualizing faculty which sees that as already perfect which is still lying in the raw material. The Scot has the lower faculty in full degree ; he has the forecasting leap of the mind which sees what to make of things—more, sees them made and in vivid operation. To him there is a railway through the desert where no railway exists, and mills along the quiet stream. And his *perfervidum ingenium* is quick to attempt the realizing of his dreams. That is why he makes the best of colonists. Galt is his type —Galt, dreaming in boyhood of the fine water power a fellow could bring round the hill, from the stream where he went a-fishing (they have done it since), dreaming in manhood of the cities yet to rise amid Ontario's woods (they are there to witness to his foresight). Indeed, so flushed and riotous can the Scottish mind become over a commercial prospect that it sometimes sends native caution by the board, and a man's really fine idea becomes an empty balloon, to carry him off to the limbo of vanities. There is a megalomaniac in every parish of Scotland. Well, not so much as that ; they're owre canny for that to be said of them. But in every district almost you may find a poor creature who for thirty years has cherished a great scheme by which he means to revolutionize the world's commerce, and amass

a fortune in monstrous degree.   He is generally to be
seen shivering at the Cross, and (if you are a nippy man)
you shout carelessly in going by, " Good-morning,
Tamson ; how's the scheme ? "   And he would be very
willing to tell you, if only you would wait to listen.
" Man," he will cry eagerly behind you, " if I only had
anither wee wheel in my invention—she would do, the
besom !   I'll sune have her ready noo."   Poor Tamson !

But these are the exceptions.   Scotsmen, more than
other men perhaps, have the three great essentials of
commercial success—imagination to conceive schemes,
common sense to correct them, and energy to push them
through.   Common sense, indeed, so far from being
wanting, is in most cases too much in evidence, perhaps,
crippling the soaring mind and robbing the idea of its
early radiance ;   in quieter language, she makes the
average Scotsman to be over-cautious.   His combinations are rarely Napoleonic until he becomes an American.
In his native dales he seldom ventures on a daring policy.
And yet his forecasting mind is always detecting " possibeelities."   So he contents himself by creeping cau-
tiously from point to point, ignoring big, reckless schemes
and using the safe and small, till he arrives at a florid
opulence.   He has expressed his love of *festina lente* in
business in a score of proverbs—" Bit-by-bit's the better
horse, though big-by-big's the baulder ; "   " Ca' canny, or
ye'll cowp ; "   " Many a little makes a mickle ; "   and
" Creep before ye gang."   This mingling of caution and
imagination is the cause of his stable prosperity.   And
its characteristic is a sure progressiveness.   That sure
progressiveness was the characteristic of Wilson's prosperity in Barbie.   In him, too, imagination and caution
were equally developed.   He was always foreseeing
" chances " and using them, gripping the good and rejecting the dangerous (had he not gripped the chance
of auld Rab Jamieson's barn ?   There was caution in
that, for it was worth the money whatever happened ;

and there was imagination in the whole scheme, for he
had a vision of Barbie as a populous centre and streets
of houses in his holm). And every "chance" he seized
led to a better one, till almost every "chance" in Barbie
was engrossed by him alone. This is how he went to
work. Note the " bit-by-bitness " of his great career.

When Mrs. Wilson was behind the counter, Wilson
was out " distributing." He was not always out, of
course—his volume of trade at first was not big enough
for that ; but in the mornings, and the long summer
dusks, he made his way to the many outlying places of
which Barbie was the centre. There, in one and the
same visit, he distributed goods and collected orders for
the future. Though his bill had spoken of " carts,"
as if he had several, that was only a bit of splurge on
his part ; his one conveyance at the first was a stout
spring cart, with a good brown cob between the shafts.
But with this he did such a trade as had never been
known in Barbie. The Provost said it was " shtupen-
dous."

When Wilson was jogging homeward in the balmy
evenings of his first summer at Barbie, no eye had he for
the large evening star, tremulous above the woods, or
for the dreaming sprays against the yellow west. It
wasn't his business ; he had other things to mind. Yet
Wilson was a dreamer too. His close, musing eye, peering at the dusky-brown nodge of his pony's hip through
the gloom, saw not that, but visions of chances, oppor-
tunities, occasions. When the lights of Barbie twinkled
before him in the dusk, he used to start from a pleasant
dream of some commercial enterprise suggested by the
country round. " Yon holm would make a fine bleach-
ing green—pure water, fine air, labour cheap, and everything handy. Or the Lintie's Linn among the woods—
water power running to waste yonder—surely something could be made of that." He would follow his idea
through all its mazes and developments, oblivious of

the passing miles. His delight in his visions was exactly the same as the author's delight in the figments of
his brain. They were the same good company along the
twilight roads. The author, happy with his thronging
thoughts (when they are kind enough to throng), is no
happier than Wilson was on nights like these.

He had not been a week on his rounds when he saw
a " chance " waiting for development. When out " de-
livering " he used to visit the upland farms to buy
butter and eggs for the Emporium. He got them
cheaper so. But more eggs and butter could be had
than were required in the neighbourhood of Barbie.
Here was a chance for Wilson ! He became a collector
for merchants at a distance. Barbie, before it got the
railway, had only a silly little market once a fortnight,
which was a very poor outlet for stuff. Wilson provided a better one. Another thing played into his
hands, too, in that connection. It is a cheese-making
countryside about Barbie, and the less butter produced
at a cheese-making place, the better for the cheese.
Still, a good many pounds are often churned on the
sly. What need the cheese merchant ken ? it keepit
the gudewife in bawbees frae week to week ; and if
she took a little cream frae the cheese now and than they
werena a pin the waur o't, for she aye did it wi' decency
and caution ! Still, it is as well to dispose of this kind
of butter quietly, to avoid gabble among ill-speakers.
Wilson, slithering up the back road with his spring cart
in the gloaming, was the man to dispose of it quietly.
And he got it dirt cheap, of course, seeing it was a kind
of contraband. All that he made in this way was not
much to be sure—threepence a dozen on the eggs, perhaps, and fourpence on the pound of butter—still, you
know, every little makes a mickle, and hained gear
helps weel.* And more important than the immediate
profit was the ultimate result. For Wilson in this

* *Hained gear*, saved money.

way established with merchants, in far-off Fechars and
Poltandie, a connection for the sale of country produce
which meant a great deal to him in future, when he
launched out as cheese-buyer in opposition to Gourlay.

It " occurred " to him also (things were always occur-
ring to Wilson) that the " Scotch cuddy " business had
as fine a chance in " Barbie and surrounding neighbourhood " as ever it had in North and Middle England.
The " Scotch cuddy " is so called because he is a beast
of burden, and not from the nature of his wits. He is
a travelling packman, who infests communities of work-
ing-men, and disposes of his goods on the credit system,
receiving payment in instalments. You go into a working-man's house (when he is away from home for prefer-
ence), and laying a swatch of cloth across his wife's
knee, " What do you think of that, mistress ? " you
inquire, watching the effect keenly. Instantly all her
covetous heart is in her eye, and, thinks she to herself,
" Oh, but John would look well in that at the kirk on
Sunday ! " She has no ready money, and would never
have the cheek to go into a draper's and order the suit ;
but when she sees it lying there across her knee, she just
cannot resist it. (And fine you knew that when you
clinked it down before her !) Now that the goods are
in the house, she cannot bear to let them out the door
again. But she hints a scarcity of cash. " Tut, woman ! "
quoth you, bounteous and kind, " there's no obstacle in
that ! You can pay me in instalments ! " How much
would the instalments be, she inquires. " Oh, a mere
trifle—half a crown a week, say." She hesitates and
hankers. " John's Sunday coat's getting quite shabby,
so it is, and Tam Macalister has a new suit, she was
noticing—the Macalisters are always flaunting in their
braws ! And, there's that Paisley shawl for herself,
too ; eh, but they would be the canty pair, cocking
down the road on Sunday in *that* rig ! they would
take the licht frae Meg Macalister's een—thae Mac-

alisters are always so en-vy-fu'!" Love, vanity, covetousness, present opportunity, are all at work upon the poor body. She succumbs. But the half-crown weekly payments have a habit of lengthening themselves out till the packman has made fifty per cent. by the business. And why not? a man must have some interest on his money! Then there's the risk of bad debts, too—that falls to be considered. But there was little risk of bad debts when Wilson took to cloth-distributing. For success in that game depends on pertinacity in pursuit of your victim, and Wilson was the man for that.

He was jogging home from Brigabee, where he had been distributing groceries at a score of wee houses, when there flashed on his mind a whole scheme for cloth-distribution on a large scale; for mining villages were clustering in about Barbie by this time, and he saw his way to a big thing.

He was thinking of Sandy Toddle, who had been a Scotch cuddy in the Midlands, and had retired to Barbie on a snug bit fortune—he was thinking of Sandy when the plan rose generous on his mind. He would soon have more horses than one on the road; why shouldn't they carry swatches of cloth as well as groceries? If he had responsible men under him, it would be their own interest, for a small commission on the profits, to see that payments were levied correctly every week. And those colliers were reckless with their cash, far readier to commit themselves to buying than the cannier country bodies round. Lord! there was money in the scheme. No sooner thought of than put in practice. Wilson gave up the cloth-peddling after five or six years—he had other fish to fry by that time—but while he was at it he made money hand over fist at the job.

But what boots it to tell of all his schemes? He had the lucky eye, and everything he looked on prospered.

Before he had been a week in Barbie he met Gourlay, just at the Bend o' the Brae, in full presence of the bodies. Remembering their first encounter, the grocer tried to outstare him ; but Gourlay hardened his glower, and the grocer blinked. When the two passed, " I declare ! " said the bodies, " did ye see yon ?—they're not on speaking terms ! " And they hotched with glee to think that Gourlay had another enemy.

Judge of their delight when they saw one day about a month later, just as Gourlay was passing up the street, Wilson come down it with a load of coals for a customer ! For he was often out Auchterwheeze road in the early morning, and what was the use of an empty journey back again, especially as he had plenty of time in the middle of the day to attend to other folk's affairs ? So here he was, started as a carrier, in full opposition to Gourlay.

"Did you see Gourlay's face ? " chuckled the bodies when the cart went by. " Yon was a bash in the eye to him. Ha, ha ! he's not to have it all his own way now ! "

Wilson had slid into the carrying in the natural development of business. It was another of the possibilities which he saw and turned to his advantage. The two other chief grocers in the place, Cunningham the dirty and Calderwood the drunken, having no carts or horses of their own, were dependent on Gourlay for conveyance of their goods from Skeighan. But Wilson brought his own. Naturally, he was asked by his customers to bring a parcel now and then, and naturally, being the man he was, he made them pay for the privilege. With that for a start the rest was soon accomplished. Gourlay had to pay now for his years of insolence and tyranny; all who had irked beneath his domineering ways got their carrying done by Wilson. Ere long that prosperous gentleman had three carts on the road, and two men under him to help in his various affairs.

Carting was only one of several new developments in

the business of J. W.   When the navvies came in about
the town and accommodation was ill to find, Wilson
rigged up an old shed in the corner of his holm as a
hostelry for ten of them—and they had to pay through
the nose for their night's lodging.   Their food they
obtained from the Emporium, and thus the Wilsons bled
them both ways.   Then there was the scheme for supply-
ing milk—another of the " possibeelities."   Hitherto in
winter, Barbie was dependent for its milk supply on
heavy farm-carts that came lumbering down the street,
about half-past seven in the morning, jangling bells to
waken sleepy customers, and carrying lanterns that
carved circles of fairy yellow out the raw air.   But Mrs.
Wilson got four cows, back-calvers who would be milking
strong in December, and supplied milk to all the folk
about the Cross.

She had a lass to help her in the house now, and the
red-headed boy was always to be seen, jinking round
corners like a weasel, running messages hot-foot, errand
boy to the " bisness " in general.   Yet, though everybody was busy and skelping at it, such a stress of work
was accompanied with much disarray.   Wilson's yard
was the strangest contrast to Gourlay's.   Gourlay's was
a pleasure to the eye, everything of the best and everything in order, since the master's pride would not allow
it to be other.   But though Wilson's Emporium was
clean, his back yard was littered with dirty straw,
broken boxes, old barrels, stable refuse, and the sky-
pointing shafts of carts, uptilted in between.   When
boxes and barrels were flung out of the Emporium they
were generally allowed to lie on the dunghill until they
were converted into firewood.   " Mistress, you're a trifle
mixed," said the Provost in grave reproof, when he went
round to the back to see Wilson on a matter of business.
But " Tut," cried Mrs. Wilson, as she threw down a
plank, to make a path for him across a dub—" Tut,"
she laughed, " the clartier the cosier ! "   And it was as

true as she said it. The thing went forward splendidly in spite of its confusion.

Though trade was brisker in Barbie than it had ever been before, Wilson had already done injury to Gourlay's business as general conveyor. But, hitherto, he had not infringed on the gurly one's other monopolies. His chance came at last.

He appeared on a market-day in front of the Red Lion, a piece of pinky brown paper in his hand. That was the first telegram ever seen in Barbie, and it had been brought by special messenger from Skeighan. It was short and to the point. It ran : " Will buy 300 stone cheese 8 shillings stone * delivery at once," and was signed by a merchant in Poltandie.

Gourlay was talking to old Tarmillan of Irrendavie, when Wilson pushed in and addressed Tarmillan, without a glance at the grain-merchant.

" Have you a kane o' cheese to sell, Irrendavie ? " was his blithe salutation.

" I have," said Irrendavie, and he eyed him suspiciously. For what was Wilson speiring for ? *He* wasna a cheese-merchant.

" How much the stane are ye seeking for't ? " said Wilson.

" I have just been asking Mr. Gourlay here for seven-and-six," said Irrendavie, " but he winna rise a penny on the seven ! "

" *I*'ll gi'e ye seven-and-six," said Wilson, and slapped his long thin flexible bank-book far too ostentatiously against the knuckles of his left hand.

" But—but," stammered Irrendavie, suspicious still, but melting at the offer, " *you* have no means of storing cheese."

" Oh," said Wilson, getting in a fine one at Gourlay,

* That is for the stone of fourteen pounds. At that time Scotch cheese was selling, *roughly*, at from fifty to sixty shillings the hundred-weight.

"there's no drawback in that! The ways o' business have changed greatly since steam came close to our doors. It's nothing but vanity nowadays when a country merchant wastes money on a ramshackle of buildings for storing—there's no need for that if he only had brains to develop quick deliveries. Some folk, no doubt, like to build monuments to their own pride, but I'm not one of that kind; there's not enough sense in that to satisfy a man like me. My offer doesna hold, you understand, unless you deliver the cheese at Skeighan Station. Do you accept the condition?"

"Oh yes," said Irrendavie, "I'm willing to agree to that."

"C'way into the Red Lion then," said Wilson, "and we'll wet the bargain with a drink to make it hold the tighter!"

Then a strange thing happened. Gourlay had a curious stick of foreign wood (one of the trifles he fed his pride on) the crook of which curved back to the stem and inhered, leaving space only for the fingers. The wood was of wonderful toughness, and Gourlay had been known to bet that no man could break the handle of his stick by a single grip over the crook and under it. Yet now, as he saw his bargain whisked away from him and listened to Wilson's jibe, the thing snapped in his grip like a rotten twig. He stared down at the broken pieces for a while, as if wondering how they came there, then dashed them on the ground while Wilson stood smiling by. And then he strode—with a look on his face that made the folk fall away.

"He's hellish angry," they grinned to each other when their foe was gone, and laughed when they heard the cause of it. "Ha, ha, Wilson's the boy to diddle him!" And yet they looked queer when told that the famous stick had snapped in his grasp like a worm-eaten larch-twig. "Lord!" cried the baker in admiring awe, "did he break it with the ae chirt! It's been tried by

scores of fellows for the last twenty years, and never a
man of them was up till't ! Lads, there's something
splendid about Gourlay's wrath. What a man he is
when the paw-sion grups him ! "

" Thplendid, d'ye ca't ? " said the Deacon.   " He may
thwing in a towe for his thplendid wrath yet."

From that day Wilson and Gourlay were a pair of
gladiators for whom the people of Barbie made a ring.
They pitted the protagonists against each other and
hounded them on to rivalry by their comments and
remarks, taking the side of the newcomer, less from
partiality to him than from hatred of their ancient
enemy.   It was strange that a thing so impalpable as
gossip should influence so strong a man as John Gourlay
to his ruin.   But it did.   The bodies of Barbie became
not only the chorus to Gourlay's tragedy, buzzing it
abroad and discussing his downfall ; they became also,
merely by their maddening tattle, a villain of the piece
and an active cause of the catastrophe.   Their gossip
seemed to materialize into a single entity, a something
propelling, that spurred Gourlay on to the schemes that
ruined him.   He was not to be done, he said ; he would
show the dogs what he thought of them.   And so he
plunged headlong, while the wary Wilson watched him,
smiling at the sight.

There was a pretty hell-broth brewing in the little
town.

CHAPTER XII.

"Ay, man, Templandmuir, it's you!" said Gourlay, coming forward with great heartiness. "Ay, man, and how are ye? C'way into the parlour!"

"Good-evening, Mr. Gourlay," said the Templar. His manner was curiously subdued.

Since his marriage there was a great change in the rubicund squireen. Hitherto he had lived in sluttish comfort on his own land, content with the little it brought in, and proud to be the friend of Gourlay, whom everybody feared. If it ever dawned on his befuddled mind that Gourlay turned the friendship to his own account, his vanity was flattered by the prestige he acquired because of it. Like many another robustious big toper, the Templar was a chicken at heart, and "to be in with Gourlay" lent him a consequence that covered his deficiency. "Yes, I'm sleepy," he would yawn in Skeighan Mart; "I had a sederunt yestreen wi' John Gourlay," and he would slap his boot with his riding-switch and feel like a hero. "I know how it is, I know how it is!" Provost Connal of Barbie used to cry; "Gourlay both courts and cowes him—first he courts and then he cowes—and the Templar hasn't the courage to break it off!" The Provost hit the mark.

But when the Templar married the miller's daughter of the Mill o' Blink (a sad come-down, said foolish neighbours, for a Halliday of Templandmuir) there was a sudden change about the laird. In our good Scots proverb, "A miller's daughter has a shrill voice," and

the new leddy of Templandmuir ("a leddy she is!"
said the frightened housekeeper) justified the proverb.
Her voice went with the skirl of an east wind through
the rat-riddled mansion of the Hallidays. She was nine-
and-twenty, and a birkie woman of nine-and-twenty
can make a good husband out of very unpromising
material. The Templar wore a scared look in those days
and went home betimes. His cronies knew the fun was
over when they heard what happened to the great punch-
bowl—she made it a swine-trough. It was the heirloom
of a hundred years, and as much as a man could carry
with his arms out, a massive curio in stone ; but to her
husband's plaint about its degradation, " Oh," she cried,
" it'll never know the difference ! It's been used to
swine ! "

But she was not content with the cessation of the
old ; she was determined on bringing in the new. For
a twelvemonth now she had urged her husband to be
rid of Gourlay. The country was opening up, she said,
and the quarry ought to be their own. A dozen times
he had promised her to warn Gourlay that he must yield
the quarry when his tack ran out at the end of the year,
and a dozen times he had shrunk from the encounter.

" I'll write," he said feebly.

" Write ! " said she, lowered in her pride to think her
husband was a coward. " Write, indeed ! Man, have
ye no spunk ? Think what he has made out o' ye !
Think o' the money that has gone to him that should
have come to you ! You should be glad o' the chance
to tell him o't. My certy, if I was you I wouldn't miss
it for the world—just to let him know of his cheatry !
Oh, it's very right that *I* "—she sounded the *I* big and
brave—" it's very right that *I* should live in this tumble-
down hole while *he* builds a palace from your plunder !
It's right that *I* should put up with this "—she flung
hands of contempt at her dwelling—" it's right that *I*
should put up with this, while yon trollop has a splendid

mansion on the top o' the brae ! And every bawbee of
his fortune has come out of you—the fool makes nothing
from his other business—he would have been a pauper
if he hadn't met a softie like you that he could do what
he liked with. Write, indeed ! I have no patience with
a wheen sumphs of men ! Them do the work o' the
world ! They may wear the breeks, but the women
wear the brains, I trow. I'll have it out with the black
brute myself," screamed the hardy dame, " if you're
feared of his glower. If you havena the pluck for it,
I have. Write, indeed ! In you go to the meeting that
oald ass of a Provost has convened, and don't show your
face in Templandmuir till you have had it out with
Gourlay ! "

No wonder the Templar looked subdued.

When Gourlay came forward with his usual calculated
heartiness, the laird remembered his wife and felt very
uncomfortable. It was ill to round on a man who
always imposed on him a hearty and hardy good-fellow-
ship. Gourlay, greeting him so warmly, gave him no
excuse for an outburst. In his dilemma he turned to
the children, to postpone the evil hour.

" Ay, man, John ! " he said heavily, " you're there ! "
Heavy Scotsmen are fond of telling folk that they are
where they are. " You're there ! " said Templandmuir.

" Ay," said John, the simpleton, " I'm here."

In the grime of the boy's face there were large white
circles round the eyes, showing where his fists had rubbed
off the tears through the day.

" How are you doing at the school ? " said the Templar.

" Oh, he's an ass ! " said Gourlay. " He takes after
his mother in that ! The lassie's more smart—she
favours our side o' the house ! Eh, Jenny ? " he inquired, and tugged her pigtail, smiling down at her in
grim fondness.

" Yes," nodded Janet, encouraged by the petting,
" John's always at the bottom of the class. Jimmy

Wilson's always at the top, and the dominie set him to teach John his 'counts the day—after he had thrashed him!"

She cried out at a sudden tug on her pigtail, and looked up, with tears in her eyes, to meet her father's scowl.

"You eediot!" said Gourlay, gazing at his son with a savage contempt, "have you no pride to let Wilson's son be your master?"

John slunk from the room.

"Bide where you are, Templandmuir," said Gourlay after a little, "I'll be back directly."

He went through to the kitchen and took a crystal jug from the dresser. He "made a point" of bringing the water for his whisky. "I like to pump it up *cold*," he used to say, "cold and cold, ye know, till there's a mist on the outside of the glass like the bloom on a plum, and then, by Goad, ye have the fine drinking! Oh no—ye needn't tell me, I wouldn't lip drink if the water wasna ice-cold." He never varied from the tipple he approved. In his long sederunts with Templandmuir he would slip out to the pump, before every brew, to get water of sufficient coldness.

To-night he would birl the bottle with Templandmuir as usual, till the fuddled laird should think himself a fine big fellow as being the intimate of John Gourlay—and then, sober as a judge himself, he would drive him home in the small hours. And when next they met, the pot-valiant squireen would chuckle proudly, "Faith, yon was a night." By a crude cunning of the kind Gourlay had maintained his ascendancy for years, and to-night he would maintain it still. He went out to the pump to fetch water with his own hands for their first libation.

But when he came back and set out the big decanter Templandmuir started to his feet.

"Noat to-night, Mr. Gourlay," he stammered—and

his unusual flutter of refusal might have warned Gourlay
—" noat to-night, if *you* please ; noat to-night, if *you*
please. As a matter of fact—eh—what I really came
into the town for, doan't you see, was—eh—to attend
the meeting the Provost has convened about the railway.
You'll come down to the meeting, will ye noat ? "

He wanted to get Gourlay away from the House with
the Green Shutters. It would be easier to quarrel with
him out of doors.

But Gourlay gaped at him across the table, his eyes
big with surprise and disapproval.

" Huh ! " he growled, " I wonder at a man like you
giving your head to that ! It's a wheen damned nonsense."

" Oh, I'm no so sure of that," drawled the Templar.
" I think the railway means to come."

The whole country was agog about the new railway.
The question agitating solemn minds was whether it
should join the main line at Fechars, thirty miles ahead,
or pass to the right, through Fleckie and Barbie, to a
junction up at Skeighan Drone. Many were the reasons
spluttered in vehement debate for one route or the other.
" On the one side, ye see, Skeighan was a big place
a'readys, and look what a centre it would be if it had
three lines of rail running out and in ! Eh, my, what
a centre ! Then there was Fleckie and Barbie—they
would be the big towns ! Up the valley, too, was the
shortest road ; it would be a daft-like thing to build
thirty mile of rail, when fifteen was enough to establish
the connection ! And was it likely—I put it to ainy
man of sense—was it likely the Coal Company wouldn't
do everything in their power to get the railway up the
valley, seeing that if it didn't come that airt they would
need to build a line of their own ? "—" Ah, but then, ye
see, Fechars was a big place too, and there was lots of
mineral up there as well ! And though it was a longer
road to Fechars and part of it lay across the moors,

there were several wee towns that airt just waiting for a chance of growth! I can tell ye, sirs, this was going to be a close question!"

Such was the talk in pot-house and parlour, at kirk and mart and tryst and fair, and wherever potentates did gather and abound. The partisans on either side began to canvass the country in support of their contentions. They might have kept their breath to cool their porridge, for these matters, we know, are settled in the great Witenagemot. But petitions were prepared and meetings were convened. In those days Provost Connal of Barbie was in constant communion with the "Pow-ers." "Yass," he nodded gravely—only "nod" is a word too swift for the grave inclining of that mighty pow—"yass, ye know, the great thing in matters like this is to get at the Pow-ers, doan't you see? Oh yass, yass; we must get at the Pow-ers!" and he looked as if none but he were equal to the job. He even went to London (to interrogate the "Pow-ers"), and simple bodies, gathered at the Cross for their Saturday at e'en, told each other with bated breath that the Provost was away to the "seat of Goaver'ment to see about the railway." When he came back and shook his head, hope drained from his fellows and left them hollow in an empty world. But when he smacked his lips on receiving an important letter, the heavens were brightened and the landscapes smiled.

The Provost walked about the town nowadays with the air of a man on whose shoulders the weight of empires did depend. But for all his airs it was not the Head o' the Town who was the ablest advocate of the route up the Water of Barbie. It was that public-spirited citizen, Mr. James Wilson of the Cross! Wilson championed the cause of Barbie with an ardour that did infinite credit to his civic heart. For one thing, it was a grand way of recommending himself to his new townsfolk, as he told his wife, " and so increasing the circle of our present

trade, don't ye understand ? "—for another, he was as
keen as the keenest that the railway should come and
enhance the value of his property.   " We must agitate,"
he cried, when Sandy Toddle murmured a doubt whether
anything they could do would be of much avail.   " It's
not settled yet what road the line's to follow, and who
knows but a trifle may turn the scale in our behalf ?
Local opinion ought to be expressed !   They're sending
a monster petition from the Fechars side ; we'll send the
Company a bigger one from ours !   Look at Skeighan
and Fleckie and Barbie—three towns at our back, and
the new Coal Company forbye !   A public opinion of
that size ought to have a great weight—if put forward
properly !   We must agitate, sirs, we must agitate ;
we maun scour the country for names in our support.
Look what a number of things there are to recommend
our route.   It's the shortest, and there's no need for
heavy cuttings such as are needed on the other side ;
the road's there a'ready—Barbie Water has cut it through
the hills.   It's the manifest design of Providence that
there should be a line up Barbie Valley !   What a position for't !—And, oh," thought Wilson, " what a site for
building houses in my holm !—Let a meeting be convened
at wunst ! "

The meeting was convened, with Provost Connal in
the chair and Wilson as general factotum.

" You'll come down to the meeting ? " said Templandmuir to Gourlay.

Go to a meeting for which Wilson had sent out the
bills !   At another, Gourlay would have hurled his usual
objurgation that he would see him condemned to eternal
agonies ere he granted his request !   But Templandmuir
was different.   Gourlay had always flattered this man
(whom he inwardly despised) by a companionship which
made proud the other.   He had always yielded to Templandmuir in small things, for the sake of the quarry,
which was a great thing.   He yielded to him now.

" Verra well," he said shortly, and rose to get his hat.
When Gourlay put on his hat the shallow meanness
of his brow was hid, and nothing was seen to impair his
dark, strong gravity of face.   He was a man you would
have turned to look at as he marched in silence by the
side of Templandmuir.   Though taller than the laird,
he looked shorter because of his enormous breadth.   He
had a chest like the heave of a hill.   Templandmuir
was afraid of him.   And fretting at the necessity he felt
to quarrel with a man of whom he was afraid, he had
an unreasonable hatred of Gourlay, whose conduct made
this quarrel necessary at the same time that his character
made it to be feared ; and he brooded on his growing rage
that, with it for a stimulus, he might work his cowardly
nature to the point of quarrelling.   Conscious of the
coming row, then, he felt awkward in the present, and
was ignorant what to say.   Gourlay was silent too.   He
felt it an insult to the House with the Green Shutters
that the laird should refuse its proffered hospitality.
He hated to be dragged to a meeting he despised.   Never
before was such irritation between them.

When they came to the hall where the meeting was
convened, there were knots of bodies grouped about the
floor.   Wilson fluttered from group to group, an important man, with a roll of papers in his hand.   Gourlay,
quick for once in his dislike, took in every feature of the
man he loathed.

Wilson was what the sentimental women of the neighbourhood called a " bonny man."   His features were
remarkably regular, and his complexion was remarkably
fair.   His brow was so delicate of hue that the blue
veins running down his temples could be traced distinctly beneath the whiteness of the skin.   Unluckily
for him, he was so fair that in a strong light (as now beneath the gas) the suspicion of his unwashedness became
a certainty—" as if he got a bit idle slaik now and than,
and never a good rub," thought Gourlay in a clean

disgust. Full lips showed themselves bright red in the middle between the two wings of a very blonde and very symmetrical moustache. The ugly feature of the face was the blue calculating eyes. They were tender round the lids, so that the white lashes stuck out in little peaks. And in conversation he had a habit of peering out of these eyes as if he were constantly spying for something to emerge that he might twist to his advantage. As he talked to a man close by and glimmered (not at the man beside him, but far away in the distance of his mind at some chance of gain suggested by the other's words) Gourlay heard him say musingly, "Imphm, imphm, imphm! there might be something *in* that!" nodding his head and stroking his moustache as he uttered each meditative "imphm."

It was Wilson's unconscious revelation that his mind was busy with a commercial hint which he had stolen from his neighbour's talk. "The damned sneck-drawer!" thought Gourlay, enlightened by his hate; "he's sucking Tam Finlay's brains, to steal some idea for himsell!" And still as Wilson listened he murmured swiftly, "Imphm! I see, Mr. Finlay; imphm! imphm! imphm!" nodding his head and pulling his moustache and glimmering at his new "opportunity."

Our insight is often deepest into those we hate, because annoyance fixes our thought on them to probe. We cannot keep our minds off them. "Why do they do it?" we snarl, and wondering why, we find out their character. Gourlay was not an observant man, but every man is in any man somewhere, and hate to-night driving his mind into Wilson, helped him to read him like an open book. He recognized with a vague uneasiness—not with fear, for Gourlay did not know what it meant, but with uneasy anger—the superior cunning of his rival. Gourlay, a strong block of a man cut off from the world by impotence of speech, could never have got out of Finlay what Wilson drew from him in two minutes' easy conversation.

Wilson ignored Gourlay, but he was very blithe with Templandmuir, and inveigled him off to a corner. They talked together very briskly, and Wilson laughed once with uplifted head, glancing across at Gourlay as he laughed. Curse them, were they speaking of him ?

The hall was crammed at last, and the important bodies took their seats upon the front benches. Gour.. lay refused to be seated with the rest, but stood near the platform, with his back to the wall, by the side of Templandmuir.

After what the Provost described " as a few prelimi‑ nary remarks "—they lasted half an hour—he called on Mr. Wilson to address the meeting. Wilson descanted on the benefits that would accrue to Barbie if it got the railway, and on the needcessity for a " long pull, and a strong pull, and a pull all together "—a phrase which he repeated many times in the course of his address. He sat down at last amid thunders of applause.

" There's no needcessity for me to make a loang speech," said the Provost.

" Hear, hear ! " said Gourlay, and the meeting was unkind enough to laugh.

" Order, order ! " cried Wilson perkily.

" As I was saying when I was grossly interrupted," fumed the Provost, " there's no needcessity for me to make a loang speech. I had thoat we were a‑all agreed on the desirabeelity of the rileway coming in our direc‑ tion. I had thoat, after the able—I must say the very able—speech of Mr. Wilson, that there wasn't a man in this room so shtupid as to utter a word of dishapproval. I had thoat we might prosheed at woance to elect a depu‑ tation. I had thoat we would get the name of every‑ body here for the great petition we mean to send the Pow‑ers. I had thoat it was all, so to shpeak, a fore‑ gone conclusion. But it seems I was mistaken, ladies

and gentlemen—or rather, I oat to say gentlemen, for
I believe there are no ladies present.   Yass, it seems I
was mistaken.   It may be there are some who would
like to keep Barbie going on in the oald way which they
found so much to their advantage.   It may be there are
some who regret a change that will put an end to their
chances of tyraneezin'.   It may be there are some who
know themselves so shtupid that they fear the new con-
deetions of trade the railway's bound to bring."—Here
Wilson rose and whispered in his ear, and the people
watched them, wondering what hint J. W. was passing
to the Provost.   The Provost leaned with pompous
gravity toward his monitor, hand at ear to catch the
treasured words.   He nodded and resumed.—" Now,
gentlemen, as Mr. Wilson said, this is a case that needs
a loang pull, and a stroang pull, and a pull all together.
We must be unanimous.   It will *noat* do to show ourselves divided among ourselves.   Therefore I think we
oat to have expressions of opinion from some of our
leading townsmen.   That will show how far we are
unanimous.   I had thoat there could be only one opinion, and that we might prosheed at once with the petition.   But it seems I was wroang.   It is best to inquire
first exactly where we stand.   So I call upon Mr. John
Gourlay, who has been the foremost man in the town for
mainy years—at least he used to be that—I call upon
Mr. Gourlay as the first to express an opinion on the
subjeck."

Wilson's hint to the Provost placed Gourlay in a fine
dilemma.   Stupid as he was, he was not so stupid as not
to perceive the general advantage of the railway.   If he
approved it, however, he would seem to support Wilson
and the Provost, whom he loathed.   If he disapproved,
his opposition would be set down to a selfish consideration for his own trade, and he would incur the anger
of the meeting, which was all for the coming of the railway.   Wilson had seized the chance to put him in a false

position. He knew Gourlay could not put forty words together in public, and that in his dilemma he would blunder and give himself away.

Gourlay evaded the question.

" It would be better to convene a meeting," he bawled to the Provost, " to consider the state of some folk's back doors."—That was a nipper to Wilson !—" There's a stink at the Cross that's enough to kill a cuddy ! "

" Evidently not," yelled Wilson, " since you're still alive ! "

A roar went up against Gourlay. All he could do was to scowl before him, with hard-set mouth and gleaming eyes, while they bellowed him to scorn.

" I would like to hear what Templandmuir has to say on the subject," said Wilson, getting up. " But no doubt he'll follow his friend Mr. Gourlay."

" No, I don't follow Mr. Gourlay," bawled Templandmuir with unnecessary loudness. The reason of his vehemence was twofold. He was nettled (as Wilson meant he should) by the suggestion that he was nothing but Gourlay's henchman. And being eager to oppose Gourlay, yet a coward, he yelled to supply in noise what he lacked in resolution.

" I don't follow Mr. Gourlay at all," he roared ; " I follow nobody but myself ! Every man in the district's in support of this petition. It would be absurd to suppose anything else. I'll be glad to sign't among the first, and do everything I can in its support."

" Verra well," said the Provost ; " it seems we're agreed after all. We'll get some of our foremost men to sign the petition at this end of the hall, and then it'll be placed in the anteroom for the rest to sign as they go out."

" Take it across to Gourlay," whispered Wilson to the two men who were carrying the enormous tome. They took it over to the grain merchant, and one of them handed him an inkhorn. He dashed it to the ground.

The meeting hissed like a cellarful of snakes. But Gourlay turned and glowered at them, and somehow the hisses died away. His was the high courage that feeds on hate, and welcomes rather than shrinks from its expression. He was smiling as he faced them.

" Let *me* pass," he said, and shouldered his way to the door, the bystanders falling back to make room. Templandmuir followed him out.

" I'll walk to the head o' the brae," said the Templar.

He must have it out with Gourlay at once, or else go home to meet the anger of his wife. Having opposed Gourlay already, he felt that now was the time to break with him for good. Only a little was needed to complete the rupture. And he was the more impelled to declare himself to-night because he had just seen Gourlay discomfited, and was beginning to despise the man he had formerly admired. Why, the whole meeting had laughed at his expense! In quarrelling with Gourlay, moreover, he would have the whole locality behind him. He would range himself on the popular side. Every impulse of mind and body pushed him forward to the brink of speech ; he would never get a better occasion to bring out his grievance.

They trudged together in a burning silence. Though nothing was said between them, each was in wrathful contact with the other's mind. Gourlay blamed everything that had happened on Templandmuir, who had dragged him to the meeting and deserted him. And Templandmuir was longing to begin about the quarry, but afraid to start.

That was why he began at last with false, unnecessary loudness. It was partly to encourage himself (as a bull bellows to increase his rage), and partly because his spite had been so long controlled. It burst the louder for its pent fury.

" Mr. Gourlay ! " he bawled suddenly, when they came

opposite the House with the Green Shutters, " I've had a crow to pick with you for more than a year."

It came on Gourlay with a flash that Templandmuir was slipping away from him. But he must answer him civilly for the sake of the quarry.

" Ay, man," he said quietly, " and what may that be ? "

" I'll damned soon tell you what it is," said the Templar. " Yon was a monstrous overcharge for bringing my ironwork from Fleckie. I'll be damned if I put up with that ! "

And yet it was only a trifle. He had put up with fifty worse impositions and never said a word. But when a man is bent on a quarrel any spark will do for an explosion.

" How do ye make that out ? " said Gourlay, still very quietly, lest he should alienate the quarry laird.

" Damned fine do I make that out," yelled Templandmuir, and louder than ever was the yell. He was the brave man now, with his bellow to hearten him. " Damned fine do I make that out. You charged me for a whole day, though half o't was spent upon your own concerns. I'm tired o' you and your cheatry. You've made a braw penny out o' me in your time. But curse me if I endure it loanger. I give you notice this verra night that your tack o' the quarry must end at Martinmas."

He was off, glad to have it out and glad to escape the consequence, leaving Gourlay a cauldron of wrath in the darkness. It was not merely the material loss that maddened him. But for the first time in his life he had taken a rebuff without a word or a blow in return. In his desire to conciliate he had let Templandmuir get away unscathed. His blood rocked him where he stood.

He walked blindly to the kitchen door, never knowing how he reached it. It was locked—at this early hour !—and the simple inconvenience let loose the fury of his wrath. He struck the door with his clenched fist till the blood streamed on his knuckles.

It was Mrs. Gourlay who opened the door to him. She started back before his awful eyes.

" John ! " she cried, " what's wrong wi' ye ? "

The sight of the she-tatterdemalion there before him, whom he had endured so long and must endure for ever, was the crowning burden of his night. Damn her, why didn't she get out of the way ? why did she stand there in her dirt and ask silly questions ? He struck her on the bosom with his great fist, and sent her spinning on the dirty table.

She rose from among the broken dishes and came towards him, with slack lips and great startled eyes. " John," she panted, like a pitiful frightened child, " what have I been doing ? . . . Man, what did you hit me for ? "

He gaped at her with hanging jaw. He knew he was a brute—knew she had done nothing to-night more than she had ever done—knew he had vented on her a wrath that should have burst on others. But his mind was at a stick ; how could he explain—to *her?* He gaped and glowered for a speechless moment, then turned on his heel and went into the parlour, slamming the door till the windows rattled in their frames.

She stared after him a while in large-eyed stupor, then flung herself in her old nursing-chair by the fire, and spat blood in the ribs, hawking it up coarsely—we forget to be delicate in moments of supremer agony. And then she flung her apron over her head and rocked herself to and fro in the chair where she had nursed his children, wailing, " It's a pity o' me, it's a pity o' me ! My God, ay, it's a geyan pity o' me ! "

The boy was in bed, but Janet had watched the scene with a white, scared face and tearful cries. She crept to her mother's side.

The sympathy of children with those who weep is

innocently selfish. The sight of tears makes them uncomfortable, and they want them to cease, in the interests of their own happiness. If the outward signs of grief would only vanish, all would be well. They are not old enough to appreciate the inward agony.

So Janet tugged at the obscuring apron, and whimpered, "Don't greet, mother, don't greet. Woman, I dinna like to see ye greetin'."

But Mrs. Gourlay still rocked herself and wailed, " It's a pity o' me, it's a pity o' me ! My God, ay, it's a geyan pity o' me ! "

CHAPTER XIII.

"Is he in himsell?" asked Gibson the builder, coming into the Emporium.

Mrs. Wilson was alone in the shop. Since trade grew so brisk she had an assistant to help her, but he was out for his breakfast at present, and as it happened she was all alone.

"No," she said, "he's no in. We're terribly driven this twelvemonth back, since trade grew so thrang, and he's aye hunting business in some corner. He's out the now after a carrying affair. Was it ainything perticular?"

She looked at Gibson with a speculation in her eyes that almost verged on hostility. Wives of the lower classes who are active helpers in a husband's affairs often direct that look upon strangers who approach him in the way of business. For they are enemies whatever way you take them; come to be done by the husband or to do him—in either case, therefore, the object of a sharp curiosity. You may call on an educated man, either to fleece him or be fleeced, and his wife, though she knows all about it, will talk to you charmingly of trifles while you wait for him in her parlour. But a wife of the lower orders, active in her husband's affairs, has not been trained to dissemble so prettily; though her face be a mask, what she is wondering comes out in her eye. There was suspicion in the big round stare that Mrs. Wilson directed at the builder. What was *he* spiering for "himsell" for? What could he be up to?

Some end of his own, no doubt.   Anxious curiosity
forced her to inquire.

" Would I do instead ? " she asked.

" Well, hardly," said Gibson, clawing his chin, and
gazing at a corded round of " Barbie's Best " just above
his head.   " Dod, it's a fine ham that," he said, to turn
the subject.   " How are ye selling it the now ? "

" Tenpence a pound retail, but ninepence only if ye
take a whole one.   Ye had better let me send you one,
Mr. Gibson, now that winter's drawing on.   It's a
heartsome thing, the smell of frying ham on a frosty
morning "—and her laugh went skelloching up the
street.

" Well, ye see," said Gibson, with a grin, " I expect
Mr. Wilson to present me with one when he hears the
news that I have brought him."

" Aha ! " said she, " it's something good, then," and
she stuck her arms akimbo.—" James ! " she shrilled,
" James ! " and the red-haired boy shot from the back
premises.

" Run up to the Red Lion, and see if your father has
finished his crack wi' Templandmuir.   Tell him Mr.
Gibson wants to see him on important business."

The boy squinted once at the visitor, and scooted, the
red head of him foremost.

While Gibson waited and clawed his chin she exam-
ined him narrowly.   Suspicion as to the object of his
visit fixed her attention on his face.

He was a man with mean brown eyes.   Brown eyes
may be clear and limpid as a mountain pool, or they may
have the fine black flash of anger and the jovial gleam,
or they may be mean things—little and sly and oily.
Gibson's had the depth of cunning, not the depth of
character, and they glistened like the eyes of a lustful
animal.   He was a reddish man, with a fringe of sandy
beard, and a perpetual grin which showed his yellow
teeth, with green deposit round their roots.   It was

more than a grin—it was a *rictus*, semicircular from cheek to cheek; and the beady eyes, ever on the watch up above it, belied its false benevolence. He was not florid, yet that grin of his seemed to intensify his red-dishness (perhaps because it brought out and made prominent his sandy valance and the ruddy round of his cheeks), so that the baker christened him long ago " the man with the sandy smile."   " Cunning Johnny " was his other nickname.   Wilson had recognized a match in him the moment he came to Barbie, and had resolved to act with him if he could, but never to act against him. They had made advances to each other—birds of a feather, in short.

The grocer came in hurriedly, white-waistcoated to-day, and a perceptibly bigger bulge in his belly than when we first saw him in Barbie, four years ago now.

" Good-morning, Mr. Gibson," he panted.   " Is it private that ye wanted to see me on ? "

" Verra private," said the sandy smiler.

" We'll go through to the house, then," said Wilson, and ushered his guest through the back premises. But the voice of his wife recalled him.   " James ! " she cried. " Here for a minute just," and he turned to her, leaving Gibson in the yard.

" Be careful what you're doing," she whispered in his ear.   " It wasna for nothing they christened Gibson ' Cunning Johnny.'   Keep the dirt out your een."

" There's no fear of that," he assured her pompously. It was a grand thing to have a wife like that, but her advice nettled him now just a little, because it seemed to imply a doubt of his efficiency—and that was quite onnecessar.   He knew what he was doing.   They would need to rise very early that got the better o' a man like him !

" You'll take a dram ? " said Wilson, when they reached a pokey little room where the most conspicuous and dreary object was a large bare flowerpot of red earthenware, on a green woollen mat, in the middle of a round table. Out of the flowerpot rose gauntly a three-sticked frame, up which two lonely stalks of a climbing plant tried to scramble, but failed miserably to reach the top. The round little rickety table with the family album on one corner (placed at what Mrs. Wilson considered a beautiful artistic angle to the window), the tawdry cloth, the green mat, the shiny horsehair sofa, and the stuffy atmosphere, were all in perfect harmony of ugliness. A sampler on the wall informed the world that there was no place like home.

Wilson pushed the flowerpot to one side, and " You'll take a dram ? " he said blithely.

" Oh ay," said Gibson with a grin; " I never refuse drink when I'm offered it for nothing."

" Hi ! hi ! " laughed Wilson at the little joke, and produced a cut decanter and a pair of glasses. He filled the glasses so brimming full that the drink ran over on the table.

" Canny, man, for God's sake canny ! " cried Gibson, starting forward in alarm. " Don't ye see you're spilling the mercies ? " He stooped his lips to the rim of his glass, and sipped, lest a drop of Scotia's nectar should escape him.

They faced each other, sitting. " Here's pith ! " said Gibson. " Pith ! " said the other in chorus, and they nodded to each other in amity, primed glasses up and ready. And then it was eyes heavenward and the little finger uppermost.

Gibson smacked his lips once and again when the fiery spirit tickled his uvula.

" Ha ! " said he, " that's the stuff to put heart in a man."

" It's no bad whisky," said Wilson complacently.

Gibson wiped the sandy stubble round his mouth with the back of his hand, and considered for a moment. Then, leaning forward, he tapped Wilson's knee in whispering importance.

"Have you heard the news?" he murmured, with a watchful glimmer in his eyes.

"No!" cried Wilson, glowering, eager and alert. "Is't ocht in the business line? Is there a possibeelity for me in't?"

"Oh, there might," nodded Gibson, playing his man for a while.

"Ay, man!" cried Wilson briskly, and brought his chair an inch or two forward. Gibson grinned and watched him with his beady eyes. "What green teeth he has!" thought Wilson, who was not fastidious.

"The Coal Company are meaning to erect a village for five hundred miners a mile out the Fleckie Road, and they're running a branch line up the Lintie's Burn that'll need the building of a dozen brigs. I'm happy to say I have nabbed the contract for the building."

"Man, Mr. Gibson, d'ye tell me that! I'm proud to hear it, sir; I am that!" Wilson was hotching in his chair with eagerness. For what could Gibson be wanting with *him* if it wasna to arrange about the carting? "Fill up your glass, Mr. Gibson, man; fill up your glass. You're drinking nothing at all. Let *me* help you."

"Ay, but I havena the contract for the carting," said Gibson. "That's not mine to dispose of. They mean to keep it in their own hand."

Wilson's mouth forgot to shut, and his eyes were big and round as his mouth in staring disappointment. Was it this he was wasting his drink for?

"Where do I come in?" he asked blankly.

Gibson tossed off another glassful of the burning heartener of men, and leaned forward with his elbows on the table.

"D'ye ken Goudie, the Company's manager? He's worth making up to, I can tell ye. He has complete control of the business, and can airt you the road of a good thing. I made a point of helping him in everything, ever since he came to Barbie, and I'm glad to say that he hasna forgotten't. Man, it was through him I got the building contract ; they never threw't open to the public. But they mean to contract separate for carting the material. That means that they'll need the length of a dozen horses on the road for a twelvemonth to come ; for it's no only the building—they're launching out on a big scale, and there's lots of other things forbye. Now, Goudie's as close as a whin, and likes to keep everything dark till the proper time comes for sploring o't. Not a whisper has been heard so far about this village for the miners—there's a rumour, to be sure, about a wheen houses going up, but nothing *near* the reality. And there's not a soul, either, that kens there's a big contract for carting to be had 'ceptna Goudie and mysell. But or a month's by they'll be advertising for estimates for a twelvemonth's carrying. I thocht a hint aforehand would be worth something to you, and that's the reason of my visit."

" I see," said Wilson briskly. " You're verra good, Mr. Gibson. You mean you'll give me an inkling in private of the other estimates sent in, and help to arrange mine according ? "

" Na," said Gibson. " Goudie's owre close to let me ken. I'll speak a word in his ear on your behalf, to be sure, if you agree to the proposal I mean to put before you. But Gourlay's the man you need to keep your eye on. It's you or him for the contract—there's nobody else to compete wi' the two o' ye."

" Imphm, I see," said Wilson, and tugged his moustache in meditation. All expression died out of his face while his brain churned within. What Brodie had christened " the considering keek " was in his eyes ; they were far away, and saw the distant village in process of erection ; busy with its chances and occasions. Then an uneasy thought seemed to strike him and recall him to the man by his side. He stole a shifty glance at the sandy smiler.

"But I thought *you* were a friend of Gourlay's," he said slowly.

"Friendship!" said Gibson. "We're speaking of business. And there's sma-all friendship atween me and Gourlay. He was nebby owre a bill I sent in the other day; and I'm getting tired of his bluster. Besides, there's little more to be made of him. Gourlay's bye wi't. But you're a rising man, Mr. Wilson, and I think that you and me might work thegither to our own advantage, don't ye see? Yes; just so; to the advantage of us both. Oom?"

"I hardly see what you're driving at," said Wilson.

"I'm driving at this," said Gibson. "If Gourlay kens you're against him for the contract, he'll cut his estimate down to a ruinous price, out o' sheer spite—yes, out o' sheer spite—rather than be licked by *you* in public competition. And if he does that, Goudie and I may do what we like, but we canna help you. For it's the partners that decide the estimates sent in, d'ye see? Imphm, it's the partners. Goudie has noathing to do wi' that. And if Gourlay once gets round the partners, you'll be left out in the cold for a very loang time. Shivering, sir, shivering! You will that!"

"Dod, you're right. There's a danger of that. But I fail to see how we can prevent it."

"We can put Gourlay on a wrong scent," said Gibson.

"But how, though?"

Gibson met one question by another.

"What was the charge for a man and a horse and a day's carrying when ye first came hereaway?" he asked.

"Only four shillings a day," said Wilson promptly. "It has risen to six now," he added.

"Exactly," said Gibson; "and with the new works coming in about the town it'll rise to eight yet. I have it for a fact that the Company's willing to gie that. Now if you and me could procure a job for Gourlay at the lower rate, before the news o' this new industry gets scattered—a job that would require the whole of his plant, you understand, and prevent his competing for the Company's business—we would clear"—he clawed his chin to help his arithmetic—" we would clear three hundred and seventy-four pounds o' difference on the twelvemonth. At least *you* would make that," he added, " but you would allow me a handsome commission of course—the odd hundred and seventy, say—for bringing the scheme before ye. I don't think there's ocht unreasonable in tha-at. For it's not the mere twelvemonth's work that's at stake, you understand ; it's the valuable connection for the fee-yuture. Now, I have influence wi' Goudie ; I can help you there. But if Gourlay gets in there's just a chance that you'll never be able to oust him."

" I see," said Wilson. " Before he knows what's coming, we're to provide work for Gourlay at the lower rate, both to put money in our own pocket and prevent him competing for the better business."

" You've summed it to the nines," said Gibson.

" Yes," said Wilson blankly, " but how on earth are *we* to provide work for him ? "

Gibson leaned forward a second time and tapped Wilson on the knee.

" Have you never considered what a chance for building there's in that holm of yours ? " he asked. " You've a fortune there, lying undeveloped."

That was the point to which Cunning Johnny had been leading all the time. He cared as little for Wilson as for Gourlay ; all he wanted was a contract for covering Wilson's holm with jerry-built houses, and a good commission on the year's carrying. It was for this he evolved the conspiracy to cripple Gourlay.

Wilson's thoughts went to and fro like the shuttle of a weaver. He blinked in rapidity of thinking, and stole shifty glances at his comrade. He tugged his mous-

tache and said " Imphm " many times.   Then his eyes
went off in their long preoccupied stare, and the sound
of the breath, coming heavy through his nostrils, was
audible in the quiet room.   Wilson was one of the men
whom you hear thinking.

"I see," he said slowly.   "You mean to bind Gourlay to cart building material to my holm at the present
price of work.   You'll bind him in general terms so
that he canna suspect, till the time comes, who in
particular he's to work for.   In the meantime I'll be
free to offer for the Company's business at the higher
price."

"That's the size o't," said Gibson.

Wilson was staggered by the rapid combinations of
the scheme.   But Cunning Johnny had him in the toils.
The plan he proposed stole about the grocer's every
weakness, and tugged his inclinations to consent.   It
was very important, he considered, that he, and no other,
should obtain this contract, which was both valuable in
itself and an earnest of other business in the future.
And Gibson's scheme got Gourlay, the only possible
rival, out of the way.   For it was not possible for Gourlay to put more than twelve horses on the road, and if
he thought he had secured a good contract already, he
would never dream of applying for another.   Then,
Wilson's malice was gratified by the thought that Gourlay, who hated him, should have to serve, as helper and
underling, in a scheme for his aggrandizement.   That
would take down his pride for him!   And the commercial imagination, so strong in Wilson, was in-
flamed by the vision of himself as a wealthy house-
owner which Gibson put before him.   Cunning Johnny
knew all this when he broached the scheme—he fore-
saw the pull of it on Wilson's nature.   Yet Wilson hesitated.   He did not like to give himself to Gibson quite
so rapidly.

"You go fast, Mr. Gibson," said he.   "Faith, you go

fast. This is a big affair, and needs to be looked at for a while."

"Fast!" cried Gibson. "Damn it, we have no time to waste. We maun act on the spur of the moment."

"I'll have to borrow money," said Wilson slowly; "and it's verra dear at the present time."

"It was never worth more in Barbie than it is at the present time. Man, don't ye see the chance you're neglecting? Don't ye see what it means? There's thousands lying at your back door if ye'll only reach to pick them up. Yes, thousands. Thousands, I'm telling ye—thousands!"

Wilson saw himself provost and plutocrat. Yet was he cautious.

"*You*'ll do well by the scheme," he said tartly, "if you get the sole contract for building these premises of mine, and a fat commission on the carrying forbye."

"Can you carry the scheme without me?" said Gibson. "A word from me to Goudie means a heap." There was a veiled threat in the remark.

"Oh, we'll come to terms," said the other. "But how will you manage Gourlay?"

"Aha!" said Gibson, "I'll come in handy for that, you'll discover. There's been a backset in Barbie for the last year—things went owre quick at the start and were followed by a wee lull; but it's only for a time, sir—it's only for a time. Hows'ever, it and you thegither have damaged Gourlay: he's both short o' work and scarce o' cash, as I found to my cost when I asked him for my siller! So when I offer him a big contract for carting stones atween the quarry and the town foot, he'll swallow it without question. I'll insert a clause that he must deliver the stuff at such places as I direct within four hundred yards of the Cross, in ainy direction—for I've several jobs near the Cross, doan't ye see, and how's he to know that yours is one o' them? Man, it's easy to

bamboozle an ass like Gourlay! Besides, he'll think
my principals have trusted me to let the carrying to
ainy one I like, and, as I let it to him, he'll fancy I'm on
his side, doan't ye see? He'll never jalouse that I mean
to diddle him. In the meantime we'll spread the news
that you're meaning to build on a big scale upon your
own land; we'll have the ground levelled, the founda-
tions dug, and the drains and everything seen to. Now,
it'll never occur to Gourlay, in the present slackness o'
trade, that you would contract wi' another man to cart
your material, and go hunting for other work yoursell.
That'll throw him off the scent till the time comes to
put his nose on't. When the Company advertise for
estimates he canna compete wi' you, because he's pre-
engaged to me; and he'll think you're out o't too, because you're busy wi' your own woark. You'll be free
to nip the eight shillings. Then we'll force him to ful-
fill his bargain and cart for us at six."

"If he refuses?" said Wilson.

"I'll have the contract stamped and signed in the
presence of witnesses," said Gibson. "Not that that's
necessary, I believe, but a double knot's aye the safest."

Wilson looked at him with admiration.

"Gosh, Mr. Gibson," he cried, "you're a warmer!
Ye deserve your name. Ye ken what the folk ca'
you?"

"Oh yes," said Gibson complacently. "I'm quite
proud o' the description."

"I've my ain craw to pick wi' Gourlay," he went on.
"He was damned ill-bred yestreen when I asked him to
settle my account, and talked about extortion. But
bide a wee, bide a wee! I'll enjoy the look on his face
when he sees himself forced to carry for you, at a rate
lower than the market price."

When Gibson approached Gourlay on the following day he was full of laments about the poor state of
trade.

" Ay," said he, " the grand railway they boasted o'
hasna done muckle for the town ! "

" Atwell ay," quoth Gourlay with pompous wisdom ;
" they'll maybe find, or a's by, that the auld way wasna
the warst way. There was to be a great boom, as they
ca't, but I see few signs o't."

" I see few signs o't either," said Gibson   " it's the
slackest time for the last twa years."

Gourlay grunted his assent.

" But I've a grand job for ye, for a' that," said Gibson, slapping his hands.   " What do ye say to the feck
of a year's carting tweesht the quarry and the town
foot ? "

" I might consider that," said Gourlay, " if the terms
were good."

" Six shillins," said Gibson, and went on in solemn
protest : " In the present state o' trade, doan't ye see,
I couldna give a penny more."   Gourlay, who had
denounced the present state of trade even now, was
prevented by his own words from asking for a penny
more.

" At the town foot, you say ? " he asked.

" I've several jobs thereaway," Gibson explained hurriedly, " and you must agree to deliver stuff ainy place
I want it within four hundred yards o' the Cross.   It's
all one to you, of course," he went on, " seeing you're
paid by the day."

"'Oh, it's all one to me," said Gourlay.

Peter Riney and the new " orra " man were called in
to witness the agreement.   Cunning Johnny had made
it as cunning as he could.

" We may as well put a stamp on't," said he.   " A
stamp costs little, and means a heap."

" You're damned particular the day," cried Gourlay
in a sudden heat.

" Oh, nothing more than my usual, nothing more
than my usual," said Gibson blandly.   " Good-morn-

ing, Mr. Gourlay," and he made for the door, buttoning
the charter of his dear revenge in the inside pocket of
his coat. Gourlay ignored him.

When Gibson got out he turned to the House with the
Green Shutters, and " Curse you ! " said he ; " you may
refuse to answer me the day, but wait till this day eight
weeks. You'll be roaring than."

On that day eight weeks Gourlay received a letter
from Gibson requiring him to hold himself in readiness
to deliver stone, lime, baulks of timber, and iron girders
in Mr. Wilson's holm, in terms of his agreement, and
in accordance with the orders to be given him from
day to day. He was apprised that a couple of carts of
lime and seven loads of stone were needed on the
morrow.

He went down the street with grinding jaws, the letter
crushed to a white pellet in his hand. It would have
gone ill with Gibson had he met him. Gourlay could
not tell why, or to what purpose, he marched on and on
with forward staring eyes. He only knew vaguely that
the anger drove him.

When he came to the Cross a long string of carts was
filing from the Skeighan Road, and passing across to
the street leading Fleckie-ward. He knew them to be
Wilson's. The Deacon was there, of course, hobbling
on his thin shanks, and cocking his eye to see everything that happened.

" What does this mean ? " Gourlay asked him, though
he loathed the Deacon.

" Oh, haven't ye heard ? " quoth the Deacon blithely.
" That's the stuff for the new mining village out the
Fleckie Road. Wilson has nabbed the contract for the
carting. They're saying it was Gibson's influence wi'
Goudie that helped him to the getting o't."

Amid his storm of anger at the trick, Gourlay was
conscious of a sudden pity for himself, as for a man most
unfairly worsted. He realized for a moment his own

inefficiency as a business man, in conflict with cleverer rivals, and felt sorry to be thus handicapped by nature. Though wrath was uppermost, the other feeling was revealed, showing itself by a gulping in the throat and a rapid blinking of the eyes. The Deacon marked the signs of his chagrin.

" Man ! " he reported to the bodies, " but Gourlay was cut to the quick. His face showed how gunkit he was. Oh, but he was chawed. I saw his breist give the great heave."

" Were ye no sorry ? " cried the baker.

" Thorry, hi ! " laughed the Deacon. " Oh, I was thorry, to be sure," he lisped, " but I didna thyow't. I'm glad to thay I've a grand control of my emotionth. Not like thum folk we know of," he added slyly, giving the baker a " good one."

All next day Gibson's masons waited for their building material in Wilson's holm. But none came. And all day seven of Gourlay's horses champed idly in their stalls.

Barbie had a weekly market now, and, as it happened, that was the day it fell on. At two in the afternoon Gourlay was standing on the gravel outside the Red Lion, trying to look wise over a sample of grain which a farmer had poured upon his great palm. Gibson approached with false voice and smile.

" Gosh, Mr. Gourlay ! " he cried protestingly, " have ye forgotten whatna day it is ? Ye havena gi'en my men a ton o' stuff to gang on wi'."

To the farmer's dismay his fine sample of grain was scattered on the gravel by a convulsive movement of Gourlay's arm. As Gourlay turned on his enemy, his face was frightfully distorted ; all his brow seemed gathered in a knot above his nose, and he gaped on his words, yet ground them out like a labouring mill, each word solid as plug shot.

" I'll see Wil-son . . . and Gib-son . . . and every

other man's son . . . frying in hell," he said slowly,
" ere a horse o' mine draws a stane o' Wilson's property.
Be damned to ye, but there's your answer ! "

Gibson's cunning deserted him for once. He put his
hand on Gourlay's shoulder in pretended friendly remonstrance.

" Take your hand off my shouther ! " said Gourlay,
in a voice the tense quietness of which should have
warned Gibson to forbear.

But he actually shook Gourlay with a feigned play-
fulness.

Next instant he was high in air ; for a moment the
hobnails in the soles of his boots gleamed vivid to the
sun ; then Gourlay sent him flying through the big window of the Red Lion, right on to the middle of the
great table where the market-folk were drinking.

For a minute he lay stunned and bleeding among the
broken crockery, in a circle of white faces and startled
cries.

Gourlay's face appeared at the jagged rent, his eyes
narrowed to fiercely gleaming points, a hard, triumphant
devilry playing round his black lips. " You damned
treacherous rat ! " he cried, " that's the game John
Gourlay can play wi' a thing like you."

Gibson rose from the ruin on the table and came
bleeding to the window, his grin a *rictus* of wrath, his
green teeth wolfish with anger.

" By God, Gourlay," he screamed, " I'll make you
pay for this ; I'll fight you through a' the law courts in
Breetain, but you'll implement your bond."

" Damn you for a measled swine ! would you grunt at
me ? " cried Gourlay, and made to go at him through the
window. Though he could not reach him, Gibson
quailed at his look. He shook his fist in impotent
wrath, and spat threats of justice through his green
teeth.

" To hell wi' your law-wers ! " cried Gourlay. " I'd

throttle ye like the dog you are on the floor o' the House o' Lords."

But that day was to cost him dear. Ere six months passed he was cast in damages and costs for a breach of contract aggravated by assault. He appealed, of course. He was not to be done ; he would show the dogs what he thought of them.

CHAPTER XIV.

IN those days it came to pass that Wilson sent his son to the High School of Skeighan—even James, the red-haired one, with the squint in his eye. Whereupon Gourlay sent *his* son to the High School of Skeighan too, of course, to be upsides with Wilson. If Wilson could afford to send his boy to a distant and expensive school, then, by the Lord, so could he ! And it also came to pass that James, the son of James the grocer, took many prizes ; but John, the son of John, took no prizes. Whereat there were ructions in the House of Gourlay.

Gourlay's resolve to be equal to Wilson in everything he did was his main reason for sending his son to the High School of Skeighan. That he saw his business decreasing daily was a reason too. Young Gourlay was a lad of fifteen now, undersized for his age at that time, though he soon shot up to be a swaggering youngster. He had been looking forward with delight to helping his father in the business—how grand it would be to drive about the country and see things !—and he had irked at being kept for so long under the tawse of old Bleach-the-boys. But if the business went on at this rate there would be little in it for the boy. Gourlay was not without a thought of his son's welfare when he packed him off to Skeighan. He would give him some book-lear, he said ; let him make a kirk or a mill o't.

But John shrank, chicken-hearted, from the prospect. Was he still to drudge at books ? Was he to go out among strangers whom he feared ? His imagination set to work on what he heard of the High School of Skeighan, and made it a bugbear. They had to do mathematics; what could *he* do wi' thae whigmaleeries? They had to recite Shakespeare in public; how could *he* stand up and spout, before a whole jing-bang o' them?

" I don't want to gang," he whined.

" Want ? " flamed his father. " What does it matter what *you* want ? Go you shall."

" I thocht I was to help in the business," whimpered John.

" Business ! " sneered his father; " a fine help *you* would be in business."

" Ay man, Johnnie," said his mother, maternal fondness coming out in support of her husband, " you should be glad your father can allow ye the opportunity. Eh, but it's a grand thing a gude education ! You may rise to be a minister."

Her ambition could no further go. But Gourlay seemed to have formed a different opinion of the sacred calling. " It's a' he's fit for," he growled.

So John was put to the High School of Skeighan, travelling backwards and forwards night and morning by the train, after the railway had been opened. And he discovered, on trying it, that the life was not so bad as he had feared. He hated his lessons, true, and avoided them whenever he was able. But his father's pride and his mother's fondness saw that he was well dressed and with money in his pocket ; and he began to grow important. Though Gourlay was no longer the only " big man " of Barbie, he was still one of the " big men," and a consciousness of the fact grew upon his son. When he passed his old classmates (apprentice grocers now, and carters and ploughboys) his febrile insolence led him to swagger and assume. And it was fine to mount the train at Barbie on the fresh, cool mornings, and be off past the gleaming rivers and the woods. Better still was the home-coming—to board the empty train at

Skeighan when the afternoon sun came pleasant through the windows, to loll on the fat cushions and read the novelettes. He learned to smoke too, and that was a source of pride. When the train was full on market days he liked to get in among the jovial farmers, who encouraged his assumptions. Meanwhile Jimmy Wilson would be elsewhere in the train, busy with his lessons for the morrow; for Jimmy had to help in the Emporium of nights—his father kept him to the grindstone. Jimmy had no more real ability than young Gourlay, but infinitely more caution. He was one of the gimlet characters who, by diligence and memory, gain prizes in their school days—and are fools for the remainder of their lives.

The bodies of Barbie, seeing young Gourlay at his pranks, speculated over his future, as Scottish bodies do about the future of every youngster in their ken.

" I wonder what that son o' Gourlay's 'ull come till," said Sandy Toddle, musing on him with the character-reading eye of the Scots peasant.

" To no good—you may be sure of that," said ex-Provost Connal. " He's a regular splurge ! When Drunk Dan Kennedy passed him his flask in the train the other day he swigged it, just for the sake of showing off. And he's a coward, too, for all his swagger. He grew ill-bred when he swallowed the drink, and Dan, to frighten him, threatened to hang him from the window by the heels. He didn't mean it, to be sure ; but young Gourlay grew white at the very idea o't—he shook like a dog in a wet sack. ' Oh,' he cried, shivering, ' how the ground would go flying past your eyes ; how quick the wheel opposite ye would buzz—it would blind ye by its quickness; how the gray slag would flash below ye ! ' Those were his very words. He seemed to see the thing as if it were happening before his eyes, and stared like a fellow in hysteerics, till Dan was obliged to give him another drink. ' You would spue with

the dizziness,' said he, and he actually bocked himsell."

Young Gourlay seemed bent on making good the
prophecy of Barbie. Though his father was spending
money he could ill afford on his education, he fooled
away his time. His mind developed a little, no doubt,
since it was no longer dazed by brutal and repeated
floggings. In some of his classes he did fairly well,
but others he loathed. It was the rule at Skeighan
High School to change rooms every hour, the classes
tramping from one to another through a big lobby.
Gourlay got a habit of stealing off at such times—it was
easy to slip out—and playing truant in the byways of
Skeighan. He often made his way to the station, and
loafed in the waiting room. He had gone there on a
summer afternoon, to avoid his mathematics and read
a novel, when a terrible thing befell him.

For a while he swaggered round the empty platform
and smoked a cigarette. Milk-cans clanked in a shed
mournfully. Gourlay had a congenital horror of eerie
sounds—he was his mother's son for that—and he fled
to the waiting room, to avoid the hollow clang. It was
a June afternoon, of brooding heat, and a band of yellow
sunshine was lying on the glazed table, showing every
scratch in its surface. The place oppressed him ; he
was sorry he had come. But he plunged into his novel
and forgot the world.

He started in fear when a voice addressed him. He
looked up, and here it was only the baker—the baker
smiling at him with his fine gray eyes, the baker with
his reddish fringe of beard and his honest grin, which
wrinkled up his face to his eyes in merry and kindly
wrinkles. He had a wonderful hearty manner with a boy.

" Ay man, John, it's you," said the baker. " Dod,
I'm just in time. The storm's at the burstin '! "

" Storm ! " said Gourlay. He had a horror of lightning since the day of his birth.

"Ay, we're in for a pelter.   What have you been doing that you didna see't?"

They went to the window.   The fronting heavens were a black purple.   The thunder, which had been growling in the distance, swept forward and roared above the town.   The crash no longer rolled afar, but cracked close to the ear, hard, crepitant.   Quick lightning stabbed the world in vicious and repeated hate. A blue-black moistness lay heavy on the cowering earth. The rain came—a few drops at first, sullen, as if loath to come, that splashed on the pavement wide as a crown piece; then a white rush of slanting spears.   A great blob shot in through the window, open at the top, and spat wide on Gourlay's cheek.   It was lukewarm.   He started violently—that warmth on his cheek brought the terror so near.

The heavens were rent with a crash, and the earth seemed on fire.   Gourlay screamed in terror.

The baker put his arm round him in kindly protection.

"Tuts, man, dinna be feared," he said.   "You're John Gourlay's son, ye know.   You ought to be a hardy man."

"Ay, but I'm no," chattered John, the truth coming out in his fear.   "I just let on to be."

But the worst was soon over.   Lightning, both sheeted and forked, was vivid as ever, but the thunder slunk growling away.

"The heavens are opening and shutting like a man's eye," said Gourlay.   "Oh, it's a terrible thing the world!" and he covered his face with his hands.

A flash shot into a mounded wood far away.   "It stabbed it like a dagger!" stared Gourlay.

"Look, look, did ye see yon?   It came down in a broad flash—then jerked to the side—then ran down to a sharp point again.   It was like the coulter of a plough."

Suddenly a blaze of lightning flamed wide, and a fork shot down its centre.

" That," said Gourlay, " was like a red crack in a white-hot furnace door."

" Man, you're a noticing boy," said the baker.

" Ay," said John, smiling in curious self-interest, " I notice things too much. They give me pictures in my mind. I'm feared of them, but I like to think them over when they're by."

Boys are slow of confidence to their elders, but Gourlay's terror and the baker's kindness moved him to speak. In a vague way he wanted to explain.

" I'm no feared of folk," he went on, with a faint return to his swagger. " But things get in on me. A body seems so wee compared with that "—he nodded to the warring heavens.

The baker did not understand. " Have you seen your faither ? " he asked.

" My faither ! " John gasped in terror. If his father should find him playing truant !

" Yes ; did ye no ken he was in Skeighan ? We come up thegither by the ten train, and are meaning to gang hame by this. I expect him every moment."

John turned to escape. In the doorway stood his father.

When Gourlay was in wrath he had a widening glower that enveloped the offender ; yet his eye seemed to stab —a flash shot from its centre to transfix and pierce. Gaze at a tiger through the bars of his cage, and you will see the look. It widens and concentrates at once.

" What are you doing here ? " he asked, with the wild-beast glower on his son.

" I—I—I—— " John stammered and choked.

" What are you doing here ? " said his father.

John's fingers worked before him ; his eyes were large and aghast on his father ; though his mouth hung open no words would come.

" How lang has he been here, baker ? "

There was a curious regard between Gourlay and the baker. Gourlay spoke with a firm civility.

" Oh, just a wee whilie," said the baker.

" I see. You want to shield him.—You have been playing the truant, have 'ee ? Am I to throw away gude money on *you* for this to be the end o't ? "

" Dinna be hard on him, John," pleaded the baker. " A boy's but a boy. Dinna thrash him."

" Me thrash him ! " cried Gourlay. " I pay the High School of Skeighan to thrash him, and I'll take damned good care I get my money's worth. I don't mean to hire dowgs and bark for mysell."

He grabbed his son by the coat collar and swung him out the room. Down High Street he marched, carrying his cub by the scruff of the neck as you might carry a dirty puppy to an outhouse. John was black in the face ; time and again in his wrath Gourlay swung him off the ground. Grocers coming to their doors, to scatter fresh yellow sawdust on the old, now trampled black and wet on the sills, stared sideways, chins up and mouths open, after the strange spectacle. But Gourlay splashed on amid the staring crowd, never looking to the right or left.

Opposite the Fiddler's Inn whom should they meet but Wilson ! A snigger shot to his features at the sight. Gourlay swung the boy up ; for a moment a wild impulse surged within him to club his rival with his own son.

He marched into the vestibule of the High School, the boy dangling from his great hand.

" Where's your gaffer ? " he roared at the janitor.

" Gaffer ? " blinked the janitor.

" Gaffer, dominie, whatever the damn you ca' him— the fellow that runs the business."

" The Headmaster ! " said the janitor.

" Heidmaister, ay," said Gourlay in scorn, and went trampling after the janitor down a long wooden corridor.   A door was flung open showing a classroom where the Headmaster was seated teaching Greek.

The sudden appearance of the great-chested figure in the door, with his fierce, gleaming eyes, and the rain-beads shining on his frieze coat, brought into the close academic air the sharp, strong gust of an outer world.

" I believe I pay *you* to look after that boy," thundered Gourlay.   " Is this the way you do your work ? " And with the word he sent his son spinning along the floor like a curling-stone, till he rattled, a wet, huddled lump, against a row of chairs.   John slunk bleeding behind the master.

" Really ! " said MacCandlish, rising in protest.

" Don't ' really ' me, sir !   I pay *you* to teach that boy, and you allow him to run idle in the streets.   What have you to seh ? ".

" But what can I do ? " bleated MacCandlish, with a white spread of deprecating hands.

The stronger man took the grit from his limbs.

" Do—do ?   Damn it, sir, am *I* to be *your* dominie ? Am *I* to teach *you* your duty ?   Do !   Flog him, flog him, flog him !   If you don't send him hame wi' the welts on him as thick as that forefinger, I'll have a word to say to you-ou, Misterr MacCandlish ! "

He was gone—they heard him go clumping along the corridor.

Thereafter young Gourlay had to stick to his books. And, as we know, the forced union of opposites breeds the greater disgust between them.   However, his school days would soon be over, and meanwhile it was fine to pose on his journeys to and fro as Young Hopeful of the Green Shutters.

He was smoking at Skeighan Station on an afternoon, as the Barbie train was on the point of starting.   He was staying on the platform till the last moment, in order to show the people how nicely he could bring the smoke down his nostrils—his " Prince of Wales's feathers " he called the great, curling puffs. As he dallied, a little aback from an open window, he heard a voice which he knew mentioning the Gourlays. It was Templandmuir who was speaking.

" I see that Gourlay has lost his final appeal in that lawsuit of his," said the Templar.

" D'ye tell me that ? " said a strange voice. Then— " Gosh, he must have lost infernal ! "

" Atweel has he that," said Templandmuir. " The costs must have been enormous, and then there's the damages. He would have been better to settle't and be done wi't, but his pride made him fight it to the hindmost ! It has made touch the boddom of his purse, I'll wager ye. Weel, weel, it'll help to subdue his pride a bit, and muckle was the need o' that."

Young Gourlay was seized with a sudden fear. The prosperity of the House with the Green Shutters had been a fact of his existence ; it had never entered his boyish mind to question its continuance. But a weakening doubt stole through his limbs. What would become of him if the Gourlays were threatened with disaster ? He had a terrifying vision of himself as a lonely atomy, adrift on a tossing world, cut off from his anchorage.

" Mother, are *we* ever likely to be ill off ? " he asked his mother that evening.

She ran her fingers through his hair, pushing it back from his brow fondly. He was as tall as herself now.

" No, no, dear ; what makes ye think that ? Your father has always had a grand business, and I brought a hantle money to the house."

" Hokey ! " said the youth, " when Ah'm in the business Ah'll have the times ! "

CHAPTER XV.

GOURLAY was hard up for money. Every day of his life taught him that he was nowhere in the stress of modern competition. The grand days—only a few years back, but seeming half a century away, so much had happened in between—the grand days when he was the only big man in the locality, and carried everything with a high hand, had disappeared for ever. Now all was bustle, hurry, and confusion, the getting and sending of telegrams, quick dispatches by railway, the watching of markets at a distance, rapid combinations that bewildered Gourlay's duller mind. At first he was too obstinate to try the newer methods; when he did, he was too stupid to use them cleverly. When he plunged it was always at the wrong time, for he plunged at random, not knowing what to do. He had lost heavily of late both in grain and cheese, and the lawsuit with Gibson had crippled him. It was well for him that property in Barbie had increased in value; the House with the Green Shutters was to prove the buttress of his fortune. Already he had borrowed considerably upon that security; he was now dressing to go to Skeighan and get more.

"Brodie, Gurney and Yarrowby" of Glasgow were the lawyers who financed him, and he had to sign some papers at Goudie's office ere he touched the cash.

He was meaning to drive, of course; Gourlay was proud of his gig, and always kept a spanking roadster. "What a fine figure of a man!" you thought, as you saw him coming swiftly towards you, seated high on his driving cushion.   That driving cushion was Gourlay's pedestal from which he looked down on Barbie for many a day.

A quick step, yet shambling, came along the lobby. There was a pause, as of one gathering heart for a venture ;   then a clumsy knock on the door.

" Come in," snapped Gourlay.

Peter Riney's queer little old face edged timorously into the room.   He only opened the door the width of his face, and looked ready to bolt at a word.

" Tam's deid ! " he blurted.

Gourlay gashed himself frightfully with his razor, and a big red blob stood out on his cheek.

" Deid ! " he stared.

" Yes," stammered Peter.   " He was right enough when Elshie gae him his feed this morning ; but when I went in enow to put the harness on, he was lying deid in the loose-box.   The batts—it's like."

For a moment Gourlay stared with the open mouth of an angry surprise, forgetting to take down his razor.

" Aweel, Peter," he said at last, and Peter went away.

The loss of his pony touched Gourlay to the quick. He had been stolid and dour in his other misfortunes, had taken them as they came, calmly ;   he was not the man to whine and cry out against the angry heavens. He had neither the weakness nor the width of nature to indulge in the luxury of self-pity.   But the sudden death of his gallant roadster, his proud pacer through the streets of Barbie, touched him with a sense of quite personal loss and bereavement.   Coming on the heels of his other calamities it seemed to make them more poignant, more sinister, prompting the question if misfortune would never have an end.

" Damn it, I have enough to thole," Gourlay muttered ;   " surely there was no need for this to happen." And when he looked in the mirror to fasten his stock, and saw the dark, strong, clean-shaven face, he stared at it for a moment, with a curious compassion for the man before him, as for one who was being hardly used. The hard lips could never have framed the words, but the vague feeling in his heart, as he looked at the dark vision, was : " It's a pity of you, sir."

He put on his coat rapidly, and went out to the stable. An instinct prompted him to lock the door.

He entered the loose-box. A shaft of golden light, aswarm with motes, slanted in the quietness. Tam lay on the straw, his head far out, his neck unnaturally long, his limbs sprawling, rigid. What a spanker Tam had been ! What gallant drives they had had together ! When he first put Tam between the shafts, five years ago, he had been driving his world before him, plenty of cash and a big way of doing. Now Tam was dead, and his master netted in a mesh of care.

" I was always gude to the beasts, at any rate," Gourlay muttered, as if pleading in his own defence.

For a long time he stared down at the sprawling carcass, musing. "Tam the powney," he said twice, nodding his head each time he said it ; "Tam the powney," and he turned away.

How was he to get to Skeighan ? He plunged at his watch. The ten o'clock train had already gone, the express did not stop at Barbie ; if he waited till one o'clock he would be late for his appointment. There was a brake, true, which ran to Skeighan every Tuesday. It was a downcome, though, for a man who had been proud of driving behind his own horseflesh to pack in among a crowd of the Barbie sprats. And if he went by the brake, he would be sure to rub shoulders with his stinging and detested foes. It was a fine day ; like enough the whole jing-bang of them would be going with the brake to Skeighan. Gourlay, who shrank from nothing, shrank from the winks that would be sure to pass when they saw him, the haughty, the aloof, forced to creep

among them cheek for jowl. Then his angry pride
rushed towering to his aid. Was John Gourlay to turn
tail for a wheen o' the Barbie dirt? Damn the fear o't!
It was a public conveyance; he had the same right to
use it as the rest o' folk!

The place of departure for the brake was the " Black
Bull," at the Cross, nearly opposite to Wilson's. There
were winks and stares and elbow-nudgings when the folk
hanging round saw Gourlay coming forward; but he
paid no heed. Gourlay, in spite of his mad violence
when roused, was a man at all other times of a grave
and orderly demeanour. He never splurged. Even his
bluster was not bluster, for he never threatened the
thing which he had not it in him to do. He walked
quietly into the empty brake, and took his seat in the
right-hand corner at the top, close below the driver.

As he had expected, the Barbie bodies had mustered
in strength for Skeighan. In a country brake it is the
privilege of the important men to mount beside the
driver, in order to take the air and show themselves off
to an admiring world. On the dickey were ex-Provost
Connal and Sandy Toddle, and between them the Deacon,
tightly wedged. The Deacon was so thin (the bodie)
that, though he was wedged closely, he could turn and
address himself to Tam Brodie, who was seated next the
door.

The fun began when the horses were crawling up the
first brae.

The Deacon turned with a wink to Brodie, and dropping a glance on the crown of Gourlay's hat, " Tum-
muth," he lisped, " what a dirty place that ith!"
pointing to a hovel by the wayside.

Brodie took the cue at once. His big face flushed
with a malicious grin. " Ay," he bellowed; " the owner
o' that maun be married to a dirty wife, I'm thinking!"

" It must be terrible," said the Deacon, " to be married
to a dirty trollop."

" Terrible," laughed Brodie ; " it's enough to give ainy man a gurly temper."

They had Gourlay on the hip at last. More than arrogance had kept him off from the bodies of the town ; a consciousness also that he was not their match in malicious innuendo. The direct attack he could meet superbly, downing his opponent with a coarse birr of the tongue ; to the veiled gibe he was a quivering hulk, to be prodded at your ease. And now the malignants were around him (while he could not get away)—talking *to* each other, indeed, but *at* him, while he must keep quiet in their midst.

At every brae they came to (and there were many braes) the bodies played their malicious game, shouting remarks along the brake, to each other's ears, to his comprehension.

The new house of Templandmuir was seen above the trees.

" What a splendid house Templandmuir has built ! " cried the ex-Provost.

" Splendid ! " echoed Brodie. " But a laird like the Templar has a right to a fine mansion such as that ! He's no' like some merchants we ken o' who throw away money on a house for no other end but vanity. Many a man builds a grand house for a show-off, when he has verra little to support it. But the Templar's different. He has made a mint of money since he took the quarry in his own hand."

" He's verra thick wi' Wilson, I notice," piped the Deacon, turning with a grin and a gleaming droop of the eye on the head of his tormented enemy. The Deacon's face was alive and quick with the excitement of the game, his face flushed with an eager grin, his eyes glittering. Decent folk in the brake behind felt compunctious visitings when they saw him turn with the flushed grin and the gleaming squint on the head of his enduring victim. " Now for another stab ! " they thought.

" You may well say that," shouted Brodie. " Wilson has procured the whole of the Templar's carterage. Oh, Wilson has become a power ! Yon new houses of his must be bringing in a braw penny.—I'm thinking, Mr. Connal, that Wilson ought to be the Provost ! "

" Strange ! " cried the former Head of the Town, " that *you* should have been thinking that ! I've just been in the same mind o't. Wilson's by far and away the most progressive man we have. What a business he has built in two or three years ! "

" He has that ! " shouted Brodie. " He goes up the brae as fast as some other folk are going down't. And yet they tell me he got a verra poor welcome from some of us the first morning he appeared in Barbie ! "

Gourlay gave no sign. Others would have shown, by the moist glisten of self-pity in the eye, or the scowl of wrath, how much they were moved ; but Gourlay stared calmly before him, his chin resting on the head of his staff, resolute, immobile, like a stone head at gaze in the desert. Only the larger fullness of his fine nostril betrayed the hell of wrath seething within him. And when they alighted in Skeighan an observant boy said to his mother, " I saw the marks of his chirted teeth through his jaw."

But they were still far from Skeighan, and Gourlay had much to thole.

" Did ye hear," shouted Brodie, " that Wilson is sending his son to the College at Embro in October ? "

" D'ye tell me that ? " said the Provost. " What a successful lad that has been ! He's a credit to moar than Wilson ; he's a credit to the whole town."

" Ay," yelled Brodie ; " the money wasna wasted on *him !* It must be a terrible thing when a man has a splurging ass for his son, that never got a prize ! "

The Provost began to get nervous. Brodie was going too far. It was all very well for Brodie, who was at the far end of the wagonette and out of danger ; but if he provoked an outbreak, Gourlay would think nothing of tearing Provost and Deacon from their perch and tossing them across the hedge.

"What does Wilson mean to make of his son?" he inquired—a civil enough question surely.

"Oh, a minister. That'll mean six or seven years at the University."

"Indeed!" said the Provost. "That'll cost an enormous siller!"

"Oh," yelled Brodie, "but Wilson can afford it! It's not everybody can! It's all verra well to send your son to Skeighan High School, but when it comes to sending him to College, it's time to think twice of what you're doing—especially if you've little money left to come and go on."

"Yeth," lisped the Deacon; "if a man canna afford to College his son, he had better put him in hith business —if he hath ainy business left to thpeak o', that ith!"

The brake swung on through merry cornfields where reapers were at work, past happy brooks flashing to the sun, through the solemn hush of ancient and mysterious woods, beneath the great white-moving clouds and blue spaces of the sky. And amid the suave enveloping greatness of the world the human pismires stung each other and were cruel, and full of hate and malice and a petty rage.

"Oh, damn it, enough of this!" said the baker at last.

"Enough of what?" blustered Brodie.

"Of you and your gibes," said the baker, with a wry mouth of disgust. "Damn it, man, leave folk alane!"

Gourlay turned to him quietly. "Thank you, baker," he said slowly. "But don't interfere on my behalf! John Gourla"—he dwelt on his name in ringing pride —"John Gourla can fight for his own hand—if so there need to be. And pay no heed to the thing before ye. The mair ye tramp on a dirt it spreads the wider!"

"Who was referring to *you*?" bellowed Brodie.

Gourlay looked over at him in the far corner of the brake, with the wide-open glower that made people blink. Brodie blinked rapidly, trying to stare fiercely the while.

"Maybe ye werena referring to me," said Gourlay slowly. "But if *I* had been in your end o' the brake *ye* would have been in hell or this!"

He had said enough. There was silence in the brake till it reached Skeighan. But the evil was done. Enough had been said to influence Gourlay to the most disastrous resolution of his life.

"Get yourself ready for the College in October," he ordered his son that evening.

"The College!" cried John aghast.

"Yes! Is there ainything in that to gape at?" snapped his father, in sudden irritation at the boy's amaze.

"But I don't want to gang!" John whimpered as before.

"Want! what does it matter what *you* want? You should be damned glad of the chance! I mean to make ye a minister; they have plenty of money and little to do—a grand, easy life o't. MacCandlish tells me you're a stupid ass, but have some little gift of words. You have every qualification!"

"It's against *my* will," John bawled angrily.

"*Your* will!" sneered his father.

To John the command was not only tyrannical, but treacherous. There had been nothing to warn him of a coming change, for Gourlay was too contemptuous of his wife and children to inform them how his business stood. John had been brought up to go into the business, and now, at the last moment, he was undeceived, and ordered off to a new life, from which every instinct of his being shrank afraid. He was cursed with an imagination in excess of his brains, and in the haze of the future he saw two pictures with uncanny vividness—

himself in bleak lodgings raising his head from Virgil, to wonder what they were doing at home to-night ; and, contrasted with that loneliness, the others, his cronies, laughing along the country roads beneath the glimmer of the stars. They would be having the fine ploys while he was mewed up in Edinburgh. Must he leave loved Barbie and the House with the Green Shutters ? must he still drudge at books which he loathed ? must he venture on a new life where everything terrified his mind ?

" It's a shame ! " he cried. " And I refuse to go. I don't want to leave Barbie ! I'm feared of Edinburgh," and there he stopped in conscious impotence of speech. How could he explain his forebodings to a rock of a man like his father ?

" No more o't ! " roared Gourlay, flinging out his hand—" not another word ! You go to College in October ! "

" Ay, man, Johnny," said his mother, " think o' the future that's before ye ! "

" Ay," howled the youth in silly anger, " it's like to be a braw future ! "

" It's the best future you can have ! " growled his father.

For while rivalry, born of hate, was the propelling influence in Gourlay's mind, other reasons whispered that the course suggested by hate was a good one on its merits. His judgment, such as it was, supported the impulse of his blood. It told him that the old business would be a poor heritage for his son, and that it would be well to look for another opening. The boy gave no sign of aggressive smartness to warrant a belief that he would ever pull the thing together. Better make him a minister. Surely there was enough money left about the house for tha-at ! It was the best that could befall him.

Mrs. Gourlay, for her part, though sorry to lose her son, was so pleased at the thought of sending him to college, and making him a minister, that she ran on in

foolish maternal gabble to the wife of Drucken Wabster.
Mrs. Webster informed the gossips, and they discussed
the matter at the Cross.

"Dod," said Sandy Toddle, "Gourlay's better off
than I supposed!"

"Huts!" said Brodie, "it's just a wheen bluff to
blind folk!"

"It would fit him better," said the Doctor, "if he
spent some money on his daughter. She ought to pass
the winter in a warmer locality than Barbie. The lassie
has a poor chest! I told Gourlay, but he only gave
a grunt. And 'oh,' said Mrs. Gourlay, 'it would be a
daft-like thing to send *her* away, when John maun be
weel provided for the College.' D'ye know, I'm beginning to think there's something seriously wrong with
yon woman's health! She seemed anxious to consult
me on her own account, but when I offered to sound her
she wouldn't hear of it. 'Na,' she cried, 'I'll keep it
to mysell!' and put her arm across her breast as if
to keep me off. I do think she's hiding some complaint! Only a woman whose mind was weak with
disease could have been so callous as yon about her
lassie."

"Oh, her mind's weak enough," said Sandy Toddle.
"It was always that! But it's only because Gourlay
has tyraneezed her verra soul. I'm surprised, however,
that *he* should be careless of the girl. He was aye said
to be browdened upon *her*."

"Men-folk are often like that about lassie-weans,"
said Johnny Coe. "They like well enough to pet them
when they're wee, but when once they're big they never
look the road they're on! They're a' very fine when
they're pets, but they're no sae fine when they're pretty
misses. And, to tell the truth, Janet Gourlay's ainything but pretty!"

Old Bleach-the-boys, the bitter dominie (who rarely
left the studies in political economy which he found a

solace for his thwarted powers), happened to be at the Cross that evening. A brooding and taciturn man, he said nothing till others had their say. Then he shook his head.

"They're making a great mistake," he said gravely, "they're making a great mistake! Yon boy's the last youngster on earth who should go to College."

"Ay, man, dominie, he's an infernal ass, is he noat?" they cried, and pressed for his judgment.

At last, partly in real pedantry, partly with humorous intent to puzzle them, he delivered his astounding mind.

"The fault of young Gourlay," quoth he, "is a sensory perceptiveness in gross excess of his intellectuality."

They blinked and tried to understand.

"Ay, man, dominie!" said Sandy Toddle. "That means he's an infernal cuddy, dominie! Does it na, dominie?"

But Bleach-the-boys had said enough. "Ay," he said dryly, "there's a wheen gey cuddies in Barbie!" and he went back to his stuffy little room to study "The Wealth of Nations."

CHAPTER XVI.

THE scion of the house of Gourlay was a most un-travelled sprig when his father packed him off to the University. Of the world beyond Skeighan he had no idea. Repression of his children's wishes to see something of the world was a feature of Gourlay's tyranny, less for the sake of the money which a trip might cost (though that counted for something in his refusal) than for the sake of asserting his authority. "Wants to gang to Fechars, indeed! Let him bide at home," he would growl; and at home the youngster had to bide. This had been the more irksome to John since most of his companions in the town were beginning to peer out, with their mammies and daddies to encourage them. To give their cubs a " cast o' the world " was a rule with the potentates of Barbie ; once or twice a year young Hopeful was allowed to accompany his sire to Fechars or Poltandie, or—oh, rare joy !—to the city on the Clyde. To go farther, and get the length of Edinburgh, was dangerous, because you came back with a halo of glory round your head which banded your fellows together in a common attack on your pretensions. It was his lack of pretension to travel, however, that banded them against young Gourlay. " Gunk " and " chaw " are the Scots for a bitter and envious disappointment which shows itself in face and eyes. Young Gourlay could never conceal that envious look when he heard of a glory which he did not share ; and the youngsters noted his weakness with the unerring precision of the urchin to mark simple difference of character. Now the boy presses fiendishly on an intimate discovery in the nature of his friends, both because it gives him a new and delightful feeling of power over them, and also because he has not learned charity from a sense of his deficiencies, the brave ruffian having none. He is always coming back to probe the raw place, and Barbie boys were always coming back to " do a gunk " and " play a chaw " on young Gourlay by boasting their knowledge of the world, winking at each other the while to observe his grinning anger. They were large on the wonders they had seen and the places they had been to, while he grew small (and they saw it) in envy of their superiority. Even Swipey Broon had a crow at him. For Swipey had journeyed in the company of his father to far-off Fechars, yea even to the groset-fair, and came back with an epic tale of his adventures. He had been in fifteen taverns, and one hotel (a temperance hotel, where old Brown bashed the proprietor for refusing to supply him gin) ; one Pepper's Ghost ; one Wild Beasts' Show ; one Exhibition of the Fattest Woman on the Earth ; also in the precincts of one jail, where Mr. Patrick Brown was cruelly incarcerate for wiping the floor with the cold refuser of the gin. " Criffens ! Fechars ! " said Swipey for a twelvemonth after, stunned by the mere recollection of that home of the glories of the earth. And then he would begin to expatiate for the benefit of young Gourlay—for Swipey, though his name was the base Teutonic Brown, had a Celtic contempt for brute facts that cripple the imperial mind. So well did he expatiate that young Gourlay would slink home to his mother and say, " Yah, even Swipey Broon has been to Fechars, though my faither 'ull no allow *me* ! " " Never mind, dear," she would soothe him ; " when once you're in the business, you'll gang a'where. And nut wan o' them has sic a business to gang intill ! "

But though he longed to go here and there for a day,

that he might be able to boast of it at home, young
Gourlay felt that leaving Barbie for good would be a
cutting of his heart-strings. Each feature of it, town
and landward, was a crony of old years. In a land like
Barbie, of quick hill and dale, of tumbled wood and fell,
each facet of nature has an individuality so separate and
so strong that if you live with it a little it becomes
your friend, and a memory so dear that you kiss the
thought of it in absence. The fields are not similar as
pancakes; they have their difference; each leaps to
the eye with a remembered and peculiar charm. That
is why the heart of the Scot dies in flat southern lands;
he lives in a vacancy; at dawn there is no Ben Agray
to nod recognition through the mists. And that is why,
when he gets north of Carlisle, he shouts with glee as
each remembered object sweeps on the sight: yonder's
the Nith with a fisherman hip-deep jigging at his rod,
and yonder's Corsoncon with the mist on his brow. It
is less the totality of the place than the individual feature
that pulls at the heart, and it was the individual feature
that pulled at young Gourlay. With intellect little or
none, he had a vast, sensational experience, and each
aspect of Barbie was working in his blood and brain.
Was there ever a Cross like Barbie Cross? Was there
ever a burn like the Lintie? It was blithe and heartsome to go birling to Skeighan in the train; it was grand
to jouk round Barbie on the nichts at e'en! Even
people whom he did not know he could locate with
warm sure feelings of superiority. If a poor workman
slouched past him on the road, he set him down in his
heart as one of that rotten crowd from the Weaver's
Vennel or the Tinker's Wynd. Barbie was in subjection
to the mind of the son of the important man. To dash
about Barbie in a gig, with a big dog walloping behind,
his coat-collar high about his ears, and the reek of a
meerschaum pipe floating white and blue many yards
behind him, jovial and sordid nonsense about home—

that had been his ideal. His father, he thought angrily, had encouraged the ideal, and now he forbade it, like the brute he was. From the earth in which he was rooted so deeply his father tore him, to fling him on a world he had forbidden him to know. His heart presaged disaster.

Old Gourlay would have scorned the sentimentality of seeing him off from the station, and Mrs. Gourlay was too feckless to propose it for herself. Janet had offered to convoy him, but when the afternoon came she was down with a racking cold. He was alone as he strolled on the platform — a youth well-groomed and well-supplied, but for once in his life not a swaggerer, though the chance to swagger was unique. He was pointed out as "Young Gourlay off to the College." But he had no pleasure in the rôle, for his heart was in his boots.

He took the slow train to Skeighan, where he boarded the express. Few sensational experiences were unknown to his too-impressionable mind, and he knew the animation of railway travelling. Coming back from Skeighan in an empty compartment on nights of the past, he had sometimes shouted and stamped and banged the cushions till the dust flew, in mere joy of his rush through the air; the constant rattle, the quick-repeated noise, getting at his nerves, as they get at the nerves of savages and Englishmen on Bank Holidays. But any animation of the kind which he felt to-day was soon expelled by the slow uneasiness welling through his blood. He had no eager delight in the unknown country rushing past; it inspired him with fear. He thought with a feeble smile of what Mysie Monk said when they took her at the age of sixty (for the first time in her life) to the top of Milmannoch Hill. "Eh," said Mysie, looking round her in amaze—"eh, sirs, it's a lairge place the world when you see it all!" Gourlay smiled because he had the same thought, but feebly, because he was cowering

at the bigness of the world.   Folded nooks in the hills
swept past, enclosing their lonely farms ;   then the open
straths, where autumnal waters gave a pale gleam to the
sky.   Sodden   moors   stretched   away   in   vast   patient
loneliness.   Then a gray smear of rain blotted the world,
penning him in with his dejection.   He seemed to be
rushing through unseen space, with no companion but
his own foreboding.   " Where are you going to ? " asked
his mind, and the wheels of the train repeated the question all the way to Edinburgh, jerking it out in two short
lines and a long one :   " Where are you going to ?   Where
are you going to ?   Ha, ha, Mr. Gourlay, where are you
going to ? "

It was the same sensitiveness to physical impression
which won him to Barbie that repelled him from the
outer world.   The scenes round Barbie, so vividly impressed, were his friends, because he had known them
from his birth ;   he was a somebody in their midst and
had mastered their familiarity ;   they were the ministers
of his mind.   Those other scenes were his foes, because,
realizing them morbidly in relation to himself, he was
cowed by their big indifference to him, and felt puny,
a nobody before them.   And he could not pass them
like more manly and more callous minds ;   they came
burdening in on him whether he would or no.   Neither
could he get above them.   Except when lording it at
Barbie, he had never a quick reaction of the mind on
what he saw ;   it possessed him, not he it.

About twilight, when the rain had ceased, his train
was brought up with a jerk between the stations.   While
the rattle and bang continued it seemed not unnatural
to young Gourlay (though depressing) to be whirling
through the darkening land ;   it went past like a pano-
rama in a dream.   But in the dead pause following the
noise he thought it " queer " to be sitting here in the
intense quietude and looking at a strange and unfamiliar
scene—planted in its midst by a miracle of speed, and

gazing at it closely through a window ! Two ploughmen
from the farmhouse near the line were unyoking at the
end of the croft ; he could hear the muddy noise (" splor-
roch " is the Scotch of it) made by the big hoofs on
the squashy head-rig. " Bauldy " was the name of the
shorter ploughman, so yelled to by his mate ; and two
of the horses were " Prince and Rab "—just like a pair in
Loranogie's stable. In the curtainless window of the
farmhouse shone a leaping flame—not the steady glow of
a lamp, but the tossing brightness of a fire—and thought
he to himself, " They're getting the porridge for the
men ! " He had a vision of the woman stirring in the
meal, and of the homely interior in the dancing firelight.
He wondered who the folk were, and would have liked
to know them. Yes, it was " queer," he thought, that
he who left Barbie only a few hours ago should be in
intimate momentary touch with a place and people he
had never seen before. The train seemed arrested by a
spell that he might get his vivid impression.

When ensconced in his room that evening he had a
brighter outlook on the world. With the curtains drawn,
and the lights burning, its shabbiness was unrevealed.
After the whirling strangeness of the day he was glad
to be in a place that was his own ; here at least was a
corner of earth of which he was master ; it reassured
him. The firelight dancing on the tea things was pleasant
and homely, and the enclosing cosiness shut out the
black roaring world that threatened to engulf his personality. His spirits rose, ever ready to jump at a trifle.

The morrow, however, was the first of his lugubrious
time.

If he had been an able man he might have found a
place in his classes to console him. Many youngsters
are conscious of a vast depression when entering the
portals of a university ; they feel themselves inadequate
to cope with the wisdom of the ages garnered in the solid
walls. They envy alike the smiling sureness of the genial

charlatan (to whom professors are a set of fools), and the easy mastery of the man of brains. They have a cowering sense of their own inefficiency. But the feeling of uneasiness presently disappears. The first shivering dip is soon forgotten by the hearty breaster of the waves. But ere you breast the waves you must swim ; and to swim through the sea of learning was more than heavy-headed Gourlay could accomplish. His mind, finding no solace in work, was left to prey upon itself.

If he had been the ass total and complete he might have loafed in the comfortable haze which surrounds the average intelligence, and cushions it against the world. But in Gourlay was a rawness of nerve, a sensitiveness to physical impression, which kept him fretting and stewing, and never allowed him to lapse on a sluggish indifference.

Though he could not understand things, he could not escape them ; they thrust themselves forward on his notice. We hear of poor genius cursed with perceptions which it can't express ; poor Gourlay was cursed with impressions which he couldn't intellectualize. With little power of thought, he had a vast power of observation ; and as everything he observed in Edinburgh was offensive and depressing, he was constantly depressed—the more because he could not understand. At Barbie his life, though equally void of mental interest, was solaced by surroundings which he loved. In Edinburgh his surroundings were appalling to his timid mind. There was a greengrocer's shop at the corner of the street in which he lodged, and he never passed it without being conscious of its trodden and decaying leaves. They were enough to make his morning foul. The middle-aged woman, who had to handle carrots with her frozen fingers, was less wretched than he who saw her, and thought of her after he went by. A thousand such impressions came boring in upon his mind and made him squirm. He could not toss them aside like the callous and manly ;

he could not see them in their due relation, and think them unimportant, like the able ; they were always recurring and suggesting woe. If he fled to his room, he was followed by his morbid sense of an unpleasant world. He conceived a rankling hatred of the four walls wherein he had to live. Heavy Biblical pictures, in frames of gleaming black like the splinters of a hearse, were hung against a dark ground. Every time Gourlay raised his head he scowled at them with eyes of gloom. It was curious that, hating his room, he was loath to go to bed. He got a habit of sitting till three in the morning, staring at the dead fire in sullen apathy.

He was sitting at nine o'clock one evening, wondering if there was no means of escape from the wretched life he had to lead, when he received a letter from Jock Allan, asking him to come and dine.

CHAPTER XVII.

THAT dinner was a turning-point in young Gourlay's career. It is lucky that a letter describing it has fallen into the hands of the patient chronicler. It was sent by young Jimmy Wilson to his mother. As it gives an idea—which is slightly mistaken—of Jock Allan, and an idea—which is very unmistakable—of young Wilson, it is here presented in the place of pride. It were a pity not to give a human document of this kind all the honour in one's power.

" Dear mother," said the wee sma' Scoatchman—so the hearty Allan dubbed him—" dear mother, I just write to inform you that I've been out to a grand dinner at Jock Allan's. He met me on Princes Street, and made a great how-d'ye-do. ' Come out on Thursday night, and dine with me,' says he, in his big way. So here I went out to see him. I can tell you he's a warmer ! I never saw a man eat so much in all my born days—but I suppose he would be having more on his table than usual to show off a bit, knowing us Barbie boys would be writing home about it all. And drink ! D'ye know, he began with a whole half tumbler of whisky, and how many more he had I really should *not* like to say ! And he must be used to it, too, for it seemed to have no effect on him whatever. And then he smoked and smoked—two great big cigars after we had finished eating, and then ' Damn it,' says he—he's an awful man to swear—' damn it,' he says, ' there's no satisfaction in cigars ; I must have a pipe,' and he actu-

ally smoked *four* pipes before I came away! I noticed
the cigars were called ' Estorellas—Best Quality,' and
when I was in last Saturday night getting an ounce of
shag at the wee shoppie round the corner, I asked the
price of ' these Estorellas.' ' Ninepence a piece!' said
the bodie. Just imagine Jock Allan smoking eighteen-
pence, and not being satisfied! He's up in the world
since he used to shaw turnips at Loranogie for sixpence
a day! But he'll come down as quick if he keeps on
at yon rate. He made a great phrase with me; but
though it keeps down one's weekly bill to get a meal like
yon—I declare I wasn't hungry for two days—for all
that I'll go very little about him. He'll be the kind
that borrows money very fast—one of those harum-
scarum ones!' "

Criticism like that is a boomerang that comes back
to hit the emitting skull with a hint of its kindred
woodenness. It reveals the writer more than the written
of. Allan was a bigger man than you would gather from
Wilson's account of his Gargantuan revelry. He had a
genius for mathematics—a gift which crops up, like
music, in the most unexpected corners—and from plough-
boy and herd he had become an actuary in Auld Reekie.
Wilson had no need to be afraid, the meagre fool, for his
host could have bought him and sold him.

Allan had been in love with young Gourlay's mother
when she herself was a gay young fliskie at Tenshillingland, but his little romance was soon ended when Gourlay came and whisked her away. But she remained the
one romance of his life. Now in his gross and jovial
middle age he idealized her in memory (a sentimentalist,
of course—he was Scotch); he never saw her in her
scraggy misery to be disillusioned; to him she was still
the wee bit lairdie's dochter, a vision that had dawned
on his wretched boyhood, a pleasant and pathetic memory.
And for that reason he had a curious kindness to her
boy. That was why he introduced him to his boon

companions. He thought he was doing him a good turn.

It was true that Allan made a phrase with a withered wisp of humanity like young Wilson. Not that he failed to see through him, for he christened him "a dried washing-clout." But Allan, like most great-hearted Scots far from their native place, saw it through a veil of sentiment ; harsher features that would have been ever-present to his mind if he had never left it disappeared from view, and left only the finer qualities bright within his memory. And idealizing the place he idealized its sons. To him they had a value not their own, just because they knew the brig and the burn and the brae, and had sat upon the school benches. He would have welcomed a dog from Barbie. It was from a like generous emotion that he greeted the bodies so warmly on his visits home—he thought they were as pleased to see him as he was to see them. But they imputed false motives to his hearty greetings. Even as they shook his hand the mean ones would think to themselves : " What does he mean by this now ? What's he up till ? No doubt he'll be wanting something off me ! " They could not understand the gusto with which the returned exile cried, " Ay, man, Jock Tamson, and how are ye ? " They thought such warmth must have a sinister intention.—A Scot revisiting his native place ought to walk very quietly. For the parish is sizing him up.

There were two things to be said against Allan, and two only—unless, of course, you consider drink an objection. Wit with him was less the moment's glittering flash than the anecdotal bang ; it was a fine old crusted blend which he stored in the cellars of his mind to bring forth on suitable occasions, as cob-webby as his wine. And it tickled his vanity to have a crowd of admiring youngsters round him to whom he might retail his anecdotes, and play the brilliant *raconteur*. He had cronies of his own years, and he was lordly and jovial amongst them—yet he wanted another *entourage*. He was one of those middle-aged bachelors who like a train of youngsters behind them, whom they favour in return for homage. The wealthy man who had been a peasant lad delighted to act the jovial host to sons of petty magnates from his home. Batch after batch as they came up to College were drawn around him—partly because their homage pleased him, and partly because he loved anything whatever that came out of Barbie. There was no harm in Allan—though when his face was in repose you saw the look in his eye at times of a man defrauding his soul. A robustious young fellow of sense and brains would have found in this lover of books and a bottle not a bad comrade. But he was the worst of cronies for a weak swaggerer like Gourlay. For Gourlay, admiring the older man's jovial power, was led on to imitate his faults, to think them virtues and a credit ; and he lacked the clear, cool head that kept Allan's faults from flying away with him.

At dinner that night there were several braw, braw lads of Barbie Water. There were Tarmillan the doctor (a son of Irrendavie), Logan the cashier, Tozer the Englishman, old Partan—a guileless and inquiring mind— and half a dozen students raw from the west. The students were of the kind that goes up to College with the hayseed sticking in its hair. Two are in a Colonial Cabinet now, two are in the poorhouse. So they go.

Tarmillan was the last to arrive. He came in sucking his thumb, into which he had driven a splinter while conducting an experiment.

" I've a morbid horror of lockjaw," he explained. " I never get a jag from a pin but I see myself in the shape of a hoop, semicircular, with my head on one end of a table, my heels on the other, and a doctor standing on my navel trying to reduce the curvature."

" Gosh ! " said Partan, who was a literal fool, " is that the treatment they purshoo ? "

" That's the treatment ! " said Tarmillan, sizing up his man. " Oh, it's a queer thing lockjaw ! I remember when I was gold-mining in Tibet, one of our carriers who died of lockjaw had such a circumbendibus in his body that we froze him and made him the hoop of a bucket to carry our water in. You see he was a thin bit man, and iron was scarce."

" Ay, man ! " cried Partan, " you've been in Tibet ? "

" Often," waved Tarmillan, " often ! I used to go there every summer."

Partan, who liked to extend his geographical knowledge, would have talked of Tibet for the rest of the evening—and Tarmie would have told him news—but Allan broke in.

" How's the book, Tarmillan ? " he inquired.

Tarmillan was engaged on a treatise which those who are competent to judge consider the best thing of its kind ever written.

" Oh, don't ask me," he writhed. " Man, it's an irksome thing to write, and to be asked about it makes you squirm. It's almost as offensive to ask a man when his book will be out as to ask a woman when she'll be delivered. I'm glad you invited me—to get away from the confounded thing. It's become a blasted tyrant. A big work's a mistake ; it's a monster that devours the brain. I neglect my other work for that fellow of mine ; he bags everything I think. I never light on a new thing, but ' Hullo ! ' I cry, ' here's an idea for the book ! ' If you are engaged on a big subject, all your thinking works into it or out of it."

" M'yes," said Logan ; " but that's a swashing way of putting it."

" It's the danger of the aphorism," said Allan, " that it states too much in trying to be small.—Tozer, what do you think ? "

" I never was engaged on a big subject," sniffed Tozer.

" We're aware o' that ! " said Tarmillan.

Tozer went under, and Tarmillan had the table. Allan was proud of him.

"Courage is the great thing," said he. "It often succeeds by the mere show of it. It's the timid man that a dog bites. Run *at* him and he runs."

He was speaking to himself rather than the table, admiring the courage that had snubbed Tozer with a word. But his musing remark rang a bell in young Gourlay. By Jove, he had thought that himself, so he had! He was a hollow thing, he knew, but a buckram pretence prevented the world from piercing to his hollowness. The son of his courageous sire (whom he equally admired and feared) had learned to play the game of bluff. A bold front was half the battle. He had worked out his little theory, and it was with a shock of pleasure the timid youngster heard great Allan give it forth. He burned to let him know that he had thought that too.

To the youngsters, fat of face and fluffy of its circling down, the talk was a banquet of the gods. For the first time in their lives they heard ideas (such as they were) flung round them royally. They yearned to show that they were thinkers too. And Gourlay was fired with the rest.

"I heard a very good one the other day from old Bauldy Johnston," said Allan, opening his usual wallet of stories when the dinner was in full swing. At a certain stage of the evening "I heard a good one" was the invariable keynote of his talk. If you displayed no wish to hear the "good one," he was huffed. "Bauldy was up in Edinburgh," he went on, "and I met him near the Scott Monument and took him to Lockhart's for a dram. You remember what a friend he used to be of old Will Overton. I wasn't aware, by-the-bye, that Will was dead till Bauldy told me. '*He was a great fellow my friend Will*,' he rang out in yon deep voice of his. '*The thumb-mark of his Maker was*

wet in the clay of him.'   Man, it made a quiver go down
my spine."

"Oh, Bauldy has been a kenned phrase-maker for the
last forty year," said Tarmillan.   "But every other
Scots peasant has the gift.   To hear Englishmen talk,
you would think Carlyle was unique for the word that
sends the picture home—they give the man the credit
of his race.   But I've heard fifty things better than 'wil-
lowy man' in the stable a-hame on a wat day in hairst—
fifty things better—from men just sitting on the corn-
kists and chowing beans."

"I know a better one than that," said Allan.   Tarmillan had told no story, you observe, but Allan was so
accustomed to saying "I know a better one than that,"
that it escaped him before he was aware.   "I remember when Bauldy went off to Paris on the spree.   He
kept his mouth shut when he came back, for he was
rather ashamed o' the outburst.   But the bodies were
keen to hear.   'What's the incense like in Notre Dame?'
said Johnny Coe, with his een big.   *Burning stink!*'
said Bauldy."

"I can cap that with a better one still," said Tarmillan, who wasn't to be done by any man.   "I was with
Bauldy when he quarrelled Tam Gibb of Hoochan-doe.
Hoochan-doe's a yelling ass, and he threatened Bauldy
—oh, he would do this, and he would do that, and he
would do the other thing.   *Damn ye, would ye threaten
me?*' cried Bauldy.   *I'll gar your brains jaup red to the
heavens!*'   And I 'clare to God, sirs, a nervous man
looked up to see if the clouds werena spattered with
the gore!'"

Tozer cleared a sarcastic windpipe.

"Why do you clear your throat like that?" said Tarmillan—"like a craw with the croup, on a bare branch
against a gray sky in November!   If I had a throat like
yours, I'd cut it and be done wi't."

"I wonder what's the cause of that extraordinary

vividness in the speech of the Scotch peasantry ? " said
Allan—more to keep the blades from bickering than
from any wish to know.

" It comes from a power of seeing things vividly inside your mind," said a voice, timorous and wheezy,
away down the table.

What cockerel was this crowing ?

They turned, and beheld the blushing Gourlay.

But Tarmillan and Tozer were at it again, and he
was snubbed. Jimmy Wilson sniggered, and the other
youngsters enjoyed his discomfiture. Huh ! What
right has *he* to set up his pipe ?

His shirt stuck to his back. He would have liked the
ground to open and swallow him.

He gulped a huge swill of whisky to cover his vexa-
tion ; and oh, the mighty difference ! A sudden courage
flooded his veins. He turned with a scowl on Wilson,
and, " What the devil are *you* sniggering at ? " he
growled. Logan, the only senior who marked the by-
play, thought him a hardy young spunkie.

The moment the whisky had warmed the cockles of
his heart Gourlay ceased to care a rap for the sniggerers.
Drink deadened his nervous perception of the critics
on his right and left, and set him free to follow his idea
undisturbed. It was an idea he had long cherished—
being one of the few that ever occurred to him. He
rarely made phrases himself—though, curiously enough,
his father often did without knowing it—the harsh
grind of his character producing a flash. But Gourlay
was aware of his uncanny gift of visualization—or of
" seeing things in the inside of his head," as he called it
—and vanity prompted the inference, that this was the
faculty that sprang the metaphor. His theory was now
clear and eloquent before him. He was realizing for the
first time in his life (with a sudden joy in the discovery)
the effect of whisky to unloose the brain ; sentences
went hurling through his brain with a fluency that

thrilled. If he had the ear of the company, now he had the drink to hearten him, he would show Wilson and the rest that he wasn't such a blasted fool! In a room by himself he would have spouted to the empty air.

Some such point he had reached in the hurrying jumble of his thoughts when Allan addressed him.

Allan did not mean his guest to be snubbed. He was a gentleman at heart, not a cad like Tozer ; and this boy was the son of a girl whose laugh he remembered in the gloamings at Tenshillingland.

" I beg your pardon, John," he said in heavy benevolence—he had reached that stage—" I beg your pardon. I'm afraid you was interrupted."

Gourlay felt his heart a lump in his throat, but he rushed into speech.

" Metaphor comes from the power of seeing things in the inside of your head," said the unconscious disciple of Aristotle—" seeing them so vivid that you see the likeness between them. When Bauldy Johnston said ' the thumb-mark of his Maker was wet in the clay of him,' he *saw* the print of a thumb in wet clay, and he *saw* the Almighty making a man out of mud, the way He used to do in the Garden of Eden lang syne. So Bauldy flashed the two ideas together, and the metaphor sprang! A man'll never make phrases unless he can see things in the middle of his brain. *I* can see things in the middle of my brain," he went on cockily—" anything I want to ! I don't need to shut my eyes either. They just come up before me."

" Man, you're young to have noticed these things, John," said Jock Allan. " I never reasoned it out before, but I'm sure you're in the right o't."

He spoke more warmly than he felt, because Gourlay had flushed and panted and stammered (in spite of inspiring bold John Barleycorn) while airing his little theory, and Allan wanted to cover him. But Gourlay

took it as a tribute to his towering mind. Oh, but he
was the proud mannikin. " Pass the watter ! " he said
to Jimmy Wilson, and Jimmy passed it meekly.

Logan took a fancy to Gourlay on the spot. He was
a slow, sly, cosy man, with a sideward laugh in his eye, a
humid gleam. And because his blood was so genial and
so slow, he liked to make up to brisk young fellows,
whose wilder outbursts might amuse him. They quickened his sluggish blood. No bad fellow, and good-
natured in his heavy way, he was what the Scotch call a
" slug for the drink." A " slug for the drink " is a man
who soaks and never succumbs. Logan was the more
dangerous a crony on that account. Remaining sober
while others grew drunk, he was always ready for another dram, always ready with an oily chuckle for the
sploring nonsense of his satellites. He would see them
home in the small hours, taking no mean advantage
over them, never scorning them because they " couldn't
carry it," only laughing at their daft vagaries. And
next day he would gurgle, " So-and-so was screwed last
night, and, man, if you had heard his talk ! " Logan
had enjoyed it. He hated to drink by himself, and
liked a splurging youngster with whom to go the
rounds.

He was attracted to Gourlay by the manly way he
tossed his drink, and by the false fire it put into him.
But he made no immediate advance. He sat smiling in
creeshy benevolence, beaming on Gourlay but saying
nothing. When the party was ended, however, he made
up to him going through the door.

" I'm glad to have met you, Mr. Gourlay," said
he. " Won't you come round to the Howff for a
while ? "

" The Howff ? " said Gourlay.

" Yes," said Logan ; " haven't ye heard o't ? It's a
snug bit house where some of the West Country billies
forgather for a nicht at e'en. Oh, nothing to speak of,

ye know—just a dram and a joke to pass the time now
and then ! ''

" Aha ! '' laughed Gourlay, " there's worse than a
drink, by Jove.   It puts smeddum in your blood ! ''

Logan nipped the guard of his arm in heavy playful-
ness and led him to the Howff.

CHAPTER XVIII.

YOUNG Gourlay had found a means of escaping from his foolish mind. By the beginning of his second session he was as able a toper as a publican could wish. The somewhat sordid joviality of Allan's ring, their wit-combats that were somewhat crude, appeared to him the very acme of social intercourse. To emulate Logan and Allan was his aim. But drink appealed to him in many ways besides. Now when his too apprehensive nerves were frightened by bugbears in his lonely room he could be off to the Howff and escape them. And drink inspired him with false courage to sustain his pose as a hardy rollicker. He had acquired a kind of prestige since the night of Allan's party, and two of the fellows whom he met there—Armstrong and Gillespie—became his friends at College and the Howff. He swaggered before them as he had swaggered at school both in Barbie and Skeighan, and now there was no Swipey Broon to cut him over the coxcomb. Armstrong and Gillespie—though they saw through him—let him run on, for he was not bad fun when he was splurging. He found, too, when with his cronies that drink unlocked his mind, and gave a free flow to his ideas. Nervous men are often impotent of speech from very excess of perception ; they realize not merely what they mean to say, but with the nervous antennæ of their minds they feel the attitude of every auditor. Distracted by lateral perceptions from the point ahead, they blunder where blunter minds would go forward undismayed. That was the experience of young Gourlay. If he tried to talk freely when sober, he always grew confused. But drink deadened the outer rim of his perception and left it the clearer in the middle for its concentration. In plainer language, when he was drunk he was less afraid of being laughed at, and free of that fear he was a better speaker. He was driven to drink, then, by every weakness of his character. As nervous hypochondriac, as would-be swaggerer, as a dullard requiring stimulus, he found that drink, to use his own language, gave him " smeddum."

With his second year he began the study of philosophy, and that added to his woes. He had nerves to feel the Big Conundrum, but not the brains to solve it ; small blame to him for that, since philosophers have cursed each other black in the face over it for the last five thousand years. But it worried him. The strange and sinister detail of the world, that had always been a horror to his mind, became more horrible beneath the stimulus of futile thought. But whisky was the mighty cure. He was the gentleman who gained notoriety on a memorable occasion by exclaiming, " Metaphysics be damned ; let us drink ! " Omar and other bards have expressed the same conclusion in more dulcet wise. But Gourlay's was equally sincere. How sincere is another question.

Curiously, an utterance of " Auld Tam," one of his professors, half confirmed him in his evil ways.

" I am speaking now," said Tam, " of the comfort of a true philosophy, less of its higher aspect than its comfort to the mind of man. Physically, each man is highest on the globe ; intellectually, the philosopher alone dominates the world. To him are only two entities that matter—himself and the Eternal ; or, if another, it is his fellow-man, whom serving he serves the ultimate of being. But he is master of the outer world. The mind, indeed, in its first blank outlook on life is terrified by the demoniac force of nature and the swarming misery of man ; by the vast totality of things, the cold remoteness of the starry heavens, and the threat of the devouring seas.   It is puny in their midst."

Gourlay woke up, and the sweat broke on him.   Great Heaven, had Tam been through it too !

" At that stage," quoth the wise man, " the mind is dispersed in a thousand perceptions and a thousand fears ; there is no central greatness in the soul.   It is assailed by terrors which men sunk in the material never seem to feel.   Phenomena, uninformed by thought, bewilder and depress."

" Just like me ! " thought Gourlay, and listened with a thrilling interest because it was " just like him."

" But the labyrinth," said Tam, with a ring in his voice as of one who knew—" the labyrinth cannot appal the man who has found a clue to its windings.   A mind that has attained to thought lives in itself, and the world becomes its slave.   Its formerly distracted powers rally home ; it is central, possessing, not possessed.   The world no longer frightens, being understood.   Its sinister features are accidents that will pass away, and they gradually cease to be observed.   For real thinkers know the value of a wise indifference.   And that is why they are often the most genial men ; unworried by the transient, they can smile and wait, sure of their eternal aim.   The man to whom the infinite beckons is not to be driven from his mystic quest by the ambush of a temporal fear ; there is no fear—it has ceased to exist.   That is the comfort of a true philosophy—if a man accepts it not merely mechanically, from another, but feels it in breath and blood and every atom of his being.   With a warm surety in his heart, he is undaunted by the outer world. That, gentlemen, is what thought can do for a man."

" By Jove," thought Gourlay, " that's what whisky does for me ! "

And that, on a lower level, was what whisky did.

He had no conception of what Tam really meant; there were people, indeed, who used to think that Tam never knew what he meant himself.   They were as little able as Gourlay to appreciate the mystic, through the radiant haze of whose mind thoughts loomed on you sudden and big, like mountain tops in a sunny mist, the grander for their dimness.   But Gourlay, though he could not understand, felt the fortitude of whisky was somehow akin to the fortitude described.   In the increased vitality it gave he was able to tread down the world.   If he walked on a wretched day in a wretched street, when he happened to be sober, his mind was hither and yon in a thousand perceptions and a thousand fears, fastening to (and fastened to) each squalid thing around.   But with whisky humming in his blood he paced onward in a happy dream.   The wretched puddles by the way, the frowning rookeries where misery squalled, the melancholy noises of the street, were passed unheeded by.   His distracted powers rallied home ; he was concentrate, his own man again, the hero of his musing mind.   For, like all weak men of a vivid fancy, he was constantly framing dramas of which he was the towering lord.   The weakling who never " downed " men in reality was always " downing " them in thought.   His imaginary triumphs consoled him for his actual rebuffs.   As he walked in a tipsy dream, he was " standing up " to somebody, hurling his father's phrases at him, making short work of *him !*   If imagination paled, the nearest tavern supplied a remedy, and flushed it to a radiant glow.   Whereupon he had become the master of his world, and not its slave.

" Just imagine," he thought, " whisky doing for me what philosophy seems to do for Tam.   It's a wonderful thing the drink ! "

His second session wore on, and when near its close Tam gave out the subject for the Raeburn.

The Raeburn was a poor enough prize—a few books for

an " essay in the picturesque ; " but it had a peculiar interest for the folk of Barbie. Twenty years ago it was won four years in succession by men from the valley ; and the unusual run of luck fixed it in their minds. Thereafter when an unsuccessful candidate returned to his home, he was sure to be asked very pointedly, " Who won the Raeburn the year ? " to rub into him their perception that he at least had been a failure. A bodie would dander slowly up, saying, " Ay, man, ye've won hame ! " Then, having mused awhile, would casually ask, " By-the-bye, who won the Raeburn the year ? Oh, it was a Perthshire man ! It used to come our airt, but we seem to have lost the knack o't ! Oh yes, sir, Barbie bred writers in those days, but the breed seems to have decayed." Then he would murmur dreamily, as if talking to himself, " Jock Goudie was the last that got it hereaway. But *he* was a clever chap."

The caustic bodie would dander away with a grin, leaving a poor writhing soul. When he reached the Cross he would tell the Deacon blithely of the " fine one he had given him," and the Deacon would lie in wait to give him a fine one too. In Barbie, at least, your returning student is never met at the station with a brass band, whatever may happen in more emotional districts of the North, where it pleases them to shed the tear.

" An Arctic Night " was the inspiring theme which Tam set for the Raeburn.

" A very appropriate subject ! " laughed the fellows ; " quite in the style of his own lectures." For Tam, though wise and a humorist, had his prosy hours. He used to lecture on the fifteen characteristics of Lady Macbeth (so he parcelled the unhappy Queen), and he would announce quite gravely, " We will now approach the discussion of the eleventh feature of the lady."

Gourlay had a shot at the Raeburn. He could not bring a radiant fullness of mind to bear upon his task (it was not in him to bring), but his morbid fancy set to work of its own accord. He saw a lonely little town far off upon the verge of Lapland night, leagues and leagues across a darkling plain, dark itself and little and lonely in the gloomy splendour of a Northern sky. A ship put to sea, and Gourlay heard in his ears the skirl of the man who went overboard—struck dead by the icy water on his brow, which smote the brain like a tomahawk.

He put his hand to his own brow when he wrote that, and, " Yes," he cried eagerly, " it would be the *cold* would kill the brain! Ooh-ooh, how it would go in ! "

A world of ice groaned round him in the night ; bergs ground on each other and were rent in pain ; he heard the splash of great fragments tumbled in the deep, and felt the waves of their distant falling lift the vessel beneath him in the darkness. To the long desolate night came a desolate dawn, and eyes were dazed by the encircling whiteness ; yet there flashed green slanting chasms in the ice, and towering pinnacles of sudden rose, lonely and far away. An unknown sea beat upon an unknown shore, and the ship drifted on the pathless waters, a white dead man at the helm.

" Yes, by Heaven," cried Gourlay, " I can see it all, I can see it all—that fellow standing at the helm, frozen white and as stiff's an icicle ! "

Yet, do what he might, he was unable to fill more than half a dozen small pages. He hesitated whether he should send them in, and held them in his inky fingers, thinking he would burn them. He was full of pity for his own inability. " I wish I was a clever chap," he said mournfully.

" Ach, well, I'll try my luck," he muttered at last, " though Tam may guy me before the whole class for doing so little o't."

The Professor, however (unlike the majority of Scottish professors), rated quality higher than quantity.

" I have learned a great deal myself," he announced on the last day of the session—" I have learned a great deal myself from the papers sent in on the subject of an ' Arctic Night.' "

" Hear, hear ! " said an insolent student at the back.

" Where, where ? " said the Professor ; " stand up, sir ! "

A gigantic Borderer rose blushing into view, and was greeted with howls of derision by his fellows. Tam eyed him, and he winced.

" You will apologize in my private room at the end of the hour," said Aquinas, as the students used to call him. " Learn that this is not a place to bray in."

The giant slunk down, trying to hide himself.

" Yes," said Tam, " I have learned what a poor sense of proportion some of you students seem to have. It was not to see who could write the most, but who could write the best, that I set the theme. One gentleman—he has been careful to give me his full name and address," twinkled Tam, and picking up a huge manuscript he read it from the outer page, " Mr. Alexander MacTavish of Benmacstronachan, near Auchnapeterhoolish, in the island of South Uist—has sent me in no less than a hundred and fifty-three closely-written pages ! I dare say it's the size of the adjectives he uses that makes the thing so heavy," quoth Tam, and dropped it thudding on his desk. " Life is short, the art of the MacTavish long, and to tell the truth, gentlemen "—he gloomed at them humorously—" to tell the truth, I stuck in the middle o't ! " (Roars of laughter, and a reproving voice, " Oh, ta pold MacTa-avish ! " whereat there was pandemonium). MacTavish was heard to groan, " Oh, why tid I leave my home ! " to which a voice responded in mocking antiphone, " Why tid you cross ta teep ? " The noise they made was heard at Holyrood.

When the tumult and the shouting died, Tam resumed

with a quiver in his voice, for " ta pold MacTavish " had tickled him too. " Now, gentlemen," he said, " I don't judge essays by their weight, though I'm told they sometimes pursue that method in Glasgow ! "

(Groans for the rival University, cries of " Oh-oh-oh ! " and a weary voice, " Please, sir, don't mention that place ; it makes me feel quite ill.")

The Professor allayed the tumult with dissuasive palm.

" I believe," he said dryly, " you call that noise of yours ' the College Tramp ; ' in the Senatus we speak o't as ' the Cuddies' Trudge.' Now gentlemen, I'm not unwilling to allow a little noise on the last day of the session, but really you must behave more quietly.—So little does that method of judging essays commend itself to me, I may tell you, that the sketch which I consider the best barely runs to half a dozen short pages."

Young Gourlay's heart gave a leap within him ; he felt it thudding on his ribs. The skin crept on him, and he breathed with quivering nostrils. Gillespie wondered why his breast heaved.

" It's a curious sketch," said the Professor. " It contains a serious blunder in grammar and several mistakes in spelling, but it shows, in some ways, a wonderful imagination."

" Ho, ho ! " thought Gourlay.

" Of course there are various kinds of imagination," said Tam. " In its lowest form it merely recalls something which the eyes have already seen, and brings it vividly before the mind. A higher form pictures something which you never saw, but only conceived as a possible existence. Then there's the imagination which not only sees but hears—actually hears what a man would say on a given occasion, and entering into his blood, tells you exactly why he does it. The highest form is both creative and consecrative, if I may use the word, merging in diviner thought. It irradiates the world. Of that high power there is no evidence in the essay before me. To be sure there was little occasion for its use."

Young Gourlay's thermometer went down.

"Indeed," said Aquinas, "there's a curious want of bigness in the sketch—no large nobility of phrase. It is written in gaspy little sentences, and each sentence begins ' and '—' and '—' and,' like a schoolboy's narrative. It's as if a number of impressions had seized the writer's mind, which he jotted down hurriedly, lest they should escape him. But, just because it's so little wordy, it gets the effect of the thing—faith, sirs, it's right on to the end of it every time ! The writing of some folk is nothing but a froth of words—lucky if it glistens without, like a blobber of iridescent foam. But in this sketch there's a perception at the back of every sentence. It displays, indeed, too nervous a sense of the external world."

"Name, name ! " cried the students, who were being deliberately worked by Tam to a high pitch of curiosity.

"I would strongly impress on the writer," said the shepherd, heedless of his bleating sheep—"I would strongly impress on the writer to set himself down for a spell of real, hard, solid, and deliberate thought. That almost morbid perception, with philosophy to back it, might create an opulent and vivid mind. Without philosophy it would simply be a curse. With philosophy it would bring thought the material to work on. Without philosophy it would simply distract and irritate the mind."

"Name, name ! " cried the fellows.

"The winner of the Raeburn," said Thomas Aquinas, "is Mr. John Gourlay."

*   *   *   *   *   *

Gourlay and his friends made for the nearest public-house. The occasion, they thought, justified a drink. The others chaffed Gourlay about Tam's advice.

"You know, Jack," said Gillespie, mimicking the sage, "what you have got to do next summer is to set yourself down for a spell of real, hard, solid, and deliberate thought. That was Tam's advice, you know."

"Him and his advice!" said Gourlay.

CHAPTER XIX.

THERE were only four other passengers dropped by the eleven o'clock express at Skeighan station, and, as it happened, young Gourlay knew them all. They were petty merchants of the neighbourhood whom he had often seen about Barbie. The sight of their remembered faces as he stepped on to the platform gave him a delightful sense that he was nearing home. He had passed from the careless world where he was nobody at all to the familiar circle where he was a somebody, a mentioned man, and the son of a mentioned man—young Mr. Gourlay!

He had a feeling of superiority to the others, too, because they were mere local journeyers, while he had travelled all the way from mighty Edinburgh by the late express. He was returning from the outer world, while they were bits of bodies who had only been to Fechars. As Edinburgh was to Fechars so was he to them. Round him was the halo of distance and the mystery of night-travelling. He felt big.

" Have you a match, Robert ? " he asked very graciously of Robin Gregg, one of the porters whom he knew. Getting his match, he lit a cigarette ; and when it was lit, after one quick puff, turned it swiftly round to examine its burning end. " Rotten ! " he said, and threw it away to light another. The porters were watching him, and he knew it. When the stationmaster appeared yawning from his office, as he was passing through the gate, and asked who it was, it flattered his

vanity to hear Robin's answer, that it was " young Mr.
Gourlay of Barbie, just back from the Univ-ai-rsity ! "

He had been so hot for home that he had left Edinburgh at twilight, too eager to wait for the morrow.
There was no train for Barbie at this hour of the night ;
and, of course, there was no gig to meet him.   Even if
he had sent word of his coming, " There's no need for
travelling so late," old Gourlay would have growled ;
" let him shank it.   We're in no hurry to have him
home."

He set off briskly, eager to see his mother and tell her
he had won the Raeburn.   The consciousness of his
achievement danced in his blood, and made the road
light to his feet.   His thoughts were not with the country round him, but entirely in the moment of his entrance, when he should proclaim his triumph, with
proud enjoyment of his mother's pride.   His fancy
swept to his journey's end, and took his body after, so
that the long way was as nothing, annihilate by the leap
forward of his mind.

He was too vain, too full of himself and his petty
triumph, to have room for the beauty of the night.   The
sky was one sea of lit cloud, foamy ridge upon ridge
over all the heavens, and each wave was brimming with
its own whiteness, seeming unborrowed of the moon.
Through one peep-hole, and only one, shone a distant
star, a faint white speck far away, dimmed by the nearer
splendours of the sky.   Sometimes the thinning edge of
a cloud brightened in spume, and round the brightness
came a circle of umber, making a window of fantastic
glory for Dian the queen ;   there her white vision peeped
for a moment on the world, and the next she was hid
behind a fleecy veil, witching the heavens.   Gourlay
was alone with the wonder of the night.   The light from
above him was softened in a myriad boughs, no longer
mere light and cold, but a spirit indwelling as their soul,
and they were boughs no longer but a woven dream.

He walked beneath a shadowed glory. But he was dead to it all. One only fact possessed him. He had won the Raeburn—he had won the Raeburn! The road flew beneath him.

Almost before he was aware, the mean gray streets of Barbie had clipped him round. He stopped, panting from the hurry of his walk, and looked at the quiet houses, all still among the gloom. He realized with a sudden pride that he alone was in conscious possession of the town. Barbie existed to no other mind. All the others were asleep; while he had a thrilling consciousness of them and of their future attitude to him, they did not know that he, the returning great one, was present in their midst. They all knew of the Raeburn, however, and ere long they would know that it was his. He was glad to hug his proud secret in presence of the sleeping town, of which he would be the talk to-morrow. How he would surprise them! He stood for a little, gloating in his own sensations. Then a desire to get home tugged him, and he scurried up the long brae.

He stole round the corner of the House with the Green Shutters. Roger, the collie, came at him with a bow-wow-wow. " Roger ! " he whispered, and cuddled him, and the old loyalist fawned on him and licked his hand. The very smell of the dog was couthie in his nose.

The window of a bedroom went up with a crash.

" Now, then, who the devil are you ? " came the voice of old Gourlay.

" It's me, faither," said John.

" Oh, it's you, is it ? This is a fine time o' night to come home."

" Faither, I have—I have won the Raeburn ! "

" It'll keep, my mannie, it'll keep "—and the window slammed.

Next moment it was up.

" Did young Wilson get onything ? " came the eager cry.

" Nut him ! " said John.

" Fine, man !   Damned, sir, I'm proud o' ye ! "

John went round the corner treading on air.   For the first time in his life his father had praised him.

He peeped through a kink at the side of the kitchen blind, where its descent was arrested by a flowerpot in the corner of the window-sill.   As he had expected, though it was long past midnight, his mother was not yet in bed.   She was folding a white cloth over her bosom, and about her, on the backs of chairs, there were other such cloths, drying by the fire.   He watched her curiously ; once he seemed to hear a whimpering moan. When she buttoned her dress above the cloth, she gazed sadly at the dying embers— the look of one who has gained short respite from a task of painful tendance on the body, yet is conscious that the task and the pain are endless, and will have to be endured, to-morrow and to-morrow, till she dies.   It was the fixed gaze of utter weariness and apathy.   A sudden alarm for his mother made John cry her name.

She flew to the door, and in a moment had him in her arms.   He told his news, and basked in her adoration.

She came close to him, and " John," she said in a smiling whisper, big-eyed, " John," she breathed, " would ye like a dram ? "   It was as if she was propounding a roguish plan in some dear conspiracy.

He laughed.   " Well," he said, " seeing we have won the Raeburn, you and I, I think we might."

He heard her fumbling in the distant pantry.   He smiled to himself as he listened to the clinking glass, and, " By Jove," said he, " a mother's a fine thing ! "

" Where's Janet ? " he asked when she returned.   He wanted another worshipper.

" Oh, she gangs to bed the moment it's dark," his mother complained, like one aggrieved.   " She's always saying that she's ill.   I thocht when she grew up that she might be a wee help, but she's no use at all.   And

I'm sure, if a' was kenned, I have more to complain o'
than she has. Atweel ay," she said, and stared at the
embers.

It rarely occurs to young folk who have never left
their homes that their parents may be dying soon;
from infancy they have known them as established facts
of nature like the streams and hills; they expect them
to remain. But the young who have been away for
six months are often struck by a tragic difference in
their elders on returning home. To young Gourlay
there was a curious difference in his mother. She was
almost beautiful to-night. Her blue eyes were large
and glittering, her ears waxen and delicate, and her
brown hair swept low on her blue-veined temples.
Above and below her lips there was a narrow margin of
the purest white.

"Mother," he said anxiously, "you're not ill, are ye?
What do ye need so many wee clouts for?"

She gasped and started. "They're just a wheen
clouts I was sorting out," she faltered. "No, no, dear,
there's noathing wrong wi' me."

"There's one sticking in your blouse," said he, and
pointed to her slack breast.

She glanced nervously down and pushed it farther in.
"I dare say I put it there when I wasna thinking," she
explained.

But she eyed him furtively to see if he were still
looking.

CHAPTER XX.

THERE is nothing worse for a weakling than a small success. The strong man tosses it beneath his feet as a step to rise higher on. He squeezes it into its proper place as a layer in the life he is building. If his memory dwells on it for a moment, it is only because of its valuable results, not because in itself it is a theme for vanity. And if he be higher than strong he values not it, but the exercise of getting it ; viewing his actual achievement, he is apt to reflect, " Is this pitiful thing, then, all that I toiled for ? " Finer natures often experience a keen depression and sense of littleness in the pause that follows a success. But the fool is so swollen by thought of his victory that he is unfit for all healthy work till somebody jags him and lets the gas out. He never forgets the great thing he fancies he did thirty years ago, and expects the world never to forget it either. The more of a weakling he is, and the more incapable of repeating his former triumph, the more he thinks of it ; and the more he thinks of it the more it satisfies his meagre soul, and prevents him essaying another brave venture in the world. His petty achievement ruins him. The memory of it never leaves him, but swells to a huge balloon that lifts him off his feet and carries him heavens-high—till it lands him on a dunghill. Even from that proud eminence he oft cock-a-doodles his former triumph to the world. " Man, you wouldn't think to see me here that I once held a great position. Thirty year back I did a big thing. It was like this, ye see." And then follows a recital of his faded glories—generally ending with a hint that a drink would be very acceptable.

Even such a weakling was young Gourlay. His success in Edinburgh, petty as it was, turned his head, and became one of the many causes working to destroy him. All that summer at Barbie he swaggered and drank on the strength of it.

On the morning after his return he clothed himself in fine raiment (he was always well dressed till the end came), and sallied forth to dominate the town. As he swaggered past the Cross, smoking a cigarette, he seemed to be conscious that the very walls of the houses watched him with unusual eyes, as if even they felt that yon was John Gourlay whom they had known as a boy, proud wearer now of the academic wreath, the conquering hero returned to his home. So Gourlay figured them. He, the disconsidered, had shed a lustre on the ancient walls. They were tributaries to his new importance—somehow their attitude was different from what it had ever been before. It was only his self-conscious bigness, of course, that made even inanimate things seem the feeders of his greatness. As Gourlay, always alive to obscure emotions which he could never express in words, mused for a moment over the strange new feeling that had come to him, a gowsterous voice hailed him from the Black Bull door. He turned, and Peter Wylie, hearty and keen like his father, stood him a drink in honour of his victory, which was already buzzed about the town.

Drucken Wabster's wife had seen to that. " Ou," she cried, " his mother's daft about it, the silly auld thing ; she can speak o' noathing else. Though Gourlay gies her very little to come and go on, she slipped him a whole sovereign this morning, to keep his pouch. Think o' that, kimmers ; heard ye ever sic extravagance ! I saw her doin'd wi' my own eyes. It's aince wud and aye waur * wi' her, I'm thinking. But the wastefu'

* " *Aince wud and aye waur*," silly for once and silly for always.

wife's the waefu' widow, she should keep in mind. She's far owre browdened upon yon boy. I'm sure I howp good may come o't, but——" and with an ominous shake of the head she ended the Websterian harangue.

When Peter Wylie left him Gourlay lit a cigarette and stood at the Cross, waiting for the praises yet to be. The Deacon toddled forward on his thin shanks.

"Man Dyohn, you're won hame, I thee. Ay, man! And how are ye?"

Gourlay surveyed him with insolent, indolent eyes. "Oh, I'm all rai-ight, Deacon," he swaggered; "how are ye-ow?" and he sent a puff of tobacco smoke down through his nostrils.

"I declare!" said the Deacon. "I never thaw onybody thmoke like that before! That'll be one of the thingth ye learn at College, no doubt."

"Ya-as," yawned Gourlay; "it gives you the full flavour of the we-eed."

The Deacon glimmered over him with his eyes. "The weed," said he. "Jutht tho! Imphm. The weed."

Then worthy Mister Allardyce tried another opening. "But, dear me!" he cried, "I'm forgetting entirely. I must congratulate ye. Ye've been doing wonderth, they tell me, up in Embro."

"Just a little bit," swaggered Gourlay, right hand on outshot hip, left hand flaunting a cigarette in air most delicate, tobacco smoke curling from his lofty nose. He looked down his face at the Deacon. "Just a little bit, Mr. Allardyce, just a little bit. I tossed the thing off in a twinkling."

"Ay man, Dyohn," said the Deacon with great solicitude; "but you maunna work that brain o' yours too hard, though. A heid like yours doesna come through the hatter's hand ilka day o' the week; you mutht be careful not to put too great a thtrain on't. Ay, ay; often the best machine's the easiest broken and the warst to mend. You should take a rest and enjoy yourself.

But there ! what need I be telling *you* that ? A College-
bred man like you kenth far better about it than a thilly
auld country bodie ! You'll be meaning to have a grand
holiday and lots o' fun—a dram now and then, eh, and
mony a rattle in the auld man's gig ? "

At this assault on his weak place Gourlay threw away
his important manner with the end of his cigarette. He
could never maintain the lofty pose for more than five
minutes at a time.

" You're *right*, Deacon," he said, nodding his head
with splurging sincerity. " I mean to have a demned
good holiday. One's glad to get back to the old place
after six months in Edinburgh."

" Atweel," said the Deacon. " But, man, have you
tried the new whisky at the Black Bull ?—I thaw ye
in wi' Pate Wylie. It'th extr'ornar gude—thaft as the
thang o' a mavis on a nicht at e'en, and fiery as a Highland charge."—It was not in character for the Deacon
to say such a thing, but whisky makes the meanest of
Scots poetical. He elevates the manner to the matter,
and attains the perfect style.—" But no doubt," the
cunning old prier went on, with a smiling suavity in
his voice—" but no doubt a man who knowth Edinburgh
tho well as you will have a favourite blend of hith own.
I notice that University men have a fine taste in thpirits."

" I generally prefer ' Kinblythmont's Cure,' " said
Gourlay, with the air of a connoisseur. " But ' Ander-
son's Sting o' Delight ' 's very good, and so's ' Balsillie's
Brig o' the Mains.' "

" Ay," said the Deacon. " Ay, ay ! ' Brig o' the
Mains ' ith what Jock Allan drinks. He'll pree noathing
else. I dare thay you thee a great deal of him in Embro."

" Oh, every week," swaggered Gourlay. " We're
always together, he and I."

" Alwayth thegither ! " said the Deacon.

It was not true that Allan and Gourlay were together
at all times. Allan was kind to Jean Richmond's son

(in his own ruinous way), but not to the extent of being burdened with the cub half a dozen times a week. Gourlay was merely boasting—as young blades are apt to do of acquaintance with older roisterers. They think it makes them seem men of the world. And in his desire to vaunt his comradeship with Allan, John failed to see that Allardyce was scooping him out like an oyster.

"Ay man," resumed the Deacon; "he's a hearty fellow, Jock. No doubt you have the great thprees?"

"Sprees!" gurgled Gourlay, and flung back his head with a laugh. "I should think we have. There was a great foy at Allan's the night before I left Edinburgh. Tarmillan was there—d'ye know, yon's the finest fellow I ever met in my life!—and Bauldy Logan—he's another great chap. Then there was Armstrong and Gillespie—great friends of mine, and damned clever fellows they are, too, I can tell you. Besides us three there were half a dozen more from the College. You should have heard the talk! And every man-jack was as drunk as a lord. The last thing I remember is some of us students dancing round a lamp-post while Logan whistled a jig."

Though Gourlay the elder hated the Deacon, he had never warned his son to avoid him. To have said "Allardyce is dangerous" would have been to pay the old malignant too great a compliment; it would have been beneath John Gourlay to admit that a thing like Allardyce could harm him and his. Young Gourlay, therefore, when once set agoing by the Deacon's deft management, blurted everything without a hanker. Even so, however, he felt that he had gone too far. He glanced anxiously at his companion. "Mum's the word about this, of course," he said with a wink. "It would never do for this to be known about the 'Green Shutters.'"

"Oh, I'm ath thound ath a bell, Dyohn, I'm ath thound ath a bell," said the Deacon. "Ay, man! You jutht bear out what I have alwayth underthood about the men o' brainth. They're the heartiest devilth after a'. Burns, that the baker raves so muckle o', was jutht another o' the thame—jutht another o' the thame. We'll be hearing o' you boys—Pate Wylie and you and a wheen mair—having rare ploys in Barbie through the thummer."

" Oh, we'll kick up a bit of a dust," Gourlay sniggered, well pleased. Had not the Deacon ranked him in the robustious great company of Burns! " I say, Deacon, come in and have a nip."

" There's your faither," grinned the Deacon.

" Eh ? what ? " cried Gourlay in alarm, and started round, to see his father and the Rev. Mr. Struthers advancing up the Fechars Road. " Eh—eh—Deacon— I—I'll see you again about the nip."

" Jutht tho," grinned the Deacon. " We'll post- pone the drink to a more convenient opportunity."

He toddled away, having no desire that old Gourlay should find him talking to his son. If Gourlay sus- pected him of pulling the young fellow's leg, likely as not he would give an exhibition of his demned unpleasant manners.

Gourlay and the minister came straight towards the student. Of the Rev. Mr. Struthers it may be said with truth that he would have cut a remarkable figure in any society. He had big splay feet, short stout legs, and a body of such bulging bulbosity that all the droppings of his spoon—which were many—were caught on the round of his black waistcoat, which always looked as if it had just been spattered by a gray shower. His eyebrows were bushy and white, and the hairs slanting up and out rendered the meagre brow even narrower than it was. His complexion, more especially in cold weather, was a dark crimson. The purply colour of his face was inten- sified by the pure whiteness of the side whiskers project- ing stiffly by his ears, and in mid-week, when he was unshaven, his redness revealed more plainly, in turn, the short gleaming stubble that lay like rime on his chin. His eyes goggled, and his manner at all times was that of a staring and earnest self - importance. " Puffy Importance " was one of his nicknames.

Struthers was a man of lowly stock who, after a ten years' desperate battle with his heavy brains, succeeded at the long last of it in passing the examinations required for the ministry. The influence of a wealthy patron then presented him to Barbie. Because he had taken so long to get through the University himself, he constantly magnified the place in his conversation, partly to excuse his own slowness in getting through it, partly that the greater glory might redound on him who had conquered it at last, and issued from its portals a fat and prosperous alumnus. Stupid men who have mastered a system, not by intuition but by a plodding effort of slow years, always exaggerate its importance—did it not take them ten years to understand it ? Whoso has passed the system, then, is to their minds one of a close corporation, of a select and intellectual few, and entitled to pose before the uninitiate. Because their stupidity made the thing difficult, their vanity leads them o exalt it. Woe to him that shall scoff at any detail ! To Struthers the Senatus Academicus was an august assemblage worthy of the Roman Curia, and each petty academic rule was a law sacrosanct and holy. He was for ever talking of the " Univairsity." " Mind ye," he would say, " it takes a long time to understand even the workings of the Univairsity—the Senatus and such-like ; it's not for every one to criticize." He implied, of course, that he had a right to criticize, having passed triumphant through the mighty test. This vanity of his was fed by a peculiar vanity of some Scots peasants, who like to discuss Divinity Halls, and so on, because to talk of these things shows that they too are intelligent men, and know the awful intellectual ordeal required of a " Meenister." When a peasant says, " He went through his

Arts course in three years, and got a kirk the moment
he was licensed," he wants you to see that he's a smart
man himself, and knows what he's talking of. There
were several men in Barbie who liked to talk in that
way, and among them Puffy Importance, when graciously inclined, found ready listeners to his pompous
blether about the "Univairsity." But what he liked
best of all was to stop a newly-returned student in full
view of the people, and talk learnedly of his courses—
dear me, ay—of his courses, and his matriculations,
and his lectures, and his graduations, and his thingum-
bobs. That was why he bore down upon our great
essayist.

"Allow me to congratulate you, John," he said, with
heavy solemnity; for Struthers always made a congre-
gation of his listener, and droned as if mounted for a
sermon. "Ye have done excellently well this session;
ye have indeed. Ex - cellently well — ex - cellently
well!"

Gourlay blushed and thanked him.

"Tell me now," said the cleric, "do you mean to take
your Arts course in three years or four? A loang Arts
course is a grand thing for a clairgyman. Even if he
spends half a dozen years on't he won't be wasting his
time!"

Gourlay glanced at his father. "I mean to try't in
three," he said. His father had threatened him that
he must get through his Arts in three years—without
deigning, of course, to give any reason for the threat.

"We-ell," said Mr. Struthers, gazing down the Fechars
Road, as if visioning great things, "it will require a
strenuous and devoted application—a strenuous and
devoted application—even from the man of abeelity
you have shown yourself to be. Tell me now," he
went on, "have ye heard ainything of the new Professor of Exegesis? D'ye know how he's doing?"

Young Gourlay knew nothing of the new Professor

of Exegesis, but he answered, " Very well, I believe,"
at a venture.

" Oh, he's sure to do well, he's sure to do well ! He's
one of the best men we have in the Church. I have
just finished his book on the Epheesians. It's most pro-
found ! It has taken me a whole year to master it."
(" Garvie on the Ephesiàns " is a book of a hundred and
eighty pages.) " And, by the way," said the parson,
stooping to Scotch in his ministerial jocoseness, " how's
auld Tam, in whose class you were a prize-winner ? He
was appointed to the professoriate the same year that
I obtained my licence. I remember to have heard him
deliver a lecture on German philosophy, and I thought
it excellently good. But perhaps," he added, with
solemn and pondering brows—" perhaps he was a little
too fond of Hegel. Yess, I am inclined to think that
he was a little too fond of Hegel." Mrs. Eccles, listening from the Black Bull door, wondered if Hegel was a
drink.

" He's very popular," said young Gourlay.

" Oh, he's sure to be popular ; he merits the very
greatest popple-arity. And he would express himself as
being excellently well pleased with your theme ? What
did he say of it, may I venture to inquire ? "

Beneath the pressure of his father's presence young
Gourlay did not dare to splurge. " He seemed to think
there was something in it," he answered, modestly
enough.

" Oh, he would be sure to think there was something
in it," said the minister, staring, and wagging his pow.
" Not a doubt of tha-at, not a doubt of tha-at ! There
must have been something in it to obtain the palm of
victory in the face of such prodigious competeetion.
It's the see-lect intellect of Scotland that goes to the
Univairsity, and only the ee-lect of the see-lect win the
palm. And it's an augury of great good for the future.
Abeelity to write is a splendid thing for the Church.

Good-bye, John, and allow me to express once moar my great satisfaction that a pareeshioner of mine is a la-ad of such brilliant promise ! "

Though the elder Gourlay disconsidered the Church, and thought little of Mr. Struthers, he swelled with pride to think that the minister should stop his offspring in the Main Street of Barbie, to congratulate him on his prospects. They were close to the Emporium, and with the tail of his eye he could see Wilson peeping from the door and listening to every word. This would be a hair in Wilson's neck ! There were no clerical compliments for *his* son ! The tables were turned at last.

His father had a generous impulse to John for the bright triumph he had won the Gourlays. He fumbled in his trouser pocket, and passed him a sovereign.

" I'm kind o' hard-up," he said, with grim jocosity, " but there's a pound to keep your pouch. No nonsense now ! " he shot at the youth with a loaded eye. " That's just for use if you happen to be in company. A Gourlay maun spend as much as the rest o' folk."

" Yes, faither," said the youngster, and Gourlay went away.

That grimly-jocose reference to his poverty was a feature of Gourlay's talk now, when he spoke of money to his family. It excused the smallness of his doles, yet led them to believe that he was only joking—that he had plenty of money if he would only consent to shell it out. And that was what he wished them to believe. His pride would not allow him to confess, even to his nearest, that he was a failure in business, and hampered with financial trouble. Thus his manner of warning them to be careful had the very opposite effect. " He has heaps o' cash," thought the son, as he watched the father up the street ; " there's no need for a fellow to be mean."

Flattered (as he fondly imagined) by the Deacon, flattered by the minister, tipped by his mother, tipped by his father, hail-fellow-well-met with Pate Wylie—Lord,

but young Gourlay was the fine fellow! Symptoms of
swell-head set in with alarming rapidity. He had a wild
tendency to splurge. And, that he might show in a
single afternoon all the crass stupidity of which he was
capable, he immediately allowed himself a veiled insult
towards the daughters of the ex-Provost. They were
really nice girls, in spite of their parentage, and as they
came down the street they glanced with shy kindness
at the student from under their broad-brimmed hats.
Gourlay raised his in answer to their nod. But the
moment after, and in their hearing, he yelled blatantly
to Swipey Broon to come on and have a drink of beer.
Swipey was a sweep now, for Brown the ragman had
added chimney-cleaning to his other occupations—plu-
rality of professions, you observe, being one of the features of the life of Barbie. When Swipey turned out of
the Fleckie Road he was as black as the ace of spades,
a most disreputable phiz. And when Gourlay yelled
his loud welcome to that grimy object, what he wanted to
convey to the two girls was: " Ho, ho, my pretty misses,
I'm on bowing terms with you, and yet when I might go
up and speak to ye, I prefer to go off and drink with a
sweep, d'ye see ? That shows what I think o' ye! "
All that summer John took an oblique revenge on those
who had disconsidered the Gourlays, but would have
liked to make up to him now when they thought he was
going to do well—he took a paltry revenge by patently
rejecting their advances and consorting instead, and in
their presence, with the lowest of low company. Thus
he vented a spite which he had long cherished against
them for their former neglect of Janet and him. For
though the Gourlay children had been welcome at well-
to-do houses in the country, their father's unpopularity
had cut them off from the social life of the town. When
the Provost gave his grand spree on Hogmanay there
was never an invitation for the Gourlay youngsters.
The slight had rankled in the boy's mind. Now, how-

ever, some of the local bigwigs had an opinion (with
very little to support it) that he was going to be a successful man, and they showed a disposition to be friendly.
John, with a rankling memory of their former coldness,
flouted every overture, by letting them see plainly that
he preferred to their company that of Swipey Broon,
Jock M'Craw, and every ragamuffin of the town. It
was a kind of back-handed stroke at them. That was
the paltry form which his father's pride took in him.
He did not see that he was harming himself rather than
his father's enemies. Harm himself he did, for you
could not associate with Jock M'Craw and the like
without drinking in every howff you came across.

When the bodies assembled next day for their " morning," the Deacon was able to inform them that young
Gourlay was back from the College, dafter than ever, and
that he had pulled his leg as far as he wanted it. " Oh,"
he said, " I played him like a kitten wi' a cork, and
found out ainything and everything I wished. I dith-
covered that he's in wi' Jock Allan and that crowd—
I edged the conversation round on purpoth! Unless
he wath blowing his trump—which I greatly doubt—
they're as thick as thieveth. Ye ken what that meanth.
He'll turn hith wee finger to the ceiling oftener than he
puts hith forefinger to the pen, I'm thinking. It theemth
he drinkth enormuth! He took a gey nip last thummer,
and this thummer I wager he takes mair o't. He avowed
his plain intention. ' I mean to kick up a bit of a dust,'
thays he. Oh, but he's the splurge ! "

" Ay, ay," said Sandy Toddle ; " thae students are
a gey squad—especially the young ministers."

" Ou," said Tam Wylie, " dinna be hard on the ministers. Ministers are just like the rest o' folk. They
mind me o' last year's early tatties. They're grand
when they're gude, but the feck o' them's frostit."

" Ay," said the Deacon, " and young Gourlay's frostit
in the shaw already. I doubt it'll be a poor ingathering."

"Weel, weel," said Tam Wylie, "the mair's the pity o' that, Deacon."

"Oh, it'th a grai-ait pity," said the Deacon, and he bowed his body solemnly with outspread hands. "No doubt it'th a grai-ait pity!" and he wagged his head from side to side, the picture of a poignant woe.

"I saw him in the Black Bull yestreen," said Brodie, who had been silent hitherto in utter scorn of the lad they were speaking of—too disgusted to open his mouth. "He was standing drinks to a crowd that were puffing him up about that prize o' his."

"It's alwayth the numskull hath the most conceit," said the Deacon.

"And yet there must be something in him too, to get that prize," mused the ex-Provost.

"A little ability's a dangerous thing," said Johnny Coe, who could think at times. "To be safe you should be a genius winged and flying, or a crawling thing that never leaves the earth. It's the half-and-half that hell gapes for. And owre they flap."

But nobody understood him. "Drink and vanity'll soon make end of *him*," said Brodie curtly, and snubbed the philosopher.

Before the summer holiday was over (it lasts six months in Scotland) young Gourlay was a habit-and-repute tippler. His shrinking abhorrence from the scholastic life of Edinburgh flung him with all the greater abandon into the conviviality he had learned to know at home. His mother (who always seemed to sit up now, after Janet and Gourlay were in bed) often let him in during the small hours, and as he hurried past her in the lobby he would hold his breath lest she should smell it. "You're unco late, dear," she would say wearily, but no other reproach did she utter. "I was taking a walk," he would answer thickly; "there's a fine moon!" It was true that when his terrible depression seized him he was sometimes tempted to seek

the rapture and peace of a moonlight walk upon the
Fleckie Road. In his crude clay there was a vein of
poetry : he could be alone in the country, and not lonely ;
had he lived in a green quiet place, he might have
learned the solace of nature for the wounded when eve
sheds her spiritual dews. But the mean pleasures to be
found at the Cross satisfied his nature, and stopped him
midway to that soothing beauty of the woods and
streams which might have brought healing and a wise
quiescence. His success—such as it was—had gained
him a circle—such as it was—and the assertive nature
proper to his father's son gave him a kind of lead amongst
them. Yet even his henchmen saw through his swaggering. Swipey Broon turned on him one night, and
threatened to split his mouth, and he went as white as
the wall behind him.

Among his other follies, he assumed the pose of a man
who could an he would—who had it in him to do great
things, if he would only set about them. In this he was
partly playing up to a foolish opinion of his more ignorant associates ; it was they who suggested the pose to
him. " Devilish clever ! " he heard them whisper one
night as he stood in the door of a tavern ; " he could do
it if he liked, only he's too fond o' the fun." Young
Gourlay flushed where he stood in the darkness—flushed
with pleasure at the criticism of his character which was,
nevertheless, a compliment to his wits. He felt that he
must play up at once to the character assigned him.
" Ho, ho, my lads ! " he cried, entering with a splurge ;
" let's make a night o't. I should be working for my
degree to-night, but I suppose I can get it easy enough
when the time comes." " What did I tell ye ? " said
M'Craw, nudging an elbow ; and Gourlay saw the nudge.
Here at last he had found the sweet seduction of a
proper pose—that of a *grand homme manqué*, of a man
who would be a genius were it not for the excess of his
qualities. Would he continue to appear a genius, then

he must continue to display that excess which—so he
wished them to believe—alone prevented his brilliant
achievements. It was all a curious, vicious inversion.
" You could do great things if you didn't drink," crooned
the fools. " See how I drink," Gourlay seemed to answer; " that is why I don't do great things. But,
mind you, I could do them were it not for this." Thus
every glass he tossed off seemed to hint in a roundabout
way at the glorious heights he might attain if he didn't
drink it. His very roistering became a pose, and his
vanity made him roister the more, to make the pose
more convincing.

CHAPTER XXI.

On a beautiful evening in September, when a new crescent moon was pointing through the saffron sky like the lit tip of a finger, the City Fathers had assembled at the corner of the Fleckie Road. Though the moon was peeping, the dying glory of the day was still upon the town. The white smoke rose straight and far in the golden mystery of the heavens, and a line of dark roofs, transfigured against the west, wooed the eye to musing. But though the bodies felt the fine evening bathe them in a sensuous content, as they smoked and dawdled, they gave never a thought to its beauty. For there had been a blitheness in the town that day, and every other man seemed to have been preeing the demijohn.

Drucken Wabster and Brown the ragman came round the corner, staggering.

"Young Gourlay's drunk!" blurted Wabster—and reeled himself as he spoke.

"Is he a wee fou?" said the Deacon eagerly.

"Wee be damned," said Wabster; "he's as fou as the Baltic Sea! If you wait here, you'll be sure to see him! He'll be round the corner directly."

"De-ar me, is he so bad as that?" said the ex-Provost, raising his hands in solemn reprobation. He raised his eyes to heaven at the same time, as if it pained them to look on a world that endured the burden of a young Gourlay. "In broad daylight, too!" he sighed. "De-ar me, has he come to this?"

" Yis, Pravast," hiccupped Brown, " he has ! He's as phull of drink as a whelk-shell's phull of whelk. He's nearly as phull as meself—and begorra, that's mighty phull." He stared suddenly, scratching his head solemnly as if the fact had just occurred to him. Then he winked.

" You could set fire to his braith ! " cried Wabster. " A match to his mouth would send him in a lowe."

" A living gas jet ! " said Brown.

They staggered away, sometimes rubbing shoulders as they lurched together, sometimes with the road between them.

" I kenned young Gourlay was on the fuddle when I saw him swinging off this morning in his greatcoat," cried Sandy Toddle. " There was debauch in the flap o' the tails o't."

" Man, have you noticed that too ! " cried another eagerly. " He's aye warst wi' the coat on ! "

" Clothes undoubtedly affect the character," said Johnny Coe. " It takes a gentleman to wear a lordly coat without swaggering."

" There's not a doubt o' tha-at ! " approved the baker, who was merry with his day's carousal ; " there's not a doubt o' tha-at ! Claes affect the disposeection. I mind when I was a young chap I had a grand pair o' breeks— Wull I ca'ed them—unco decent breeks they were, I mind, lang and swankie like a ploughman ; and I aye thocht I was a tremendous honest and hamely fallow when I had them on ! And I had a verra disreputable hat," he added—" Rab I christened him, for he was a perfect devil—and I never cocked him owre my lug on nichts at e'en but ' Baker ! ' he seemed to whisper, ' Baker ! Let us go out and do a bash ! ' And we generally went."

" You're a wonderful man ! " piped the Deacon.

" We may as well wait and see young Gourlay going by," said the ex-Provost. " He'll likely be a sad spectacle."

" Ith auld Gourlay on the thtreet the nicht ? " cried
the Deacon eagerly. " I wonder will he thee the youngster afore he gets hame ! Eh, man "—he bent his knees
with staring delight—" eh, man, if they would only
meet forenenst uth ! Hoo ! "

" He's a regular waster," said Brodie. " When a silly
young blood takes a fancy to a girl in a public-house
he's always done for; I've observed it times without
number. At first he lets on that he merely gangs in
for a drink ; what he really wants, however, is to see the
girl. Even if he's no great toper to begin with, he must
show himself fond o' the dram, as a means of getting to
his jo. Then, before he kens where he is, the habit
has gripped him. That's a gate mony a ane gangs."

" That's verra true, now that ye mention't," gravely
assented the ex-Provost. His opinion of Brodie's
sagacity, high already, was enhanced by the remark.
" Indeed, that's verra true. But how does't apply to
young Gourlay in particular, Thomas ? Is *he* after
some damsel o' the gill-stoup ? "

" Ou ay—he's ta'en a fancy to yon bit shilp in the
bar-room o' the Red Lion. He's always hinging owre
the counter talking till her, a cigarette dropping from
his face, and a half-fu' tumbler at his elbow. When a
young chap takes to hinging round bars, ae elbow on
the counter and a hand on his other hip, I have verra
bad brows o' him always—verra bad brows, indeed. Oh
—oh, young Gourlay's just a goner ! a goner, sirs—a
goner ! "

" Have ye heard about him at the Skeighan Fair ? "
said Sandy Toddle.

" No, man," said Brodie, bowing down and keeking
at Toddle in his interest ; " I hadna heard about tha-at !
Is this a *new* thing ? "

" Oh, just at the fair ; the other day, ye know ! "

" Ay, man, Sandy ! " said big Brodie, stooping down to
Toddle to get near the news; " and what was it, Sandy ? "

" Ou, just drinking, ye know, wi'—wi' Swipey Broon
—and, eh, and that M'Craw, ye know—and Sandy Hull
—and a wheen mair o' that kind—ye ken the kind ; a
verra bad lot ! " said Sandy, and wagged a disapproving
pow.   " Here they all got as drunk as drunk could be, and
started fighting wi' the colliers !   Young Gourlay got a
bloodied nose !   Then nothing would serve him but he
must drive back wi' young Pin-oe, who was even drunker
than himsell.   They drave at sic a rate that when they
dashed from this side o' Skeighan Drone the stour o'
their career was rising at the far end.   They roared and
sang till it was a perfect affront to God's day, and frae
sidie to sidie they swung till the splash-brods were
skreighing on the wheels.   At a quick turn o' the road
they wintled owre ; and there they were, sitting on their
doups in the atoms o' the gig, and glowering frae them !
When young Gourlay slid hame at dark he was in such
a state that his mother had to hide him frae the auld
man.   She had that, puir body !   The twa women were
obliged to carry the drunk lump to his bedroom—and
yon lassie far ga'en in consumption, too, they tell me !
Ou, he was in a perfectly awful condition — perfectly
awful ! "

" Ay, man," nodded Brodie.   " I hadna heard o't.
Curious that I didna hear o' that ! "

" It was Drucken Wabster's wife that telled it. There's
not a haet that happens at the Gourlays but she clypes.
I speired her mysell, and she says young Gourlay has a
black eye."

" Ay, ay ; there'th thmall hope for the Gourlayth
in *him !* " said the Deacon.

" How do *you* ken ? " cried the baker.   " He's no the
first youngster I've seen the wiseacres o' the world wagging their sagacious pows owre ; and, eh, but he was *this*
waster !—according to their way of it—and, oh, but he
was the *other* waster ! and, ochonee, but he was the *wild*
fellow.   And a' the while they werena fit to be his door-

mat ; for it was only the fire in the ruffian made him seem sae daft."

"True !" said the ex-Provost, "true ! Still there's a decency in daftness. And there's no decency in young Gourlay. He's just a mouth ! 'Start canny, and you'll steer weel,' my mother used to say ; but he has started unco ill, and he'll steer to ruin."

"Dinna spae ill-fortune !" said the baker, "dinna spae ill-fortune ! And never despise a youngster for a random start. It's the blood makes a breenge."

"Well, I like young men to be quiet," said Sandy Toddle. "I would rather have them a wee soft than rollickers."

"Not I !" said the baker. "If I had a son, I would rather an ill deil sat forenenst me at the table than parratch in a poke. Burns (God rest his banes !) struck the he'rt o't. Ye mind what he said o' Prince Geordie :

> ' Yet mony a ragged cowte's been known
>   To mak a noble aiver ;
> And ye may doucely fill a throne,
>   For a' their clishmaclaver.
> There him at Agincourt wha shone,
>   Few better were or braver ;
> And yet wi' funny queer Sir John
>   He was an unco shaver
>   For mony a day.'

Dam't, but Burns is gude."

"Huts, man, dinna sweer sae muckle !" frowned the old Provost.

"Ou, there's waur than an oath now and than," said the baker. "Like spice in a bun it lends a briskness. But it needs the hearty manner wi't. The Deacon there couldna let blatter wi' a hearty oath to save his withered sowl. I kenned a trifle o' a fellow that got in among a jovial gang lang syne that used to sweer tremendous, and he bude to do the same the bit bodie ; so he used to say 'Dim it !' in a wee, sma voice that was clean rideec'lous. He was a lauchable dirt, that."

"What was his name?" said Sandy Toddle.

"Your ain," said the baker. (To tell the truth, he was gey fou.) "Alexander Toddle was his name: '*Dim it!*' he used to squeak, for he had been a Scotch cuddy in the Midlands, and whiles he used the English. '*Dim it!*' said he. I like a man that says '*Dahm't.*'"

"Ay; but then, you thee, *you*'re an artitht in wordth," said the Deacon.

"Ye're an artist in spite," said the baker.

"Ah, well," said the ex-Provost, "Burns proved to be wrang in the end o't, and you'll maybe be the same. George the Fort' didna fill the throne verra doucely for a' their clishmaclaver, and I don't think young Gourlay'll fill the pulpit verra doucely for a' ours. For he's saftie and daftie baith, and that's the deidly combination. At least, that's my opinion," quoth he, and smacked his lips, the important man.

"Tyuts," said the baker, "folk should be kind to folk. There may be a possibeelity for the Gourlays in the youngster yet!"

He would have said more, but at that moment his sonsy big wife came out, with oh, such a roguish and kindly smile, and, "Tom, Tom," said she, "what are ye havering here for? C'way in, man, and have a dish o' tea wi' me!"

He glanced up at her with comic shrewdness from where he sat on his hunkers—for fine he saw through her—and "Ou ay," said he, "ye great muckle fat hotch o' a dacent bodie, ye—I'll gang in and have a dish o' tea wi' ye." And away went the fine fuddled fellow.

"She's a wise woman that," said the ex-Provost, looking after them. "She kenned no to flyte, and he went like a lamb."

"I believe he'th feared o' her," snapped the Deacon, "or he wudny-un went thae lamb-like!"

"Leave him alone!" said Johnny Coe, who had been

drinking too. " He's the only kind heart in Barbie.
And Gourlay's the only gentleman."

" Gentleman ! " cried Sandy Toddle. " Lord save us !
Auld Gourlay a gentleman ! "

" Yes, gentleman ! " said Johnny, to whom the drink
gave a courage. " Brute, if ye like, but aristocrat frae
scalp to heel. If he had brains, and a dacent wife, and
a bigger field—oh, man," said Johnny, visioning the
possibility, " Auld Gourla could conquer the world, if
he swalled his neck till't."

" It would be a big conquest that ! " said the Deacon.
—" Here comes his son, taking his ain share o' the earth,
at ony rate."

Young Gourlay came staggering round the corner,
" a little sprung " (as they phrase it in Barbie), but not
so bad as they had hoped to see him. Webster and the
ragman had exaggerated the condition of their fellow-
toper. Probably their own oscillation lent itself to
everything they saw. John zigzagged, it is true, but
otherwise he was fairly steady on his pins. Unluckily,
however, failing to see a stone before on the road, he
tripped, and went sprawling on his hands and knees.
A titter went.

" What the hell are you laughing at ? " he snarled,
leaping up, quick to feel the slight, blatant to resent it.

" Tyuts, man," Tam Wylie rebuked him in a careless
scorn.

With a parting scowl he went swaggering up the
street.

" Ay," said Toddle dryly, " that's the Gourlay possibeelity."

CHAPTER XXII.

" AHA, Deacon, my old cock, here you are ! " The speaker smote the Deacon between his thin shoulder-blades till the hat leapt on his startled cranium. " No, not a lengthy stay—just down for a flying visit to see my little girl. Dem'd glad to get back to town again— Barbie's too quiet for my tastes. No life in the place, no life at all ! "

The speaker was Davie Aird, draper and buck. " No life at all," he cried, as he shot down his cuffs with a jerk, and swung up and down the bar-room of the Red Lion. He was dressed in a long fawn overcoat reaching to his heels, with two big yellow buttons at the waist behind, in the most approved fashion of the horsy. He paused in his swaggering to survey the backs of his long white delicate hands, holding them side by side before him, as if to make sure they were the same size. He was letting the Deacon see his ring. Then pursing his chin down, with a fastidious and critical regard, he picked a long fair hair off his left coat sleeve. He held it high as he had seen them do on the stage of the Theatre Royal. " Sweet souvenir ! " he cried, and kissed it, " most dear remembrance ! "

The Deacon fed on the sight. The richness of his satiric perception was too great to permit of speech. He could only gloat and be dumb.

" Waiting for Jack Gourlay," Aird rattled again. " He's off to College again, and we're driving in his father's trap to meet the express at Skeighan Station.

Wonder what's keeping the fellow. I like a man to be punctual. Business training, you see ; yes, by Gad, two thousand parcels a week go out of our place, and all of 'em up to time ! Ah, there he is," he added, as the harsh grind of wheels was heard on the gravel at the door. " Thank God, we'll soon be in civilization."

Young Gourlay entered, greatcoated and lordly, through the two halves of that easy-swinging door.

" Good ! " he cried. " Just a minute, Aird, till I get my flask filled."

" My weapon's primed and ready," Aird ha-haed, and slapped the breast pocket of his coat.

John birled a bright sovereign on the counter, one of twenty old Gourlay had battered his brains to get together for the boy's expenses. The young fellow rattled the change into his trouser pocket like a master of millions.

The Deacon and another idler or two gathered about the steps in the darkness, to see that royal going off. Peter Riney's bunched-up little old figure could be seen on the front seat of the gig ; Aird was already mounted behind. The mare (a worthy successor to Spanking Tam) pawed the gravel and fretted in impatience ; her sharp ears, seen pricked against the gloom, worked to and fro. A widening cone of light shone out from the leftward lamp of the gig, full on a glistering laurel, which Simpson had growing by his porch. Each smooth leaf of the green bush gave back a separate gleam, vivid to the eye in that pouring yellowness. Gourlay stared at the bright evergreen, and forget for a moment where he was. His lips parted, and—as they saw in the light from the door—his look grew dreamy and far-away.

The truth was that all the impressions of a last day at home were bitten in on his brain as by acid, in the very middle of his swaggering gusto. That gusto was largely real, true, for it seemed a fine thing to go splurging off to College in a gig; but it was still more largely assumed, to combat the sorrow of departure. His heart was in his boots at the thought of going back to accursed Edinburgh—to those lodgings, those dreary, damnable lodgings. Thus his nature was reduced to its real elements in the hour of leaving home; it was only for a swift moment he forgot to splurge, but for that moment the cloak of his swaggering dropped away, and he was his naked self, morbidly alive to the impressions of the world, afraid of life, clinging to the familiar and the known. That was why he gazed with wistful eyes at that laurel clump, so vivid in the pouring rays. So vivid there, it stood for all the dear country round which was now hidden by the darkness; it centred his world among its leaves. It was a last picture of loved Barbie that was fastening on his mind. There would be fine gardens in Edinburgh, no doubt; but oh, that couthie laurel by the Red Lion door! It was his friend; he had known it always.

The spell lasted but a moment, one of those moments searching a man's nature to its depths, yet flitting like a lonely shadow on the autumn wheat. But Aird was already fidgeting. "Hurry up, Jack," he cried; "we'll need to pelt if we mean to get the train."

Gourlay started. In a moment he had slipped from one self to another, and was the blusterer once more. "Right!" he splurged. "Hover a blink till I light my cigar."

He was not in the habit of smoking cigars, but he had bought a packet on purpose, that he might light one before his admiring onlookers ere he went away. Nothing like cutting a dash.

He was seen puffing for a moment with indrawn cheeks, his head to one side, the flame of the flickering vesta lighting up his face, his hat pushed back till it rested on his collar, his fair hair hanging down his brow. Then he sprang to the driving seat and gathered up the reins. "Ta-ta, Deacon ; see and behave your-self ! " he flung across his shoulder, and they were off with a bound.

" Im-pidenth ! " said the outraged Deacon.

Peter Riney was quite proud to have the honour of driving two such bucks to the station. It lent him a consequence ; he would be able to say when he came back that he had been " awa wi' the young mester "— for Peter said " mester," and was laughed at by the Barbie wits who knew that " maister " was the proper English. The splurging twain rallied him and drew him out in talk, passed him their flasks at the Brownie's Brae, had him tee-heeing at their nonsense. It was a full-blooded night to the withered little man.

That was how young Gourlay left Barbie for what was to prove his last session at the University.

*　　*　　*　　*　　*　　*

All Gourlay's swankie chaps had gone with the going of his trade ; only Peter Riney, the queer little oddity, remained. There was a loyal simplicity in Peter which never allowed him to question the Gourlays. He had been too long in their service to be of use to any other ; while there was a hand's turn to be done about the House with the Green Shutters he was glad to have the chance of doing it. His respect for his surly tyrant was as great as ever ; he took his pittance of a wage and was thankful. Above all he worshipped young Gour-lay ; to be in touch with a College-bred man was a re-flected glory ; even the escapades noised about the little town, to his gleeful ignorance, were the signs of a man of the world. Peter chuckled when he heard them talked of. " Terr'ble clever fallow, the young mester ! " the bowed little man would say, sucking his pipe of an evening, " terr'ble clever fallow, the young mester ; and hardy, too — infernal hardy ! " Loyal Peter be-lieved it.

But ere four months had gone Peter was discharged.

It was on the day after Gourlay sold Black Sally, the mare, to get a little money to go on with.

It was a bright spring day, of enervating softness; a fosie day—a day when the pores of everything seemed opened. People's brains felt pulpy, and they sniffed as with winter's colds. Peter Riney was opening a pit of potatoes in the big garden, shovelling aside the foot-deep mould, and tearing off the inner covering of yellow straw—which seemed strange and unnatural, somehow, when suddenly revealed in its glistening dryness, beneath the moist dark earth. Little crumbles of mould trickled down, in among the flattened shining straws. In a tree near Peter two pigeons were gurgling and *rookety-cooing*, mating for the coming year. He fell to sorting out the potatoes, throwing the bad ones on a heap aside—" tattie-walin'," as they call it in the north. The enervating softness was at work on Peter's head, too, and from time to time, as he waled, he wiped his nose on his sleeve.

Gourlay watched him for a long time without speaking. Once or twice he moistened his lips, and cleared his throat, and frowned, as one who would broach unpleasant news. It was not like him to hesitate. But the old man, encased in senility, was ill to disturb; he was intent on nothing but the work before him; it was mechanical and soothing, and occupied his whole mind. Gourlay, so often the trampling brute without knowing it, felt it brutal to wound the faithful old creature dreaming at his toil. He would have found it much easier to discharge a younger and a keener man.

" Stop, Peter," he said at last; " I don't need you ainy more."

Peter rose stiffly from his knees and shook the mould with a pitiful gesture from his hands. His mouth was fallen slack, and showed a few yellow tusks.

" Eh ? " he asked vaguely. The thought that he must leave the Gourlays could not penetrate his mind.

" I don't need you ainy more," said Gourlay again, and met his eye steadily.

" I'm gey auld," said Peter, still shaking his hands with that pitiful gesture, " but I only need a bite and a sup. Man, I'm willin' to tak onything."

" It's no that," said Gourlay sourly—" it's no that. But I'm giving up the business."

Peter said nothing, but gazed away down the garden, his sunken mouth forgetting to munch its straw, which dangled by his chin. " I'm an auld servant," he said at last, " and, mind ye," he flashed in pride, " I'm a true ane."

" Oh, you're a' that," Gourlay grunted ; " you have been a good servant."

" It'll be the poorhouse, it's like," mused Peter. " Man, have ye noathing for us to do ? " he asked pleadingly.

Gourlay's jaw clamped. " Noathing, Peter," he said sullenly, " noathing ; " and slipped some money into Peter's heedless palm.

Peter stared stupidly down at the coins. He seemed dazed. " Ay, weel," he said ; " I'll feenish the tatties, at ony rate."

" No, no, Peter," and Gourlay gripped him by the shoulder as he turned back to his work—" no, no ; I have no right to keep you. Never mind about the money ; you deserve something, going so suddenly after sic a long service. It's just a bit present to mind you o'—to mind you o'—" he broke suddenly and scowled across the garden.

Some men, when a feeling touches them, express their emotion in tears ; others by an angry scowl—hating themselves inwardly, perhaps, for their weakness in being moved, hating, too, the occasion that has probed their weakness. It was because he felt parting with Peter so keenly that Gourlay behaved more sullenly than usual. Peter had been with Gourlay's father in

his present master's boyhood, had always been faithful
and submissive ; in his humble way was nearer the grain
merchant than any other man in Barbie. He was the
only human being Gourlay had ever deigned to joke
with, and that in itself won him an affection. More—
the going of Peter meant the going of everything. It
cut Gourlay to the quick. Therefore he scowled.

Without a word of thanks for the money, Peter
knocked the mould off his heavy boots, striking one
against the other clumsily, and shuffled away across the
bare soil. But when he had gone twenty yards he
stopped, and came back slowly. " Good-bye, sir," he
said with a rueful smile, and held out his hand.

Gourlay gripped it. " Good-bye, Peter ! good-bye ;
damn ye, man, good-bye ! "

Peter wondered vaguely why he was sworn at. But
he felt that it was not in anger. He still clung to his
master's hand. " I've been fifty year wi' the Gourlays,"
said he. " Ay, ay ; and this, it seems, is the end o't."

" Oh, gang away ! " cried Gourlay, " gang away,
man ! " And Peter went away.

Gourlay went out to the big green gate where he had
often stood in his pride, and watched his old servant
going down the street. Peter was so bowed that the
back of his velveteen coat was halfway up his spine, and
the bulging pockets at the corners were midway down
his thighs. Gourlay had seen the fact a thousand times,
but it never gripped him before. He stared till Peter
disappeared round the Bend o' the Brae.

" Ay, ay," said he, " ay, ay. There goes the last
o' them."

It was a final run of ill-luck that brought Gourlay to
this desperate pass. When everything seemed to go
against him he tried several speculations, with a gam-
bler's hope that they might do well, and retrieve the
situation. He abandoned the sensible direction of
affairs, that is, and trusted entirely to chance, as men are

apt to do when despairing. And chance betrayed him. He found himself of a sudden at the end of his resources.

Through all his troubles his one consolation was the fact that he had sent John to the University. That was something saved from the wreck, at any rate. More and more, as his other supports fell away, Gourlay attached himself to the future of his son. It became the sheet-anchor of his hopes. If he had remained a prosperous man, John's success would have been merely incidental, something to disconsider in speech, at least, however pleased he might have been at heart. But now it was the whole of life to him. For one thing, the son's success would justify the father's past and prevent it being quite useless; it would have produced a minister, a successful man, one of an esteemed profession. Again, that success would be a salve to Gourlay's wounded pride; the Gourlays would show Barbie they could flourish yet, in spite of their present downcome. Thus, in the collapse of his fortunes, the son grew all-important in the father's eyes. Nor did his own poverty seem to him a just bar to his son's prosperity. " I have put him through his Arts," thought Gourlay ; " surely he can do the rest himsell. Lots of young chaps, when they warstle through their Arts, teach the sons of swells to get a little money to gang through Diveenity. My boy can surely do the like ! " Again and again, as Gourlay felt himself slipping under in the world of Barbie, his hopes turned to John in Edinburgh. If that boy would only hurry up and get through, to make a hame for the lassie and the auld wife !

CHAPTER XXIII.

YOUNG Gourlay spent that winter in Edinburgh pretty much as he had spent the last. Last winter, however, it was simply a weak need for companionship that drew him to the Howff. This winter it was more: it was the need of a formed habit that must have its wonted satisfaction. He had a further impulse to conviviality now. It had become a habit that compelled him.

The diversions of some men are merely subsidiary to their lives, externals easy to be dropped ; with others they usurp the man. They usurp a life when it is never happy away from them, when in the midst of other occupations absent pleasures rise vivid to the mind, with an irresistible call. Young Gourlay's too-seeing imagination, always visioning absent delights, combined with his weakness of will, never gripping to the work before him, to make him hate his lonely studies and long for the jolly company of his friends. He never opened his books of an evening but he thought to himself, " I wonder what they're doing at the Howff to-night ? " At once he visualized the scene, imagined every detail, saw them in their jovial hours. And, seeing them so happy, he longed to be with them. On that night, long ago, when his father ordered him to College, his cowardly and too vivid mind thought of the ploys the fellows would be having along the Barbie roads, while he was mewed up in Edinburgh. He saw the Barbie rollickers in his mind's eye, and the student in his lonely rooms, and contrasted them mournfully. So now, every night, he saw the cosy companions in their Howff, and shivered at his own isolation. He felt a tugging at his heart to be off and join them. And his will was so weak that, nine times out of ten, he made no resistance to the impulse.

He had always a feeling of depression when he must sit down to his books. It was the start that gravelled him. He would look round his room and hate it, mutter " Damn it, I must work ; " and then, with a heavy sigh, would seat himself before an outspread volume on the table, tugging the hair on a puckered forehead. Sometimes the depression left him, when he buckled to his work ; as his mind became occupied with other things the vision of the Howff was expelled. Usually, however, the stiffness of his brains made the reading drag heavily, and he rarely attained the sufficing happiness of a student eager and engrossed. At the end of ten minutes he would be gaping across the table, and wondering what they were doing at the Howff. " Will Logan be singing ' Tam Glen ' ? Or is Gillespie fiddling Highland tunes, by Jing, with his elbow going it merrily ? Lord ! I would like to hear ' Miss Drummond o' Perth ' or ' Gray Daylicht '—they might buck me up a bit. I'll just slip out for ten minutes, to see what they're doing, and be back directly." He came back at two in the morning, staggering.

On a bleak spring evening, near the end of February, young Gourlay had gone to the Howff, to escape the shuddering misery of the streets. It was that treacherous spring weather which blights. Only two days ago the air had been sluggish and balmy ; now an easterly wind nipped the gray city, naked and bare. There was light enough, with the lengthening days, to see plainly the rawness of the world. There were cold yellow gleams in windows fronting a lonely west. Uncertain little puffs of wind came swirling round corners, and

made dust and pieces of dirty white paper gyrate on
the roads.   Prosperous old gentlemen pacing home,
rotund in their buttoned-up coats, had clear drops at
the end of their noses.   Sometimes they stopped—their
trousers legs flapping behind them—and trumpeted
loudly into red silk handkerchiefs.   Young Gourlay
had fled the streets.   It was the kind of night that
made him cower.

By eight o'clock, however, he was merry with the
barley-bree, and making a butt of himself to amuse the
company.   He was not quick-witted enough to banter
a comrade readily, nor hardy enough to essay it un-
provoked ; on the other hand, his swaggering love of
notice impelled him to some form of talk that would
attract attention.   So he made a point of always coming
with daft stories of things comic that befell him—at least,
he said they did.   But if his efforts were greeted with too
loud a roar, implying not only appreciation of the stories,
but also a contempt for the man who could tell them
of himself, his sensitive vanity was immediately wounded,
and he swelled with sulky anger.   And the moment
after he would splurge and bluster to reassert his dignity.

" I remember when I was a boy," he hiccupped, " I
had a pet goose at home."

There was a titter at the queer beginning.

" I was to get the price of it for myself, and so when
Christmas drew near I went to old MacFarlane, the
poulterer in Skeighan.   ' Will you buy a goose ? ' said I.
' Are ye for sale, my man ? ' was his answer."

Armstrong flung back his head and roared, prolonging the loud *ho-ho !* through his big nose and open mouth
long after the impulse to honest laughter was exhausted.
He always laughed with false loudness, to indicate his
own superiority, when he thought a man had been
guilty of a public silliness.   The laugh was meant to
show the company how far above such folly was Mr.
Armstrong.

Gourlay scowled. " Damn Armstrong ! " he thought, " what did he yell like that for ?   Does he think I didn't see the point of the joke against myself ?   Would I have told it if I hadn't ?   This is what comes of being sensitive.   I'm always too sensitive !   I felt there was an awkward silence, and I told a story against myself to dispel it in fun, and this is what I get for't.   Curse the big brute ! he thinks I have given myself away.   But I'll show him ! "

He was already mellow, but he took another swig to hearten him, as was his habit.

" There's a damned sight too much yell about your laugh, Armstrong," he said, truly enough, getting a courage from his anger and the drink.   " No gentleman laughs like that."

" ' Risu inepto res ineptior nulla est,' " said Tarmillan, who was on one of his rare visits to the Howff.   He was too busy and too wise a man to frequent it greatly.

Armstrong blushed ; and Gourlay grew big and brave, in the backing of the great Tarmillan.   He took another swig on the strength of it.   But his resentment was still surging.   When Tarmillan went, and the three students were left by themselves, Gourlay continued to nag and bluster, for that blatant laugh of Armstrong's rankled in his mind.

" I saw Hepburn in the street to-day," said Gillespie, by way of a diversion.

" Who's Hepburn ? " snapped Gourlay.

" Oh, don't you remember ?   He's the big Border chap who got into a row with auld Tam on the day you won your prize essay."   (That should surely appease the fool, thought Gillespie.)   " It was only for the fun of the thing Hepburn was at College, for he has lots of money ; and, here, he never apologized to Tam !   He said he would go down first."

" He was damned right," spluttered Gourlay.   " Some of these profs. think too much of themselves.   They

wouldn't bully *me!* There's good stuff in the Gourlays," he went on with a meaning look at Armstrong ;
" they're not to be scoffed at. I would stand insolence
from no man."

" Ay, man," said Armstrong, " would you face up to
a professor ? "

" Wouldn't I ? " said the tipsy youth ; " and to you,
too, if you went too far."

He became so quarrelsome as the night went on that
his comrades filled him up with drink, in the hope of
deadening his ruffled sensibilities. It was, " Yes, yes,
Jack ; but never mind about that ! Have another
drink, just to show there's no ill-feeling among friends."

When they left the Howff they went to Gillespie's and
drank more, and after that they roamed about the
town. At two in the morning the other two brought
Gourlay to his door. He was assuring Armstrong he
was not a gentleman.

When he went to bed the fancied insult he had suffered
swelled to monstrous proportions in his fevered brain.
Did Armstrong despise him ? The thought was poison !
He lay in brooding anger, and his mind was fluent in
wrathful harangues in some imaginary encounter of the
future, in which he was a glorious victor. He flowed
in eloquent scorn of Armstrong and his ways. If I could
talk like this always, he thought, what a fellow I would
be ! He seemed gifted with uncanny insight into Armstrong's character. He noted every weakness in the
rushing whirl of his thoughts, set them in order one by
one, saw himself laying bare the man with savage glee
when next they should encounter. He would whiten
the big brute's face by showing he had probed him to
the quick. Just let him laugh at me again, thought
Gourlay, and I'll analyze each mean quirk of his dirty
soul to him !

The drink was dying in him now, for the trio had
walked for more than an hour through the open air

when they left Gillespie's rooms. The stupefaction of alcohol was gone, leaving his brain morbidly alive. He was anxious to sleep, but drowsy dullness kept away. His mind began to visualize of its own accord, independent of his will ; and, one after another, a crowd of pictures rose vivid in the darkness of his brain. He saw them as plainly as you see this page, but with a different clearness—for they seemed unnatural, belonging to a morbid world. Nor did one suggest the other ; there was no connection between them ; each came vivid of its own accord.

First it was an old pit-frame on a barren moor, gaunt, against the yellow west. Gourlay saw bars of iron, left when the pit was abandoned, reddened by the rain ; and the mounds of rubbish, and the scattered bricks, and the rusty clinkers from the furnace, and the melancholy shining pools. A four-wheeled old trolley had lost two of its wheels, and was tilted at a slant, one square end of it resting on the ground.

" Why do I think of an old pit ? " he thought angrily ; " curse it ! why can't I sleep ? "

Next moment he was gazing at a ruined castle, its mouldering walls mounded atop with decaying rubble ; from a loose crumb of mortar a long, thin film of the spider's weaving stretched bellying away to a tall weed waving on the crazy brink. Gourlay saw its glisten in the wind. He saw each crack in the wall, each stain of lichen ; a myriad details stamped themselves together on his raw mind. Then a constant procession of figures passed across the inner curtain of his closed eyes. Each figure was cowled ; but when it came directly opposite, it turned and looked at him with a white face. " Stop, stop ! " cried his mind ; " I don't want to think of you, I don't want to think of you, I don't want to think of you ! Go away ! " But as they came of themselves, so they went of themselves. He could not banish them.

He turned on his side, but a hundred other pictures

pursued him.   From an inland hollow he saw the great
dawn flooding up from the sea, over a sharp line of
cliff, wave after wave of brilliance surging up the heavens.
The landward slope of the cliff was gray with dew.
The inland hollow was full of little fields, divided by
stone walls, and he could not have recalled the fields
round Barbie with half their distinctness.   For a moment they possessed his brain.   Then an autumn wood
rose on his vision.   He was gazing down a vista of yellow
leaves ; a long, deep slanting cleft, framed in lit foliage.
Leaves, leaves ; everywhere yellow leaves, luminous,
burning.   He saw them falling through the lucid air.
The scene was as vivid as fire to his brain, though of
magic stillness.   Then the foliage changed suddenly to
great serpents twined about the boughs.   Their colours
were of monstrous beauty.   They glistened as they
moved.

He leapt in his bed with a throb of horror.   Could
this be the delirium of drink ?   But no ; he had often
had an experience like this when he was sleepless ; he
had the learned description of it pat and ready ; it was
only automatic visualization.

Damn !   Why couldn't he sleep ?   He flung out of
bed, uncorked a bottle with his teeth, tilted it up, and
gulped the gurgling fire in the darkness.   Ha ! that was
better.

His room was already gray with the coming dawn.
He went to the window and opened it.   The town was
stirring uneasily in its morning sleep.   Somewhere in
the distance a train was shunting ; *clank, clank, clank*
went the wagons.   What an accursed sound !   A dray
went past the end of his street rumbling hollowly, and
the rumble died drearily away.   Then the footsteps of
an early workman going to his toil were heard in the
deserted thoroughfare.   Gourlay looked down and saw
him pass far beneath him on the glimmering pavement.
He was whistling.   Why did the fool whistle ?   What

had he got to whistle about ? It was unnatural that one man should go whistling to his work, when another had not been able to sleep the whole night long.

He took another vast glut of whisky, and the moment after was dead to the world.

He was awakened at eight o'clock by a monstrous hammering on his door. By the excessive loudness of the first knock he heard on returning to consciousness, he knew that his landlady had lost her temper in trying to get him up. Ere he could shout she had thumped again. He stared at the ceiling in sullen misery. The middle of his tongue was as dry as bark.

For his breakfast there were thick slabs of rancid bacon, from the top of which two yellow eggs had spewed themselves away among the cold gravy. His gorge rose at them. He nibbled a piece of dry bread and drained the teapot ; then shouldering into his greatcoat, he tramped off to the University.

It was a wretched morning. The wind had veered once more, and a cold drizzle of rain was falling through a yellow fog. The reflections of the street lamps in the sloppy pavement went down through spiral gleams to an infinite depth of misery. Young Gourlay's brain was aching from his last night's debauch, and his body was weakened with the want both of sleep and food. The cold yellow mist chilled him to the bone. What a fool I was to get drunk last night, he thought. Why am I here ? Why am I trudging through mud and misery to the University ? What has it all got to do with me ? Oh, what a fool I am, what a fool !

" Drown dull care," said the devil in his ear.

He took a sixpence from his trousers pocket, and looked down at the white bit of money in his hand till it was wet with the falling rain. Then he went into a flashy tavern, and, standing by a sloppy bar, drank sixpenny-worth of cheap whisky. It went to his head at once, owing to his want of food, and with a dull warm feeling

in his body he lurched off to his first lecture for the
day. His outlook on the world had changed. The fog
was now a comfortable yellowness. " Freedom and
whisky gang thegither : tak aff your dram," he quoted
to his own mind. " That stuff did me good. Whisky's
the boy to fettle you."

He was in his element•the moment he entered the
classroom. It was a bear garden. The most moral
individual has his days of perversity when a malign fate
compels him to show the worst he has in him. A Scottish
university class—which is many most moral individuals
—has a similar eruptive tendency when it gets into the
hands of a weak professor. It will behave well enough
for a fortnight, then a morning comes when nothing can
control it. This was a morning of the kind. The lecturer, who was an able man but a weakling, had begun
by apologizing for the condition of his voice, on the
ground that he had a bad cold. Instantly every man
in the class was blowing his nose. One fellow, of a
most portentous snout, who could trumpet like an
elephant, with a last triumphant snort sent his handkerchief across the room. When called to account for
his conduct, " Really, sir," he said, " er-er-oom—bad
cold ! " Uprose a universal sneeze. Then the " rough-
ing " began, to the tune of " John Brown's body lies
a-mouldering in the grave "—which no man seemed to
sing, but every man could hear. They were playing the
tune with their feet.

The lecturer glared with white repugnance at his tor-
mentors.

Young Gourlay flung himself heart and soul into the
cruel baiting. It was partly from his usual love of
showing off, partly from the drink still seething within
him, but largely, also, as a reaction from his morning's
misery. This was another way of drowning reflection.
The morbidly gloomy one moment often shout madly
on the next.

At last the lecturer plunged wildly at the door and flung it open. "Go!" he shrieked, and pointed in superb dismissal.

A hundred and fifty barbarians sat where they were, and laughed at him; and he must needs come back to the platform, with a baffled and vindictive glower.

He was just turning, as it chanced, when young Gourlay put his hands to his mouth and bellowed "*Cock-a-doodle-do!*"

Ere the roar could swell, the lecturer had leapt to the front of the rostrum with flaming eyes. "Mr. Gourlay," he screamed furiously—"you there, sir; you will apologize humbly to me for this outrage at the end of the hour."

There was a womanish shrillness in the scream, a kind of hysteria on the stretch, that (contrasted with his big threat) might have provoked them at other times to a roar of laughter. But there was a sincerity in his rage to-day that rose above its faults of manner, and an immediate silence took the room—the more impressive for the former noise. Every eye turned to Gourlay. He sat gaping at the lecturer.

If he had been swept to the anteroom there and then, he would have been cowed by the suddenness of his own change, from a loud tormentor in the company of others, to a silent culprit in a room alone. And apologies would have been ready to tumble out, while he was thus loosened by surprise and fear.

Unluckily he had time to think, and the longer he thought the more sullen he became. It was only an accident that led to his discovery, while the rest escaped; and that the others should escape, when they were just as much to blame as he was, was an injustice that made him furious. His anger was equally divided between the cursed mischance itself, the teacher who had "jumped" on him so suddenly, and the other rowdies who had escaped to laugh at his discomfiture; he had the same

burning resentment to them all. When he thought of
his chuckling fellow-students, they seemed to engross his
rage ; when he thought of the mishap, he damned it and
nothing else ; when he thought of the lecturer, he felt
he had no rage to fling away upon others—the Snuffler
took it all. As his mind shot backwards and forwards
in an angry gloom, it suddenly encountered the image of
his father. Not a professor of the lot, he reflected,
could stand the look of black Gourlay. And he wouldn't
knuckle under, either, so he wouldn't. He came of a
hardy stock. He would show them ! He wasn't going
to lick dirt for any man. Let him punish all or none,
for they had all been kicking up a row—why, big Cunningham had been braying like an ass only a minute
before.

He spied Armstrong and Gillespie glinting across at
him with a curious look : they were wondering whether
he had courage enough to stand to his guns with a professor. He knew the meaning of the look, and resented
it. He was on his mettle before them, it seemed. The
fellow who had swaggered at the Howff last night about
" what *he* would do if a professor jumped on *him*,"
mustn't prove wanting in the present trial, beneath the
eyes of those on whom he had imposed his blatancy.

When we think of what Gourlay did that day, we must
remember that he was soaked in alcohol—not merely
with his morning's potation, but with the dregs of previous carousals. And the dregs of drink, a thorough
toper will tell you, never leave him. He is drunk on
Monday with his Saturday's debauch. As " Drucken
Wabster " of Barbie put it once, " When a body's hard
up, his braith's a consolation." If that be so—and
Wabster, remember, was an expert whose opinion on
this matter is entitled to the highest credence—if that
be so, it proves the strength and persistence of a thorough alcoholic impregnation, or, as Wabster called it, of
" a good soak." In young Gourlay's case, at any rate,

the impregnation was enduring and complete. He was like a rag steeped in fusel oil.

As the end of the hour drew near, he sank deeper in his dogged sullenness. When the class streamed from the large door on the right, he turned aside to the little anteroom on the left, with an insolent swing of the shoulders. He knew the fellows were watching him curiously—he felt their eyes upon his back. And, therefore, as he went through the little door, he stood for a moment on his right foot, and waggled his left, on a level with his hip behind, in a vulgar derision of them, the professor, and the whole situation. That was a fine taunt flung back at them !

There is nothing on earth more vindictive than a weakling. When he gets a chance he takes revenge for everything his past cowardice forced him to endure. The timid lecturer, angry at the poor figure he had cut on the platform, was glad to take it out of young Gourlay for the wrongdoing of the class. Gourlay was their scapegoat. The lecturer had no longer over a hundred men to deal with, but one lout only, sullen yet shrinking in the room before him. Instead of coming to the point at once, he played with his victim. It was less from intentional cruelty than from an instinctive desire to recover his lost feeling of superiority. The class was his master, but here was one of them he could cow at any rate.

" Well ? " he asked, bringing his thin finger-tips together, and flinging one thigh across the other.

Gourlay shuffled his feet uneasily.

" Yes ? " inquired the other, enjoying his discomfiture.

Gourlay lowered. " Whatna gate was this to gang on ? Why couldn't he let a blatter out of his thin mouth, and ha' done wi't ? "

" I'm waiting ! " said the lecturer.

The words " I apologize " rose in Gourlay, but refused to pass his throat. No, he wouldn't, so he wouldn't !

He would see the lecturer far enough, ere he gave an apology before it was expressly required.

"Oh, that's the line you go on, is it?" said the lecturer, nodding his head as if he had sized up a curious animal. "I see, I see! You add contumacy to insolence, do you? . . . Imphm."

Gourlay was not quite sure what contumacy meant, and the uncertainty added to his anger.

"There were others making a noise besides me," he blurted. "I don't see why *I* should be blamed for it all."

"Oh, you don't see why *you* should be had up, indeed? I think we'll bring you to a different conclusion. Yes, I think so."

Gourlay, being forced to stand always on the one spot, felt himself swaying in a drunken stupor. He blinked at the lecturer like an angry owl—the blinking regard of a sodden mind, yet fiery with a spiteful rage. His wrath was rising and falling like a quick tide. He would have liked one moment to give a rein to the Gourlay temper, and let the lecturer have it hot and strong; the next, he was quivering in a cowardly horror of the desperate attempt he had so nearly made. Curse his tormentor! Why did he keep him here, when his head was aching so badly? Another taunt was enough to spring his drunken rage.

"I wonder what you think you came to College for?" said the lecturer. "I have been looking at your records in the class. They're the worst I ever saw. And you're not content with that, it seems. You add misbehaviour to gross stupidity."

"To hell wi' ye!" said Gourlay.

There was a feeling in the room as if the air was stunned. The silence throbbed.

The lecturer, who had risen, sat down suddenly as if going at the knees, and went white about the gills. Some men would have swept the ruffian with a burst of generous wrath, a few might have pitied in their anger;

but this young Solomon was thin and acid, a vindictive rat. Unable to cow the insolent in present and full-blooded rage, he fell to thinking of the great machine he might set in motion to destroy him. As he sat there in silence, his eyes grew ferrety, and a sleek revenge peeped from the corners of his mouth. " I'll show him what I'll do to him for this ! " is a translation of his thought. He was thinking, with great satisfaction to himself, of how the Senatus would deal with young Gourlay.

Gourlay grew weak with fear the moment the words escaped him. They had been a thunderclap to his own ears. He had been thinking them, but—as he pleaded far within him now—had never meant to utter them ; they had been mere spume off the surge of cowardly wrath seething up within him, longing to burst, but afraid. It was the taunt of stupidity that fired his drunken vanity to blurt them forth.

The lecturer eyed him sideways where he shrank in fear. " You may go," he said at last. " I will report your conduct to the University."

* * * * * *

Gourlay was sitting alone in his room when he heard that he had been expelled. For many days he had drunk to deaden fear, but he was sober now, being newly out of bed. A dreary ray of sunshine came through the window, and fell on a wisp of flame blinking in the grate. As Gourlay sat, his eyes fixed dully on the faded ray, a flash of intuition laid his character bare to him. He read himself ruthlessly. It was not by conscious effort ; insight was uncanny and apart from will. He saw that blatancy had joined with weakness, morbidity with want of brains ; and that the results of these, converging to a point, had produced the present issue, his expulsion. His mind recognized how logical the issue was, assenting wearily as to a problem proved. Given those qualities, in those circumstances, what else could have happened ? And such a weakling as he knew himself to be could never—he thought—make effort sufficient to alter his qualities. A sense of fatalism came over him, as of one doomed. He bowed his head, and let his arms fall by the sides of his chair, dropping them like a spent swimmer ready to sink. The sudden revelation of himself to himself had taken the heart out of him. " I'm a waster ! " he said aghast. And then, at the sound of his own voice, a fear came over him, a fear of his own nature ; and he started to his feet and strode feverishly, as if by mere locomotion, to escape from his clinging and inherent ill. It was as if he were trying to run away from himself.

He faced round at the mirror on his mantel, and looked at his own image with staring and startled eyes, his mouth open, the breath coming hard through his nostrils. " You're a gey ill ane," he said ; " you're a gey ill ane ! My God, where have you landed yourself ? "

He went out to escape from his thoughts. Instinctively he turned to the Howff for consolation.

With the panic despair of the weak, he abandoned hope of his character at its first collapse, and plunged into a wild debauch, to avoid reflecting where it would lead him in the end. But he had a more definite reason for prolonging his bout in Edinburgh. He was afraid to go home and meet his father. He shrank, in visioning fear, before the dour face, loaded with scorn, that would swing round to meet him as he entered through the door. Though he swore every night in his cups that he would " square up to the Governor the morn, so he would ! " always, when the cold light came, fear of the interview drove him to his cups again. His courage zigzagged, as it always did ; one moment he towered in imagination, the next he grovelled in fear.

Sometimes, when he was fired with whisky, another element entered into his mood, no less big with destruction. It was all his father's fault for sending him to Edinburgh, and no matter what happened, it would serve the old fellow right! He had a kind of fierce satisfaction in his own ruin, because his ruin would show them at home what a mistake they had made in sending him to College. It was the old man's tyranny, in forcing him to College, that had brought all this on his miserable head. Well, he was damned glad, so he was, that they should be punished at home by their own foolish scheme—it had punished *him* enough, for one. And then he would set his mouth insolent and hard, and drink the more fiercely, finding a consolation in the thought that his tyrannical father would suffer through his degradation too.

At last he must go home. He drifted to the station aimlessly ; he had ceased to be self-determined. His compartment happened to be empty ; so, free to behave as he liked, he yelled music-hall snatches in a tuneless voice, hammering with his feet on the wooden floor. The noise pleased his sodden mind, which had narrowed to a comfortable stupor—outside of which his troubles seemed to lie, as if they belonged not to him but to somebody else. With the same sodden interest he was staring through the window, at one of the little stations on the line, when a boy, pointing, said, " *Flat white nose !* " and Gourlay laughed uproariously, adding at the end, " He's a clever chield, that ; my nose *would* look flat and white against the pane." But this outbreak of mirth seemed to break in on his comfortable vagueness ; it roused him by a kind of reaction to think of home, and of what his father would say. A minute after he had been laughing so madly, he was staring sullenly in front of him. Well, it didn't matter ; it was all the old fellow's fault, and he wasn't going to stand any of his jaw. " None of your jaw, John Gourlay ! " he said, nodding his head viciously, and thrusting out his clenched fist—" none of your jaw ; d'ye hear ? "

He crept into Barbie through the dusk. It had been market-day, and knots of people were still about the streets. Gourlay stole softly through the shadows, and turned his coat-collar high about his ears. He nearly ran into two men who were talking apart, and his heart stopped dead at their words.

"No, no, Mr. Gourlay," said one of them; "it's quite impossible. I'm not unwilling to oblige ye, but I cannot take the risk."

John heard the mumble of his father's voice.

"Well," said the other reluctantly, "if ye get the baker and Tam Wylie for security? I'll be on the street for another half-hour."

"Another half-hour!" thought John with relief. He would not have to face his father the moment he went in. He would be able to get home before him. He crept on through the gloaming to the House with the Green Shutters.

CHAPTER XXIV.

THERE had been fine cackling in Barbie as Gourlay's men dropped away from him one by one ; and now it was worse than ever. When Jimmy Bain and Sandy Cross were dismissed last winter, " He canna last long now," mused the bodies; and then when even Riney got the sack, " Lord ! " they cried, " this maun be the end o't." The downfall of Gourlay had an unholy fascination for his neighbours, and that not merely because of their dislike to the man. That was a whet to their curiosity, of course ; but, over and above it, they seemed to be watching, with bated breath, for the final collapse of an edifice that was bound to fall. Simple expectation held them. It was a dramatic interest—of suspense, yet certainty—that had them in its grip. " He's *bound* to come down," said Certainty. " Yes ; but *when*, though ? " cried Curiosity, all the more eager because of its instinct for the coming crash. And so they waited for the great catastrophe which they felt to be so near. It was as if they were watching the tragedy near at hand, and noting with keen interest every step in it that must lead to inevitable ruin. That invariably happens when a family tragedy is played out in the midst of a small community. Each step in it is discussed with a prying interest that is neither malevolent nor sympathetic, but simply curious. In this case it was chiefly malevolent—only because Gourlay had been such a brute to Barbie.

Though there were thus two reasons for public interest, the result was one and the same—a constant tittle-tattling.   Particular spite and a more general curiosity brought the grain merchant's name on to every tongue. Not even in the gawcey days of its prosperity had the House with the Green Shutters been so much talked of.

"Pride *will* have a downcome," said some, with a gleg look and a smack of the lip, trying to veil their personal malevolence in a common proverb.   "He's simply in debt in every corner," goldered the keener spirits; "he never had a brain for business.   He's had money for stuff he's unable to deliver!   Not a day gangs by but the big blue envelopes are coming.   How do I ken? say ye!   How do I ken, indeed?   Oh-ooh, I ken perfectly.   Perfectly!   It was Postie himsell that telled me."

Yet all this was merely guesswork.   For Gourlay had hitherto gone away from Barbie for his moneys and accommodations, so that the bodies could only surmise; they had nothing definite to go on.   And through it all the gurly old fellow kept a brave front to the world. He was thinking of retiring, he said, and gradually drawing in his business.   This offhand and lordly, to hide the patent diminution of his trade.

"Hi-hi!" said the old Provost, with a cruel laugh, when he heard of Gourlay's remark—"drawing in his business, ay!   It's like Lang Jean Lingleton's waist, I'm thinking.   It's thin eneugh drawn a'readys!"

On the morning of the last market-day he was ever to see in Barbie, old Gourlay was standing at the green gate, when the postman came up with a smirk, and put a letter in his hand.   He betrayed a wish to hover in gossip, while Gourlay opened his letter, but "Less lip!" said surly John, and the fellow went away.

Ere he had reached the corner, a gowl of anger and grief struck his ear, and he wheeled eagerly.

Gourlay was standing with open mouth and outstretched arm, staring at the letter in his clenched fist with a look of horror, as if it had stung him.

"My God!" he cried, "had *I* not enough to thole?"

"Aha!" thought Postie, "yon letter Wilson got this morning was correct, then! His son had sent the true story. That letter o' Gourlay's had the Edinburgh postmark; somebody has sent him word about his son.—Lord! what a tit-bit for my rounds."

Mrs. Gourlay, who was washing dishes, looked up to see her husband standing in the kitchen door. His face frightened her. She had often seen the blaze in his eye, and often the dark scowl, but never this bloodless pallor in his cheek. Yet his eyes were flaming.

"Ay, ay," he birred, "a fine job you have made of him!"

"Oh, what is it?" she quavered, and the dish she was wiping clashed on the floor.

"That's it!" said he, "that's it! Breck the dishes next; breck the dishes! Everything seems gaun to smash. If ye keep on lang eneugh, ye'll put a bonny end till't or ye're bye wi't—the lot o' ye."

The taunt passed in the anxiety that stormed her.

"Tell me, see!" she cried, imperious in stress of appeal. "Oh, what is it, John?" She stretched out her thin, red hands, and clasped them tightly before her. "Is it from Embro? Is there ainything the matter with *my* boy? Is there ainything the matter with *my* boy?"

The hard eye surveyed her a while in grim contempt of her weakness. She was a fluttering thing in his grip.

"*Every* thing's the matter with *your* boy." he sneered slowly, "*every* thing's the matter with *your* boy. And it's your fault too, damn you, for you always spoiled him!"

With sudden wrath he strode over to the famous range and threw the letter within the great fender.

"What is it?" he cried, wheeling round on his wife. "The son you were so wild about sending to College has been flung in disgrace from its door! That's what it is!" He swept from the house like a madman.

Mrs. Gourlay sank into her old nursing chair and wailed, "Oh, my wean, my wean; my dear, my poor dear!" She drew the letter from the ashes, but could not read it for her tears. The words "drunkenness" and "expulsion" swam before her eyes. The manner of his disgrace she did not care to hear; she only knew her first-born was in sorrow.

"Oh, my son, my son," she cried; "my laddie, my ·wee laddie!" She was thinking of the time when he trotted at her petticoat.

It was market-day, and Gourlay must face the town. There was interest due on a mortgage which he could not pay; he must swallow his pride and try to borrow it in Barbie. He thought of trying Johnny Coe, for Johnny was of yielding nature, and had never been unfriendly.

He turned, twenty yards from his gate, and looked at the House with the Green Shutters. He had often turned to look back with pride at the gawcey building on its terrace, but never as he looked to-day. All that his life meant was bound up in that house—it had been the pride of the Gourlays; now it was no longer his, and the Gourlays' pride was in the dust—their name a by-word. As Gourlay looked, a robin was perched on the quiet roof-tree, its breast vivid in the sun. One of his metaphors flashed at the sight. "Shame is sitting there too," he muttered, and added with a proud, angry snarl, "on the riggin' o' *my* hoose!"

He had a triple wrath to his son. He had not only ruined his own life; he had destroyed his father's hope that by entering the ministry he might restore the Gourlay reputation. Above all, he had disgraced the House with the Green Shutters. That was the crown of his offending. Gourlay felt for the house of his pride even more than for himself—rather the house was himself ; there was no division between them. He had built it bluff to represent him to the world. It was his character in stone and lime. He clung to it, as the dull, fierce mind, unable to live in thought, clings to a material source of pride. And John had disgraced it. Even if fortune took a turn for the better, Green Shutters would be laughed at the country over, as the home of a prodigal.

As he went by the Cross, Wilson (Provost this long while) broke off a conversation with Templandmuir, to yell, " It's gra-and weather, Mr. Gourlay ! " The men had not spoken for years. So to shout at poor Gourlay in his black hour, from the pinnacle of civic greatness, was a fine stroke : it was gloating, it was rubbing in the contrast. The words were innocent, but that was nothing ; whatever the remark, for a declared enemy to address Gourlay in his shame was an insult : that was why Wilson addressed him. There was something in the very loudness of his tones that cried plainly, " Aha, Gourlay ! Your son has disgraced you, my man !" Gourlay glowered at the animal and plodded dourly. Ere he had gone ten yards a coarse laugh came bellowing behind him. They saw the colour surge up the back of his neck, to the roots of his hair.

He stopped. Was his son's disgrace known in Barbie already ? He had hoped to get through the market-day without anybody knowing. But Wilson had a son in Edinburgh ; he had written, it was like. The salutation, therefore, and the laugh, had both been uttered in derision. He wheeled, his face black with the passionate blood. His mouth yawed with anger. His voice had a moan of intensity.

" What are 'e laughing at ? " he said, with a mastering quietness. . . " Eh ? . . . Just tell me, please, what you're laughing at."

He was crouching for the grip, his hands out like a gorilla's. The quiet voice, from the yawing mouth, be-

neath the steady, flaming eyes, was deadly. There is
something inhuman in a rage so still.

" Eh ? " he said slowly, and the moan seemed to come
from the midst of a vast intensity rather than a human
being. It was the question that must grind an answer.

Wilson was wishing to all his gods that he had not
insulted this awful man. He remembered what had
happened to Gibson. This, he had heard, was the very
voice with which Gourlay moaned, " Take your hand
off *my* shouther ! " ere he hurled Gibson through the
window of the Red Lion. Barbie might soon want a
new Provost, if he ran in now.

But there is always one way of evading punishment
for a veiled insult, and of adding to its sting by your
evasion. Repudiate the remotest thought of the pro-
tester. Thus you enjoy your previous gibe, with the
additional pleasure of making your victim seem a fool
for thinking you referred to him. You not only insult
him on the first count, but send him off with an additional hint that he isn't worth your notice. Wilson was
an adept in the art.

" Man," he lied blandly, but his voice was quivering
—" ma-a-an, I wasn't so much as giving ye a thoat !
It's verra strange if I cannot pass a joke with my o-old
friend Templandmuir without *you* calling me to book.
It's a free country, I shuppose ! Ye weren't in my mind
at a-all. I have more important matters to think of,"
he ventured to add, seeing he had baffled Gourlay.

For Gourlay was baffled. For a directer insult, an
offensive gesture, one fierce word, he would have ham-
mered the road with the Provost. But he was helpless
before the bland, quivering lie. Maybe they werena
referring to him ; maybe they knew nothing of John in
Edinburgh ; maybe he had been foolishly suspeecious.
A subtle yet baffling check was put upon his anger.
Madman as he was in wrath, he never struck without
direct provocation ; there was none in this pulpy gentle-

ness.   And he was too dull of wit to get round the
common ruse and find a means of getting at them.

He let loose a great breath through his nostrils, as
if releasing a deadly force which he had pent within
him, ready should he need to spring.   His mouth opened
again, and he gaped at them with a great, round, unsee-
ing stare.   Then he swung on his heel.

But wrath clung round him like a garment.   His
anger fed on its uncertainties.   For that is the beauty
of the Wilson method of insult : you leave the poison
in your victim's blood, and he torments himself.   " Was
Wilson referring to *me*, after all ? " he pondered slowly ;
and his body surged at the thought.   " If he was, I
have let him get away unkilled," and he clutched the
hands whence Wilson had escaped.   Suddenly a flashing thought stopped him dead in the middle of his walk,
staring hornily before him.   He had seen the point at
last that a quicker man would have seized on at the
first.   Why had Wilson thrust his damned voice on him
on this particular morning of all days in the year, if he
was not gloating over some news which he had just
heard about the Gourlays ?   It was as plain as daylight :
his son had sent word from Edinburgh.   That was why
he brayed and ho-ho-hoed when Gourlay went by.
Gourlay felt a great flutter of pulses against his collar ;
there was a pain in his throat, an ache of madness in
his breast.   He turned once more.   But Wilson and the
Templar had withdrawn discreetly to the Black Bull ;
the street wasna canny.   Gourlay resumed his way, his
being a dumb gowl of rage.   His angry thought swept
to John.   Each insult, and fancied insult, he endured
that day was another item in the long account of
vengeance with his son.   It was John who had brought
all this flaming round his ears—John whose colleging
he had lippened to so muckle.   The staff on which he
leaned had pierced him.   By the eternal heavens he would
tramp it into atoms.   His legs felt John beneath them.

As the market grew busy, Gourlay was the aim of
innumerable eyes. He would turn his head to find himself the object of a queer, considering look; then the
eyes of the starer would flutter abashed, as though detected spying the forbidden. The most innocent look
at him was poison. " Do they know ? " was his constant thought ; " have. they heard the news ? What's
Loranogie looking at me like that for ? "

Not a man ventured to address him about John—he
had cowed them too long. One man, however, showed
a wish to try. A pretended sympathy, from behind the
veil of which you probe a man's anguish at your ease,
is a favourite weapon of human beasts anxious to wound.
The Deacon longed to try it on Gourlay. But his courage failed him. It was the only time he was ever
worsted in malignity. Never a man went forth, bowed
down with a recent shame, wounded and wincing from
the public gaze, but that old rogue hirpled up to him,
and lisped with false smoothness : " Thirce me, neebour,
I'm thorry for ye ! Thith ith a *terrible* affair ! It'th on
everybody'th tongue. But ye have my thympathy, neebour, ye have tha-at — my warmetht thympathy."
And all the while the shifty eyes above the lying mouth
would peer and probe, to see if the soul within the other
was writhing at his words.

Now, though everybody was spying at Gourlay in the
market, all were giving him a wide berth ; for they knew
that he was dangerous. He was no longer the man
whom they had baited on the way to Skeighan ; then
he had some control, now three years' calamities had
fretted his temper to a raw wound. To flick it was
perilous. Great was the surprise of the starers, therefore, when the idle old Deacon was seen to detach himself and hail the grain merchant. Gourlay wheeled, and
waited with a levelled eye. All were agog at the sight
—something would be sure to come o' this—here would
be an encounter worth the speaking o'. But the Deacon,

having toddled forward a bittock on his thin shanks, stopped half-roads, took snuff, trumpeted into his big red handkerchief, and then, feebly waving, " I'll thee ye again, Dyohn," clean turned tail and toddled back to his cronies.

A roar went up at his expense.

" God ! " said Tam Wylie, " did ye see yon ? Gourlay stopped him wi' a glower."

But the laugh was maddening to Gourlay. Its readiness, its volume, showed him that scores of folk had him in their minds, were watching him, considering his position, cognizant of where he stood. " They ken," he thought. " They were a' waiting to see what would happen. They wanted to watch how Gourlay tholed the mention o' his son's disgrace. I'm a kind o' show to them."

Johnny Coe, idle and well-to-pass, though he had no business of his own to attend to, was always present where business men assembled. It was a gra-and way of getting news. To-day, however, Gourlay could not find him. He went into the cattle mart to see if he was there. For two years now Barbie had a market for cattle, on the first Tuesday of the month.

The auctioneer, a jovial dog, was in the middle of his roaring game. A big red bullock, the coat of which made a rich colour in the ring, came bounding in, scared at its surroundings—staring one moment and the next careering.

" There's meat for you," said he of the hammer ; " see how it runs ! How much am I offered for *this* fine bullock ? " He sing-songed, always saying " *this* fine bullock " in exactly the same tone of voice. " Thirteen pounds for *this* fine bullock ; thirteen-five ; thirteen-ten ; thirteen-ten for *this* fine bullock ; thirteen-ten ; any further bids on thirteen-ten ? why, it's worth that for the colour o't ; thank ye, sir—thirteen-fifteen ; fourteen pounds ; fourteen pounds for *this* fine bullock ; see how the stot stots * about the ring; that joke should raise him another half-sovereign; ah, I knew it would—fourteen-five; fourteen-five for *this* fine bullock; fourteen-ten; no more than fourteen-ten for *this* fine bullock; going at fourteen-ten; gone—Irrendavie."

Now that he was in the circle, however, the mad, big, handsome beast refused to go out again. When the cattlemen would drive him to the yard, he snorted and galloped round, till he had to be driven from the ring with blows. When at last he bounded through the door, he flung up his heels with a bellow, and sent the sand of his arena showering on the people round.

" I seh!" roared Brodie in his coarsest voice, from the side of the ring opposite to Gourlay. " I seh, owctioner! That maun be a College-bred stot, from the way he behaves. He flung dirt at his masters, and had to be expelled."

" Put Brodie in the ring and rowp him!" cried Irrendavie. " He roars like a bill, at ony rate."

There was a laugh at Brodie, true; but it was at Gourlay that a hundred big red faces turned to look. He did not look at them, though. He sent his eyes across the ring at Brodie.

" Lord!" said Irrendavie, " it's weel for Brodie that the ring's acqueesh them! Gourlay'll murder somebody yet. Red hell lap out o' his e'en when he looked at Brodie."

Gourlay's suspicion that his son's disgrace was a matter of common knowledge had now become a certainty. Brodie's taunt showed that everybody knew it. He walked out of the building very quietly, pale but resolute; no meanness in his carriage, no cowering. He was an arresting figure of a man as he stood for a moment in the door and looked round for the man whom he was seeking. " Weel, weel," he was thinking, " I maun thole, I suppose. They were under *my*

* *Stot*, a bullock; *to stot*, to bound.

feet for many a day, and they're taking their advantage now."

But though he could thole, his anger against John was none the less. It was because they had been under his feet for many a day that John's conduct was the more heinous. It was his son's conduct that gave Gourlay's enemies their first opportunity against him, that enabled them to turn the tables. They might sneer at his trollop of a wife, they might sneer at his want of mere cleverness ; still he held his head high amongst them. They might suspect his poverty ; but so far, for anything they knew, he might have thousands behind him. He owed not a man in Barbie. The appointments of Green Shutters were as brave as ever. The selling of his horses, the dismissal of his men, might mean the completion of a fortune, not its loss. Hitherto, then, he was invulnerable—so he reasoned. It was his son's disgrace that gave the men he had trodden under foot the first weapon they could use against him. That was why it was more damnable in Gourlay's eyes than the conduct of all the prodigals that ever lived. It had enabled his foes to get their knife into him at last, and they were turning the dagger in the wound. All owing to the boy on whom he had staked such hopes of keeping up the Gourlay name ! His account with John was lengthening steadily.

Coe was nowhere to be seen. At last Gourlay made up his mind to go out and make inquiries at his house, out the Fleckie Road. It was a quiet, big house, standing by itself, and Gourlay was glad there was nobody to see him.

It was Miss Coe herself who answered his knock at the door.

She was a withered old shrew, with fifty times the spunk of Johnny. On her thin wrists and long hands there was always a pair of bright red mittens, only her finger-tips showing. Her far-sunken and toothless mouth was always working, with a sucking motion of the lips; and her round little knob of a sticking-out chin munched up and down when she spoke, a long, stiff whitish hair slanting out its middle. However much you wished to avoid doing so, you could not keep your eyes from staring at that solitary hair while she was addressing you. It worked up and down so, keeping time to every word she spoke.

"Is your brother in?" said Gourlay. He was too near reality in this sad pass of his to think of "mistering." "Is your brother in?" said he.

"No-a!" she shrilled—for Miss Coe answered questions with an old-maidish scream, as if the news she was giving must be a great surprise both to you and her. "No-a!" she skirled; "he's no-a in-a. Was it ainything particular?"

"No," said Gourlay heavily. "I—I just wanted to see him," and he trudged away.

Miss Coe looked after him for a moment ere she closed the door. "He's wanting to barrow money," she cried; "I'm nearly sure o't! I maun caution Johnny when he comes back frae Fleckie, afore he gangs east the toon. Gourlay could get him to do ocht! He always admired the brute—I'm sure I kenna why. Because he's siccan a silly body himsell, I suppose!"

It was after dark when Gourlay met Coe on the street. He drew him aside in the shadows, and asked for a loan of eighty pounds.

Johnny stammered a refusal. "Hauf the bawbees is mine," his sister had skirled, "and I daur ye to do ony siccan thing, John Coe!"

"It's only for a time," pleaded Gourlay; "and, by God," he flashed, "it's hell in *my* throat to ask from any man."

"No, no, Mr. Gourlay," said Johnny, "it's quite impossible. I've always looked up to ye, and I'm not unwilling to oblige ye, but I cannot take the risk."

" Risk ! " said Gourlay, and stared at the darkness. By hook or by crook he must raise the money to save the House with the Green Shutters. It was no use trying the bank; he had a letter from the banker in his desk, to tell him that his account was overdrawn. And yet if the interest were not paid at once, the lawyers in Glasgow would foreclose, and the Gourlays would be flung upon the street. His proud soul must eat dirt, if need be, for the sake of eighty pounds.

" If I get the baker or Tam Wylie to stand security," he asked, " would ye not oblige me ? I think they would do it. I have always felt they respected me."

" Well," said Johnny slowly, fearing his sister's anger, " if ye get the baker and Tam Wylie for security. I'll be on the street for another half-hour."

A figure, muffled in a greatcoat, was seen stealing off through the shadows.

" God's curse on whoever that is," snarled Gourlay, " creeping up to listen to our talk ! "

" I don't think so," said Johnny ; " it seemed a young chap trying to hide himself."

Gourlay failed to get his securities. The baker, though a poor man, would have stood for him, if Tam Wylie would have joined ; but Tam would not budge. He was as clean as gray granite, and as hard.

So Gourlay trudged home through the darkness, beaten at last, mad with shame and anger and foreboding.

The first thing he saw on entering the kitchen was his son—sitting muffled in his coat by the great fender.

CHAPTER XXV.

JANET and her mother saw a quiver run through Gourlay as he stood and glowered from the threshold. He seemed of monstrous bulk and significance, filling the doorway in his silence.

The quiver that went through him was a sign of his contending angers, his will struggling with the tumult of wrath that threatened to spoil his revenge. To fell that huddled oaf with a blow would be a poor return for all he had endured because of him. He meant to sweat punishment out of him drop by drop, with slow and vicious enjoyment. But the sudden sight of that living disgrace to the Gourlays woke a wild desire to leap on him at once and glut his rage—a madness which only a will like his could control. He quivered with the effort to keep it in.

To bring a beaten and degraded look into a man's face, rend manhood out of him in fear, is a sight that makes decent men wince in pain; for it is an outrage on the decency of life, an offence to natural religion, a violation of the human sanctities. Yet Gourlay had done it once and again. I saw him " down " a man at the Cross once, a big man with a viking beard, dark brown, from which you would have looked for manliness. Gourlay, with stabbing eyes, threatened, and birred, and " downed " him, till he crept away with a face like chalk, and a hunted, furtive eye. Curiously it was his manly beard that made the look such a pain, for its contrasting colour showed the white face of the coward—and a coward had no right to such a beard. A grim and cruel smile went after him as he slunk away. "*Ha!*" barked Gourlay, in lordly and pursuing scorn, and the fellow leapt where he walked as the cry went through him. To break a man's spirit so, take that from him which he will never recover while he lives, send him slinking away *animo castrato*—for that is what it comes to—is a sinister outrage of the world. It is as bad as the rape of a woman, and ranks with the sin against the Holy Ghost—derives from it, indeed. Yet it was this outrage that Gourlay meant to work upon his son. He would work him down and down, this son of his, till he was less than a man, a frightened, furtive animal. Then, perhaps, he would give a loose to his other rage, unbuckle his belt, and thrash the grown man like a wriggling urchin on the floor.

As he stood glowering from the door Mrs. Gourlay rose, with an appealing cry of "*John!*" But Gourlay put his eye on her, and she sank into her chair, staring up at him in terror. The strings of the tawdry cap she wore seemed to choke her, and she unfastened them with nervous fingers, fumbling long beneath her lifted chin to get them loose. She did not remove the cap, but let the strings dangle by her jaw. The silly bits of cloth waggling and quivering, as she turned her head repeatedly from son to husband and from husband to son, added to her air of helplessness and inefficiency. Once she whispered with ghastly intensity, "*God have mercy!*"

For a length of time there was a loaded silence.

Gourlay went up to the hearth, and looked down on his son from near at hand. John shrank down in his greatcoat. A reek of alcohol rose from around him. Janet whimpered.

But when Gourlay spoke it was with deadly quietude. The moan was in his voice. So great was his controlled wrath that he drew in great, shivering breastfuls of air between the words, as if for strength to utter them ; and they quavered forth on it again. He seemed weakened by his own rage.

"Ay, man ! " he breathed. . . . "Ye've won hame, I observe ! . . . Dee-ee-ar me ! . . . Im-phm ! "

The contrast between the lowness of his voice and his steady, breathing anger that possessed the air (they felt it coming as on waves) was demoniac, appalling.

John could not speak ; he was paralyzed by fear. To have this vast hostile force touch him, yet be still, struck him dumb. Why did his father not break out on him at once ? What did he mean ? What was he going to do ? The jamb of the fireplace cut his right shoulder as he cowered into it, to get away as far as he could.

" I'm saying . . . ye've won hame ! " quivered Gourlay in a deadly slowness, and his eyes never left his son.

And still the son made no reply. In the silence the ticking of the big clock seemed to fill their world. They were conscious of nothing else. It smote the ear.

"Ay," John gulped at last from a throat that felt closing. The answer seemed dragged out of him by the insistent silence.

" Just so-a ! " breathed his father, and his eyes opened in wide flame. He heaved with the great breath he drew. . . . "Im-phm ! " he drawled.

He went through to the scullery at the back of the kitchen to wash his hands. Through the open door Janet and her mother—looking at each other with affrighted eyes—could hear him sneering at intervals, "Ay, man ! " . . . "Just that, now ! " . . . "Im-phm ! " And again, "Ay, ay ! . . . Dee-ee-ar me ! " in grim, falsetto irony.

When he came back to the kitchen he turned to Janet, and left his son in a suspended agony.

"Ay, woman, Jenny, ye're there ! " he said, and

nipped her ear as he passed over to his chair. "Were ye in Skeighan the day ? "

"Ay, faither," she answered.

"And what did the Skeighan doctor say ? "

She raised her large pale eyes to his with a strange look. Then her head sank low on her breast.

"Nothing ! " she said at last.

"Nothing ! " said he. "Nothing for nothing, then. I hope you didna pay him ? "

"No, faither," she answered. "I hadna the baw-bees."

"When did ye get back ? " he asked.

"Just after—just after——" Her eyes flickered over to John, as if she were afraid of mentioning his name.

"Oh, just after this gentleman ! But there's noathing strange in tha-at ; you were always after him. You were born after him, and considered after him ; he aye had the best o't.—I howp *you* are in good health ? " he sneered, turning to his son. "It would never do for a man to break down at the outset o' a great career ! . . . For ye *are* at the outset o' a great career ; are ye na ? "

His speech was as soft as the foot of a tiger, and sheathed as rending a cruelty. There was no escaping the crouching stealth of it. If he had leapt with a roar, John's drunken fury might have lashed itself to rage. But the younger and weaker man was fascinated and helpless before the creeping approach of so monstrous a wrath.

"Eh ? " asked Gourlay softly, when John made no reply ; "I'm saying you're at the outset o' a great career ; are ye no ? Eh ? "

Soft as his "Eh " was in utterance, it was insinuating, pursuing ; it had to be answered.

"No," whimpered John.

"Well, well ; you're maybe at the end o't ! Have ye been studying hard ? "

" Yes," lied John.

" That's right ! " cried his father with great heartiness. " There's my brave fellow ! Noathing like studying ! . . . And no doubt "—he leaned over suavely—
" and no doubt ye've brought a wheen prizes home wi'
ye as usual ? Eh ? "

There was no answer.

" Eh ? "

" No," gulped the cowerer.

" *Nae* prizes ! " cried Gourlay, and his eyebrows went
up in a pretended surprise. " *Nae-ae* prizes ! Ay,
man ! Fow's that, na ? "

Young Gourlay was being reduced to the condition
of a beaten child, who, when his mother asks if he has
been a bad boy, is made to sob " Yes " at her knee.
" Have you been a good boy ? " she asks—" No," he
pants ; and " Are you sorry for being a bad boy ? "—
" Yes," he sobs ; and " Will you be a good boy now,
then ? "—" Yes," he almost shrieks, in his desire to be
at one with his mother. Young Gourlay was being
equally beaten from his own nature, equally battered
under by another personality. Only he was not asked
to be a good boy. He might gang to hell for anything
auld Gourlay cared—when once he had bye with him.

Even as he degraded his son to this state of unnatural
cowardice, Gourlay felt a vast disgust swell within him
that a son of his should be such a coward. " Damn
him ! " he thought, glowering with big-eyed contempt
at the huddled creature ; " he hasna the pluck o' a pig !
How can he stand talk like this without showing he's
a man ? When I was a child on the brisket, if a man
had used me as I'm using him, I would have flung mysell
at him. He's a pretty-looking object to carry the name
o' John Gourla' ! My God, what a ke-o of *my* life I've
made—that auld trollop for my wife, that sumph for
my son, and that dying lassie for my dochter ! Was it I
that bred him ? *That !* "

He leapt to his feet in devilish merriment.

" Set out the spirits, Jenny ! " he cried ; " set out the spirits ! My son and I must have a drink together—to celebrate the occeesion ; ou ay," he sneered, drawling out the word with sharp, unfamiliar sound, " just to celebrate the occeesion ! "

The wild humour that seized him was inevitable, born of a vicious effort to control a rage that was constantly increasing, fed by the sight of the offender. Every time he glanced across at the thing sitting there he was swept with fresh surges of fury and disgust. But his vicious constraint curbed them under, and refused them a natural expression. They sought an unnatural. Some vent they must have, and they found it in a score of wild devilries he began to practise on his son. Wrath fed and checked iṅ one brings the hell on which man is built to the surface. Gourlay was transformed. He had a fluency of speech, a power of banter, a readiness of tongue, which he had never shown before. He was beyond himself. Have you heard the snarl with which a wild beast arrests the escaping prey which it has just let go in enjoying cruelty ? Gourlay was that animal. For a moment he would cease to torture his son, feed his disgust with a glower ; then the sight of him huddled there would wake a desire to stamp on him ; but his will would not allow that, for it would spoil the sport he had set his mind on ; and so he played with the victim which he would not kill.

" Set out the speerits, Jenny," he birred, when she wavered in fear. " What are ye shaking for ? Set out the speerits—just to shelebrate the joyful occeesion, ye know — ay, ay, just to shelebrate the joyful occee- sion ! "

Janet brought a tray, with glasses, from the pantry. As she walked, the rims of the glasses shivered and tinkled against each other, from her trembling. Then she set a bottle on the table.

Gourlay sent it crashing to the floor. " A bottle ! "
he roared. " A bottle for huz twa ! To hell wi' bottles !
The jar, Jenny, the jar ; set out the jar, lass, set out the
jar. For we mean to make a night of it, this gentleman
and me. Ay," he yawed with a vicious smile, " we'll
make a night o't—we two. A night that Barbie'll remember loang ! "

" Have ye skill o' drink ? " he asked, turning to his
son.

" No," wheezed John.

" No ! " cried his father. " I thought ye learned
everything at College ! Your education's been neglected. But I'll teach ye a lesson or *this* nicht's by.
Ay, by God," he growled, " I'll teach ye a lesson."

Curb his temper as he might, his own behaviour was
lashing it to frenzy. Through the moaning intensity
peculiar to his vicious rage there leapt at times a wild-
beast snarl. Every time they heard it, it cut the veins
of his listeners with a start of fear—it leapt so suddenly.

" Ha'e, sir ! " he cried.

John raised his dull, white face and looked across at
the bumper which his father poured him. But he felt
the limbs too weak beneath him to go and take it.

" Bide where ye are ! " sneered his father, " bide where
ye are ! I'll wait on ye ; I'll wait on ye. Man, I waited
on ye the day that ye were bo-orn ! The heavens were
hammering the world as John Gourla' rode through the
storm for a doctor to bring hame his heir. The world
was feared, but *he* wasna feared," he roared in Titanic
pride, " *he* wasna feared ; no, by God, for he never met
what scaured him ! . . . Ay, ay," he birred softly
again, " ay, ay, ye were ushered loudly to the world,
serr ! Verra appropriate for a man who was destined to
make such a name ! . . . Eh ? . . . Verra appropriate,
serr ; verra appropriate ! And you'll be ushered just as
loudly out o't. Oh, young Gourlay's death maun make
a splurge, ye know—a splurge to attract folk's attention ! "

John's shaking hand was wet with the spilled whisky.
"Take it off," sneered his father, boring into him
with a vicious eye; "take it off, serr; take off your
dram! Stop! Somebody wrote something about that
—some poetry or other. Who was it?"

"I dinna ken," whimpered John.

"Don't tell lies now. You do ken. I heard you
mention it to Loranogie. Come on now—who was it?"

"It was Burns," said John.

"Oh, it was Burns, was it? And what had Mr. Burns
to say on the subject? Eh?"

"'Freedom and whisky gang thegither: tak aff your
dram,'" stammered John.

"A verra wise remark," said Gourlay gravely. "'Freedom and whisky gang thegither;'" he turned the quota-
tion on his tongue, as if he were savouring a tit-bit.
"That's verra good," he approved. "You're a great
admirer of Burns, I hear. Eh?"

"Yes," said John.

"Do what he bids ye, then. Take off your dram!
It'll show what a fine free fellow you are!"

It was a big, old-fashioned Scotch drinking-glass, con-
taining more than half a gill of whisky, and John drained
it to the bottom. To him it had been a deadly thing at
first, coming thus from his father's hand. He had
taken it into his own with a feeling of aversion that
was strangely blended of disgust and fear. But the
moment it touched his lips, desire leapt in his throat
to get at it.

"Good!" roared his father in mock admiration.
"God, ye have the thrapple! When I was your age
that would have choked me. I must have a look at that
throat o' yours. Stand up! . . . *Stand up when I
tall 'ee!*"

John rose swaying to his feet. Months of constant
tippling, culminating in a wild debauch, had shattered
him. He stood in a reeling world. And the fear weak-

ening his limbs changed his drunken stupor to a heart-heaving sickness. He swayed to and fro, with a cold sweat oozing from his chalky face.

"What's ado wi' the fellow?" cried Gourlay. "Oom? He's swinging like a saugh-wand. I must wa-alk round this and have a look!"

John's drunken submissiveness encouraged his father to new devilries. The ease with which he tortured him provoked him to more torture; he went on more and more viciously, as if he were conducting an experiment, to see how much the creature would bear before he turned. Gourlay was enjoying the glutting of his own wrath.

He turned his son round with a finger and thumb on his shoulder, in insolent inspection, as you turn an urchin round to see him in his new suit of clothes. Then he crouched before him, his face thrust close to the other, and peered into his eyes, his mouth distent with an infernal smile. "My boy, Johnny," he said sweetly, "my boy, Johnny," and patted him gently on the cheek. John raised dull eyes and looked into his father's. Far within him a great wrath was gathering through his fear. Another voice, another self, seemed to whimper, with dull iteration, "I'll *kill* him; I'll *kill* him; by God, I'll *kill* him—if he doesna stop this—if he keeps on like this at me!" But his present and material self was paralyzed with fear.

"Open your mouth!" came the snarl—"*wider, damn ye! wider!*"

"Im-phm!" said Gourlay, with a critical drawl, pulling John's chin about to see into him the deeper. "Im-phm! God, it's like a furnace! What's the Latin for throat?"

"Guttur," said John.

"Gutter," said his father. "A verra appropriate name! Yours stinks like a cesspool! What have you been doing till't? I'm afraid ye aren't in very good

health, after a-all. . . . Eh ? . . . Mrs. Gourla', Mrs.
Gourla' ! He's in very bad case, this son of yours, Mrs.
Gourla' ! Fine I ken what he needs, though.—Set out
the brandy, Jenny, set out the brandy," he roared ;
" whisky's not worth a damn for him ! Stop ; it was
you gaed the last time—it's *your* turn now, auld wife,
it's *your* turn now ! Gang for the brandy to your
twa John Gourla's. We're a pair for a woman to be
proud of ! "

He gazed after his wife as she tottered to the pantry.

" Your skirt's on the gape, auld wife," he sang ; " your
skirt's on the gape ; as use-u-al," he drawled ; " as use-
u-al. It was always like that ; and it always scunnered
me, for I aye liked things tidy—though I never got
them. However, I maunna compleen when ye bore sic
a braw son to my name. He's a great consolation !
Imphm, he is that—a great consolation ! "

The brandy bottle slipped from the quivering fingers
and was smashed to pieces on the floor.

" Hurrah ! " yelled Gourlay.

He seemed rapt and carried by his own devilry. The
wreck and ruin strewn about the floor consorted with
the ruin of his fortunes ; let all go smash—what was the
use of caring ? Now in his frenzy, he, ordinarily so
careful, seemed to delight in the smashings and the
breakings ; they suited his despair.

He saw that his spirit of destruction frightened them,
too, and that was another reason to indulge it.

" To hell with everything," he yelled, like a mock-
bacchanal. " *We*'re the hearty fellows ! We'll make a
red night now we're at it ! " And with that he took the
heel of a bottle on his toe and sent it flying among the
dishes on the dresser. A great plate fell, split in two.

" Poor fellow ! " he whined, turning to his son ;
" poo-oor fellow ! I fear he has lost his pheesic. For
that was the last bottle o' brandy in my aucht ; the last
John Gourlay had, the last he'll ever buy. What am

I to do wi' ye now ? . . . Eh ? . . . I must do something ; it's coming to the bit now, sir."

As he stood in a heaving silence the sobbing of the two women was heard through the room. John was still swaying on the floor.

Sometimes Gourlay would run the full length of the kitchen, and stand there glowering on a stoop ; then he would come crouching up to his son on a vicious little trot, pattering in rage, the broken glass crunching and grinding beneath his feet. At any moment he might spring.

" What do ye think I mean to do wi' ye now ? " he moaned. . . . " Eh ? . . . What do ye think I mean to do wi' ye now ? "

As he came grinning in rage his lips ran out to their full width, and the tense slit showed his teeth to their roots. The gums were white. The stricture of the lips had squeezed them bloodless.

He went back to the dresser once more and bent low beside it, glancing at his son across his left shoulder, with his head flung back sideways, his right fist clenched low and ready from a curve of the elbow. It swung heavy as a mallet by his thigh. Janet got to her knees and came shuffling across the floor on them, though her dress was tripping her, clasping her outstretched hands, and sobbing in appeal, " Faither, faither ; O faither ; for God's sake, faither ! " She clung to him. He unclenched his fist and lifted her away. Then he came crouching and quivering across the floor slowly, a gleaming devilry in the eyes that devoured his son. His hands were like outstretched claws, and shivered with each shiver of the voice that moaned, through set teeth, " What do ye think I mean to do wi' ye now ? . . . What do ye think I mean to do wi' ye now ? . . . Ye damned sorrow and disgrace that ye are, what do ye think I mean to do wi' ye now ? "

" Run, John ! " screamed Mrs. Gourlay, leaping to her

feet. With a hunted cry young Gourlay sprang to the door. So great had been the fixity of Gourlay's wrath, so tense had he been in one direction, as he moved slowly on his prey, that he could not leap to prevent him. As John plunged into the cool, soft darkness, his mother's " Thank God ! " rang past him on the night.

His immediate feeling was of coolness and width and spaciousness, in contrast with the hot grinding hostility that had bored so closely in on him for the last hour. He felt the benignness of the darkened heavens. A tag of some forgotten poem he had read came back to his mind, and, " Come, kindly night, and cover me," he muttered, with shaking lips ; and felt how true it was. My God, what a relief to be free of his father's eyes ! They had held him till his mother's voice broke the spell. They seemed to burn him now.

What a fool he had been to face his father when empty both of food and drink ! Every man was down-hearted when he was empty. If his mother had had time to get the tea, it would have been different ; but the fire had been out when he went in. " He wouldn't have downed me so easy if I had had anything in me," he muttered, and his anger grew as he thought of all he had been made to suffer. For he was still the swaggerer. Now that the incubus of his father's tyranny no longer pressed on him directly, a great hate rose within him for the tyrant. He would go back and have it out when he was primed. " It's the only hame I have," he sobbed angrily to the darkness ; " I have no other place to gang till ! Yes, I'll go back and have it out with him when once I get something in me, so I will." It was no disgrace to suck courage from the bottle for that encounter with his father, for nobody could stand up to black Gourlay—nobody. Young Gourlay was yielding to a peculiar fatalism of minds diseased : all that affects them seems different from all that affects everybody else ; they are even proud of their separate and peculiar doom. Young Gourlay not thought but felt it—he was different from everybody else. The heavens had cursed nobody else with such a terrible sire. It was no cowardice to fill yourself with drink before you faced him.

A drunkard will howl you an obscene chorus the moment after he has wept about his dead child. For a mind in the delirium of drink is no longer a coherent whole, but a heap of shattered bits, which it shows one after the other to the world. Hence the many transformations of that semi-madness, and their quick variety. Young Gourlay was showing them now. His had always been a wandering mind, deficient in application and control, and as he neared his final collapse it became more and more variable, the prey of each momentary thought. In a short five minutes of time he had been alive to the beauty of the darkness, cowering before the memory of his father's eyes, sobbing in self-pity and angry resolve, shaking in terror—indeed he was shaking now. But his vanity came uppermost. As he neared the Red Lion he stopped suddenly, and the darkness seemed on fire against his cheeks. He would have to face curious eyes, he reflected. It was from the Red Lion he and Aird had started so grandly in the autumn. It would never do to come slinking back like a whipped cur ; he must carry it off bravely in case the usual busybodies should be gathered round the bar. So with his coat flapping lordly on either side of him, his hands deep in his trousers pockets, and his hat on the back of his head, he drove at the swing-doors with an outshot chest, and entered with a " breenge." But for all his swagger he must have had a face like death, for there was a cry among the idlers. A man breathed, " My God ! What's the matter ? " With shaking knees Gourlay advanced to the bar, and, " For God's sake, Aggie," he whispered, " give me a Kinblythmont ! "

It went at a gulp.

" Another ! " he gasped, like a man dying of thirst, whom his first sip maddens for more. " Another ! Another ! "

He had tossed the other down his burning throat when Deacon Allardyce came in.

He knew his man the moment he set eyes on him, but, standing at the door, he arched his hand above his brow, as you do in gazing at a dear unexpected friend, whom you pretend not to be quite sure of, so surprised and pleased are you to see him there.

" Ith it Dyohn ? " he cried. " It *ith* Dyohn ! " And he toddled forward with outstretched hand. " Man Dyohn ! " he said again, as if he could scarce believe the good news, and he waggled the other's hand up and down, with both his own clasped over it. " I'm proud to thee you, thir ; I am that. And tho you're won hame, ay ! Im-phm ! And how are ye tummin on ? "

" Oh, *I'm* all right, Deacon," said Gourlay with a silly laugh. " Have a wet ? " The whisky had begun to warm him.

" A wha-at ? " said the Deacon, blinking in a puzzled fashion with his bleary old eyes.

" A dram—a drink—a drop o' the Auld Kirk," said Gourlay, with a stertorous laugh down through his nostrils.

" Hi ! hi ! " laughed the Deacon in his best falsetto. " Ith that what ye call it up in Embro ? A wet, ay ! Ah, well, maybe I will take a little drope, theeing you're tho ready wi' your offer."

They drank together.

" Aggie, fill me a mutchkin when you're at it," said Gourlay to the pretty barmaid with the curly hair. He had spent many an hour with her last summer in the bar. The four big whiskies he had swallowed in the last half-hour were singing in him now, and he blinked at her drunkenly.

There was a scarlet ribbon on her dark curls, coquettish, vivid, and Gourlay stared at it dreamily, partly in

a drunken daze, and partly because a striking colour
always brought a musing and self-forgetting look within
his eyes.   All his life he used to stare at things dreamily,
and come to himself with a start when spoken to.   He
forgot himself now.

"Aggie," he said, and put his hand out to hers clumsily where it rested on the counter—"Aggie, that ribbon's infernal bonny on your dark hair!"

She tossed her head, and perked away from him on
her little high heels.   Him, indeed!—the drunkard!   She
wanted none of his compliments!

There were half a dozen in the place by this time, and
they all stared with greedy eyes.   "That's young Gourlay—him that was *expelled*," was heard, the last an
emphatic whisper, with round eyes of awe at the offence
that must have merited such punishment.   "*Expelled*,
mind ye!"—with a round shake of the head.   "Watch
Allardyce.   We'll see fun."

"What's this 'expelled' is, now?" said John Toodle,
with a very considering look and tone in his uplifted
face—"properly speaking, that is," he added, implying
that of course he knew the word in its ordinary sense,
but was not sure of it "properly speaking."

"Flung oot," said Drucken Wabster, speaking from
the fullness of his own experience.

"Whisht!" said a third.   "Here's Tam Brodie.
Watch what *he* does."

The entrance of Brodie spoiled sport for the Deacon.
He had nothing of that malicious *finesse* that made
Allardyce a genius at flicking men on the raw.   He
went straight to his work, stabbing like an awl.

"Hal-lo!" he cried, pausing with contempt in the
middle of the word, when he saw young Gourlay.
"Hal-lo!   *You* here!—Brig o' the Mains, miss, if *you*
please.—Ay, man!   God, you've been making a name
up in Embro.   I hear you stood up till him gey weel,"
and he winked openly to those around.

Young Gourlay's maddened nature broke at the insult. " Damn you," he screamed, " leave *me* alone, will you ? I have done nothing to *you*, have I ? "

Brodie stared at him across his suspended whisky glass, an easy and assured contempt curling his lip. " Don't greet owre't, my bairn," said he, and even as he spoke John's glass shivered on his grinning teeth. Brodie leapt on him, lifted him, and sent him flying.

" That's a game of your father's, you damned dog," he roared. " But there's mair than him can play the game ! "

" Canny, my freendth, canny ! " piped Allardyce, who was vexed at a fine chance for his peculiar craft being spoiled by mere brutality of handling. All this was most inartistic. Brodie never had the fine stroke.

Gourlay picked himself bleeding from the floor, and holding a handkerchief to his mouth, plunged headlong from the room. He heard the derisive roar that came after him stop, strangled by the sharp swing-to of the door. But it seemed to echo in his burning ears as he strode madly on through the darkness. He uncorked his mutchkin and drank it like water. His swollen lip smarted at first, but he drank till it was a mere dead lump to his tongue, and he could not feel the whisky on the wound.

His mind at first was a burning whirl through drink and rage, with nothing determined and nothing definite. But thought began to shape itself. In a vast vague circle of consciousness his mind seemed to sit in the centre and think with preternatural clearness. Though all around was whirling and confused, drink had endowed some inner eye of the brain with unnatural swift vividness. Far within the humming circle of his mind he saw an instant and terrible revenge on Brodie, acted it, and lived it now. His desires were murderers, and he let them slip, gloating in the cruelties that hot fancy wreaked upon his enemy. Then he suddenly remembered his father. A rush of fiery blood seemed to drench all his body as he thought of what had passed between them. "But, by Heaven," he swore, as he threw away his empty bottle, " he won't use me like that another time ; I have blood in me now." His maddened fancy began building a new scene, with the same actors, the same conditions, as the other, but an issue gloriously diverse. With vicious delight he heard his father use the same sneers, the same gibes, the same brutalities ; then he turned suddenly and had him under foot, kicking, bludgeoning, stamping the life out. He would do it, by Heaven, he would do it ! The memory of what had happened came fierily back, and made the pressing darkness burn. His wrath was brimming on the edge, ready to burst, and he felt proudly that it would no longer ebb in fear. Whisky had killed fear, and left a hysterical madman, all the more dangerous because he was so weak. Let his father try it on now ; he was ready for him !

And his father was ready for him, for he knew what had happened at the inn. Mrs. Webster, on her nightly hunt for the man she had sworn to honour and obey, having drawn several public-houses blank, ran him to earth at last in the bar-room of the Red Lion. " Yes, yes, Kirsty," he cried, eager to prevent her tongue, " I know I'm a blagyird ; but oh, the terrible thing that has happened ! " He so possessed her with his graphic tale that he was allowed to go chuckling back to his potations, while she ran hot-foot to the Green Shutters.

" Eh, poo-oor Mrs. Gourlay ; and oh, your poo-oor boy, too ; and eh, that brute Tam Brodie——" Even as she came through the door the voluble clatter was shrilling out the big tidings, before she was aware of Gourlay's presence. She faltered beneath his black glower.

" Go on ! " he said, and ground it out of her.

" The damned sumph ! " he growled, " to let Brodie

hammer him ! " For a moment, it is true, his anger was divided, stood in equipoise, even dipped " Brodie-ward." " I've an account to sattle wi' *him* ! " he thought grimly. " When *I* get my claw on his neck, I'll teach him better than to hit a Gourlay ! I wonder," he mused, with a pride in which was neither doubt nor wonder—" I wonder will he fling the father as he flang the son ! " But that was the instinct of his blood, not enough to make him pardon John. On the contrary, here was a new offence of his offspring. On the morrow Barbie would be burning with another affront which he had put upon the name of Gourlay. He would waste no time when he came back, be he drunk or be he sober ; he would strip the flesh off him.

" Jenny," he said, " bring me the step-ladder."

He would pass the time till the prodigal came back— and he was almost certain to come back, for where could he go in Barbie ?—he would pass the time by trying to improve the appearance of the house. He had spent money on his house till the last, and even now had the instinct to embellish it. Not that it mattered to him now ; still he could carry out a small improvement he had planned before. The kitchen was ceiled in dark timber, and on the rich brown rafters there were wooden pegs and bars, for the hanging of Gourlay's sticks and fishing-rods. His gun was up there, too, just above the hearth. It had occurred to him about a month ago, however, that a pair of curving steel rests, that would catch the glint from the fire, would look better beneath his gun than the dull pegs, where it now lay against a joist. He might as well pass the time by putting them up.

The bringing of the steps, light though they were, was too much for Janet's weak frame, and she stopped in a fit of coughing, clutching the ladder for support, while it shook to her spasms.

" Tuts, Jenny, this'll never do," said Gourlay, not

unkindly. He took the ladder away from her and laid his hand on her shoulder. "Away to your bed, lass. You maunna sit so late."

But Janet was anxious for her brother, and wanted to sit up till he came home. She answered, "Yes," to her father, but idled discreetly, to consume the time.

"Where's my hammer?" snarled Gourlay.

"Is it no by the clock?" said his wife wearily. "Oh, I remember, I remember! I gied it to Mrs. Webster to break some brie-stone, to rub the front doorstep wi'. It'll be lying in the porch."

"Oh, ay, as usual," said Gourlay—" as usual."

"John!" she cried in alarm, "you don't mean to take down the gun, do ye?"

"Huts, you auld fule, what are you skirling for? D'ye think I mean to shoot the dog? Set back on your creepie and make less noise, will ye?"

Ere he had driven a nail in the rafter John came in, and sat down by the fire, taking up the great poker, as if to cover his nervousness. If Gourlay had been on the floor he would have grappled with him there and then. But the temptation to gloat over his victim from his present height was irresistible. He went up another step, and sat down on the very summit of the ladder, his feet resting on one of the lower rounds. The hammer he had been using was lying on his thigh, his hand clutched about its haft.

"Ay, man, you've been taking a bit walk, I hear."

John made no reply, but played with the poker. It was so huge, owing to Gourlay's whim, that when it slid through his fingers it came down on the muffled hearthstone with a thud like a pavior's hammer.

"I'm told you saw the Deacon on your rounds? Did he compliment you on your return?"

At the quiet sneer a lightning-flash showed John that Allardyce had quizzed him too. For a moment he was conscious of a vast self-pity. "Damn them, they're all down on me," he thought. Then a vindictive rage against them all took hold of him, tense, quivering.

"Did you see Thomas Brodie when ye were out?" came the suave inquiry.

"I saw him," said John, raising fierce eyes to his father's. He was proud of the sudden firmness in his voice. There was no fear in it, no quivering. He was beyond caring what happened to the world or him.

"Oh, you saw him," roared Gourlay, as his anger leapt to meet the anger of his son. "And what did he say to you, may I speir? . . . Or maybe I should speir what he did . . . Eh?" he grinned.

"By God, I'll kill ye," screamed John, springing to his feet, with the poker in his hand. The hammer went whizzing past his ear. Mrs. Gourlay screamed and tried to rise from her chair, her eyes goggling in terror. As Gourlay leapt, John brought the huge poker with a crash on the descending brow. The fiercest joy of his life was the dirl that went up his arm as the steel thrilled to its own hard impact on the bone. Gourlay thudded on the fender, his brow crashing on the rim.

At the blow there had been a cry as of animals from the two women. There followed an eternity of silence, it seemed, and a haze about the place; yet not a haze, for everything was intensely clear; only it belonged to another world. One terrible fact had changed the Universe. The air was different now—it was full of murder. Everything in the room had a new significance, a sinister meaning. The effect was that of an unholy spell.

As through a dream Mrs. Gourlay's voice was heard crying on her God.

John stood there, suddenly weak in his limbs, and stared, as if petrified, at the red poker in his hand. A little wisp of grizzled hair stuck to the square of it, severed, as by scissors, between the sharp edge and the bone. It was the sight of that bit of hair that roused him from his stupor—it seemed so monstrous and horrible, sticking all by itself to the poker. " I didna strike him so hard," he pleaded, staring vaguely, " I didna strike him so hard." Now that the frenzy had left him, he failed to realize the force of his own blow. Then with a horrid fear on him, " Get up, faither," he entreated ; " get up, faither ! O man, you micht get up ! "

Janet, who had bent above the fallen man, raised an ashen face to her brother, and whispered hoarsely, " His heart has stopped, John ; you have killed him ! "

Steps were heard coming through the scullery. In the fear of discovery Mrs. Gourlay shook off the apathy that held her paralyzed. She sprang up, snatched the poker from her son, and thrust it in the embers.

" Run, John ; run for the doctor," she screamed.— " O Mrs. Webster, Mrs. Webster, I'm glad to see ye. Mr. Gourlay fell from the top o' the ladder, and smashed his brow on the muckle fender."

CHAPTER XXVI.

" MOTHER ! " came the startled whisper, "mother ! O woman, waken and speak to me ! "

No comforting answer came from the darkness to tell of a human being close at hand ; the girl, intently listening, was alone with her fear. All was silent in the room, and the terror deepened. Then the far-off sound in the house was heard once more.

" Mother—mother, what's that ? "

" What is it, Janet ? " came a feebly complaining voice ; " what's wrong wi' ye, lassie ? "

Janet and her mother were sleeping in the big bedroom, Janet in the place that had been her father's. He had been buried through the day, the second day after his murder. Mrs. Gourlay had shown a feverish anxiety to get the corpse out the house as soon as possible ; and there had been nothing to prevent it. " Oh," said Doctor Dandy to the gossips, " it would have killed any man to fall from such a height on to the sharp edge of yon fender. No ; he was not quite dead when I got to him. He opened his eyes on me, once—a terrible look—and then life went out of him with a great quiver."

Ere Janet could answer her mother she was seized with a racking cough, and her hoarse bark sounded hollow in the silence. At last she sat up and gasped fearfully, " I thocht—I thocht I heard something moving ! "

" It would be the wind," plained her mother ; " it would just be the wind. John's asleep this strucken hour and mair. I sat by his bed for a lang while, and he prigged and prayed for a dose o' the whisky ere he won away. He wouldna let go my hand till he slept, puir fallow. There's an unco fear on him—an unco fear. But try and fa' owre," she soothed her daughter. " That would just be the wind ye heard."

" There's nae wind ! " said Janet.

The stair creaked. The two women clung to each other, gripping tight fingers, and their hearts throbbed like big separate beings in their breasts. There was a rustle, as of something coming ; then the door opened, and John flitted to the bedside with a candle in his hand. Above his nightshirt his bloodless face looked gray.

" Mother," he panted, " there's something in my room ! "

" What is it, John ? " said his mother, in surprise and fear.

" I—I thocht it was himsell ! O mother, I'm feared, I'm feared ! O mother, I'm *feared !* " He sang the words in a hysterical chant, his voice rising at the end.

The door of the bedroom clicked. It was not a slamming sound, only the door went to gently, as if some one closed it. John dropped the candle from his shaking hand, and was left standing in the living darkness.

" *Save me !* " he screamed, and leaped into the bed, burrowing down between the women till his head was covered by the bedclothes. He trembled so violently that the bed shook beneath them.

" Let me bide wi' ye ! " he pleaded, with chattering jaws ; " oh, let me bide wi' ye ! I daurna gang back to that room by mysell again."

His mother put her thin arm round him. " Yes, dear," she said ; " you may bide wi' us. Janet and me wouldna let anything harm you." She placed her hand on his brow caressingly. His hair was damp with a cold sweat. He reeked of alcohol.

Some one went through the Square playing a concertina. That sound of the careless world came strangely in upon their lonely tragedy. By contrast the cheerful, silly noise out there seemed to intensify their darkness and isolation here. Occasional far-off shouts were heard from roisterers going home.

Mrs. Gourlay lay staring at the darkness with intent eyes. What horror might assail her she did not know, but she was ready to meet it for the sake of John. " Ye brought it on yoursell," she breathed once, as if defying an unseen accuser.

It was hours ere he slept, but at last a heavy sough told her he had found oblivion. " He's won owre," she murmured thankfully. At times he muttered in his sleep, and at times Janet coughed hoarsely at his ear.

" Janet, dinna hoast sae loud, woman ! You'll waken your brother."

Janet was silent. Then she choked—trying to stifle another cough.

" Woman," said her mother complainingly. " that's surely an unco hoast ye hae ! "

" Ay," said Janet, " it's a gey hoast."

Next morning Postie came clattering through the paved yard in his tackety boots, and handed in a blue envelope at the back door with a business-like air, his ferrety eyes searching Mrs. Gourlay's face as she took the letter from his hand. But she betrayed nothing to his curiosity, since she knew nothing of her husband's affairs, and had no fear, therefore, of what the letter might portend. She received the missive with a vacant unconcern. It was addressed to " John Gourlay, Esquire." She turned it over in a silly puzzlement, and, " Janet ! " she cried, " what am I to do wi' this ? "

She shrank from opening a letter addressed to her dead tyrant, unless she had Janet by her side. It was so many years since he had allowed her to take an active interest in their common life (indeed he never had) that she was as helpless as a child.

"It's to faither," said Janet. "Shall I waken John?"

"No; puir fellow, let him sleep," said his mother. "I stole in to look at him enow, and his face was unco wan lying down on the pillow. I'll open the letter mysell; though, as your faither used to tell me, I never had a heid for business."

She broke the seal, and Janet, looking over her shoulder, read aloud to her slower mind :—

"GLASGOW, *March* 12, 18—.

"SIR,—We desire once more to call your attention to the fact that the arrears of interest on the mortgage of your house have not been paid. Our client is unwilling to proceed to extremities, but unless you make some arrangement within a week, he will be forced to take the necessary steps to safeguard his interests.—Yours faithfully,   BRODIE, GURNEY, & YARROWBY."

Mrs. Gourlay sank into a chair, and the letter slipped from her upturned palm, lying slack upon her knee.

"Janet," she said appealingly, "what's this that has come on us? Does the house we live in, the House with the Green Shutters, not belong to us ainy more? Tell me, lassie. What does it mean?"

"I don't ken," whispered Janet, with big eyes. "Did faither never tell ye of the bond?"

"He never telled me about anything," cried Mrs. Gourlay, with a sudden passion. "I was aye the one to be keepit in the dark—to be keepit in the dark and sore hadden doon. Oh, are we left destitute, Janet— and us was aye sae muckle thocht o'! And me, too, that's come of decent folk, and brought him a gey pickle bawbees—am I to be on the parish in my auld age? Oh, *my* faither, *my* faither!"

Her mind flashed back to the jocose and well-to-do father who had been but a blurred thought to her for twenty years. That his daughter should come to a pass like this was enough to make him turn in his grave. Janet was astonished by her sudden passion in feebleness. Even the murder of her husband had been met by her weak mind with a dazed resignation. For her natural horror at the deed was swallowed by her anxiety to shield the murderer ; and she experienced a vague relief—felt but not considered—at being freed from the incubus of Gourlay's tyranny. It seemed, too, as if she was incapable of feeling anything poignantly, deadened now by these quick calamities. But that *she*, that Tenshillingland's daughter, should come to be an object of common charity, touched some hidden nerve of pride, and made her writhe in agony.

" It mayna be sae bad," Janet tried to comfort her.

" Waken John," said her mother feverishly—" waken John, and we'll gang through his faither's desk. There may be something gude amang his papers. There may be something gude ! " she gabbled nervously ; " yes, there may be something gude ! In the desk—in the desk— there may be something gude in the desk ! "

John staggered into the kitchen five minutes later. Halfway to the table where his mother sat he reeled and fell over on a chair, where he lay with an ashen face, his eyes mere slits in his head, the upturned whites showing through. They brought him whisky, and he drank and was recovered. And then they went through to the parlour, and opened the great desk that stood in the corner. It was the first time they had ever dared to raise its lid. John took up a letter lying loosely on the top of the other papers, and after a hasty glance, " This settles it ! " said he. It was the note from Gourlay's banker, warning him that his account was overdrawn.

" God help us ! " cried Mrs. Gourlay, and Janet began

to whimper. John slipped out of the room. He was still in his stocking-feet, and the women, dazed by this sudden and appalling news, were scarcely aware of his departure.

He passed through the kitchen, and stood on the step of the back door, looking out on the quiet little paved yard. Everything there was remarkably still and bright. It was an early spring that year, and the hot March sun beat down on him, paining his bleared and puffy eyes. The contrast between his own lump of a body, drink-dazed, dull-throbbing, and the warm, bright day came in on him with a sudden sinking of the heart, a sense of degradation and personal abasement. He realized, however obscurely, that he was an eyesore in nature, a blotch on the surface of the world, an offence to the sweet-breathing heavens. And that bright silence was so strange and still ; he could have screamed to escape it.

The slow ticking of the kitchen clock seemed to beat upon his raw brain. Damn the thing, why didn't it stop—with its monotonous tick-tack, tick-tack, tick-tack? He could feel it inside his head, where it seemed to strike innumerable little blows on a strained chord it was bent on snapping.

He tiptoed back to the kitchen on noiseless feet, and cocking his ear to listen, he heard the murmur of women's voices in the parlour. There was a look of slyness and cunning in his face, and his eyes glittered with desire. The whisky was still on the table. He seized the bottle greedily, and tilting it up, let the raw liquid gurgle into him like cooling water. It seemed to flood his parched being with a new vitality.

"Oh, I doubt we'll be gey ill off ! " he heard his mother whine, and at that reminder of her nearness he checked the great, satisfied breath he had begun to blow. He set the bottle on the table, bringing the glass noiselessly down upon the wood, with a tense, unnatural precision possible only to drink - steadied nerves — a steadiness like the humming top's whirled to its fastest. Then he sped silently through the courtyard and locked himself into the stable, chuckling in drunken triumph as he turned the key. He pitched forward on a litter of dirty straw, and in a moment sleep came over his mind in a huge wave of darkness.

An hour later he woke from a terrible dream, flinging his arms up to ward off a face that had been pressing on his own. Were the eyes that had burned his brain still glaring above him ? He looked about him in drunken wonder. From a sky-window a shaft of golden light came slanting into the loose-box, living with yellow motes in the dimness. The world seemed dead ; he was alone in the silent building, and from without there was no sound. Then a panic terror flashed on his mind that those eyes had actually been here—and were here with him still—where he was locked up with them alone. He strained his eyeballs in a horrified stare at vacancy. Then he shut them in terror, for why did he look ? If he looked, the eyes might burn on him out of nothing-ness. The innocent air had become his enemy—pregnant with unseen terrors to glare at him. To breathe it stifled him ; each draught of it was full of menace. With a shrill cry he dashed at the door, and felt in the clutch of his ghostly enemy when he failed to open it at once, breaking his nails on the baffling lock. He mowed and chattered and stamped, and tore at the lock, frustrate in fear. At last he was free ! He broke into the kitchen, where his mother sat weeping. She raised her eyes to see a dishevelled thing, with bits of straw scattered on his clothes and hair.

" Mother ! " he screamed, " mother ! " and stopped suddenly, his starting eyes seeming to follow something in the room.

" What are ye glowering at, John ? " she wailed.

" Thae damned een," he said slowly, " they're burn-ing my soul ! Look, look ! " he cried, clutching her thin wrist; "see, there, there—coming round by the dresser! A-ah!" he screamed, in hoarse execration. "Would ye, then?" and he hurled a great jug from the table at the pursuing unseen.

The jug struck the yellow face of the clock, and the glass jangled on the floor.

Mrs. Gourlay raised her arms, like a gaunt sibyl, and spoke to her Maker, quietly, as if He were a man before her in the room. "Ruin and murder," she said slowly, "and madness; and death at my nipple like a child! When will Ye be satisfied?"

Drucken Wabster's wife spread the news, of course, and that night it went humming through the town that young Gourlay had the horrors, and was throwing tumblers at his mother!

"Puir body!" said the baker, in the long-drawn tones of an infinite compassion—"puir body!"

"Ay," said Toddle dryly, "he'll be wanting to put an end to *her* next, after killing his faither."

"Killing his faither?" said the baker, with a quick look. "What do you mean?"

"Mean? Ou, I just mean what the doctor says! Gourlay was that mad at the drucken young swine that he got the 'plexies, fell aff the ladder, and felled himsell deid! That's what I mean, no less!" said Toddle, nettled at the sharp question.

"Ay, man! That accounts for't," said Tam Wylie. "It did seem queer Gourlay's dying the verra nicht the prodigal cam hame. He was a heavy man too; he would come down with an infernal thud. It seems uncanny, though, it seems uncanny."

"Strange!" murmured another; and they looked at each other in silent wonder.

"But will this be true, think ye?" said Brodie— "about the horrors, I mean. *Did* he throw the tumbler at his mother?"

"Lord, it's true!" said Sandy Toddle. "I gaed into

the kitchen on purpose to make sure o' the matter with my own eyes. I let on I wanted to borrow auld Gourlay's keyhole saw. I can tell ye he had a' his orders—his tool-chest's the finest I ever saw in my life! I mean to bid for some o' yon when the rowp comes. Weel, as I was saying, I let on I wanted the wee saw, and went into the kitchen one end's errand. The tumbler (Johnny Coe says it was a bottle, however; but I'm no avised o' that—I speired Webster's wife, and I think my details are correct)—the tumbler went flying past his mother, and smashed the face o' the eight-day. It happened about the mid-hour o' the day. The clock had stoppit, I observed, at three and a half minutes to the twelve."

"Hi!" cried the Deacon, "it'th a pity auld Gourlay wathna alive thith day!"

"Faith, ay," cried Wylie. "*He* would have sorted him; *he* would have trimmed the young ruffian!"

"No doubt," said the Deacon gravely—"no doubt. But it wath scarcely that I wath thinking of. Yah!" he grinned, "thith would have been a thlap in the face till him!"

Wylie looked at him for a while with a white scunner in his face. He wore the musing and disgusted look of a man whose wounded mind retires within itself to brood over a sight of unnatural cruelty. The Deacon grew uncomfortable beneath his sideward, estimating eye.

"Deacon Allardyce, your heart's black-rotten," he said at last.

The Deacon blinked and was silent. Tam had summed him up. There was no appeal.

* * * * * *

"John dear," said his mother that evening, "we'll take the big sofa into our bedroom, and make up a grand bed for ye, and then we'll be company to one another. Eh, dear?" she pleaded. "Winna that be a fine way?

When you have Janet and me beside you, you winna be feared o' ainything coming near you. You should gang to bed early, dear. A sleep would restore your mind."

" I don't mean to go to bed," he said slowly. He spoke staringly, with the same fixity in his voice and gaze. There was neither rise nor fall in his voice, only a dull level of intensity.

" You don't mean to go to bed, John! What for, dear? Man, a sleep would calm your mind for ye."

" Na-a-a! " he smiled, and shook his head like a cunning madman who had detected her trying to get round him. " Na-a-a! No sleep for me—no sleep for me! I'm feared I would see the red een," he whispered, " the red een, coming at me out o' the darkness, the darkness "—he nodded, staring at her and breathing the word—" the darkness, the darkness! The darkness is the warst, mother," he added, in his natural voice, leaning forward as if he explained some simple, curious thing of every day. " The darkness is the warst, you know. I've seen them in the broad licht; but in the lobby," he whispered hoarsely—" in the lobby when it was dark— in the lobby they were terrible. Just twa een, and they aye keep thegither, though they're aye moving. That's why I canna pin them. And it's because I ken they're aye watching me, watching me, watching me that I get so feared. They're red," he nodded and whispered —" they're red—they're red." His mouth gaped in horror, and he stared as if he saw them now.

He had boasted long ago of being able to see things inside his head; in his drunken hysteria he was to see them always. The vision he beheld against the darkness of his mind projected itself and glared at him. He was pursued by a spectre in his own brain, and for that reason there was no escape. Wherever he went it followed him.

" O man John," wailed his mother, " what are ye

feared for your faither's een for ?   He wouldna perse-
cute his boy."

"Would he no ? " he said slowly.   "You ken yoursell
that he never liked me !   And naebody could stand his
glower.   Oh, he was a terrible man, *my* faither !   You
could feel the passion in him when he stood still.   He
could throw himsell at ye without moving.   And he's
throwing himsell at *me* frae beyond the grave."

Mrs. Gourlay beat her desperate hands.   Her feeble
remonstrance was a snowflake on a hill to the dull intensity of this conviction.   So colossal was it that it
gripped herself, and she glanced dreadfully across her
shoulder.   But in spite of her fears she must plead
with him to save.

"Johnnie dear," she wept passionately, "there's no
een !   It's just the drink gars you think sae."

"No," he said dully;   "the drink's my refuge.   It's
a kind thing, drink—it helps a body."

"But, John, nobody believes in these things nowadays.   It's just fancy in you.   I wonder at a college-
bred man like you giving heed to a wheen nonsense ! "

"Ye ken yoursell it was a byword in the place that he
would haunt the House with the Green Shutters."

"God help me ! " cried Mrs. Gourlay;   "what am I
to do ? "

She piled up a great fire in the parlour, and the three
poor creatures gathered round it for the night.   (They
were afraid to sit in the kitchen of an evening, for even
the silent furniture seemed to talk of the murder it had
witnessed.)   John was on a carpet stool by his mother's
feet, his head resting on her knee.

They heard the rattle of Wilson's brake as it swung
over the townhead from Auchterwheeze, and the laughter
of its jovial crew.   They heard the town clock chiming
the lonesome passage of the hours.   A dog was barking
in the street.

Gradually all other sounds died away.

"Mother," said John, "lay your hand alang my shouther, touching my neck. I want to be sure that you're near me."

"I'll do that, my bairn," said his mother. And soon he was asleep.

Janet was reading a novel. The children had their mother's silly gift—a gift of the weak-minded, of forgetting their own duties and their own sorrows in a vacant interest which they found in books. She had wrapped a piece of coarse red flannel round her head to comfort a swollen jaw, and her face appeared from within like a tallowy oval.

"I didna get that story finished," said Mrs. Gourlay vacantly, staring at the fire open-mouthed, her mutch-strings dangling. It was the remark of a stricken mind that speaks vacantly of anything. "Does Herbert Montgomery marry Sir James's niece?"

"No," said Janet; "he's killed at the war. It's a gey pity of him, isn't it?—Oh, what's that?"

It was John talking in his sleep.

"I have killed my faither," he said slowly, pausing long between every phrase—"I have killed my faither . . . I have killed my faither. And he's foll-owing me . . . he's foll-owing me . . . he's foll-owing me." It was the voice of a thing, not a man. It swelled and dwelt on the "follow," as if the horror of the pursuit made it moan. "He's foll-owing me . . . he's foll-owing me . . . he's foll-owing me. A face like a dark mist—and een like hell. Oh, they're foll-owing me . . . they're foll-owing me . . . they're foll-owing me!" His voice seemed to come from an infinite distance. It was like a lost soul moaning in a solitude.

The dog was barking in the street. A cry of the night came from far away.

That voice was as if a corpse opened its lips and told of horrors beyond the grave. It brought the other world into the homely room, and made it all demoniac. The women felt the presence of the unknown. It was their own flesh and blood that spoke the words, and by their own quiet hearth. But hell seemed with them in the room.

Mrs. Gourlay drew back from John's head on her lap, as from something monstrous and unholy. But he moaned in deprivation, craving her support, and she edged nearer to supply his need. Possessed with a devil or no, he was her son.

"Mother!" gasped Janet suddenly, the white circles of her eyes staring from the red flannel, her voice hoarse with a new fear—"mother, suppose—suppose he said that before anybody else!"

"Don't mention't," cried her mother with sudden passion. "How daur ye? how daur ye? My God!" she broke down and wept, "they would hang him, so they would! They would hang *my* boy—they would take and hang *my* boy!"

They stared at each other wildly. John slept, his head twisted over on his mother's knee, his eyes sunken, his mouth wide open.

"Mother," Janet whispered, "you must send him away."

"I have only three pounds in the world," said Mrs. Gourlay; and she put her hand to her breast where it was, but winced as if a pain had bitten her.

"Send him away wi't," said Janet. "The furniture may bring something. And you and me can aye thole."

In the morning Mrs. Gourlay brought two greasy notes to the table, and placed them in her son's slack hand. He was saner now; he had slept off his drunken madness through the night.

"John," she said, in pitiful appeal, "you maunna stay here, laddie. Ye'll gie up the drink when you're away —will ye na?—and then thae een ye're sae feared of 'll no trouble you ony mair. Gang to Glasgow and see the lawyer folk about the bond. And, John dear," she pleaded, "if there's nothing left for us, you'll try to work for Janet and me, will ye no? You've a grand education, and you'll surely get a place as a teacher or something; I'm sure you would make a grand teacher. Ye wouldna like to think of your mother trailing every week to the like of Wilson for an awmous, streeking out her auld hand for charity. The folk would stand in their doors to look at me, man—they would that— they would cry ben to each other to come oot and see Gourlay's wife gaun slinkin' doon the brae. Doon the brae it would be," she repeated, " doon the brae it would be "—and her mind drifted away on the sorrowful future which her fear made so vivid and real. It was only John's going that roused her.

Thomas Brodie, glowering abroad from a shop door festooned in boots, his leather apron in front, and his thumbs in the armholes of his waistcoat, as befitted an important man, saw young Gourlay pass the Cross with his bag in his hand, and dwindle up the road to the station.

"Where's *he* off to now?" he muttered. "There's something at the boddom o' this, if a body could find it out!"

CHAPTER XXVII.

WHEN John had gone his mother roused herself to a feverish industry. Even in the early days of her strength she had never been so busy in her home. But her work was aimless and to no purpose. When tidying she would take a cup without its saucer from the table, and set off with it through the room, but stopping suddenly in the middle of the floor, would fall into a muse with the dish in her hand; coming to herself long afterwards to ask vaguely, "What's this cup for? . . . Janet, lassie, what was it I was doing?" Her energy, and its frustration, had the same reason. The burden on her mind constantly impelled her to do something to escape from it, and the same burden paralyzed her mind in everything she did. So with another of her vacant whims. Every morning she rose at an unearthly hour, to fish out of old closets rag-bags bellied big with the odds and ends of thirty years' assemblage. "I'll make a patchwork quilt o' thir!" she explained, with a foolish, eager smile; and she spent hours snatching up rags and vainly trying to match them. But the quilt made no progress. She would look at a patch for a while, with her head on one side, and pat it all over with restless hands; then she would turn it round, to see if it would look better that way, only to tear it off when it was half sewn, to try another and yet another. Often she would forget the work on her lap, and stare across the room, openmouthed, her fingers plucking at her withered throat. Janet became afraid of her mother.

Once she saw her smiling to herself, when she thought nobody was watching her—an uncanny smile as of one who hugged a secret to her breast—a secret that, eluding others, would enable its holder to elude them too.

" What can *she* have to laugh at ? " Janet wondered.

At times the haze that seemed gathering round Mrs. Gourlay's mind would be dispelled by sudden rushes of fear, when she would whimper lest her son be hanged, or herself come on the parish in her old age. But that was rarely. Her brain was mercifully dulled, and her days were passed in a restless vacancy.

She was sitting with the rags scattered round her when John walked in on the evening of the third day. There were rags everywhere—on the table, and all about the kitchen ; she sat in their midst like a witch among the autumn leaves. When she looked towards his entrance the smell of drink was wafted from the door.

" John ! " she panted, in surprise—" John, did ye not go to Glasgow, boy ? "

" Ay," he said slowly, " I gaed to Glasgow."

" And the bond, John — did ye speir about the bond ? "

" Ay," he said, " I speired about the bond. The whole house is sunk in't."

" Oh ! " she gasped, and the whole world seemed to go from beneath her, so weak did she feel through her limbs.

" John," she said, after a while, " did ye no try to get something to do, that you might help me and Janet now we're helpless ? "

" No," he said : " for the een wouldna let me. Nicht and day they follow me a'where—nicht and day."

" Are they following ye yet, John ? " she whispered, leaning forward seriously. She did not try to disabuse him now ; she accepted what he said. Her mind was on a level with his own. " Are they following ye yet ? " she asked, with large eyes of sympathy and awe.

" Ay, and waur than ever too. They're getting

redder and redder. It's not a dull red," he said, with a faint return of his old interest in the curious physical; "it's a gleaming red. They lowe. A' last nicht they wouldna let me sleep. There was nae gas in my room, and when the candle went out I could see them everywhere. When I looked to one corner o' the room, they were there; and when I looked to another corner, they were there too — glowering at me; glowering at me in the darkness; glowering at me. Ye mind what a glower he had! I hid from them ablow the claes; but they followed me—they were burning in my brain. So I gaed oot and stood by a lamp-post for company. But a constable moved me on; he said I was drunk because I muttered to mysell. But I wasna drunk then, mother; I wa-as *not*. So I walkit on, and on, and on the whole nicht; but I aye keepit to the lamp-posts for company. And than when the public-houses opened I gaed in and drank and drank. I didna like the drink, for whisky has no taste to me now. But it helps ye to forget.

"Mother," he went on complainingly, "is it no queer that a pair of een should follow a man? Just a pair of een! It never happened to onybody but me," he said dully—"never to onybody but me."

His mother was panting open-mouthed, as if she choked for air, both hands clutching at her bosom. "Ay," she whispered, "it's queer;" and kept on gasping at intervals with staring eyes, "It's gey queer; it's gey queer; it's gey queer."

She took up the needle once more and tried to sew; but her hand was trembling so violently that she pricked the left forefinger which upheld her work. She was content thereafter to make loose stabs at the cloth, with a result that she made great stitches which drew her seam together in a pucker. Vacantly she tried to smooth them out, stroking them over with her hand, constantly stroking and to no purpose. John watched the aimless work with dull and heavy eyes.

For a while there was silence in the kitchen.   Janet was coughing in the room above.

"There's just ae thing'll end it ! " said John.   " Mother, give me three shillings."

It was not a request, and not a demand ; it was the dull statement of a need.   Yet the need appeared so relentless, uttered in the set fixity of his impassive voice, that she could not gainsay it.   She felt that this was not merely her son making a demand ; it was a compulsion on him greater than himself.

" There's the money ! " she said, clinking it down on the table, and flashed a resentful smile at him, close upon the brink of tears.

She had a fleeting anger.   It was scarcely at him, though ; it was at the fate that drove him.   Nor was it for herself, for her own mood was, " Well, well ; let it gang."   But she had a sense of unfairness, and a flicker of quite impersonal resentment, that fate should wring the last few shillings from a poor being.   It wasna fair. She had the emotion of it ; and it spoke in the strange look at her son, and in the smiling flush with the tears behind it.   Then she sank into apathy.

John took up the money and went out, heedless of his mother where she sat by the table; he had a doom on him, and could see nothing that did not lie within his path.   Nor did she take any note of his going ; she was callous.   The tie between them was being annulled by misery.   She was ceasing to be his mother, he to be her son ;   they were not younger and older, they were the equal victims of necessity.   Fate set each of them apart to dree a separate weird.

In a house of long years of misery the weak become callous to their dearest's agony.   The hard, strong characters are kindest in the end ; they will help while their hearts are breaking.   But the weak fall asunder at the last.   It was not that Mrs. Gourlay was thinking of herself rather than of him.   She was stunned by fate—as was he—and could think of nothing.

Ten minutes later John came out of the Black Bull with a bottle of whisky.

It was a mellow evening, one of those evenings when Barbie, the mean and dull, is transfigured to a gem-like purity, and catches a radiance. There was a dreaming sky above the town, and its light less came to the earth than was on it, shining in every path with a gracious immanence. John came on through the glow with his burden undisguised, wrapped in a tissue paper which showed its outlines. He stared right before him like a man walking in his sleep, and never once looked to either side. At word of his coming the doors were filled with mutches and bald heads, keeking by the jambs to get a look. Many were indecent in their haste, not waiting till he passed ere they peeped—which was their usual way. Some even stood away out in front of their doors to glower at him advancing, turning slowly with him as he passed, and glowering behind him as he went. They saw they might do so with impunity; that he did not see them, but walked like a man in a dream. He passed up the street and through the Square, beneath a hundred eyes, the sun shining softly round him. Every eye followed till he disappeared through his own door.

He went through the kitchen, where his mother sat, carrying the bottle openly, and entered the parlour without speaking. He came back and asked her for the corkscrew, but when she said "Eh?" with a vague wildness in her manner, and did not seem to understand, he went and got it for himself. She continued making stabs at her cloth and smoothing out the puckers in her seam.

John was heard moving in the parlour. There was the sharp *plunk* of a cork being drawn, followed by a clink of glass. And then came a heavy thud like a fall.

To Mrs. Gourlay the sounds meant nothing; she heard them with her ear, not her mind. The world around her had retreated to a hazy distance, so that it had no meaning. She would have gazed vaguely at a shell about to burst beside her.

In the evening, Janet, who had been in bed all the afternoon, came down and lit the lamp for her mother. It was a large lamp which Gourlay had bought, and it shed a rich light through the room.

" I heard John come in," she said, turning wearily round ; " but I was too ill to come down and ask what had happened. Where is he ? "

" John ? " questioned her mother—" John ? . . . Ou ay," she panted, vaguely recalling, " ou ay. I think —I think . . . he gaed ben the parlour."

" The parlour ! " cried Janet ; " but he must be in the dark ! And he canna thole the darkness ! "

" John ! " she cried, going to the parlour door, " John ! " There was a silence of the grave.

She lit a candle, and went into the room. And then she gave a squeal like a rabbit in a dog's jaws.

Mrs. Gourlay dragged her gaunt limbs wearily across the floor. By the wavering light, which shook in Janet's hand, she saw her son lying dead across the sofa. The whisky-bottle on the table was half empty, and of a smaller bottle beside it he had drunk a third. He had taken all that whisky that he might deaden his mind to the horror of swallowing the poison. His legs had slipped to the floor when he died, but his body was lying back across the couch, his mouth open, his eyes staring horridly up. They were not the eyes of the quiet dead, but bulged in frozen fear, as if his father's eyes had watched him from aloft while he died.

" There's twa thirds of the poison left," commented Mrs. Gourlay.

" Mother ! " Janet screamed, and shook her. " Mother, John's deid ! John's deid ! Don't ye see John's deid ? "

" Ay, he's deid," said Mrs. Gourlay, staring. " He winna be hanged now ! "

"Mother!" cried Janet, desperate before this apathy, "what shall we do? what shall we do? Shall I run and bring the neebours?"

"The neebours!" said Mrs. Gourlay, rousing herself wildly—"the neebours! What have *we* to do with the neebours? We are by ourselves—the Gourlays whom God has cursed; we can have no neebours. Come ben the house, and I'll tell ye something," she whispered wildly. "Ay," she nodded, smiling with mad significance, "I'll tell ye something . . . I'll tell ye something," and she dragged Janet to the kitchen.

Janet's heart was rent for her brother, but the frenzy on her mother killed sorrow with a new fear.

"Janet!" smiled Mrs. Gourlay, with insane soft interest, "Janet! D'ye mind yon nicht langsyne when your faither came in wi' a terrible look in his een and struck me in the breist? Ay," she whispered hoarsely, staring at the fire, "he struck me in the breist. But I didna ken what it was for, Janet . . . No," she shook her head, "he never telled me what it was for."

"Ay, mother," whispered Janet, "I have mind o't."

"Weel, an abscess o' some kind formed—I kenna weel what it was, but it gathered and broke, and gathered and broke, till my breist's near eaten awa wi't. Look!" she cried, tearing open her bosom, and Janet's head flung back in horror and disgust.

"O mother!" she panted, "was it that that the wee clouts were for?"

"Ay, it was that," said her mother. "Mony a clout I had to wash, and mony a nicht I sat lonely by mysell, plaistering my withered breist. But I never let onybody ken," she added with pride; "na-a-a, I never let onybody ken. When your faither nipped me wi' his tongue it nipped me wi' its pain, and, woman, it consoled me. 'Ay, ay,' I used to think; 'gibe awa, gibe awa; but I hae a freend in my breist that'll end it some day.' I likit to keep it to mysell. When it bit me it

seemed to whisper I had a freend that nane o' them
kenned o'—a freend that would deliver me! The mair
he badgered me, the closer I hugged it; and when my
he'rt was br'akin I enjoyed the pain o't."

"O my poor, poor mother!" cried Janet with a
bursting sob, her eyes raining hot tears. Her very body
seemed to feel compassion; it quivered and crept near,
as though it would brood over her mother and protect
her. She raised the poor hand and kissed it, and fondled
it between her own.

But her mother had forgotten the world in one of her
wild lapses, and was staring fixedly.

"I'll no lang be a burden to onybody," she said to
herself. "It should sune be wearing to a heid now. But
I thought of something the day John gaed away; ay,
I thought of something," she said vaguely. "Janet,
what was it I was thinking of?"

"I dinna ken," whispered Janet.

"I was thinking of something," her mother mused.
Her voice all through was a far-off voice, remote from
understanding. "Yes, I remember. Ye're young, Jenny,
and you learned the dressmaking; do ye think ye could
sew, or something, to keep a bit garret owre my heid
till I dee? Ay, it was that I was thinking of; though
it doesna matter much now—eh, Jenny? I'll no
bother you for verra lang. But I'll no gang on the
parish," she said in a passionless voice, "I'll no gang on
the parish. I'm Miss Richmond o' Tenshillingland."

She had no interest in her own suggestion. It was an
idea that had flitted through her mind before, which
came back to her now in feeble recollection. She
seemed not to wait for an answer, to have forgotten
what she said.

"O mother," cried Janet, "there's a curse on us
all! I would work my fingers raw for ye if I could, but
I canna," she screamed, "I canna, I canna! My lungs
are bye wi't. On Tuesday in Skeighan the doctor telled

me I would soon be deid; he didna say't, but fine I saw what he was hinting. He advised me to gang to Ventnor in the Isle o' Wight," she added wanly; " as if I could gang to the Isle of Wight. I cam hame trembling, and wanted to tell ye; but when I cam in ye were ta'en up wi' John, and, ' O lassie,' said you, ' dinna bother me wi' your complaints enow.' I was hurt at that, and ' Well, well,' I thocht, ' if she doesna want to hear, I'll no tell her.' I was huffed at ye. And then my faither came in, and ye ken what happened. I hadna the heart to speak o't after that; I didna seem to care. I ken what it is to nurse daith in my breist wi' pride, too, mother," she went on. " Ye never cared verra much for me; it was John was your favourite. I used to be angry because you neglected my illness, and I never telled you how heavily I hoasted blood. ' She'll be sorry for this when I'm deid,' I used to think; and I hoped you would be. I had a kind of pride in saying nothing. But, O mother, I didna ken *you* were just the same; I didna ken *you* were just the same." She looked. Her mother was not listening.

Suddenly Mrs. Gourlay screamed with wild laughter, and, laughing, eyed with mirthless merriment the look of horror with which Janet was regarding her. " Ha, ha, ha ! " she screamed, " it's to be a clean sweep o' the Gourlays ! Ha, ha, ha ! it's to be a clean sweep o' the Gourlays ! "

There is nothing uglier in life than a woman's cruel laugh; but Mrs. Gourlay's laugh was more than cruel, it was demoniac—the skirl of a human being carried by misery beyond the confines of humanity. Janet stared at her in speechless fear.

" Mother," she whispered at last, " what are we to do ? "

" There's twa-thirds of the poison left," said Mrs. Gourlay.

" Mother ! " cried Janet.

"Gourlay's dochter may gang on the parish if she likes, but his wife never will. *You* may hoast yourself to death in a garret in the poorhouse, but *I'll* follow my boy."

The sudden picture of her own lonely death as a pauper among strangers, when her mother and brother should be gone, was so appalling to Janet that to die with her mother seemed pleasanter. She could not bear to be left alone.

"Mother," she cried in a frenzy, "I'll keep ye company!"

"Let us read a chapter," said Mrs. Gourlay.

She took down the big Bible, and "the thirteent' chapter o' First Corinthians," she announced in a loud voice, as if giving it out from the pulpit, "the thirteent' —o' the First Corinthians:"—

"'*Though I speak with the tongues of men and of angels, and have not charity, I am become as sounding brass, or a tinkling cymbal.*

"'*And though I have the gift of prophecy, and understand all mysteries, and all knowledge; and though I have all faith, so that I could remove mountains, and have not charity, I am nothing.*'"

Mrs. Gourlay's manner had changed: she was in the high exaltation of madness. Callous she still appeared, so possessed by her general doom that she had no sense of its particular woes. But she was listless no more. Willing her death, she seemed to borrow its greatness and become one with the law that punished her. Arrogating the Almighty's function to expedite her doom, she was the equal of the Most High. It was her feebleness that made her great. Because in her feebleness she yielded entirely to the fate that swept her on, she was imbued with its demoniac power.

"'*Charity suffereth long, and is kind; charity envieth not; charity vaunteth not itself, is not puffed up,*

"'*Doth not behave itself unseemly, seeketh not her own, is not easily provoked, thinketh no evil;*

" ' Rejoiceth not in iniquity, but rejoiceth in the truth ;

" ' Beareth all things, believeth all things, hopeth all things, endureth all things.

" ' Charity never faileth : but whether there be prophecies, they shall fail ; whether there be tongues, they shall cease ; whether there be knowledge, it shall vanish away.

" ' For we know in part, and we prophesy in part.

" ' But when that which is perfect is come, then that which is in part shall be done away.' "

Her voice rose high and shrill as she read the great verses. Her large blue eyes shone with ecstasy. Janet looked at her in fear. This was more than her mother speaking ; it was more than human ; it was a voice from beyond the world. Alone, the timid girl would have shrunk from death, but her mother's inspiration held her.

" ' And now abideth faith, hope, charity, these three : but the greatest of these is charity.' "

Janet had been listening with such strained attention that the " Amen " rang out of her loud and involuntary, like an answer to a compelling Deity. She had clung to this reading as the one thing left to her before death, and out of her nature thus strained to listen the " Amen " came, as sped by an inner will. She scarcely knew that she said it.

They rose, and the scrunt of Janet's chair on the floor, when she pushed it behind her, sent a thrilling shiver through her body, so tense was her mood. They stood with their hands on their chair backs, and looked at each other, in a curious palsy of the will. The first step to the parlour door would commit them to the deed ; to take it was to take the poison, and they paused, feeling its significance. To move was to give themselves to the irrevocable. When they stirred at length they felt as if the ultimate crisis had been passed ; there could be no return. Mrs. Gourlay had Janet by the wrist.

She turned and looked at her daughter, and for one fleeting moment she ceased to be above humanity.

" Janet," she said wistfully, "*I* have had a heap to thole! Maybe the Lord Jesus Christ'll no' be owre sair on me."

"O mother!" Janet screamed, yielding to her terror when her mother weakened. "O mother, I'm feared! I'm feared! O mother, I'm feared!"

"Come!" said her mother; "come!" and drew her by the wrist. They went into the parlour.

*   *   *   *   *   *

The post was a square-built, bandy-legged little man, with a bristle of grizzled hair about his twisted mouth, perpetually cocking up an ill-bred face in the sight of Heaven. Physically and morally he had in him something both of the Scotch terrier and the London sparrow—the shagginess of the one, the cocked eye of the other; the one's snarling temper, the other's assured impudence. In Gourlay's day he had never got by the gateway of the yard, much as he had wanted to come further. Gourlay had an eye for a thing like him. "Damn the gurly brute!" Postie complained once; "when I passed a pleasand remark about the weather the other morning, he just looked at me and blew the reek of his pipe in my face. And that was his only answer!"

Now that Gourlay was gone, however, Postie clattered through the yard every morning, right up to the back door.

"A heap o' correspondence *thir* mornin's!" he would simper, his greedy little eye trying to glean revelations from the women's faces as they took the letters from his hand.

On the morning after young Gourlay came home for the last time, Postie was pelting along with his quick thudding step near the head of the Square, when whom should he meet but Sandy Toddle, still unwashed and yawning from his bed. It was early, and the streets were empty, except where in the distance the bent figure of an old man was seen hirpling off to his work, first twisting round stiffly to cock his eye right and left at the sky, to forecast the weather for the day.

From the chimneys the fair white spirlies of reek were rising in the pure air. The Gourlays did not seem to be stirring yet ; there was no smoke above their roof-tree to show that there was life within.

Postie jerked his thumb across his shoulder at the House with the Green Shutters.

" There'll be chynges there the day," he said, chirruping.

" Wha-at ! " Toddle breathed in a hoarse whisper of astonishment, " sequesteration ? " and he stared, big-eyed, with his brows arched.

" Something o' that kind," said the post carelessly. " I'm no' weel acquaint wi' the law-wers' lingo."

" Will't be true, think ye ? " said Sandy.

" God, it's true," said the post. " I had it frae Jock Hutchison, the clerk in Skeighan Goudie's. He got fou yestreen on the road to Barbie and blabbed it—he'll lose his job, yon chap, if he doesna keep his mouth shut. True! ay, it's true! There's damn the doubt o' that."

Toddle corrugated his mouth to whistle. He turned and stared at the House with the Green Shutters, gawcey and substantial on its terrace, beneath the tremulous beauty of the dawn. There was a glorious sunrise.

" God ! " he said, " what a downcome for that hoose ! "

" Is it no' ? " chuckled Postie.

" Whose account is it on ? " said Toddle.

" Oh, I don't ken," said Postie carelessly. " He had creditors a' owre the country. I was ay bringing the big blue envelopes from different airts. Don't mention this, now," he added, his finger up, his eye significant; " it shouldn't be known at a-all." He was unwilling that Toddle should get an unfair start, and spoil his own market for the news.

" *Nut* me ! " Toddle assured him grandly, shaking his

head as who should conduct of that kind a thousand miles off—"*nut* me, Post! I'll no breathe it to a living soul."

The post clattered in to Mrs. Gourlay's back door. He had a heavy under-stamped letter on which there was threepence to pay. He might pick up an item or two while she was getting him the bawbees.

He knocked, but there was no answer.

"The sluts!" said he, with a humph of disgust; "they're still on their backs, it seems."

He knocked again. The sound of his knuckles on the door rang out hollowly, as if there was nothing but emptiness within. While he waited he turned on the step and looked idly at the courtyard. The inwalled little place was curiously still.

At last in his impatience he turned the handle, when to his surprise the door opened, and let him enter.

The leaves of a Bible fluttered in the fresh wind from the door. A large lamp was burning on the table. Its big yellow flame was unnatural in the sunshine.

"H'mph!" said Postie, tossing his chin in disgust, "little wonder everything gaed to wreck and ruin in this house! The slovens have left the lamp burning the whole nicht lang. But less licht'll serve them now, I'm thinking!"

A few dead ashes were sticking from the lower bars of the range. Postie crossed to the fireplace and looked down at the fender. That bright spot would be the place, now, where auld Gourlay killed himself. The women must have rubbed it so bright in trying to get out the blood. It was an uncanny thing to keep in the house that. He stared at the fatal spot till he grew eerie in the strange stillness.

"Guidwife!" he cried, "Jennet! Don't ye hear?"

They did not hear, it seemed.

"God!" said he, "they sleep sound after all their misfortunes!"

At last—partly in impatience, and partly from a wish to pry—he opened the door of the parlour. "*Oh, my God!*" he screamed, leaping back,·and with his bulky bag got stuck in the kitchen door, in his desperate hurry to be gone.

He ran round to the Square in front, and down to Sandy Toddle, who was informing a bunch of unshaven bodies that the Gourlays were " sequestered."

" Oh, my God, Post, what have you seen, to bring that look to your eyes ? What have you seen, man ? Speak, for God's sake ! What is it ? "

The post gasped and stammered; then " Ooh ! " he shivered in horror, and covered his eyes, at a sudden picture in his brain.

" Speak ! " said a man solemnly.

" They have—they have—they have a' killed themselves," stammered the postman, pointing to the Gourlays.

Their loins were loosened beneath them. The scrape of their feet on the road, as they turned to stare, sounded monstrous in the silence. No man dared to speak. They gazed with blanched faces at the House with the Green Shutters, sitting dark there and terrible beneath the radiant arch of the dawn.

THE END.